The LAST NIGHT

C.D. MAJOR

ABOUT THE AUTHOR

C. D. Major writes books inspired by events in the recent past. Cesca worked in television and teaching before writing full time. Alongside her thrillers she writes feel-good reads under the pseudonym Rosie Blake. She teaches creative writing and vlogs writing tips over on her website www.cdmajor.com. Cesca lives in Berkshire with her husband, son and twin daughters. She can be found on Twitter, Facebook and Instagram and enjoys connecting with readers.

ALSO BY C.D.MAJOR:

The Silent Hours

The Other Girl

Writing as Rosie Blake:

How to Get a (Love) Life

How to Stuff Up Christmas

How to Find Your (First) Husband

The Hygge Holiday

The Gin O'Clock Club

To my daddy.

PROLOGUE

Monday 18th August 1952

She hadn't told her mother where she was going but had slipped out early before she woke. Betty had been easy to persuade; the housekeeper was far too soft a touch. She tied Jenny's hair into a loose plait and tapped her on the back of the legs, telling her not to be too long. She did the smile that Jenny knew meant she was complicit in her secret.

She set off down the path behind the house, the air already warm, the ground giving off that sweet damp smell, soft from the recent rainfall. The sun was leaking across the sea as she looked down the garden and out over the cliff edge to the water beyond. There were oranges and pinks and a pale blue shimmering above it all. It always made her suck in all her breath, how wide it was, how enormous, and there she was, this little ant, a speck really, sneaking down the garden and out onto the cliff path.

She looked back towards the house, guilty for a moment for not kissing her mother good morning. Her mother was up later and later these days, since her father had gone away. Her bedroom curtains were still closed, the dull cream fabric hanging still, Betty's silhouette moving past the downstairs windows as she bustled about preparing for the day. Jenny swallowed the feeling that she shouldn't be leaving her, desperate to be out and exploring. She loved the clifftop and the coves at this time of day; she had seen two dolphins the week before, splashing out of the water at the same moment before plunging under and doing it again. They had crossed the cove, the early-morning sun glistening on their backs slick with water. Jenny thought she'd never seen anything more incredible.

There was no one up on the clifftop in either direction, the path fell away from her on either side and she could see along it for ages. A shadow appeared on her side, startling her, a hand flying to her chest, moving quickly across her, a seagull, its enormous beak hooked and orange. Jenny felt her shoulders drop as it came to rest a little way off, on the top of a fence post, one wary eye watching her. She saluted it and ran off down the path that led to the little cove below their house. Perhaps she would find more shells for her collection. She wondered where the tide would be, how much of the sand would be exposed.

She dodged puddles, patches of mud drying at the edges, small pools of water collected in the bottom. Clumps of grass made the path uneven as she picked her way down to the rocks that formed a jutting, wonky staircase to a shelf overlooking the bay. From there she could jump down, take off her shoes and get sucked into the sand, the wet grains squelching right over her toes and feet. Sometimes she imagined sinking down further and that thought would make her heart pitter-patter a bit faster and she would scold herself for thinking it at all.

She was always careful when she made her way down,

putting both hands out to hold onto the grass and rocks that seemed to emerge from the cliff face to help her. She would cling to the clumps of soil, find her footing, and lean her weight into the cliff. She could hear the waves crashing against the rocks somewhere beneath her, relentless and unstoppable. Sometimes they sounded enormous, sometimes pathetic, as if they had no energy for it. Last week's waves had been high, spitting white foam into the air to land back down on the already darkened wet rocks. She could smell the change in the air, the stench of seaweed and salt; she could taste it on her lips.

The sun was firmly in the sky now, pushing aside clouds. It was going to be hot and Jenny hoped her mother would want to sit outside today. She pictured the curtains shut again and then tried to push that thought aside like she was the sun. She felt for the next rock, always careful here as it was the steepest part, checking the rock with her foot, making sure it was safe and secure before she lowered her foot down. She went to stand and moved her hands too, finding the next place, when a gentle gust seemed to brush past her and her left foot wobbled, her hands shooting out desperately to grasp onto something. She righted herself, sweat breaking out in her hairline as she seized a patch of long grass firmly in her fist, took a breath, surprised that she could hear it in her own ears. *Careful, Jenny.* She thought of her mother then. Just them now. *Careful, Jenny.*

She made it to the bottom and a smile stretched across her face as she saw that most of the cove was uncovered. She unbuckled her shoes, took her socks off quickly and left them on the shelf of rock, feeling the warmth of the stone as she prepared to jump down. Underneath the shelf to the left was a semi-circle of rocks, a deep pool carpeted in seaweed, a tempting place for crabs and smaller fish. She peered down to look at it, frowning when she saw something trapped between the rocks in the gulley where the sea washed in and out.

She jumped down, felt the sand give and gasped at the sudden shock of cold up to her ankles. There was a strip of sand ahead of her still wet from the water rolling in and getting sucked back out again. Two birds flew high above, coming to rest on the ledges of the cliff with others already nestled in the walls. She felt they had come to watch and turned her body towards the rock pool.

Whatever was trapped was large, bumping up against the walls of the gulley in the froth and white of the surf. Jenny stepped towards it, her body in shadow as a rock ahead of her blocked out the sun, plunging the space into a dull grey light. Her eyes had to adjust to the sudden change and she blinked, freezing for a second as she thought she saw something impossible.

She could feel goosebumps breaking out on her skin now the sun had disappeared and she hugged herself to warm up. As she neared the rock pool the sea swept in, nearly reaching her toes and moving through the gulley, lifting the object to the surface. The sound she made was drowned out by the water draining away. *A leg,* she thought. *A monster's leg.* She stepped backwards quickly, once, twice, falling into the sand on her bottom, the water instantly seeping through the thin cotton of her skirt and underclothes. She scrambled backwards, not wanting to turn her back but needing to get away. Her hands sank hopelessly, her fingers covered in the grainy sand that stuck to her skin, speckled her legs and arms. The leg again, not at all the colour of human flesh, but a leg definitely.

Jenny finally managed to stand, wavering on the spot now, wanting to lift herself back up onto the shelf, clamber up to the clifftop, run up the path, through the garden, to the back door and into a warm embrace from Betty, who would smell of cinnamon and cigarettes. She would stay firmly nuzzled into Betty's chest as her breathing calmed and she was able to tell her the story. They would telephone the policemen from the telephone box on the road by the lookout point.

But she would have to be sure of what she had seen; she couldn't very well run all the way back and then make her mother get the police if she wasn't sure. It didn't look like a leg; it was double the size really and the wrong colour entirely. Perhaps she had dreamt it, confused things in the light.

She would have to check; she knew that now. She licked her lips and wiped the hair off her forehead. She heard the waves flood in, and back, taking their next breath, waiting for her.

Do it quickly, Jenny, she thought. Like when Betty had pulled that thorn out of her foot in one quick swipe rather than tug at it and drag on the skin. She stepped forward, determined, quickening her pace and looping around wider so she could see right down the gulley. And there it was, trapped between the two rocks, the feet facing her, a whole body, no underclothes, a sleeve of pink material, hair fanned out over where the face should have been. It was enough. It wasn't natural, didn't look like anything she had seen or even imagined before. She knew that the image wouldn't leave her. For her whole life it would be the worst thing she'd ever see.

She turned then, fast, diving onto the shelf, lifting her legs up quickly and pushing her feet into her shoes, abandoning her socks; they would slow her. The leather protested and stuck to her wet feet, there was sand all over her, coating her. She climbed swiftly, the clifftop impossibly far away, hands reaching, pulling herself up, not looking back at what she had left.

She couldn't get the image out of her mind though. Her hand on the rock; the feet, blue and stiff, toes swollen huge like bumblebee stings. Her hand on the grass, heaving herself up; the hair splayed in strips across the skin. Her hand clutching weeds; the leg that didn't look like a leg. Right up onto the clifftop, grateful for the whistle of the wind then, the sound of the water on the rocks fading, replaced by the cry of a bird. Jenny ran; the body rotating in the gulley, no clothes. She ran all the way to the house. The body in the water always with her.

Her mother's face in the kitchen window, blank at first and then worried as she saw her daughter's expression, her wet clothes. Greeted at the back door, urgent, hands on her shoulders. 'What is it? What's wrong?'

Jenny panting, snatching breaths, pointing behind her; the body bumping up against the walls of the gulley, again and again.

ABIGAIL

THREE MONTHS EARLIER

'Come on, you daft bint, keep up.' The bicycle wobbled underneath her as she turned to yell at her best friend. Mary was always slower than her, her legs tucked in neatly, back straight, hair tidily pinned, an even circular movement as she pedalled.

Abigail, on the other hand, loved to get some speed up, to feel the bump of the ground beneath her, the wind lifting her hair, twisting it this way and that, loved to hear the high screech of the brakes. Rising out of her seat, she lurched forward as she came to a dramatic stop.

She put her foot down on the ground, peered behind her and saw a man in a pin-striped suit and bowler hat on his way to work, his mouth moving into a thin line of disapproval as she giggled at Mary descending the hill slowly in the neatest line.

Mary came to a stop just behind her, her breathing a little heavier perhaps as she rolled her eyes at Abigail's expression.

'Oh, do shut up! I won't be the one to get run over by a motor car.'

'This is true, not unless it's being driven by someone very, very blind.'

Mary was holding a loose strand of her hair back, a pin in her mouth, which stopped her poking her tongue out. Abigail laughed, gazing down the hill that swept round and down to Bristol harbour. It was a grey day, the weather stubbornly refusing to shift, the buildings muted. Even the pigeons looked rather fed up and jaded, pecking half-heartedly at something under a bench across the road. Behind them the top of the Wills Memorial Building could just be spotted, rising above Park Street at the centre of the city.

'Where are we even going?' Mary called.

Abigail didn't answer, just pushed herself off, pedalling furiously, laughing at the thought of Mary's open-mouthed face as she swept down the hill, freewheeling over the concrete, down Joshua's Wells Road, past a newly built block of apartments on a site that she'd thought would stay rubble for eternity.

Mary took so long to catch up that Abigail had time to prop up her bicycle and lie flat on a bench near the quay. She stretched out, her eyes shut, smiling to herself. A shadow fell across her body and she opened one eye.

'What are you doing?' Mary had her hands on her hips.

'I am lounging,' Abigail stated, sighing and closing her eyes again. 'I am rather weary from the ride and I need to rest.'

'You are impossible. Well budge up then.'

'Get your own bench.'

Mary was quiet but the shadow hadn't left. Abigail opened an eye.

'Yes, I am still here,' Mary said, her mouth twitching.

'Fine, but I am old and weary and you should feel terrible for making me mov—'

'Oh, budge up,' Mary said, swatting Abigail and laughing as she sat on the end of the bench.

Abigail sat up straight and grinned at her.

They stayed like that for a while just looking out over the river, the water lapping gently against the quay. On the other side, men and women moved past in clusters, like shoals of fish shifting together. Builders called to each other from scaffolding and a swan glided past, oblivious to the two girls sitting watching him. The morning sun was still obscured by banks of cloud. Abigail loved Bristol in the morning.

'I need to get back,' Mary said, glancing at her wristwatch.

'Oh no, don't! How dull. Can't we stay here all morning and talk about nothing?'

'Some of us have work to go to.' Mary folded her arms.

'I have sandwich making,' Abigail said with mock horror. 'That counts as work, it's deadly.'

'The way you make them it is.'

Abigail sighed and nodded. 'How true.'

'Abigail Lovatt, you are hopeless and why are you making sandwiches anyway?'

'We're off to Bath today. Like proper ladies.' She giggled, pouting at Mary and making her laugh.

'I'd forgotten,' Mary said, stretching her arms up and moving her neck from side to side.

'I can buy you some material there if you like, you're so good with that sewing machine, it's thrilling to watch you.'

'Don't be silly, you've been saving forever.'

'Yes, but I'll make you make me something too. I am not completely idiotic.'

Mary laughed. 'Of course I will,' she said, a glint of excitement in her eyes. 'I saw a photograph of Vivien Leigh the other day in the most marvellous skirt and I think I can pull it off.'

'Oh, that would be grand, she has the most fantastic cheekbones.'

'I'm not sure a skirt will give you them,' Mary said, shaking her head.

A man had emerged from a side street in front of them, on crutches, his right trouser leg pinned up around his knee. He passed them slowly, nodding an acknowledgement as he went by. They both fell silent, smiling at him with closed lips. He paused by the quay, fiddling with a box of matches as he tried to light a cigarette. The matches fell to the ground.

Abigail jumped up, walked towards him. 'Let me.'

He was half-bending down to get them but she put a hand on his arm. He raised his eyes to hers, a cigarette drooping from his lips, then shrugged and stood up. She struck the match, cupped it quickly with one hand and held it to the cigarette.

'Thanks,' he said, drawing on it.

She handed the box back and stood by his side for a second. The swan was circling back towards them. She sneaked a look at the man's profile. He wasn't a great deal older than her, maybe thirty, maybe younger. He had rounded cheeks, like a cherub, flushed pink. He seemed so like all the men before the war except a part of him was missing.

She had grown used to seeing the broken bits, men who had returned shockingly thin, with sunken faces, dark eyes and shaking hands, young men who had sparse, white hair at their temples. Abigail's fists curled at the injustice of it; all these years later, the war leaving its reminders on their bodies.

The reminders were visible on Bristol too: the gaps in a terrace of houses, a pile of bricks waiting to be removed. He was looking across at the scaffolding, at the men working. 'We're getting there,' he said. 'You won't know in a few years.'

She didn't look at his leg, just nodded in agreement, wanting that to be true. Yet she knew they would always carry the war with them; you couldn't just build a new house over the shell of the old one without seeing it in your mind as you passed.

'You have a wonderful day, miss,' he said, grinding his cigarette with the end of his crutch and smiling at her.

'You too.'

She returned to the bench and watched the man move away. As she sat back down, Mary gave her a small smile.

'Do you think we'll ever get used to it?' Abigail sighed.

'No, and we shouldn't,' Mary said decisively, both hands resting on her thighs.

Abigail scooted along the bench to her friend and dropped her head on her shoulder. 'You are marvellous, Mary.'

Mary shrugged her off. 'Don't start,' she said gruffly, despite the corner of her mouth lifting. Then without a pause Mary leapt to her feet, ran to her bicycle and wheeled it down the pavement. Swinging herself up, she raced off into the distance, laughing and calling, 'Got you!'

'Damn.'

IRINA

SPRING 2016

To Irina Woods the shadowy silence of the shop was a comfort, the early mornings her favourite time. The sign was still turned around, the door locked and bolted, and people moved past oblivious as she calculated the previous day's takings and checked the stock.

In the back her workshop waited for her, the table pockmarked and covered in a light film of dust, tools littering its surface. The rickety shelves above the woodstove were crammed with rusting pots, smeared jam jars and old paintbrushes. Her latest project, an ancient wooden oar newly restored for a former Oxford rowing blue, awaited collection. It stuck out into the room and she would continue automatically skirting round it even after it was gone.

The smell of the bakery next door tripped on a breeze through the cracks of the flaking bay window, the glass in need of a polish. Irina's coffee had grown cold, a white skin forming on its surface. Chin resting on her hand, she doodled idly, her eyes scanning the street outside as she waited for the computer to load.

The early-morning traffic inched slowly past the window, a tired-looking man in a suit yawning in the driving seat, his mouth stretched wide, unaware he was being watched. An elderly lady in a grey cloche hat bustled past, handbag tucked neatly under one arm as she stepped aside for a teenager on a smartphone. The enormous stone wall of Petworth House cast a long shadow over the street and the shop, muting the start of the day. She looked down at her drawings, squiggles of a person, floppy hair, a wary blue eye, repeated. A horn outside and the pen slipped, a thick blue line scratched over the image.

Soon the calm would be disrupted. Patricia, chatty and indomitable, would sweep in, indignant about something, declaring war on the postman for having left a parcel in the porch, on her sister for having forgotten her birthday. The sign would be flipped, the bell would ring out and the mutterings and pleasantries from the shop would clash and hum in the air as Irina worked silently next door.

For now though this was her time to be still. She admired a recent piece she'd acquired from Ardingly market, a large, French, crested, gilt mirror, propped up against the tiled fireplace. Her face was just visible in it, peeking out over the counter, her blonde hair darker in this light, her skin waxy and pale. She blinked once, bringing the rest of the shop back into focus and turned to the computer screen.

There was an email from one of her regulars. A contact in New York who'd just purchased a property somewhere in the West Country and had sent her a few items over the years. The email told her to expect a large delivery later that week and to invoice him for the work. He never asked her for a quote before a job, trusting her to be fair, perhaps. He signed off as he always did, with warmest regards. She gave a small smile at the screen, her curiosity piqued as to the nature of the delivery. He was normally more specific in his emails, the tone of this one was even vaguer than usual.

The sound of a key turning in the lock and Irina found herself swivelling towards it, one hand automatically moving to her cheek, feeling the ridges beneath. Patricia bundled in, pulling out her key with a gloved hand and muttering something at the lock. When she looked up she jumped a fraction, startled perhaps to see Irina there, the feather in her hat quivering with the movement.

'Oh now,' she gasped.

She switched on the light and the room transformed from a wash of greys to a warm yellow, light seeking out the corners, highlighting the ceramic figurines, reflecting off the glass doors of the mahogany cabinet and making Irina blink again. She stood up from the stool she'd been perching on, ready to escape to the workshop.

'That's better,' Patricia said, shrugging off her coat and moving past the wooden trunks and tables loaded with fraying lace covers, tattered books on their surfaces, to hook it on the hat stand behind the counter. 'Isn't that better?' she remarked to Irina, giving her a smile, the gap between her middle teeth prominent.

'Much,' Irina said, busying herself with clearing away her paper, pen and coffee cup.

'You and your drawings,' Patricia remarked, taking in the doodle. 'Talented,' she said, patting Irina on the arm, eyes flicking to the side of Irina's face before sliding away as if they shouldn't linger.

Irina looked down, a curtain of hair falling over her cheek. Always aware.

'I think my granddaughter is going to be an artist too.'

'Patricia, she's two.'

'I can tell. Right, I'll get the kettle on and bring you something through to the back,' Patricia called out, moving through the shop with a duster on a stick, straightening a lampshade as she passed, clicking her tongue in satisfaction.

Irina had been dismissed. The shop was Patricia's domain; it smelt of beeswax and her rosewater scent and she kept it in jumbled order.

Irina smiled at her back as she stretched up to reach the corner. 'Thanks, Patricia,' she said and moved towards the beaded-curtain door to the workshop. She caught sight of herself again as she walked past the mirror. She was close enough now to see the damage to her face. With the light overhead and the mirror at an angle it seemed worse somehow, the scar shadowed and livid red against the paleness of her skin. She automatically covered it with her hand, pushing through the curtain with the other, letting the beads fall behind her. She wouldn't think about it today, she would focus only on the here and now.

ABIGAIL

'Mum!' Abigail called out as she pushed her way through their front door and down the hallway, poking her head into the sitting room, the velvet sofa bare, and then on into the kitchen. 'Ma!' she called over her shoulder, smiling at the shopping list left out from the day before. Her mum often left a list in her careful, rounded hand. Old lists were scratched out in pencil with new ones to the side and below; she was not yet used to the end of paper rationing. Her mum still reused everything, assembling the week's scraps into a casserole – there was always a pot of bones on the boil for a soup – turning up clothes, darning socks. During wartime others had complained about the limited food but her mum had managed to turn most things into a decent meal. The most she ever asked was for Abigail to make her a warm bath for her feet after she'd queued for hours, often at one shop after another if the first didn't have what she needed. Abigail felt a spark of guilt for not doing more for her. She would make some exceptional sandwiches.

'Mum...' Abigail walked to the bottom of the stairs, one hand on the bannister. 'I'm putting a pot on.'

They'd got so used to tea; they were now completely hooked on it. Her mum had gone for years without coffee and Abigail had anyway always found the smell more enticing than the taste. They began most days with a pot of tea, only usually it was Abigail up last, yawning in the doorway of the kitchen, hair sticking up so her mum fussed and told her she'd never find a husband if she didn't use a comb.

'I don't want a man who wants me with combed hair,' she'd say, throwing her arms out wide and making her mum laugh: a quick set of snuffles and an admonishing 'Abigail' as Abigail danced around the kitchen holding her hair up at the ends. 'He will love me for who I am, combed or uncombed.'

'Honestly!'

Abigail walked back into the hallway to glance at the grandfather clock they'd inherited a couple of years before from a great-aunt she'd never met. They were due to set off for Bath in less than half an hour.

Returning to the kitchen, she searched the larder for the tinned meat and thought about starting on their sandwiches. The hamper sat open on the kitchen table: a couple of apples, two bottles of ginger beer, a pork pie wrapped in brown paper. They'd eat their picnic in Royal Victoria Park and throw the crusts to the ducks that were better fed than half of Europe. Abigail had been saving up for months and Bath seemed the ideal place to search for a dress. She was desperate to finally own something new. Her mum's friend, Mrs Hoxley, had offered to take them both in the back of her motor car. Mrs Hoxley didn't feel right driving with just her husband, she was only happy when they weren't being wasteful, and Abigail's mum had been quick to say yes. She adored the grand, sandblasted, Georgian buildings set out in sweeping crescents of neat, uniform terraces. She had been terribly upset to hear that two of them had been gutted in the Bath Blitz.

Abigail walked up the stairs frowning. It wasn't like her mum to ignore her. Maybe she was up in the attic sorting something or bent over more mending and couldn't hear her. She wavered for a second, briefly remembering being a child and standing outside her parents' bedroom door after a nightmare. They would throw the covers back and let her crawl in next to them, shushing her back to sleep, cocooned by her pyjama-clad father and snatching a handful of her mum's cotton nightie.

'You call me a lazybones,' she said, knocking once before turning the doorknob and stepping inside. The darkness made her put her hands on her hips ready to waggle a finger in admonishment. 'Still in bed, Your Majesty.' She lowered her arms slowly, her sentence fading away.

Even with the curtains closed she could see her mum's inert body; something different about it. She wasn't lying on her side, one hand tucked under her cheek, she was lying on her back. The room was sepia-coloured; the morning light filtered through the closed curtains, seeking gaps in the material, turning her mum's face and arms a shade of orange. The room was still, utterly silent except for Abigail's quickening breaths as she took in the scene. Her mum's eyes were open and as Abigail moved forward, her brain seeing but not registering, she wondered whether her mum might suddenly move, whether her chest might rise and fall, her lips start to speak even though they remained frozen in her pale face.

She reached an arm out to touch her, flinching as she felt the cool flesh, unmoving. Her mum continued looking up at the ceiling as if examining a spot on the plaster. Abigail followed her stare, dumb and motionless by the side of the bed.

'I was making a pot,' she said, her voice seeming to bounce round the four small walls and hit straight back at her. Her mum's eyes were still staring at the ceiling. Abigail knew she should try to close them, she didn't like the glassy nothingness, her mum gone, somewhere else now but not behind those eyes.

She backed away, leaving the room without opening the curtains, clattering down the staircase and along the hallway, exploding out into the street. The daylight was a shock, the street in technicolour, the sky too blue, the clouds too white, the redbrick of the houses around her startling. She panted on the steps of the house, whirling left and right for help, for something.

Two women chatting, one pushing a large navy pram on the other side of the road, looked up. A gloved hand pointed to her standing there, another hand redirected the pram. They started to cross the road. Their faces were filled with questions, one of them was asking her something. She couldn't hear exactly what. She felt the tears that were falling without restraint and her voice came as if from far away. 'My mum, she's... I found her... She's...'

She couldn't bring herself to say the words. She wanted to turn straight round, shut the front door, call her mum down for tea and hear a response, as if the last few minutes had happened in an alternative world, to another version of themselves.

One of the women came towards her. Abigail could see her mouth moving a few seconds before she heard the words penetrate her head. 'Do you need us to get help?'

'No, she can't... She's dead.'

The woman sucked air through her teeth as Abigail collapsed against her. 'She's dead. My mum's dead.'

They wouldn't be going anywhere together today. They wouldn't be going anywhere together anymore.

IRINA

When Patricia left for lunch every day, Irina was alone in the shop. With a weary gait she would emerge from the sanctuary of her workshop, the beads clacking behind her as she moved over to the till. The hour would be spent having to smile at people as they entered, answer any questions, explain the prices. Perched on the edge of the stool like a nervous bird about to take flight, she tried to avoid their gazes; she dreaded the moment when they would approach her, when they would notice. No words were ever spoken, perhaps a light cough into a hand, the stuttering of their first sentence as their tongue seemed too big for their mouth.

Today was no different. Irina waited as a woman with tight blonde curls and bright pink glasses pottered through the shop, lifting pieces, examining them in the light from the window. The sun was now over the wall of Petworth House, casting rays into the shop that sliced through the air in speckled ribbons, the dust particles softening the effect. Sniffing, the woman put down a ceramic leprechaun and drew a hand across the surface of an oak side table. She called something over her shoulder to Irina, who leant forward to answer.

The woman repeated the question without looking up. 'Have you noticed this?' Her finger, bony and tipped with a thick, dark orange nail, pressed on the surface.

Irina untangled her feet from the lower bar of the stool and moved across to see what the woman was pointing at. Her head was bowed and her pink glasses had slid to the end of her nose. Her finger was tracing a line in the wood, a hairline split in the grain. Irina bent forward to examine it and in that moment the woman looked sideways. The whole of Irina's face was highlighted, damaged and shocking in the daylight. Irina felt the woman suck in all her breath; there was a tiny whistle of her teeth and a step backwards.

Irina gabbled the explanation. 'I refinished the top, trying to get the colour as close to the original stain, but you don't want to make it entirely perfect…' The woman wasn't listening but tried to nod at the facts, the shake of her head coming a second too late. Irina's hands were clammy, her throat dry; she trailed off as the woman smiled a thank you, effusive, her eyes crinkling and maximized by the lenses in the bright frames. Irina held her gaze, deliberately unwavering, like she was testing herself. Her eyes watered, unblinking.

Eventually Irina backed off to the stool, wanting the barrier of the counter between them, wondering why she felt upset. This was nothing new and yet today she felt fragile, tired of it all. The woman left the shop shortly afterwards with a hearty goodbye, the words filled with feeling. Irina raised a hand, the reply sticking. Then she was left alone again. The ticking of two clocks clashed in the air as she waited for Patricia to return so that she could escape.

ABIGAIL

'I'll go with you,' Mary said tearfully. They were going round in circles.

It had been a couple of hours since they'd watched Abigail's mum being lowered into the ground. They were dressed in identical black, the woollen material sticking to them, too hot for the unseasonably warm spring day. Their abandoned pillbox hats with squares of veil were lying on the grass between them, their flattened hair as lank as the mood of the day.

'But your work...'

Abigail was biting on her lip. Since her mum had died she'd felt eerily removed from things, as if she were floating above her own life, watching it unfold. She kept walking into rooms and expecting her mum to be there, kept answering the door to people thinking they were her. Imagined her popping in, pulling up a chair. 'Silly you! I was here all the time.' People came with casseroles and pitying looks and Abigail had to keep the kettle on the boil so that the permanent scream from the escaping steam sounded exactly like the noise in her head.

'Maybe they'll have something for me there?'

'But where would you live?' Abigail knew she wasn't helping but she felt a brittleness about it all. Her mum had died. She was leaving. This life was over, a full stop, a very definite end. As if the past had a large line drawn next to it and she could never cross back.

That was the past in which she and Mary had discussed their futures in light-hearted voices, sipping cider for the first time, patching clothes, drawing lines on their legs to pretend they were wearing nylons. They were going to find work as secretaries, travel, marry American lads, or not. Mary admitted to Abigail once that she didn't much fancy working for a man at home as well as working outside. Abigail wanted to be in love though, wanted to be kissed, held tilted backwards by a wavy-haired man like Marlon Brando. That was before when she'd felt something. Now she would do anything to be able to stay living with her mum, looking after her, bringing her cups of sweet tea and reading to her, remaining an old maid; anything to cross that line back into the past.

They were leaning against the Clifton Downs tower, their heads resting on the stonework, both hopelessly lost in the misery of the moment, the spring sunshine, the hopeful blossom on the trees, the clumps of waving daffodils incongruous with their mood.

'You can't go,' Mary said simply.

Abigail wanted to bundle her friend into her arms and never let go but, again, she saw her as if through a thick lens, as if she had picked up binoculars and failed to adjust them, so that everything was squiffy and blurry. She didn't want to leave; she knew that much; she didn't want to be alone. But the house was only rented – her mum had taken in mending from a lot of the grand houses in Clifton, working at it day in, day out until the light failed – and now the landlord's patience was waning and Abigail knew she had to go.

She was headed to Devon, to a sister she hadn't seen since long before the war, who had married in a church in Aspley Road when Abigail was wearing frocks, pulled-up socks and sandals, and pigtails in her hair. Her sister hadn't made the funeral, had sent a vast arrangement of flowers for the coffin and her apologies that 'family circumstances' prevented her from attending. Abigail had been too swept up in everything else at the time but now it made her fists clench. How could her sister have stayed away?

She had distant memories of her sister as a child. She'd had a line of three china dolls, all dressed in velvet and with cherubic cheeks and beady eyes, sitting on a trunk at the foot of the bed. She had been sent to her room once when she had stamped her foot at their daddy. She had loved drawing, producing neat pictures with all the colour inside the lines, not like Abigail's, a mad mess of scrawls and mismatched shades. She had pinched her: that Abigail remembered.

They were older now though and she would have changed. She wouldn't be the girl who had locked her in the outside lavatory for the longest afternoon in winter so that Abigail had clawed at the wooden boards and got splinters in her fingers; or the girl who had shown her how to put on lipstick, creeping into their mum's room to prance and preen in the mirror, giggling and slopping around in high-heeled shoes that were much too big.

When she made herself, Abigail could picture them both picking their way carefully across the fields of north Devon, heads bent together, laughing. Then that scene would melt away, replaced by a blank face on a body she didn't recognize. A hard woman with thin lips, glaring at Abigail through narrowed eyes, wondering why Abigail was there. Abigail shook her head to get rid of the image. The picture postcards her sister sent promised sunny days, promenading in hats, ice-creams, open space. She felt lighter at the thought then, wanting to convince herself, needing the comfort of family, needing something on this earth of her mum. They would cling to each other and cry and Abigail would feel something again.

Abigail wanted to believe she wouldn't miss the bustle and dirt of Bristol, wouldn't miss picking up Mary from her shift at the pub, the thrill of walking into the cramped, low-ceilinged room hung about with pots. The sweaty, heaving mass as she pushed past men holding tankards of ale; the toothy grins of the regulars as they beckoned her over to the tables where they sat on upturned barrels and chairs drinking thick cider, the dregs creeping up the sides of their glasses. The room smelling of noisy men, tobacco and the sweet tang of apples. The heat all around her, hemming her in, caressing her, leaving patches under her arms, trickles down her back. The walk back along the river to Mary's house, the boats gently rocking, the cranes reaching over the surface of the water, the steam trains hissing in the station. Clifton overlooking it all in its glorious pomp: manicured lawns, sloping roads lined with impressive stone houses behind high walls and heavy gates. Bristol seemed greyer now, a body without its heart: no reason to stay.

But Mary, her friend, watching her now with large brown eyes, always ready to smile sweetly from one side of her mouth, a blush creeping over her milky cheeks when she laughed. She had felt more like a sister to her these last few years. During he war; they'd spent their days dipping in and out of each other's houses, Mary quick to appear of a morning, escaping her dad's bleak moods. Mary's mum had walked out on it all, but Mary had had nowhere to go. Abigail and her mum had become Mary's family and the girls had shared everything with each other. They had so many plans for the future, for the adventures they would go on, their travels taking them across the Atlantic. And now she was leaving her. For a moment Abigail could feel the guilt stealing into her veins, pumping round her body, straining to be felt.

She had dreamt about Mary last night, standing in the middle of the Downs, turning slowly in a circle. Not a soul around. And Abigail had watched her lost in this sea of grass, unable to call to her. Mary circling, the long grass tickling her ankles as she turned, her eyes scanning the edges of the Downs, moving along the lines of bushes, past the tower, searching for someone, hoping for someone. And Abigail stuck to her spot, looking on, helpless.

Abigail stood up suddenly and Mary jolted upright as Abigail brushed her thighs with the palm of her hands. She was brusque, ducking out of Mary's proffered arm, wrapping her coat around her like a shield, tucking her hands under her armpits, still feeling cold.

'I need to get back, I've got so much to pack up, to do.'

Mary stood opposite her, placing her hat on her head, smoothing the strands of hair that had broken free. 'I can help.'

'No, I… You have work and I need to…' She wasn't sure what she needed, but her tone was enough to ensure Mary didn't argue. Her friend's mouth closed; her expression hurt. It made Abigail turn on her heel.

She left her standing by the tower looking after her. She left her abruptly, as if she were leaving for Devon that day, as if she had already left.

IRINA

Irina wrapped the cardigan around herself and stepped outside. Although the days were getting longer there was still a chill in the air, like winter wanted to cling on, wasn't yet ready to say goodbye. She opened the back gate of the garden, reaching to unlatch it, the flimsy planks of wood worn over the years, bending to the weather. The sound of it clicking back into place made Irina feel lighter. The narrow alleyway behind the gardens smelt of damp and weeds. Ivy spilled over the backs of gardens, out of control, twisting into the thin branches that invaded the space overhead and hid the sun from view; the slits of light never reached far and the ground was soft and pockmarked with puddles, leaving mud on the soles of her boots.

Emerging onto the high street always came as a shock, the sky opening up in front of her, the high stone wall to her side snaking around the backs of the houses and out of view. The high street was picture-postcard pretty with its chocolate-box cottages, thatched roofs, single chimneys, roses clambering up trellises and window boxes crammed with different-coloured flowers. Shops had tables under awnings in front of them and people stepped out into the narrow street to manoeuvre round shoppers gossiping on the pavement.

Today clouds hung plump and still above the scene, the bright patchwork greens of the fields rolling away behind the town. Irina moved down the road, past bookshops and other antique stores, their windows loaded up with treasures: lace, wood, mirrors, miniature oil paintings in oval gold frames. Irina's attention was always half-caught by them – a hunting scene, a silver-backed hairbrush, porcelain figurines – the sight of them a comfort as she headed towards the corner of a side street and a small café with its striped awning rolled up and one or two customers sitting inside.

Pushing into the café, automatically ducking her head despite being a good foot shorter than the door, she said a quiet hello to the man behind the counter. His features, weathered and wild, seemed at odds with the tiny shop, his frame too large to be contained by such a feminine environment of chintz and china. He gave her a warm smile of recognition, a gold filling glinting from a back tooth, and pointed to a table in the centre of the room. 'I'll be over in a second.'

The polished pine table rocked on the uneven floor as she leant on it, and the centrepiece, a single flower sitting in a delicate vintage teacup of water, wobbled. Around her the bumpy stone of the whitewashed walls was broken up with black and white photographs of seaside scenes from the turn of the last century: men with their trousers rolled to the ankle and flat caps on their heads, woman wearing large hats draped in ribbons tiptoeing gingerly over the sands. On the counter was a side plate filled with coins and an ageing till with a RNLI donation box in the shape of a plastic boat.

In the back she could make out the sound of water running, pans clashing and the gentle buzz of a kitchen. A blend of different aromas billowed softly around the café – coffee, basil, cheeses – as she waited for the menu. She knew what she was ordering but she liked the calming atmosphere, the measured process; she felt her back relaxing, the knots loosening in her shoulders. Blurred shapes of people moved past a thin curtain of gauze, an inch-wide crack in the middle showing every detail as they passed, but only for a second.

She ate in silence, chewing carefully on the food and reading her book, turning the pages slowly. She was lost in the story, running through a house in Norfolk, deep inside the heroine's head. She asked for the bill by making a neat sign in the air and, as ever, it was carried over to her on a small silver tray. She left money on top of the receipt and smiled a thank you, closing her book in the process and making to put it back in her bag. It was in that moment, as she turned her head, that she saw him. A brief second, so clear, in the crack where the curtains didn't quite meet.

His floppy blonde hair pushed off his forehead with a huff; his favourite jumper, the blue knitted one he never took off. Her hand reached out for the table, which tipped up towards her as she held the edge and followed the boy with her eyes. He had moved behind the gauze now, was another indistinct blur behind netting, anonymous. She uncrossed her legs quickly, her book still in one hand, her bag in the other, forgetting everything else as she made it to the door of the café.

She stepped out onto the street and looked left, her lips pursed tightly, breath suspended as she wondered what she would see. The street ahead was empty: no boy, no anybody. It curved away downhill; on the other side a couple hovered outside a row of small shops. A man at the post box with a walking stick was looking over at her. She blinked once, then a puff of frustration behind her from a woman with a pram jolted her out of her reverie.

'I'm sorry,' she mumbled, feeling goosebumps break out on her skin. She stepped back inside the café and the woman pushed on with a brief glare of annoyance.

The man behind the counter glanced up briefly, giving her a quizzical look as she returned to her table to collect her cardigan from the back of her chair. Leaving without a word to him, she walked quickly back along the road in the direction of the shop and the shady quiet of her workspace. Before stepping into the cool of the alleyway she couldn't help looking behind her once more, hoping for another glimpse of that blue jumper, of that fair hair. He was nowhere to be seen.

ABIGAIL

It was strange seeing her sister, dressed in a fitted pattern dress with a full skirt, her waist nipped in, a cardigan thrown over her shoulders, dark brown hair pinned in curls, patent heels clip-clopping towards her. She seemed to be of another time, to have stepped straight out of the pre-war years, the sun bright behind her, haloing her in light.

Abigail had never felt drearier. She glanced down at her own dress, the hem decidedly wonky after a last-minute effort to fix it before she left Bristol, her brown suede heels scuffed at the toe, a grease stain on the arm of her jumper, which was faded and worn. She looked as if she had travelled, all stale smells and hair loose and mussed up after she'd fallen asleep waiting for the connection in Minehead.

Abigail wanted to duck out of the greeting as she stepped off the coach, embraced in a cloud of Miss Dior which overpowered the rest: the smells of the sea, the seaweed lining the banks of the harbour. Her sister stayed there, her hug tight, sharp, definite. Abigail was frozen, both hands clutching her luggage. Then she allowed herself a moment of relief. This was someone who was certain, sure-footed. She let herself be hugged and pressed; she would be told what to do, she could relax as, for the first time in weeks, someone took away the need to make a decision.

She had stumbled off the coach, relieved to be on solid ground after the rattling descent into the village down Countisbury Hill. The screech of the brakes and the momentary alarm that they would end up in a scrunched heap of metal at the bottom had made her squeak with nervousness. The bang and clatter of everyone piling out, pushing down the aisle with children dressed in long socks and shorts, carpet bags clutched to chests, a hat case bumping past the seats, an elderly woman oblivious to the commotion, a Yorkshire terrier asleep on her lap.

'How was the journey? You poor thing, it's a long way. Is that all you've brought? I'd have bags and bags.' Her sister's voice rose, unfamiliar and confident. Abigail watched her mouth moving as if from a distance, slow to respond.

'It was fine. I had an Eccles cake.'

'... I've got Edith to put out some lunch, I hope you're hungry, you must be, and we have so much to do...'

The voice faded in and out. The climb and subsequent drop down the hill had made Abigail's ears pop; now sounds were louder than before, her head fuzzy. She turned to wave at the coach driver, who raised a hand in return.

Her sister was already walking away in the direction from which she'd arrived as Abigail rushed to keep up, her suitcase and hat case banging against her legs. Her head was snapping left and right as she took in the village. It was as if she'd been dropped into a world entirely different from the one she'd left: the place was surrounded by banks of green rising sharply at every turn, and churning water below them. Along one riverbank was a line of cottages, people walking arm in arm, neat flowered borders, smoke rising from chimneys. In the harbour boats idled, two men called to each other, hands shielding their eyes. And then her sister: years older, a completely different person from the teenage girl she remembered. Her lips were plumper, outlined in a deep pink, and she had winged brown lines on her eyelids, thin but noticeable, rouge on her cheeks and nylon stockings on her legs. As she marched a little way ahead, back straight, chin tilted up, she looked like a model in a picture magazine, spectacular in this tiny corner of north Devon. It gave Abigail hope that all was not lost.

Connie turned in profile, her snub nose perfect. 'It isn't far; it is a little steep towards the end. I did tell Larry it might have been nice to use the car, but he...' She trailed off, head twisting back around.

'That's fine, I don't mind walking.' Abigail huffed, keen to please, feeling twelve again, traipsing around the streets of Bristol after her.

'We'll go up behind the Pavilion, there are steps there. Do you dance? There are sometimes dances.' She threw the question behind her.

Abigail nodded, her breaths coming out in short gasps. 'Yes... dance.'

'Good. We will, we will,' Connie muttered, seemingly to herself. 'Come on.' She paused at the bottom of a set of stairs. 'Halfway there now.'

Abigail looked at the small café built into one of the sea walls, the steamed-up windows, the cake stands on display through the glass, and felt her stomach rumble, the Eccles cake a rather long time ago. Connie wasn't pausing, marching them across a bridge where two rivers met, Abigail peeking over the side to see the water hurtling past.

She was sweating by the time they reached the house, the

narrow path, very steep in places, making her thighs burn with the effort. The leather handles of the suitcase were slippery and unpleasant in her hand and the hat-case string bit into her palm. She could feel her hair sticking to her neck and forehead as she followed her sister onto a gated driveway, two stone-ball finials marking the entrance.

The house was perched on the side of the cliff, a line of trees obscuring the sea behind it. Irina stared up at the vast redbrick building, its dormer windows seeming miles away, the tall, double chimney stacks silhouetted against the sky. They moved through the porch, past a cast-iron boot scraper and a pair of boots abandoned next to the mat. Her sister fiddled in her bag for a key to the front door, which had a polished brass ring in the centre of the glossy paint.

They entered a wide hallway bordered with an elaborate cornice. There was a hat stand and hooks for their coats and a gleaming oak table with a mirror suspended above it. The door to her right opened onto an enormous living room that looked out over the sea. French doors led out onto a large semi-circular stone terrace that provided the best views from its white wrought-iron table and two chairs surrounded by pots full of lavender. The house was decorated like the centre spread in *My Home* magazine. Elegant sculptures of sinewy women, bare-breasted and lounging on plinths, were scattered about the room; there was a peppermint chaise longue; a book lay abandoned on a mahogany table with spindly legs that sat beneath an enormous gilt-framed mirror. Abigail couldn't help comparing the Bristol house with this grandeur, worrying already that she should have wiped her shoes at the door.

'I hope you don't mind stairs,' Connie said with a tinkling laugh.

They climbed to a first-floor landing, the carpet springy

beneath their feet, and turned up another flight: oil paintings hanging in spaces, polished furniture, freshly plucked flowers in cut-crystal vases. The air was sweet with perfume and Abigail felt her head spinning with everything she was taking in. She could feel the sweat collecting in her hairline and under her arms, the suitcase heavy in her hand as she puffed up the last set of stairs.

Connie stood, impeccable, at the doorway, a smile on her painted lips as she prepared to push open the door. With a flourish she showed Abigail inside. The single bed was covered in a baby-pink rug and an ancient teddy bear was propped up against the pillow, perhaps a sign that her sister also imagined she was still the young girl she had left in Bristol all those years ago. A posy of daisies sat in fresh water alongside a small lamp and a Bible squeezed onto the bedside table. An oak dressing table in the bay window looked out over the sea.

'It's beautiful, it's all lovely, thank you,' Abigail said, looking around at the space, the sun warming the room, the glass polished. She swallowed as a flash of her mum's face in the dull quiet of their Bristol house appeared in her mind. It was really over, she was here now, in this place with a sister she hadn't seen in over a decade.

There was a noise downstairs and Connie patted her hair, checking her appearance in the dressing-table mirror.

'That's Larry,' she said quickly, pursing her lips and then releasing them.

Abigail could hear keys being thrown down onto a metal surface, a pause followed by footsteps, then a quick call to his wife.

'We're up here,' Connie trilled in a new voice, two tones higher.

The footsteps were on the stairs now, then came the top of

a man's head, a thick neck on too-narrow shoulders and finally, crowding into the corridor, turning the corner and blocking the view behind him, a man who seemed all limbs. Thick dark eyebrows that almost met in the middle, fair hair receding at the crown. His shoulders filled the doorway, his eyebrows pulled together as he stood on the threshold, staring at them both.

'Well, well, well,' he said, turning to Abigail, starting at her shoes, pausing over the scuff marks, rising slowly to her knees, making her suddenly want to cross her legs or curl herself into a ball before this scrutiny, over her dress, waist, breasts, a flicker in his expression and then her face. Not a word.

Her sister's high laugh filled the silence. 'Larry, meet Abigail.'

'My little sister-in-law,' he said, taking a step towards her, tipping an imaginary hat. A slow smile crept over his face. 'Welcome.'

IRINA

Irina had finished for the day; the walnut lamp base was now packaged in brown paper and ready for pick-up the next day. She had worked late, switching on the overhead strip light as the sun seeped away from the window. Outside, the garden was a patch of greyish shadow and the few stars were muffled by cloud. She washed out her coffee mug in the stained butler's sink in the corner and placed it upturned on the side, the wood marked with wet rings from earlier that day.

Leaving the workshop locked up, she checked the doors of the shop, the furniture forming unfamiliar shapes in the darkness as she pressed past. With everything quiet she climbed the stairs at the back, a worn runner dampening her footsteps on the wood, her hand reaching up automatically for the light switch. A flicker and the landing was illuminated: the pot plant that had seen better days, and her flat door with the brush mat outside. She turned the key in the lock, heard the latch give, stepped inside, and threw her keys onto a plate on the sideboard.

Moving though to her living room, feeling the night weigh

down on her, she turned on lamps and filled the space with noise. The flat had been hers now for four years; her mother had helped her with the deposit, had said she'd been saving it, that Dad would have wanted it. All the furniture in it was reclaimed and restored: the sofa was made of soft brown leather, the Persian rug a pattern of fine thread, its colours deeper in the lamplight, the swept empty fireplace was surrounded by ceramic tiles, its mantelpiece bare apart from two candlesticks and a photograph of back then. In the corner a wooden trunk contained letters and diaries from a half-forgotten time.

She drew the heavy plum curtains across, glimpsing the empty high street beyond. She thought back to the boy from earlier and felt a sharp pang in her chest. Running a hand along the trunk, she shook her head. She had promised herself that today was not a day for going back over things, she shouldn't give in to the constant desire to linger on the past.

Pepper snuck around the kitchen door and wound herself round Irina's legs until she bent to pick her up. Her soft fur tickled Irina's face as she moved through to the kitchen. She spooned out food for her, then opened the fridge for some eggs to make an omelette, automatically twisting to turn on the radio so that voices crammed into her galley kitchen with her, removing herself from her head. She stirred the mixture slowly, hearing the sizzle of the pan, chopped the parsley quickly and neatly, fingers tucked under. The heat from the pan filled the air with a warm cloud. The voices were arguing, a familiar comfort as she loaded up her plate, poured herself a drink and propped herself up on the bar, the stool scraping along the wooden floorboards. She focused on their words, followed the debate with half-hearted nods, a mouthful of omelette on a fork. When she was finished she switched off the radio, picked up her book from her bag and moved back through to the living room, pausing as she did every night to look at the photograph on the mantelpiece. Four of them, all smiling. They had been in an ice-cream parlour in Tenby.

She couldn't remember the booth in the parlour, she couldn't remember the flavour she chose, she couldn't remember posing for the photographer. Perhaps a waiter her dad had summoned over? She couldn't remember her mother pulling her towards her, her dad throwing an arm over her shoulder and around her brother. She couldn't remember if they said 'cheese'. She did remember the car journey down and listening to her new Walkman; it was yellow and black and she'd gone everywhere with it. Joshua sat next to her, mouth tight with concentration, both hands on the plastic wheel stuck to the back of their dad's seat. He made engine noises, so she had to twist the volume up; he beeped his plastic horn loudly and begged their dad to do the same. She remembered her mother swivelling round from the passenger seat, telling him to quieten down, a big smile on her face as she said it, so Joshua would laugh and carry on.

She blinked once, a finger hovering in the air ready to trace the familiar faces; she snatched it back. She forced herself to turn away and curled up in her favourite armchair, upholstered in light pinks and yellows and so large she could tuck herself into it entirely. Surrounded by bookshelves crammed with well-worn favourites lined up and stacked on top, in every available space, she breathed out slowly and focused on her book, the words dancing in front of her for a second, her eyes flicking upwards to the photograph, then back to the page, then settled into the routine.

MARY

She couldn't shake off the last look, Abigail – drawn and pale – stepping onto the coach, a man in a flat cap and brown trousers lifting her suitcase up onto the rack, her bewildered face in the window, one hand up to rest on it as the coach drew away, the blurred behind as Mary let the tears fall.

For the last few years it seemed Abigail and her mum had become her family. Mary was drawn to the small terraced house, her whole body relaxing as she turned into the street, eyes resting on the painted door, the glow of the windows either side, the smell of a casserole as she stepped into the corridor with its chintz wallpaper. The gentle laughter coming from the front room, abandoned knitting, plumped cushions, well-worn books left lying around. They'd crowded around the fire in winter, listening to the radio, falling into companionable silence. It had seemed like home, unlike her cold bedsit with stockings drying over the back of a chair, mismatched furniture, and a single faded photograph of her father before it all. Noises from her flatmate below – a student who seemed to spend his days playing jazz, shrieks punctuating the silence, muted giggles and hushing so that their ancient landlord wouldn't appear – made her feel all the lonelier.

Everyone asked after Abigail in the pub. She'd appeared more colourful somehow in that setting. The fug-filled air fuller as she chatted and laughed with the customers. She could charm anyone, even Ken the landlord, scrubbing furiously at the bar, rushing round to flick fruitlessly at her stool, offer a hand to help her up, raised eyebrows from the semicircle of men behind him. Abigail teaching them absurd new card games before their shifts, sitting at the upright piano banging out songs, hopelessly out of tune and yet perfect, filling the bar with noise.

Now she had gone, the terraced house had new occupants, a young family, flushed and happy looking, a baby in a pram outside, a mother sitting on the doorstep with a half-smile on her face. Abigail would have liked them, would have bent over the pram to fuss and coo at the baby with its plump cheeks and tiny fists. Mary had waved at Mrs Brent who lived next door, swallowing her hello as she turned away, not wanting to face this new reality.

She wondered then what Abigail was doing, whether she was eating ice-pops and lounging around in striped deckchairs. She imagined Devon was ten degrees warmer, everyone living on the beach, trousers rolled up, spotted handkerchiefs on heads as they felt the sun on their backs. Could she see the sea from her window, could she hear the gulls, watch the ships passing? Abigail's sister had always seemed impossibly glamorous. While they were roaming around, hair barely combed, grass stains on their skirts, Connie had been a composed and prettier version. Her wedding photograph that had stood in the centre of the mantelpiece in Abi's house showed a grown-up in lace and make-up. She wondered what the house was like and imagined it to be impeccably tidy and spacious.

Mary sat on the harbourside, legs dangling down into the nothingness, the walls streaked with dried-out seaweed, the smell overpowering for those not used to it, forcing a besuited passer-by to cover his mouth and nose with his handkerchief. She was part of the bustling life of the port, the smeared dockers who came into the pub with salt on their skin, speckling their arms with white, their hair stiff with it, sculpted into clumped peaks.

For a moment Mary felt an ache for the loss of things, wanting to be sitting at the bottom of Abigail's bed again playing cat's cradle with wool as they swapped gossip and dreamt about the exciting lives they were going to lead. Now she'd been left alone and their talk of travelling the world together seemed ridiculous, impossible. She pictured Abigail morphing into her sister, meeting new friends, forgetting Bristol and Mary. It would take Mary an age to save the money she needed, and even then she felt uncertain; without Abigail's confidence she felt lost. She swallowed, slapping the side of her calf as something bit into her, knowing this was probably it for her and that she would never leave.

ABIGAIL

Her sister lived like a movie star, her bedroom a fairy tale: paisley curtains, the hems stitched with delicate gold thread, a Windsor armchair in the corner and a careful spray of magazines fanned out on a low glass table. The four-poster bed with a canopy stood imposingly in the centre of the room. Raised on a platform, two carpeted steps leading up to it, it took Abigail's breath from her. She wanted to rush across the room and fling herself down on top of the quilt, plunge her head into the goose-down pillows and look out over the tops of the trees to the blue beyond.

'It's breath-taking! How do you ever leave it?' Abigail said in a reverential whisper.

Was it a flicker of uncertainty that crossed her sister's face then or something she imagined?

'I was allowed to design it myself,' she said, drawing her hand along the dressing table in the corner, littered with pots and brushes and creams.

'Well you've done it brilliantly.' Abigail was gratified to see her sister blushing at the compliment in the triptych-mirror.

'Sometimes I've been… Well…' Her sister was smoothing an eyebrow. 'I'm glad you're here, that's all,' she said, turning to look at her.

For the first time since her mum had died Abigail felt a swell of relief, a little puncture in the hurt so that some of the blackness was released. 'I miss her,' she said, her voice cracking, her eyes filling with tears. So many tears recently; they seemed to spring up without warning.

'You must, of course,' her sister said, returning to the triptych-mirror.

Abigail felt her body stiffen at the words. Did Connie not miss her too? Did she not remember those days when they would crowd round her legs as she read to them, the meals she'd made, the noses she'd wiped? She had hand-sewn a thousand tiny beads onto Connie's wedding dress, sitting beneath a lamp, straining her eyes late into the night. Abigail had barrelled in to find her after a nightmare, her mum soothing her forehead as she curled up next to her on the sofa.

Connie placed one hand on her stomach, her fingers splayed as she stood, embarrassed perhaps by Abigail's tears that were falling so freely. 'Come on now,' she chided, neatening a row of brushes in front of her, not meeting Abigail's eye in the mirror.

'Why did you not come?' The sentence spilled out before Abigail could stop it.

'Hmm…' Connie was frowning at a blemish on the glass.

'The funeral, why did you stay away?'

For a moment it seemed Connie's face dissolved, eyes drooping, a light gone from them. 'I wanted to, I asked, but he…' She knocked a brush off the dressing table, bent to pick it up. 'Oh, silly me.' The high laugh, the words said in a sing-song voice, a lipstick smile plastered back on her face.

Abigail stepped forward, needing to hear her answer, the

hurt of the past few weeks blocking her throat, stoppering her voice. She was frightened she would start to shout and then there would be no stopping.

'Well we can't idle about here all morning, best get on,' her sister said. She chattered all the way to the door, bustling Abigail out of the room as she did so.

Abigail was propelled along, her confidence ebbing away as she found herself back in the corridor, the gleaming staircase ahead of her, her sister already moving away down the stairs, calling to Edith about polishing the bedroom.

IRINA

The two delivery men wore black T-shirts and weary expressions. Irina had forgotten it was arriving today, until she heard Patricia's click of annoyance as the van stopped, half on the pavement, half on the road, prompting a cacophony of horn-honking. They carried it through the shop, pausing halfway to lower it and clear a wide enough path through to the workshop.

The piece was covered in a dust sheet and Irina wondered what she had taken on, feeling the familiar thrill she experienced before any job. Her New York client had a wonderful eye for beautiful pieces. She directed the men to a space in the corner of the room where she had laid a sheet on the floor and they placed it there slowly, a drawer sliding forward so that the handle could be seen poking at the cloth.

The men lingered, perhaps in the hope of being offered a mug of tea, and Patricia had to bundle them back out to their van. A line of cars was skirting it slowly and there were annoyed glances from drivers, knuckles strained on the steering wheels.

Irina turned towards the dustsheet, tentatively reaching out a hand to unveil it. She pulled it back, snagging it on a corner so that she had to reach around and free it. The lights in the room buzzed and flickered for a second, making her glance up.

'What is it?' Patricia asked as she swept through the beaded curtain, heading for the kettle and flicking it on.

'A bureau,' Irina said, her eyes drinking in the details as she moved around it. It was made of mahogany, from the Georgian period she would say, and it had pigeonhole drawers and smaller rectangular drawers beneath them. She carefully lowered the writing desk, jumping as Patricia walked up behind her.

'What's wrong with it?'

Irina frowned, feeling along the edges of the wood. The smell of old paper, damp wood and a faint whisper of another scent underneath, something familiar.

'It doesn't look too major. The leatherette needs replacing, it needs to be cleaned, another layer of polish, some of the pigeonhole drawers need attention.'

Her fingers explored the surface of the wood: scratches on the top, the splintered edges of the unpolished wood underneath bubbled and uneven. Her hand traced the corners, rounded and smooth, into the middle of the piece; the handle of the drawer was made of brass, grubby and unloved. She felt further along, inch by inch. A shot of pain in her hand, sharp, like a bite and she snatched it back, clutching it to her chest, her fingers curled into themselves, protective.

As she stared at the bureau a sudden unease settled over her; she was pleased then at the interruption of the kettle switching itself off, a faint cloud of steam making a pattern on the mirror above it. Irina squinted, her brain slow to catch up with what she was seeing. For a second she was certain she could make out a face through the steam, faint, impossible. Her head snapped back round to look behind her. The bureau stood sentinel, waiting for her. Back to the mirror, just a circle of steam. She stared, not wanting to take her eyes from it, seizing on Patricia's offer of a mug of tea, accepting it in a too-loud voice.

ABIGAIL

She found the quiet unsettling. The swooping screech of a seagull punctuated the stillness, which made her pull the covers up so that only her face peeked out. She lay on the bed, the sheets warm, straining to hear the noises she was used to in the morning – the rumble of motor cars over the cobbled street by her house, the whistle of the milkman, the chink of the bottles as he unloaded them from his cart. Instead it was the gentle wash of the sea somewhere below, the sleepy start in the village.

She should be getting up, ready to help her mum in the kitchen and make the soup for their lunch, but of course all that was over now. She felt her chest tighten. What would she do now? Who was she now? She had heard them last night through the thin walls of the house, muttered voices no doubt asking the same questions. She wouldn't be a nuisance but she would need money, to claw her way back to the city. She and Mary were going to America. It seemed an impossible idea now and the thought made her shiver.

She heard footsteps on the stairs beyond the door, steady,

slow, heavy on the bare wood, echoing in the confined space of the hall. They paused for a moment and she imagined someone on the other side of the door. Seconds passed and Abigail realized she was holding her breath. The footsteps lingered, then back down the stairs, one, two, quick and decisive.

Abigail got up, removed a sheaf of paper to write to Mary, tell her everything about her arrival, the village, try to ease the loneliness. Thinking of her face made tears prick at the back of her eyes and she looked up to the ceiling, blinking slowly.

She perched on the small chair by the window, the sea stretching into the distance, iron-grey and covered in a low mist, her pen in her mouth, lost in the past. Mist seemed to cling to the clifftop beyond, sticky on the treetops, not wanting to let go just yet. The jutting rocks spilled down the side to the beach below, the shingle a mix of purples and greys. She could just make out a couple of figures walking along the front.

A knock at her door and her sister pushed her way in, already looking preened and pressed and ready for the day. Abigail felt vulnerable in her threadbare dressing gown and worn slippers. She pulled the thin cotton around her body, shivering in the draught from the door. The pen dropped to the floor and she bent to pick it up.

Connie looked around the room, the rumpled bed, clothes erupting from the leather bag.

'I thought we could walk into the village.'

Abigail nodded and stepped over to the bed, self-consciously tugging on the covers, smoothing them down with her hand.

'Leave that. Edith will do it later. Come on.' Her sister laughed, walking across to pick up Abigail's jacket, blue cotton in an old-fashioned shape, found in a flea market in Bristol beloved by her mum.

Connie sniffed, her cheeks powdered, lines barely there. 'You could do with a couple of things and it's been ages since I've had the excuse to shop for anything new. You'd think clothes were still rationed round here, the way they patch and darn everything.'

Her sister's voice was different to her memory of it. Lower, with altered emphasis on the consonants, like the vowels were often missing.

Abigail didn't want to admit she had hardly any money; she and her mum had had to be so careful, setting aside the month's money for the rent and food. They'd been saving to buy a television set. Her mum had been swept along in Abigail's enthusiasm for it, even though she was perfectly happy to sit and listen to the wireless herself. Abigail felt a stab of guilt, wished she could rewind time, let her mum make up her own mind, not give in so easily.

'We have money,' Connie said as if she were rifling through Abigail's thoughts. 'We're family.' She turned to pat her hair in the mirror.

'I better...' Abigail indicated her dressing gown, vowing to wake up earlier the next day and be ready. She felt wrong-footed, absurdly young, and unsure of herself. She had to adjust to this new her, setting aside confident Abigail who had reassured Mary, cajoled her mum.

Connie left and Abigail had a quick splash in the bathtub in the bathroom next door, her teeth clenched from the shock of the cold. She stepped into her old clothes, noticing, as if she had new eyes, the repairs, the loose thread, another hem not quite fixed. Buttoning her skirt and twisting it round to the back, she tucked in her blouse, rolling her eyes at herself in the small square of mirror, feeling ridiculous for her scrutiny.

Poking her tongue out at herself, she felt better, a laugh escaping through the window startling a bird that had been resting on the drainpipe above. She watched it soar away, out and down. The mist had lifted slightly and she almost imagined she could see south Wales; she looked right, blowing a kiss to Bristol.

Connie was waiting in the hall, a soft woollen coat buttoned up to her throat, a basket looped over one arm. Adjusting her hat in the hall mirror, she pursed her fuchsia lips. 'Right then,' she said in a voice that sounded loud in the narrow space.

Abigail felt a surge of sisterly love as she stood next to her in the mirror. Their reflections showing two women with rich brown hair and the same hazel eyes but different in so many ways. Abigail had a longer face, a dimple in her cheek when she smiled, darker lashes fringing her eyes. Her sister had more of a snub nose, a neater version of her face.

Connie smiled at her, her eyes crinkling slightly at the edges. 'We'll go down to Lynmouth today, the meat in the butcher's is better and we need some lamb chops. I haven't been shopping in Lynmouth in ages and yesterday reminded me how pretty it is.'

'It's so close,' remarked Abigail, her eyes rounding in the mirror.

'We tend to stick to Lynton, the two don't really have a great deal to do with each other, but we are half one, half the other, so I do go down there sometimes. I like the Pavilion, and the sea pool in the summer.'

'A pool?'

'It's in the harbour; it's thrilling when it's sunny. Oh, it will be marvellous when it warms up.'

Abigail felt a slow smile spread across her face as she imagined them both in bathing suits sitting on the side of a pool.

She had learnt to swim in the local pool, thrashing about, clinging to the sides. Her mum had always been too scared to go in, but Abigail loved it. She was a fish, her mum had told her.

'Edith, we're going down to Lynmouth,' Connie called before linking an arm through Abigail's. 'I can't wait to show you off,' she trilled.

The path down to Lynmouth was twisty and steep, tree roots breaking through the concrete, bursting out of the earth like they couldn't be held down. Abigail walked carefully, with tight little bird-like steps, her hand looking for anything to hold onto, until the ground levelled out and they emerged onto a cobbled street that widened and disappeared around the corner before the harbour wall.

They wove their way down and around, emerging from stone steps onto the road beneath. The high street snaked away from them up into the trees beyond, running parallel with the East Lyn river, which tumbled over rocks, rushing past them, merging with the West Lyn river further down. The noise of the water could probably be heard in every house in the village.

'Round the corner's where the pool is, the clifftop railway's behind us, we'll go on that of course, and oh, the Rhenish tower, obviously, just up there.' She pointed at the end of the harbour, to a square stone tower with an open brazier on top. Abigail recognized it from the sepia postcard her mum had kept on the mantelpiece for a year.

Connie swept along, past a row of cottages on a slope just above the road. 'In the middle's The Rising Sun,' she said through tight lips, pointing to an old pub, whitewashed, an empty bench outside. 'We're headed to the butcher's although I must show you the café on Watersmeet Road, it's divine. We didn't really have time to stop when you arrived yesterday, but

I'm sure we do today. They do the most delicious rock cakes, so soft on the inside. Edith's tried, but she can't seem to get the recipe right.' She rolled her eyes at that last sentence and Abigail tried to look sympathetic.

They idled about, Connie picking up trinkets, mouth pressed tight as she held things up to Abigail. She bought her a thin woollen cardigan, rose pink and so soft to the touch. Abigail hadn't owned anything new for years, she clutched the bag to her chest as they walked. They shared a rock cake and a pot of tea in the café, Connie's high laugh making the woman behind the counter look up and smile at them both. Connie had told her they were sisters. That sentence had made Abigail feel lighter, that she still belonged somewhere and, as they came back out onto the street, she couldn't help smiling too at the light bouncing off the river below them, the haze of sea in the distance.

'Oh, I forgot the chops!' Connie said, clapping a hand to her mouth. 'What a dolt. I won't be long, you stay here, I'll be right back.'

'But I…'

Her sister didn't give her a chance to interrupt, twisting quickly on her heel and heading back down the cobbled street, pausing once next to a woman pushing a pram, a brief look inside before she moved away, slower than before.

Abigail sat on the edge of the harbour wall, tempted to spin round and dangle her legs over the water as if she were ten again. Instead she leant out towards the sea, looking across at the navy line of the horizon, her hair whipping over her cheeks as the wind swept round her in a sudden gust.

Up ahead a boat was turning into the harbour, men in long galoshes or string vests and long trousers moving down, carrying buckets to be hauled up over the wall. Buckets that brimmed with fish, their silver bodies catching the sunlight so they might have been full of molten silver.

The men were tanned from the outdoor work, calling instructions to one another as they moved straight past her. One man stood out, white teeth flashing even from that distance, grinning and shouting something over his shoulder to a wiry man in round spectacles. His shirt was rumpled and loose, his braces crisscrossing over his back where a patch of sweat had spread. Wiping his brow, he took off his cap, his hair flat before he pushed a hand through it, and caught her eye, his face breaking into a grin she couldn't help but return.

Her sister appeared then, frowning at Abigail as if she had just witnessed it. 'They didn't have any, which means we'll have to try in Lynton. So irritating, but it can't be helped.'

'Oh.' Abigail spun back round; glad her blushes went unnoticed as her sister chided her to come along.

She moved away from him, the boat. But just at the last moment before they climbed up the path by The Rising Sun, she couldn't resist, she turned to stare back, and there he was, looking straight at her. She sucked in her breath as he waved one hand in acknowledgement. He was nudged then by a neighbour in spectacles, his head shaking, white teeth flashing and she turned away, following her sister's calves back up the side of the cliff, still thinking about the boy in braces.

IRINA

Irina hadn't realized she was avoiding it, but as the day wore on she prioritized yet another repair not due for another month. She snuck a look. The bureau seemed to take over one half of the workshop, squeezing her back into an ever-smaller space. She was unwilling to move across the workbench, sitting hunched over a stool as she adjusted the small desk lamp and used her jewellery loupe to examine the hallmark on the bottom of a silver salver, scraping out the grime around it in delicate strokes.

Yet again her eyes were drawn to it, the large bulk in the shadowy corner of the room. It wasn't a big job, she assured herself, it wasn't damaged in any serious way and it shouldn't take long. The email from the client had been clear: it was to be restored and returned to an address in the West Country. She'd have to phone her contact in Brighton who helped her with leathering on desks, but otherwise she'd be removing the top coats of varnish, sanding it down, reapplying a stain, checking the compartments, ensuring the drawers ran smoothly.

She wondered briefly why he had sent it through; most of the items he sent her needed extensive repair work, a unique part that only she could source. This bureau seemed different from the other items he'd commissioned her to work on. The last had been a mahogany chair missing a slat from the back. He had been impressed before by her ability to conjure up wood that could no longer be found. She kept an old stock of wood, and it was a thrill to match it, like fitting the last piece into a jigsaw puzzle. She went back to the salver, aware of the bureau watching her work, in the room with her like a second person.

The end of the day seemed to trudge round. Irina felt a strong desire to be outside. The air was balmier and the hint of better weather coming seemed to tug at her as she locked up the shop for the evening.

Changing into her running outfit, a polo shirt and leggings, Irina laced up her muddy trainers and planned the route she would take. It was getting dark later now, the sky at that moment a wonderfully opaque shade, a bluish silver, the thin crescent of a moon suspended above her. Hearing the brief wail of sirens in the distance, she paused, holding her hair into a ponytail. The sound always made her wonder if someone's life was about to change. She remembered sirens from that day, a momentary glance in the direction they'd come from, not a thought for who they were racing to, not realizing they were heading for the house.

She finished tying up her hair and stepped out into the street. The streetlamps had come on and she decided to stay within the village itself, feeling safer, pounding along, manoeuvring round a couple off for dinner, an elderly man loaded down with shopping bags. The wall of Petworth House rose up above her, blank and impenetrable as she followed it round.

She imagined then the people living beyond the walls in the house itself, generations before, when they'd needed the wall to keep the people out. She imagined the family, dripping in jewels, bouffant hair, velvet dresses, complicated patterns intricately woven into their surface, at the end of a long, polished-oak dining table. The small, bewigged servants standing underneath enormous gilt-edged portraits in the vast room, hands clasped behind their backs, awaiting instruction. Now the house was open to curious, camera-snapping tourists, teenagers taking selfies in front of sombre-looking ancestors. She visited the house on occasion when she wanted inspiration; some of the pieces in there were spectacular, rooms made up in different periods. They had created Christmas in the 1950s, leaving vintage magazines on top of tattered children's board games.

She wiped at her face, a sheen on her top lip as she turned to make her way slowly back. The exercise had cleared her mind as she knew it would, her head now filled with the sounds of her feet slapping the pavement, her even breathing and the gentle hubbub of the high street, windows glowing orange, curtains drawn, shapes and shadows enjoying their evening. She pictured candles burning down to stubs, half-finished bottles of red wine, weary feet on upholstered pouffes, TVs on but being ignored in the corners.

As she turned the last corner to her apartment, her own windows blank in the distance, she heard a noise that stopped her running. A shout, somewhere up ahead. She squinted in the direction it had come from, trying to make out shapes in the distance. The sun had long since set and a handful of stars could be glimpsed through moving piles of cloud. The pavement, punctuated by light from lamps or windows, was grey and empty ahead of her. She moved on, the shop a minute away, already picturing the bath she would run when she got in. The noise came again, behind her now so that she stopped, half-spun round, her head snapping behind her. She came to a stop, her breathing faster, loud and insistent in her ears. She stepped forward, the hairs on her arms standing on end. She couldn't pinpoint what was different about the noise but it seemed so unfamiliar.

She found herself walking quickly, glancing behind and around herself warily as she headed home, wanting to be inside, to shut the door behind her. Something about the sound. She could make out the shop window up ahead, the silhouettes of the furniture in the glass, the burgundy facade almost black in this light. Her eyes instinctively moved to her flat above, the opaque glass of her bathroom, next to that a square of light, the curtains of her sitting room, and then... She froze, her body rooted to the pavement, the breath catching in her throat.

Silhouetted in the light of her living room was a figure, the face staring back, straight at her. Hair hanging limply on either side of pale skin, one palm up on the glass. Irina made a noise in her throat, her eyes flicking to check the shop; the windows, they couldn't be hers, she'd made a mistake, her brain chugged into gear. When she looked back there was nothing there at all, the curtains hanging still, the light on, no woman, no face, no palm. Irina wrapped her arms around herself protectively, her mind already doubting what she'd seen.

It was the darkness, the sounds behind her, the high street now eerily quiet. She returned, a half-glance, eyes unable to resist: there was nothing but the blank window. And yet she remembered the face, the wide eyes, focused on her, she was sure of it, the hand up on the glass. She reached the shop door, flinching at the sound of the bell as she pushed through into the shop, stepping carefully in the half-light to the beaded curtain, wavering in front of it, her hands damp as she reached to pull it back.

She wished she was with someone, that Patricia was in the shop, that it was twelve hours later and the sun was up and customers were bustling about, bringing noise and chatter and the sounds of the till opening and closing, the bell jangling. Not this awful silence, just her own hammering chest as she told herself to stop being stupid.

As she pushed the beaded curtain aside she felt the temperature drop a fraction, fumbled to find the key to the staircase and the apartment. The air seemed weighted and the sound of her breathing was still in her ears. She could make out the workbench, a couple of the tools on the sink, silvery in the half-light. To her right the bureau, its bulk outlined by a dust sheet. She dropped the key, swearing as she heard it bounce away, losing sight of it.

Calm down.

She wasn't normally in the workshop this late, that must be it, she assured herself, crouching to pick up the key. Creeping forward, brushing the floor with her hands, sawdust in a thin layer coating her palms, there was a wave of smell, a salty tang, sharp, sticking in her nose, reminding her of her last trip to Brighton, being on the beach there. She looked over her shoulder at the workshop, the pieces waiting for the morning. The smell had gone, disappeared as if she'd imagined it. Only the familiar clash of animal glue, resin and polish, which never seemed to fade.

'Stupid.' She huffed quietly, straightened up to put the key in the lock, then took the stairs two at a time up to the apartment. She didn't allow herself to think about things, just turned the key in her front door and stepped inside. She swept through each room. Nothing, no one there, her wallet and phone where she'd left them, the plate and glass still on the side table next to the armchair. She checked the whole flat, knowing she wouldn't relax without having looked.

She felt her body calm as she finished searching every room, behind doors, only scaring herself once when she caught her own startled expression in her bedroom mirror. She walked slowly back into the living room, moving to turn on the radio. It was only when she crossed the room to the windowsill that she saw the drops of water on the glass and scattered along the frame, as if it had been raining inside.

ABIGAIL

Connie had an appointment, she told Abigail in a lowered voice over breakfast, tight-lipped. Larry looked sharply across the table at her as her hand wavered protectively over her stomach. Abigail glanced down, wanting to ask, the expression on her sister's face closed, the colour draining out of her cheeks; but she felt the words halting within her, aware of Larry's look.

She was getting up from the table when Larry put a hand on her arm. Abigail froze, half in and half out of her chair, as he reached across to pluck something from her cardigan, his two fingers brushing her chest. She arched up and away from him, her eyes widening.

Larry laughed as he dabbed at the crumbs on his lips. 'Loose thread,' he said, scraping back his chair.

Connie busied herself with the marmalade, a small laugh as if trying to lighten things. Abigail found her chest was rising and falling as she stayed standing once he'd left the room.

Connie left shortly after, adjusting her hat in the mirror,

opening her mouth to speak before shutting it quickly and reaching for her coat. Abigail wandered around the house, mindlessly picking up things to examine, planning to wait for her sister to return. She traced her outline on a photograph of them all standing outside St John's Church in Bristol all those years ago, her mum looking unusually sombre in her wedding suit, mouth a thin line, the black and white photograph dulling her features. She moved away, not wanting to look anymore, reclined theatrically for a moment on the peppermint chaise longue, briefly imagining she was Joan Crawford or Marilyn Monroe, a quick grin into the silence as she thought of Mary there with her, pouting and preening as they imagined themselves as Hollywood stars.

Edith walked in to dust and Abigail strained herself rearing up into a seated position, feeling the heat creep up her neck and into her cheeks as Edith looked at her. Abigail knew she should introduce herself and half-rose to say something, wondering why she was so tongue-tied. Edith was wearing an apron, her hair tied back from her face, strands escaping from the pins. She was a little older than Abigail perhaps.

'I...'

'Miss?'

Her accent was hard to place. Not English. Scottish perhaps? Or Irish? Perhaps it was this that threw Abigail into a further spin. She got up quickly, feeling that she should be occupied with something. She left to go to her room, mumbling something inaudible as explanation on the way out. She took the stairs two at a time, closing the door to her room behind her, idly folding her clothes from the day before, then sitting at the stool in front of the dressing table and twisting her hair up into a low chignon, pinning it in place. She had an urge to escape. Seizing her coat from the hook on the back of the door, she tripped down the stairs, listening to the sounds of Edith in the kitchen, the mangle being wound down, the soft hum of an unfamiliar song.

She found herself wandering down the hill back towards Lynmouth. Something calmed in her as she descended, caught glimpses of the sea, the rooftops below. She breathed out. The trees formed a canopy above her, speckling the path with light. There was a strong breeze: a seagull hovered, its wings ruffled by it, and a man on the beach below chased after a loose sheet of newspaper.

The sea was out, low tide, the seaweed exposed in a line along the shore, boats tilted into the mud of the harbour. She wrapped her coat around herself, moving past the Pavilion, the café and pub, grateful to recognize the same landmarks, feeling that these places could become familiar to her.

She hadn't been paying a great deal of attention as she wound her way past the shops and harbour, but she stopped short when she recognized him from the boat that day. He was walking as if on a tightrope along the sea wall, arms wide, grin enormous, winking at her as she passed. She wanted to keep a straight face, perhaps even look affronted, but found herself returning the smile. He stopped, twisted on one foot, took his flat cap off with a flourish and bowed.

She turned away, smiling stupidly behind her gloved hand, knowing she shouldn't encourage him. What would her sister think? After being in the village for two seconds. It was this thought that made her brusquer with him than she might have been. She felt her face move into a frown; eyes narrowed. Then all that was forgotten as he jumped down from the wall, landing on two feet in front of her.

'You're that girl.'

She didn't know what to say to that, felt a jolt as words tumbled from her mouth. 'I am.'

He nodded, an easy smile erupting on his face. 'I'm Richard.' He held out a hand, large, palm up.

She paused for a moment. His hand stayed there, unwavering, and she found herself taking it, her cream glove lost in it as they shook.

'Good. Now that I've introduced myself, I can ask you out.'

His confidence made her bristle. 'No, I don't think…'

'I saw you, in the harbour, it's fate, something in the stars…' He held his arms out wide and she rolled her eyes at him.

'That's not fate. That's shop opening hours.'

His forehead wrinkled and his mouth fell. 'That's what you think. But I say it's fate. Where have you come from?'

'Bristol,' she said grudgingly.

He whistled out loud. 'Very fancy.'

'Hardly.' She laughed, not able to remain serious with him for long.

'Well it's fancier than here. Here there's fish and not a lot else,' he said, indicating the village behind them with a jerk of his head. 'Why did you leave?' he asked, tipping his chin to the left.

'I…' She thought then of her mum, a stab of pain as she remembered the sepia face in the bed, the unseeing eyes. She blinked once, quick to return to the tanned face of the boy. 'I'm sorry.' She bit her lip.

'No…' He held up a hand in apology. 'I can be so nosy, ignore me, it was rude.' His voice sped up, tripping over itself. 'I just ramble on, I know I do, the lads on the boat just tell me to pipe down. I'm a dreadful rambler, Dad tells me that he can't get a word in edgeways at home.'

'I thought ramblers were more about walking?'

'Are they?' he said. 'Oh, I'm not a rambler then.' He trailed off, looking anywhere but at her face. She realized he was embarrassed. It made her feel better, taller, as if maybe he didn't have all the answers.

'Do you work on the boats?' she asked, shielding her eyes to look out at the hint of sea beyond, imagining the fishing boats tied up at every angle in the harbour.

'I'm a fisherman,' he said, nodding.

'I'd love to be out on the sea. I've only ever looked at it.'

'Why's that?'

'Well I've never had the chance.'

'No, I mean, why do you want to be out on it?'

Abigail felt her own words speed up as she pictured herself at the helm of a ship, imagined herself bouncing over waves, water flying up around her. 'To be out and free and heading to who knows where. It's exciting.'

'Well you do know most days. But you're not wrong.'

'Have you always been a fisherman?'

He nodded. 'There are days I dread it.' He stopped then, abruptly, looking guiltily over his shoulder up the valley. 'My dad would hate to hear me say that.'

'Why do you dread it?'

'There's just so much...' He paused to think of the word and then shrugged. 'Water.'

'But that's what I think is so marvellous,' Abigail said, surprising herself with the passion in her voice. She pictured an endless stretch of ocean, the waves rolling past, the miles of nothingness.

'You're right. I'm whining. I just get sick of being soaked; I suppose.'

'You're allowed to whine. I don't have a clue what I'm talking about, I'd probably topple overboard or get seasick in the first hour.'

He laughed. 'My friend Bill has to drink ginger tea from a flask that his mum makes him, to stop him, you know...'

Abigail felt her nose wrinkle. 'How horrid. Poor Bill.'

'Pity us when he forgets the flask.'

'Oh,' Abigail squeaked, half at the image, half because she could see her sister's hat in the distance. 'My sister's coming.'

He turned in the direction of her finger. 'I've seen her before,' he mused.

Abigail tried to suppress the spark of jealousy as it flared. Of course he would notice her. She found herself folding her arms to her chest.

Richard turned back to her; his green eyes focused once more on her face. 'Well I'll leave you in peace.'

She felt her shoulders lower, relieved she wouldn't have to make the introductions, glad when he tipped his hat and turned away. 'Was a pleasure to meet you… Harbour Girl.'

Her sister was nearing. Abigail could feel her palms getting slippery as she turned, not wanting her sister to see her, wanting to get back to the house and wait there.

'It's Abigail,' she said, biting her lip again.

'Abigail.'

It was strange hearing her name spoken aloud by this stranger. Her insides seemed to flip and squirm. Her face twitched into a half-smile.

She giggled quietly to herself as he walked away whistling a tune she hadn't heard before. She thought it was beautiful.

IRINA

As she lay in her bed the next morning, the mood seemed to cling to her, a dread that was hard to shake. It made her pull the covers up to her chin and lie there staring at the ceiling, the swirls of plaster, the dove-grey shade. Glancing at the time, which seemed to be shifting forward rapidly, she swung her legs from the bed and started to get ready, the feeling stubbornly remaining on her skin in the shower as the water ran down her body and into the drain. She scrubbed then in fast small circles, determinedly, until her skin was pink, the memories were scoured away, and she had reclaimed her body.

Stamping down the stairs, louder than normal, she burst into the workshop, ready to take on the day. The bureau was standing there and she breathed in through her nose slowly and deliberately, feeling her lungs expand, her shoulders lift, and then out again, quickly, in a puff of relief.

She forced herself to work on it all morning: removing the bottle-green leather writing surface that curled at the edges. One of the pigeonhole drawers was jammed shut, she tried to prise it open gently with the edge of her knife but it wouldn't budge. She would return to it when she had finished the rest.

She emailed the client, curious to know more about the piece, asking him how long he had owned it, where it had come from. Within seconds an email pinged back and Irina opened it immediately without taking in the subject heading. The email announced that he was out of the country, leaving no alternative email or number. Irina had only ever communicated with him by email and now, with no other way of contacting him, her shoulders sank at the realization that she wouldn't get any answers. Worse perhaps was the slow acknowledgement that the bureau would be staying a while.

That thought seemed to trigger a reaction. Grabbing her coat, she called to Patricia in the shop. 'Just leaving for a bit, do you need anything?'

Patricia's head appeared through the beaded curtain a few seconds later, her body still in the shop. 'Nothing for me,' she said, craning her neck to the side. 'All OK?'

Irina didn't usually go out in the day like this; she could see the question in Patricia's face, the frown lines creasing her make-up. 'Yes, all OK,' she replied in a voice that was two pitches higher than normal.

She walked down the alleyway quickly, no specific destination in mind but keen to get out into the day. As she brushed past brambles curving into the path, something caught on her coat, making her stop and untangle herself; she pictured the wide road at the other end, eager to look up into the open and see the sky. She emerged onto the street where a narrow pavement dropped sharply down the hill and she turned left and walked along it. There was a field beyond that and she stepped over the turnstile, dropping into a patch of dried mud on the other side.

It was getting warmer now and her coat was almost too

much. She shook it off and threw it over one arm, revelling in the spring sunshine. The meadow was a patchwork of wild gorse and tiny flowers, the hedges tumbled over each other, barely restrained around the border. She imagined the butterflies and bees of the summer months dipping in and out of it all. Very few families came here, it was an uneven patch of beauty, no place for ball games or cricket, so they preferred to make the drive down the A285 to the beach at West Wittering on sunny days.

There was a spot at the top of an incline where you could stand and look out over the South Downs, the view a brilliant mishmash of fields and trees in every shade, the colours overlapping each other one after the other all the way to the South Downs themselves and then the sky above it all, the clouds creating shadows that moved across the landscape, grey patches that only highlighted the yellows, ochres, browns and greens of the scene beneath them.

She walked up there through the long grass, feeling a welcome burn in her thighs as she climbed higher, needing to steady herself on occasion as the ground tricked her. Then it opened out before her and she felt, for the first time that day, free of things, reminded that she was a small speck in a much bigger place, the workshop, the bureau, even the memories that could sneak up on her at any given moment, such tiny considerations really in the scheme of things.

Today the sun was unashamedly bright but the wind could still nip at her up there, playing with strands of loose hair. She wondered for a second what she might look like then to others, a heroine in a novel perhaps, atop a hill staring at the horizon, then their surprise as she turned to them, the right side of her face livid in this light and their expressions changing, her image dissolved in that moment, shifting to something else. She chastised herself for thinking in this way and turned back to take in the village, the houses and shops in their higgledy-piggledy lines, behind them the walls of Petworth House hemming them in. It was a few moments before she heard her mobile ringing.

'Irina?' Patricia sounded so brusque on the phone. 'We might have to ring a plumber, there's been a leak, although I'm not absolutely sure where it's from. Don't panic, dear, none of the furniture is damaged, it's in the workshop. I'll wait for you to get back.'

Irina rolled her eyes at the news. The pipes in the house were ancient. She'd had a nasty cold spell the year before when the boiler had packed in and the pipes had frozen, cracking when they melted and flooding her kitchen, right through the ceiling into the workshop. The plumber had assured her he'd fixed it, but you never knew with old houses. She started walking immediately, the wind gently nudging her in the back, steering her to the shop.

Patricia was with a customer, packaging up three or four figurines from one of the displays, china birds in an assortment of sizes. She grimaced as Irina passed her, which only made Irina worry more. How bad was the damage, she wondered as she pushed aside the beaded curtain. Automatically her eyes flew to the ceiling and ran along the moulding, checking for damp patches. Certainly the room smelt different, a scent she couldn't place. She pictured seaweed and lavender. She stopped examining the ceiling; nothing there appeared to be an issue, there was perhaps a small dark patch in one corner but it had been there as long as Irina had had the workshop, she kept meaning to paint over it.

Her eyes scanned the floor, where she could just make out the edge of a puddle beyond a worktop. She moved across, over shavings that needed sweeping up, to peer down at it. There was a lot of water, pooled in a mass about three feet wide and three feet across in the middle of the stone floor. It hadn't fallen on any of the tops or furniture, so they'd been lucky; it had reached one of the legs of the bureau but had gone no further. Irina looked above it, her forehead bunched up in a question. Nothing. Perhaps the water had come from the floor, seeped up between the stone cracks from somewhere? She went to fetch the mop, turning towards the cupboard in the corner.

They were in front of her then. She wondered how she'd missed them. Her skin prickled, an uneasiness shivering across her body. Her mouth felt dry as she examined them. Two fading watery footprints, their outlines barely there, on the floor next to the puddle. They would vanish soon enough. They were small and narrow. Irina stared at them for a long while, rooted to the workshop floor. Perhaps Patricia had stepped into the puddle? Yet it seemed they were prints from bare feet. Perhaps it was a coincidence, like when a cloud looks like a skeleton or there's a face in the toast. Irina wanted to laugh into the empty space, throw off the feeling, stop her heart from speeding up and get her brain thinking logically again.

She edged round them, not looking anymore at where they were, opened the door to the cupboard, chastised herself for jumping as the mop handle fell out. Lowering her hand from her chest, she did laugh then, a quick release of noise in the silence.

The beads moved aside. 'Are you alright?'

Irina spun round, holding the mop in both hands.

Patricia had moved into the room and was standing next to the worktop. 'Did you find the leak? Bit odd,' she said, eyes roving across the ceiling.

'Hmm, a mystery,' Irina said, relieved at having company for a moment, the mood already lighter. She slapped the mop down in the water, circling it and squeezing it out into the bucket.

'Well, a relief, I suppose, that nothing was damaged,' said Patricia, moving back towards the curtain, taking one last look at Irina.

Irina glanced up from her mopping, a pause, and then she nodded.

'Yes, a relief.'

She put her head back down and continued to wipe the floor. She didn't say anything about the footprints. They had gone completely now anyway.

ABIGAIL

She wasn't used to sitting around all day. Her sister held coffee mornings in the drawing room and the ladies in the village would pick their way up to the house and sit primly on a semi-circle of chairs in assorted sizes, some lost to the bear hug of an armchair, looking tiny among the cushions, some straining on the edge of a flimsy wooden straight-backed chair, perching their saucer on one hand as they lifted the tea cup to their mouth.

The women had welcomed Abigail to that first meeting. She had sat trying not to slurp her tea, joining in the moans about the continued rationing of tea – 'Absurd!' – and commenting on articles about the young queen's 'lovely skin'. She smoothed her skirt down as her sister moved elegantly across the room, remarking on one woman's ring, another's hat, ensuring all the guests were included somehow. Abigail cocked her head to one side, watching her. Her sister, born to be a hostess. She had a sudden image of her dolls' tea parties, her endless chatter, righting their positions, pouring from a miniature teapot, a much-loved present from their parents.

The talk of the day was an accident at the bottom of Countisbury Hill, a busload of people, the brakes failing and the small stone wall that continually had to be rebuilt.

'Happens once a month. We live just down Tors Road and we hear the bangs.'

'How dreadful,' Abigail said, shivering at the thought of a runaway vehicle, imagining the winter months, surely no one able to get in or out of the village. The thought made her itch at her palms and neck.

The woman raised a finely plucked eyebrow and shifted in her chair, a wall of lilac jacket blocking further conversation.

'Connie tells us you've lived in Bristol,' called a woman across the room, her cheeks stained an unnatural pink.

'I did.' Abigail smiled, nibbling on her Huntley and Palmers biscuit, wondering why the question made her eyes sting.

'Do you play whist?' the woman asked, eyes bright.

'I'm afraid not,' admitted Abigail, wondering whether she should get up and help serve things. She felt frozen on the sofa.

'Our mother never played,' Connie said.

Abigail looked at her sharply. Her hand gripped her saucer a little too tightly and she placed it slowly on the side table. 'She was terribly busy,' she said, wondering why she was jumping in.

The woman seemed to shift in her seat, turned her attention elsewhere. Had Abigail offended her somehow? Was she suggesting the woman wasn't busy if she had time for cards? The eternal run of questions was exhausting and she smoothed her skirt again, hoping the carriage clock might suddenly speed up.

She escaped into the corridor, resting her back against the door for a second, glad to be free of the babble and polite clinking of teacups on saucers, the slow stir, the talk behind gloved hands. She felt a lurch then for the quiet solitude of their home in Bristol, her mum's gentle snores, head lolled to the side, the distant sounds of the street beyond, the quiet turning of the page of her book, walks with Mary along the Downs. She wasn't used to this clucking and fussing, and that her sister seemed so at ease in there made her feel lonelier than ever.

She shook herself, feeling foolish for being such a misery, determined to return to the room and ensure she was pulling her weight, make her sister proud. She didn't want to be a drain on her, a dull weight Connie had to heave around the village. She was so lost in her thoughts; she hadn't heard the door opening. The first thing that alerted her was the sharp breeze that swept around her ankles, the sudden noise of seagulls and sea, and then the silence again, a shadow behind the inner door.

He stepped inside, eyes rounded as he took her in, leaning back against the door in the semi-darkness of the corridor. Hearing then the sounds of the coffee morning, a slow smile crept across his face as he stepped towards her, a finger to his lips. She returned the smile, feeling embarrassed to have been caught like this. His grey eyes danced with mischief as he walked over to her, bent towards the door, almost brushing her ear as he whispered, 'Running away, eh?'

She felt herself hold in her breath, felt the warmth of his words on her ear, fusty and metallic. She couldn't step back, hemmed in between him and the door. The corridor seemed tiny, like she was Alice and things were just getting smaller and smaller.

He didn't move away, stayed by her ear, his hand moving inches from her face as if he were about to cup her cheek. She looked at his hand, feeling the muscles in her neck straining.

'I best get back,' she whispered.

A bubble of laughter spilled out of him then and he steadied himself with a hand on the corridor wall. 'Stay,' he pleaded, staring at her as if they were colluding together. 'It will be unbelievably dull for you: you're not like them.'

She felt terrible for having had the same thought moments before, disloyal. He was really close now; she could see a couple of bristles on his chin that he'd missed when shaving. Her eyes crossed as she looked up at him, inches away from her.

'What are we going to do with you?' he said in a low voice, his breath smelling of pipe smoke that seeped into her pores.

She moved her gaze down, away from his, wishing she had stayed inside with the glow and heat of the other women. She could hear her sister asking where she'd gone, a sentence suspended. He was leaning right into her now, the smell from his jacket, rain-soaked tweed, overwhelming her senses. She stared resolutely at the buttons on his shirt; a thread was coming loose.

'She just stepped out,' one of the women said, so close to the door it made her start.

As if the sentence had alerted him to the others, he melted away down the corridor and she turned back towards the women. She felt like she had been gone an age, saw her sister's momentary frown, a smile quickly plastered over before anyone could tell.

'Would you like more tea, Abigail?' she called out.

She stepped inside the room, feeling the hubbub and chatter encircle her. She felt a release inside her, cast a quick glance back at the corridor before closing the door again.

'I'd love some,' she said, returning to her teacup and saucer, the milky grey remnants of her last cup still lying in the bottom. 'Please.'

IRINA

Though most people she knew looked forward to weekends, Irina often found the stretch of time unsettling. She found herself going through the motions, forcing herself to lie in even when she was twitching to get up, keen to fill the space with clatter and activity. She would go to pub lunches, see friends with babies, catch up on paperwork and sometimes find an excuse to work on something in the shop.

Today she was seeing her mother, had bought plain scones from the bakery next door. She'd left there with her nostrils full of the smells from their kitchen at home when her mother used to make them, flour on her arms and clothes as she rolled out the dough, punched it back into a ball and then rolled it out again. They would eat them with large dollops of clotted cream and homemade raspberry jam at the small table in their kitchen, Joshua with a dash of flour on his cheek as he reached for a second one.

Irina brushed off the seat, put the bag of scones down and started the engine. The car seemed chilled by its week-long wait and the engine sputtered into life, as if it were a dying man choking one last time. She backed out of the spot, a hand on the passenger seat. It had started to rain, droplets dotting the windscreen, the wipers making occasional efforts to clear it as she joined the cars heading out of the village.

Staring at the back seat in the rear-view mirror, she had a memory from years ago. Sitting in the seat next to Joshua squealing as he sang along to her favourite tape, getting all the words wrong and roaring with laughter. She wondered whether she would mention it to her mother, whether it might make her smile or whether today wouldn't be a good day for stories like that. She felt a familiar tightness in her stomach as she drove on. What sort of day would it be?

The greens gave way to the tarmac-covered A-road to Brighton, and then the buildings, shops and people of the town. A couple holding an umbrella and a child who was straining to be released, a woman walking quickly, a folded newspaper held above her head. Irina parked outside the block of flats, the number 5 sign on the parking spot perpetually tilted even though she straightened it every time she visited. Her mother lived on the second floor and Irina buzzed the intercom and stood, patting pointlessly at her hair, which was damp with rain and already frizzing.

They hugged, one armed and awkward. Irina turned her cheek away from her mother, presenting her with smooth skin to kiss. Her mother smelt of talcum powder, her lips brief and dry but there.

'Ready?' she asked, watching her mother reach for her coat.

They walked down to the pier, through the iron grilles of the arched entrance, the sweet smell of doughnuts and coffee clinging to their clothes. Their footsteps were soft on the wooden planks of the pier, the water washing in somewhere below them, just visible through the narrow slats.

Irina loved piers, the neon colours, victorious shouts, the

buzz and flash of a hundred games under one roof. She moved through the hall, the sounds changing as they crossed the swirled carpet, the whole place a clash of lights and noise. The rattle of coins, the distant screams of someone winning, the persistent thud of a song played over and over again, a siren. Her mother was shoving 2ps into the machine, the coins standing on their sides before dropping down and pushing others off the ledge. For a moment it seemed her mother was twenty years younger, that they were back in Southsea, that they were all together. Her eyes crinkled as she reached to scoop the coins into her hand, a triumphant look as she saw how many had fallen. Irina felt lighter then, as she allowed herself to enjoy simply being with her, no need to fill a silence, no need for anything but to enjoy the day.

The rain had stopped, the boards of the pier still slick with water as they moved outside. Irina tucked her hands into her coat, watched people milling along the promenade. She felt her mother join her, her hands up on the balustrade. They looked out in silence for a while, the muted sounds of the pier behind them. And then, perhaps instinctively, they both turned in the direction of the skeleton of the West Pier, its crippled rusting remains gradually being reclaimed by the sea, stubbornly sitting out in the water, not ready to give up yet. The top a twisted, sunken mass of metal. Irina looked sideways at her mother, who had turned away from it.

'It's getting cold, we should get back,' she said with an irritated swipe at an errant strand of hair.

Irina wished they'd left via the other side of the pier. They could have looked out over an unblemished stretch of sea, a length of golden sand, the painted arches of the pier, the rotating big wheel crammed with happy faces in its glass capsules. Why had she guided her out this side? Had she known? Had she wanted the reminder? Like a small thorn in her palm, wanting to press at it tentatively, see if it still hurt, wanting to talk about it, complain?

She opened her mouth to reply; perhaps this was the moment they should take. They should talk about it; it was absurd to continually skirt the thing that seemed to drag around behind them. How many times had she opened her mouth to do just that? She turned her back to the sea too, taking a breath, tapping her feet on the wooden planks beneath her, jumping as a seagull swept right past them. She opened her mouth, imagined how she might begin things. 'Mum, do you think we could…' 'Mum, do you ever wonder…' She raced through the false starts, the pathetic attempts to initiate something she wasn't even sure she wanted to, but her mother had already pushed herself from the balustrade and was walking towards the exit.

'We can get back and put a kettle on,' she called over her shoulder, her voice stretched thin.

Irina followed in her wake, like she was eight years old again and struggling to catch up with her, not wanting to leave the pier, the mindless fun. 'Kettle,' she repeated. 'Great idea.'

On the left, the West Pier stood, its rusting bones admonishing her for failing once more to talk about it all. Soon it would be called back to the sea, its body would fail and crumble, part by part, with a roar, a splash, a whine and a screech as things came loose and fell in. It would move slowly down through the water, swaying gently with the pull of the sea floor, throwing up sand in puffs as it landed on the seabed, resting there to be eaten away over time, algae on its surface, climbing over every edge, tickling the water.

Irina turned. For a brief second she thought she saw a small boy standing on one of the pier's bare arms, a tiny dot above the water. He was waving at her or gesturing to her.

Then he was gone and there was nothing but the rays of the sun bouncing off the water and the whitewashed buildings.

Her mother didn't speak at all on the walk back, stayed silent as she put the tea on and took the scones from the oven. Irina drew the small table to their spot by the window and pulled out the wooden tray. There was an unspoken assumption that they would play a round of Yahtzee, safe, just the sound of the rolling dice, the tiny changes in their breathing if the roll was a good one, a fraction faster, the next roll a little harder.

She went to fetch the dice, unable to avoid the space where the one photograph on the mantelpiece had stood. Where had her mother moved it? They had been on the pier in Southsea, sticky with sun cream and candyfloss, smeared smiles under straw hats, their parents both grinning in sunglasses. Her mother with long hair, not the neat iron-grey bob. Irina got up for her tea, feeling her stomach roll a protest, the familiar queasiness of the memory as if she had eaten candyfloss until she was full; her mouth seemed sticky with it now. The tea washed the taste away as she returned to her spot, a winged armchair with a flattened cushion.

Her mother had licked her finger and was pulling away another sheet. 'Last week Brenda scored over a thousand,' she commented, looking at a score sheet.

'Did she get a lot of straights?'

'None. Four Yahtzees.'

'Gosh.'

'She was absurdly lucky on the last roll, four threes in one roll, it seemed impossible.'

'Well let's see how we get on.' Irina took a sip of her tea and waited for her mother to get comfortable, take up the five dice in her hand and roll.

The room was warm, woozily so. Irina's eyes were drooping. The peach floor-to-ceiling curtains were shut, making everything the same shade and blocking out the view of the tops of houses and then somewhere behind them a strip of beach and the sea. Invisible from the window but you still knew it was there. The thought made Irina relax, the velvety softness of the armchair enclosing her in the space.

Her mother smiled at her, the creases around her eyes like ripples on the surface of a lake, extending down to her cheeks and around her mouth. The skin folded; the powder, dashed on that morning, caught in the cracks. Irina couldn't remember her mother without lines on her face. Where was the photo?

'I thought I saw Joshua the other day.' She blurted it out quickly, loudly, as if she had no control.

There was a heavy silence then, her mother's fist clenching the dice, her knuckles strained and white. The room was filled with the ticking of the kitchen clock, the gentle hum from the computer left on. Her mother didn't say anything for a second, seemed suspended. Irina didn't know why she had said it, wanted to take it back immediately, pile the words back into her mouth, cram them in there and shut her lips over them tight. She bit down on the inside of her cheek, cleared her throat.

'I was in a café, I thought he walked past...'

Where had it come from? Why did she have to ruin the morning with it?

The words seemed to pull her mother back into the moment. She rolled the dice then, not looking at her. She didn't make a comment.

'Well now. Brenda's husband is ill again,' she said, writing '15' in the third box, a thin smile of sympathy on her lips as she looked back up.

'Oh, that's a shame,' Irina replied, taking her mother's lead as if nothing had happened. Another day when they wouldn't prise anything open, his name dissolving into another moment they wouldn't talk about.

'He does have a very weak immune system,' her mother said, rolling the dice once more. Five sixes spilled onto the table. 'Yahtzee,' she said, clapping her hands once.

'Well done.'

MARY

Joe was back in the pub, ordering pints of cider as if it were about to run out. He didn't have a shift behind the bar, but he didn't seem to have anywhere else to be. He was slurring his words and sloshing the liquid over the sides as he spoke. Mary didn't like to see him like that, his eyes slipping and sliding about the place, his mouth in a thin line when he thought no one was looking. He told her more about his war, sometimes she forgot he was only twenty-six, his face seemed to carry extra years in the lines. It still hurt to think of her father like that, not even twenty years older but ancient when he'd returned from the prisoner-of-war camp. She didn't remember him ever sitting down when she was a child; he'd be restless, bent over the kitchen table, greasy parts of a bicycle laid out on newspaper, tinkering, screwing, hopping up to reattach things. Now he sat in a chair by the window, clouds skittering past, his eyes not focusing on them, lost somewhere, jumping if she laid a hand on his shoulder.

Joe called her Abigail that night, leaning on her as she put one of his arms over her shoulder, feeling the weight of him as she pulled him up from the stool. She'd laughed at him, pointing out the ankles that merged into her calves, the stubborn roll around her middle that didn't seem to shift. Abigail had a nipped-in waist and legs men would stop and stare at. Still, she couldn't resist the teeny glow as he muttered it. 'You're a lovely girl, Abi, a lovely girl.'

'Thanks, Joe.'

She propped him up on the way out and he patted her on the arm before weaving over the cobbled street, one foot stumbling in the gutter so she thought he might knock his teeth out on the pavement. He'd perked up for a moment earlier when she'd read to him from Abigail's last letter. She told him about the peppermint chaise longue. He'd chuckled at that.

Abigail's letters were filled with descriptions of the house, her sister's exceptionally fine clothes, her hair that somehow didn't seem to get mussed up the moment she went out the door. Abigail's hair, on the other hand, was permanently salty, the wind on the moors tossing every strand about so that it looked like she'd been burrowing through hedges; and she hid her dreadful darning efforts under other layers.

Sometimes Abigail sounded wistful, as if she wanted to say something bigger but the page was too small. Mary knew what that felt like, struggling to translate the thoughts in her head through the pen in her hand, gazing at the blank space that she needed to fill, but missing their chats on a rug on the Downs, spilling every thought onto the grass, clutching their sides with their secrets and their laughter. She thought her looping, rounded handwriting looked childish, Abigail's elegant scrawl highlighting the difference.

She walked back through Bedminster after her shift, her

legs aching from doing a double, her hands and clothes smelling of cigarette smoke; she imagined her insides filled with the stuff, swirling around her body. The apartment was dark when she got back, the lights off in the flats' downstairs. Mary cringed at the cranking sound as she switched the geyser on over the bath and stepped gingerly into the tub. She washed quickly, a threadbare towel round her as she shivered on the bare boards of her room. Rubbing at her skin, she looked over at the tips from that night, collected in a small pile of change on her chest of drawers. She was saving money now, wanting to get on with the life she had planned, get out of Bristol and see the world. She needed to get to Abigail first and then on to somewhere exciting.

She hugged the blankets over her that night, smiling to herself as she remembered Abigail's ability to tell long stories plucked from her imagination. There had been an evening during the war when bombs were being dropped on Bristol and Mary had stayed on the floor of Abigail's room, Abi's mum in the bedroom next door. They'd eaten pork casserole for dinner and lit candles behind the black-out curtains and told ghost stories, blocking out the distant thuds and shakes. Abigail had always loved being dramatic and she'd recounted a particularly nasty story about a headless woman who haunted a hotel corridor, her mum on the sofa rolling her eyes at Mary at the more absurd moments. Mary had held a cushion to her chest and listened to every word, her flesh breaking into goosebumps as Abigail made the most of it, arching an eyebrow as she described the ghostly figure, the bloodcurdling reaction of the guests.

She wished Abigail were there now in the empty flat to tell stories or talk to her more about their future travels. They were going to head to Hollywood, drive up the coastal roads, see the desert. She wondered whether, somewhere, Abigail's mum was still smiling at them in that quiet way. The days were getting longer and the moon was bright, turning the room a silvery blue. For a second Mary imagined Abigail looking out on the same moon, imagined the beams shimmering on the surface of the sea beneath her window.

ABIGAIL

The next few days dragged by in a haze of fog, spitting rain and grey. The sea churned, a moody purple, beneath the house. Abigail would wake in the morning and need to switch on the bedside lamp, looking out through the spattered panes of glass. Spring appeared to have left them, time seemed to be turning backwards now.

The room was too hot, the window stuck in place. The whistle and howl of the weather tore through the trees and around the house. She wanted to open the windows and thrust her head out into it, see the curtains billowing with energy, hear the sounds of the sea rousing her, the distant calls from birds high up on the cliffs forcing her to face each day. Instead she lay in the sticky semi-darkness, living out the past in her mind, sheets tucked up to her chin, a cloudy nothing sky in the top squares of her window.

Connie had been distant with her since the coffee morning, running errands without her, making calls in the village. She thought back to the attic room Connie and she had shared in Bristol all those years ago, the window seat looking out over the Downs, the games they had played as the last embers in the fire glowed, their podgy ginger cat stubbornly refusing to move from her spot in front of it, the whispered card games as their parents slept on next door, hushed giggling as they slapped the cards down in triumph or misery. They had spent hours on that window seat together. Why couldn't she recapture that closeness? Why couldn't they sit and play games and talk of nothing?

She thought of Mary then, missed their chattering nonsense, lying on the Downs on a picnic rug as they made daisy chains and pretended to be princesses with daisy crowns, laughing at each other, reading books, swapping gossip, giggling behind pages as men walked past in bowler hats. She missed telling her things, sharing secrets, memories from the war days, which still felt like a strangely golden time spent in a crowded room of women, days with a purpose and an energy about them. Writing letters to her wasn't the same, but they filled the endless hours and she wanted to make things vivid, pour her heart into them. Mary's, when they arrived, were horribly absent of detail, the rounded letters careful on the page; she imagined Mary self-conscious as she stuck out her tongue and bent over the sheet.

She ached for her mum, the lonely pain of wanting someone to listen, to hold her, to rest a forehead against hers and tell her the melancholy would pass. She missed her mum's scent, a mixture of soapsuds and herbs, she missed watching her work, the peace as she was bent over a dress that needed darning, some shorts that needed the hem taken up. Her face relaxed, just the delicate lines on her forehead as she focused on the work on her lap.

She left the house with all these thoughts chasing each other, faces merging, overlapping, making her eyes sting. The weather had eased but the rain still clung to the leaves and branches, the smell of the bark, the mud on the ground overwhelming everything else. She stumbled half-blind down the path to the bottom, wrapping her coat around her, still cold beneath the layers. She wandered through the village, past the shops, deserted outside, benches collecting pools of water, rain dripping from the drainpipes in a rhythm, past people hurrying, scarves knotted under their chins, a quick glance and nothing more.

Richard emerged from a cottage on a patch of land between the two rivers, shrugging on a jacket as he called out her name. She thought she saw a face in the downstairs window, just for a second. When she looked again it had gone, disappeared into the murk of the room behind the dead glass.

'Wait up,' he said, as if they had arranged to meet, as if she had strode off without him.

She felt thrown into a panic, wiping quickly at her eyes, pushing her shoulders back. He seemed to be talking to her from a distance, his mouth moving but her brain too slow to keep up.

'You haven't heard a word I just said,' he commented, a half-smile creeping over his face. Then he looked at her, serious now, his green eyes darker, his thick eyebrows lowered, his mouth a line as he stated, 'You are not alright.'

This statement, his confident gaze, the first person to notice and see it, tipped her over the edge. The tears that had been lingering behind her eyes leaked out slowly and she made a pathetic attempt to rub at them with her coat sleeve, horrified. 'I'm sorry… I'm… Please ignore me, I…'

'Come on,' he said, marching ahead of her and throwing a look over his shoulder. 'You need to follow me.'

They walked together up Watersmeet Road, away from the houses, following the curve of the East Lyn river. Richard was quiet now, walking a short pace ahead so that Abigail had to make little catch-up footsteps to keep up. His eyes were on the mouth of the valley ahead, the trees rising up on either side so that you had to crane your neck to see the tops. His cheeks were flushed pink as he turned to check she was following.

They neared the river, turning left past a row of cottages, their miniature windows facing onto the street, their doors opening almost straight into the road, the narrowest of pavements to walk along. Abigail could make out a sitting room, a doll's house standing against a wall, a crucifix on the wall of a dining room, a face peering round from an armchair. She kept following him, up to where the cottages ended and the road veered to the left.

'Here,' he said, motioning to the bridge a little further on.

She frowned, wondering whether following him had been a sensible idea. She was new to the area and didn't want to pick up a reputation. She knew how easily it could happen, had watched as girls became topics of conversations on doorsteps, stories whispered behind hands, gossip that raised the eyebrows of the listener. She had been silly to let him get this far, no doubt he thought she was fair game, she knew what they might think of someone from the city, someone like her.

She was about to turn back, went to speak, when he turned down onto the bridge and beckoned her with a hand, like she was a pet or something to be cared for.

She was curious now, wondering why he had brought her here, to this point. She wanted to laugh, to lighten the mood, but his expression seemed to stifle the sound before it could get out. He gestured to the river below and pointed up the valley, where the water pounded down past rocks, penetrating every part of the gulley, racing around stones, throwing up showers, bubbling with energy, constant, always flowing.

He had to raise his voice to compete with the noise. 'I

come here when I feel like you do, when I just want to yell it out.'

She frowned at him, caught out that he had seen right through her. She had been in just that sort of mood, wanting to scream and kick the wall in her frustration. She felt the familiar anger bubble to the surface again as she stood, swallowing once, getting herself back under control.

Then she watched as he turned away from her, leant over the edge of the railing, his head and shoulders tipped forward, his mouth suddenly open.

'You get it out!' he screamed, making her take a step backwards. Her mouth dropped open as he carried on. 'You just yell it out. The river takes it.'

She could barely hear him over the hubbub of the water below and when he stopped she walked towards him.

Putting both hands on the railings, she looked down at the river, at the relentless charge of the water as it poured over rocks and around boulders. The noise seemed to grow with the same spit and hiss, droplets thrown up, lingering in the air before falling back into the river to be flushed beneath them. She felt energized just watching it, felt her body get swept up in the shout of it.

Richard had turned towards her, was leaning over to cup his hand round his mouth. 'Try it,' he said in her ear. His breath was warm. She felt herself blush. She was going to refuse, she was going to turn around and go back, but there was something in his face, something utterly innocent. He was willing her to have a go and her resolve melted.

Standing on the first rung of the railings, she lifted herself off the ground, her hands gripping the top rung, the metal cold and rusting in her clenched hands. She felt the wind whistle around and past her, throwing her hair back. She opened her mouth, pictured her mum, sewing under the lampshade in their living room, the armchair now empty; Mary, her face when she left her; her sister, their differences; Larry, the house, her room now, the village, the feeling of smallness, of losing herself; and she screamed it at the water in shouted gasps, over and over she yelled it.

She forgot herself, where she was, clinging to the rungs of a bridge at the bottom of a valley. She screamed hoarse, snatched sentences, and let the river have them, absorb them, run on with them, battering them against the stones in its path, shattering them on the rocks into tiny manageable splinters of memory.

Then she heard a new noise, his shouts as he joined her, both of them standing on the rungs of the bridge, shoulder to shoulder, their mouths thrown open as they wailed at the water and let the river have it.

They seemed to stop at the same time and she stepped back onto the bridge, turning her body so that her back leant against the railings, her chest rising and falling from the effort. She looked down through the village to the sea, which seemed impossibly flat and calm. That was where their thoughts had ended up? Were her words being found by fishes in the Bristol Channel? The thought made her giggle, then laugh, and her whole body felt lighter.

'Thank you,' she said, turning towards Richard. He brushed a hand through his hair, tiny droplets clinging to the hairs on the back of his hand.

He shrugged. 'Makes you feel better, don't it?'

'What do you shout about?' she asked, knowing she was being bold but unable not to wonder. This boy–man, who seemed so open, his face wide and generous. She knew he would probably bat the question away. He paused, pulling a hat out of his coat pocket and tugging it down so that his fringe tickled his eyelids. She was used to the sound of his voice now, sentences spilling over one another, but he opened his mouth and shut it again.

She was about to turn away when he finally spoke. 'Feeling helpless... You know, like things can't be stopped. And my dad, he's not good and it's hard sometimes, you want to shout at someone and the river doesn't seem to mind...'

She nodded then, sorry for the darkness that had crossed his face as he mentioned his dad's illness. 'What's wrong with him? Your dad?'

'It's his legs,' he said, not divulging more.

'I'm sorry,' she said quietly.

'Me too.'

They looked down the river in silence and then with a smile he offered her his arm. 'Come on then, Your Majesty, let's show you some of the best places in the village. They do the finest chips in Devon down by the sea wall.'

She took his arm without really thinking about it, hers looping through his at the right height, his body reassuring as they departed the bridge, leaving their shouts and words in the water.

He bought a newspaper cone filled with chips, steam rising from the top, the smell divine, and they moved across to a bench overlooking the water, side by side enjoying the quiet burble of the village around them as they ate.

'I feel bad for the people in the photos when I eat them.'

'I don't think the queen will mind – she seems awfully nice, don't you think?'

'She does,' he agreed, popping a chip in his mouth, and laughing through it. 'She's a fancy one, like you.'

She grinned at him, wiping grease from her mouth with a napkin. 'And don't you forget it.'

He leapt off the bench, screwing up the newspaper and throwing it into the centre of the bin. 'How could I?'

And then he was off, a cheeky chap winking at her like they hadn't shared anything of meaning. But something in his eyes, something had shifted, like he could see inside her head. She felt a warmth spread through her stomach that she had shared that with someone. The day would always smell of batter, vinegar and him.

IRINA

Irina drove without thinking, pulling the car up next to the stone arches on the lower promenade and paying the meter. The sun was bright now, the greenery on the back wall bold, curved shadows on the promenade from the arches. She stepped across the road, walking towards the beach, her hair tickling her face before she tucked it behind an ear. The tide was out now, sunken footsteps along the shore, a couple sitting on a rug further along, wrapped up and reading.

She always missed them the most after seeing her mother, wondered how life might have turned out if they were still all together. She wondered if her mother ever shared things with others, whether she spoke with friends, Brenda perhaps? When Brenda was talking about her husband, what did her mother say in return? Didn't Brenda ask where her family were now? Irina wished she could discuss these things. She wondered why she didn't.

They'd got close to talking once. They'd been clearing out her mother's last flat and Irina had found a box. She'd thought it impossible that there could still be things from their life back then, but it had been sitting on the top of an old chest of drawers, smeared with finger marks.

Her mother noticed Irina staring. 'It was in my handbag – you know how he was always hiding things,' she'd said, her voice rusty, as if she'd forgotten how to talk about him.

Irina moved over to it in a trance, reaching out her hand, needing to touch it. She hadn't thought about it in years, but Joshua had loved it, had moved from room to room with it hanging limply at his side.

She traced the face of the familiar Ninja Turtle action figure, remembering Joshua's delight at the thing: Michelangelo, pizza-lover, the joker. He'd sit with it at meals, resting the toy on its back, nunchucks frozen in bent plastic arms, the drawn-on smile, one eyebrow permanently raised. He'd take it in the car, hold it to him when he slept, as if it were a talisman to ward off evil. Her mother had found it in her handbag afterwards. So, it hadn't been in the house.

Irina imagined his other belongings, scattered on the blue-and-white-spotted rug in his room – cars, pieces of Lego, Panini football stickers – the condition they'd be in. The image made her blink, rub at her eyes.

Don't do this, Irina.

She walked, relishing the taste of salt on her lips. She hadn't realized where she was headed until she found herself looking up at the line of hotels along the seafront, lingering over the large white facade of a Georgian townhouse, watching couples, arms thrown around each other, children pulling miniature suitcases, bumping them up the steps with two hands, all checking in to spend the weekend together. She'd been here before, with Andrew.

They were staying in a suite on the top floor. The living room had enormous double sliding doors leading to a balcony with a picnic table and they'd eaten breakfast that morning listening to the sound of the waves below them, croissant flakes littering the table and sticking to their lips, a brimming cafetière now half-empty and going cold. It was going to be a scorching day and Irina had felt excited as she pulled on a purple maxi dress, shaking out her hair. For a second the livid scar seemed to disappear, her face nothing but lips and teeth and bright eyes. A bare-chested Andrew passed her, kissed her on her shoulder and looked back at her in the mirror with a grin before slapping her bottom.

'Hey,' she said, spinning around and batting him.

He stopped her hand and pulled her into him, his body damp from the shower. Tilting her chin, he bent to kiss her, encircling her body in his arms.

'Right,' he said, drawing back and clapping his hands as if he were a schoolboy. 'Let's go.'

They were heading down to the beach and Andrew had promised to build her a castle fit for a princess. She knew he would begin it, get distracted and spend the rest of the day on the rug they'd brought, reading his book, her head resting on his chest as she read hers, every now and again muttering about heading off to rent surfboards, before falling asleep in the sunshine. They would watch swimmers, toddlers with armbands splashing in the shallows, kayakers idling like insects in the water.

There was more of a breeze that day and Irina had pulled her cardigan on, sitting up, hugging her knees, her feet sunk deep into the sand that tickled her toes. Andrew had fallen asleep, his book resting over his face. The anonymous snoozer. She smiled as he roused himself, calling from behind the book, 'I know you're staring at me,' then lifting the book and opening one eye., 'Ha! Knew it. I can feel it.'

She laughed, not denying it and picked up his hand to kiss it.

It had been a wonderful week and she hadn't wanted to return to their lives just yet; the shop could wait for a while longer. Patricia had packed her off with a raised eyebrow. She liked Andrew, ever since he'd once complimented her on a new cardigan. She thought he had an 'open face'. Irina had almost enjoyed having the spotlight on her as Patricia lumbered around the topic, bringing her over an antique ring set with topaz and announcing in a loud voice that she thought it would make an excellent engagement ring. Irina had laughed and moved through to the workshop, the smile still on her lips as she sharpened her tools, on automatic, her head full of him.

She hadn't realized she'd been following the boy with her eyes for the last few minutes. He had the same frame as Joshua, but when he turned, his face was all wrong, his eyes wider apart, his colouring a little fairer, his hair darker, more caramel. His laugh, though, that was the same; explosive, excitable. He was tugging on his mother's hand, wanting to show her something at the water's edge; he was insistent, bent double and pulling at her with both hands while she pretended to resist, giggling at him in her too-large sunhat and then relenting and taking his hand.

Andrew was sitting up next to her, watching them both too. Then he turned to face her and said in a low voice, 'Tell me about him.'

At first Irina pretended she didn't know what he meant. She tore her eyes away from the pair and went to pick up her book.

'Reena...' he said, one hand on her arm, a gentle reminder he was there.

A laugh bubbled out of her, once, strangled and distorted.

The boy at the water's edge looked up, frowning in her direction before his attention was back on whatever was on the sand. She kept her eyes staring straight ahead, the sea a glittering mass of silver and blue, the horizon blurring before her. 'Don't, Andrew.' It was a warning, issued with a half-smile frozen to her face.

'I want to know, and you need to talk about it.' He shuffled forward as he said it, went to take her hand. 'Just tell me something, anything.'

She could hear the faint panic in his voice, realized that perhaps he had been wondering for months, repressing the questions. Her mind shut down and she pulled her hand away from him. 'There's nothing to say, it's in the past.'

Was it really, she wondered, as she said the words. Did she not drag her story around with her through every waking day? For a fraction of a second she thought she could share it. It would help her, surely, to talk about it, let it out. This was what she had wanted with her mother, the great topic they manoeuvred around, ever present yet never discussed.

He had seen the photo in her flat, but she had diverted the questions away that time, and since then, whenever he'd asked her, she'd changed the subject or left the room or simply asked him not to discuss it. She could feel him now braced for her rejection. Biting on his lower lip, eyes not wavering from hers. Perhaps he thought the week had softened her and she would give in, perhaps he thought it was too fine a day to ruin, that she would still be lingering over the memory of their kisses, his body next to hers in a tangle of bed sheets and wine, that she would ease up and let him in.

She looked at him, his tan that ended abruptly below his waist – she'd laughed about it as he'd showered the day before – his eyes still searching her face. He did have an open face, Patricia was right; he had a face that encouraged you to share things. She went to open her mouth. The boy's laugh caused her head to snap around, so alike. He'd run off, his mother chasing him, holding her hat with one hand as she raced after him along the shoreline, both throwing up seawater as they ran. Irina blinked back the tears that were threatening, forced herself to look elsewhere, to think of something else. She couldn't do it, this wasn't fair, why was he ruining this holiday with his questions? How dare he do this to her, she hadn't asked for it.

When she turned back to him her face was closed and he shrank back, perhaps recognizing the expression. 'I really don't want to talk about it.'

He nodded once, his lips in a thin line, his eyes off in the direction of the surfers, and then, after a beat, he quietly rose to his feet, looking down at her as she sat in the shadow his body made. 'I can't do this then,' he said simply. There was no threat, no raised voice, no ultimatum, no drama. His voice was tinged with sadness as he cocked his head to one side. 'I'm sorry, but I can't keep ignoring it and I won't let you do this to yourself.'

She looked up at him, shielding her eyes with one hand as if she were about to ask him if he wanted a sandwich. The sun was behind him, creating a halo of light and throwing his face into shadow. She licked her lips to say something and knew that it was pointless. What could she say? She didn't want to tell him. She felt a stubborn digging in, a sharp flicker of annoyance that he had forced them into this corner.

She looked away. 'Why are you doing this?'

'I'm not doing anything,' he said with an exasperated gesture, both palms facing up. 'It's ridiculous to keep me out like this. You are clearly hurting and you need to tell me, shout it at me if you like.' His voice got louder as he talked so that by the end of the sentence she could feel the attention of nearby families flickering towards them.

'Don't,' she said, teeth grinding, feeling her face flush with more than sunburn. 'People are looking.'

'I don't give a damn,' he said, really shouting now, half-turning to face the others on the beach. 'Let them. It's you I'm interested in.'

She sat there, still, silent, avoiding his gaze until, with a huff, he reached down and collected up his things.

'I can't,' she said with finality.

'Fine,' he said. 'Fine.'

His voice broke on the last word and she glanced towards him, but his back was already to her. He was walking away, as quickly as he could, stumbling over the loose, hot sand, throwing a shirt over his shoulders, pushing his arm into the sleeve. He didn't look back towards her, took the steps two at a time up to the hotel. She could see the balcony where they had sat that morning, the picnic table empty.

She hugged her knees and looked in the other direction, down the sand. The boy had gone, lost along the shore and blended into the crowds of other beachgoers by now. She was left there on the rug looking out at the surf as it swept in relentlessly, rolling into a rhythm, already blanking Andrew out of her mind, as if he'd never been there, as if they were strangers. When Patricia asked her about the holiday, remarked on her scattering of freckles, her tanned skin, she had accepted the compliments, melting into her workshop to work on the pieces in silence, and when Andrew didn't appear for a day, a week, a month, Patricia stopped asking her questions and stopped bringing her antique rings.

She imagined herself on the spot a year or so ago. They had come here, gone out for a meal in Kemp Town, to a place with low lighting, the steady throb of chatter, cutlery tinging in the silence, muffled noises from the busy kitchen beyond. She'd worn a dress, low-cut and deep green with a pleated skirt. He'd worn a suit, a crisp white shirt and brown leather brogues. They had looked the part. He had held her hand between a tea light that had long gone out and a solitary flower in a narrow vase. She blinked the memory away, her eyes refocused on the hotel front. Her body ached for him, she wondered why she had ever let him go, why she hadn't done more to stop him walking away. Staring up at the windows one last time, she turned for her car, got in and left the town behind her.

RICHARD

They were sitting on a bench that looked out over the sea. They'd met there occasionally since the day down at the river with both of them screaming at the water. He walked along there more often than usual, hoping for a glimpse of her on the shoreline, hair whipped to the side, picking her way over the stones in heeled shoes, peach cheeks, her arms out to the sides. She'd been there today and he joined her wordlessly on the same bench, feeling his insides glow as she turned, unsurprised, a smile suggesting she'd expected him.

She was reading a book, although she now seemed to be stuck on the same page, as he stretched out his legs in front of him. The beach curved around the bay, the rocky outcrop jutting steeply, casting a thick shadow over one end. Every now and again a car would appear on the coastal road above before disappearing down behind the line of trees on Countisbury Hill. Richard couldn't drive but was fascinated by the automobiles parked up in the village, the shine of metal, the leather seats, the headlamps sticking out like toads' eyes on the front. He was lost in a daydream, Abigail sitting alongside him in the passenger seat, a scarf holding back her hair, her skin flushed as they swept along the sea road, over Exmoor.

'What are you thinking about?'

It was a moment before he realized she had put her book down, spine facing up, a smile playing on her lips as she raised an eyebrow.

'Oh, I...'

'You seemed to be on the verge of a great joke. Do tell.'

'I was thinking about... Well...' He was floundering. 'An automobile...'

She rolled her eyes at him. 'Oh dear. I thought it would be a state secret at the very least.'

He wanted then to share the image, to turn and describe their journey through Exmoor, past red deer, a hamper in the back bursting with a picnic, the automobile bouncing on tarmac as the wind rushed in through the windows and the landscape sped past. Devon seemed to have become a wilder, more romantic place these last few weeks.

On the promenade that ran along the beach he could make out a woman standing next to an enormous perambulator, the navy hood up as she stood looking out at the sea. The man she was with had stopped and was leaning over to look inside the pram; he gave a smile as he straightened and Richard lifted a hand in acknowledgement.

The toddler who had been circling the pram and his parents followed his father's gaze, face melting into a huge grin as he started a bow-legged run along the promenade, looking as if he might fall to the ground at any time.

'Bichard, Bichard.'

Abigail turned to him, an inquisitive look on her face. 'A friend?' She laughed as the plump toddler waddled up to the bench.

'Definitely a friend.' Richard grinned and bent down to

scoop the young boy into his arms, making him shriek with delight as he lifted him right over his head and down again.

'A'gen, 'gen.'

'OK, OK.' He repeated the move.

'Abigail, this is George. George, this is Abigail.'

'Hello,' Abigail said, standing up from the bench, a sweet smile splitting her face.

The small boy scrunched himself tightly against Richard's chest, slowly peeking at her with one eye.

'Don't pretend to be all shy now,' Richard teased as the boy wriggled to get down, ready to run off for the next activity.

Abigail laughed as he whistled past them both, back behind the legs of the woman next to the pram.

'Hi, Tom,' Richard said, putting out a hand to shake the man's hand. 'How's the new little man?'

The baby, eyes scrunched up, both arms flung above his head, a knitted blanket tucked tightly around him, looked utterly content.

'Oh, he's adorable,' Abigail said, leaning in. 'And so snug.'

The woman looked over at her, her cheeks pale and with bags under her eyes; she smiled at the compliment.

'Abigail, these are our neighbours, Tom and Beth.'

'Lovely to meet you. How old is he?' Abigail asked. Richard was always thrown by her easy confidence.

'Two weeks.'

'He's divine.'

'Are you headed back?' Richard asked, a thought springing into his head, keen for Abigail to come home with him, to meet his dad.

'We were. George wanted us to make the world's biggest sandcastle.'

'Did you manage it?'

'We got close.' Tom laughed, two dimples appearing on

either side of his mouth. 'George wanted to make a moat, but it will be time for the little one's feed and all hell breaks loose if we miss that.'

'Sounds like you've had experience of that.'

'I thought he'd shatter the windows. I'm amazed you haven't looked at moving.'

They turned to head back into the village.

'We'll walk with you.'

Abigail had fallen into step with Beth. There were hushed giggles as they moved along the promenade together, Abigail placing one hand on the handlebar of the pram. Richard watched the curve of her waist, the loose strand of hair that she was tucking behind her ear.

Tom lifted his eyes at him, a small smile threatening to spill out.

'Alright,' Richard said, feeling his cheeks warm as he readjusted his flat cap.

'Bichard, lift,' piped up George, a welcome interruption.

He scooped up George and trotted with him along the promenade, the toddler gurgling with laughter, his feet encased in tiny leather shoes, his body bundled into a pea coat. Abigail looked back at them, her cheeks flushed from the walk, her eyes sparkling.

Richard put George down, caught her up. 'Do you want to meet my father?' He could see Beth behind her glance at him and then her husband, knowing what they were both thinking but not caring.

Abigail nodded once. 'Absolutely, of course.'

He thought he'd never been this excited.

IRINA

It had started raining again, solidly so that the windows were permanently smeared with lines running down the surface, distorting the outside into a wash of blacks and greys. Irina spent the evening in the living room, crowded into her chair as Pepper lay curled up on a cushion in front of the radiator. Her eyes had fluttered closed, an abandoned glass of wine on the table beside her, the dishwasher going next door, a steady gurgle of noise. She blearily dragged herself to bed.

Her dreams were jumbled and full of foreign places. Faces she didn't recognize, a cottage by a river, a sweep of beach, a man in a window, a woman holding a baby in the room behind him, whispering into his hair. A shout; watching a wave head up the beach towards a chubby toddler playing in the sand. She woke, sitting up quickly, her eyes trained on the foot of her bed. The cat had joined her on the covers and seemed alert now too, focused on the same spot. Its head raised in a question. They both seemed to hold their breath, staring at the same space.

Looking around at the other shapes in the dark – her

dressing gown hanging from the door, the outline of her side table, a pile of books forgotten, the lampshade – she felt her hair sticking to her forehead. There was nothing there and Irina wondered why her heart was hammering loudly, why her hands felt clammy. Lying back down, she plumped the pillow beneath her, feeling the soothing presence of Pepper, and fell asleep again.

The next day was Sunday and she found herself back in the workshop, staring determinedly at the bureau. She had an empty day stretching ahead and she knew she needed to make progress. She sanded down the surface; she was working her way slowly through all the drawers, pulling them out, lying them on newspaper, working on them so that the bureau was left with gaping holes as if it were missing its vital organs.

There was one drawer still closed, stubbornly refusing to move, in the left-hand side of the bureau: a long thin drawer with a small brass handle. There was no keyhole and yet it remained jammed shut. Irina searched around for a way in, something niggling at her as she worked. She'd seen a piece like this before, when she was working as an apprentice in a bigger workshop just outside Chichester.

She moved systematically over it, inching across the top and down the sides, realizing as she did so that the bureau had a false bottom, the wood higher inside than it appeared from the outside. She felt her pulse quicken and she licked her lips. She wondered if there was a way to access the space. She felt along the edges of the bottom panel. She could sense something there, smaller than her fingertip but solid beneath her touch. She sucked in her breath, leaning deeper into the desk to try and look at what she'd found.

The ringing of her phone made her jump and she narrowly avoided hitting her head on the frame. Sitting on the floor next to the bureau, she fumbled to bring the phone out of her pocket, the screen announcing 'ANDREW'. She accepted the call before stopping to think about it. She curled her body over the phone as she answered.

'Irina,' Andrew said, sounding surprised. Perhaps he hadn't expected her to answer. This wasn't the first call to her in the last few weeks.

'Hi, Andrew,' she said, her breathing still fast from her find. She stood up, moving across the room to sit on a stool by the workbench, remembering yesterday, standing outside the hotel.

'I was in Brighton...' He spoke quickly. 'Thought of you and... What are you up to?'

'Nothing much. Well, I'm working on something.' As she said it she looked back at the bureau, wondered whether she had discovered something, or whether it was just a nail or an old metal bracket.

'New piece?'

'Something like that,' Irina said, not wanting to mention things in detail.

'Do you still have that stuffed ferret?' he asked, injecting a laugh into the sentence.

'It was a stoat!' She giggled without really meaning to, a hand raised over her lips. The bedraggled stoat had sold a month before. She couldn't understand how people loved taxidermy so much. 'Sold, I'm afraid,' she said, trying to match his jocular tone. What did Andrew want? They had broken up over a year ago, but she received these calls every month or so.

'Right.' He sounded distant, as if he were holding the phone away from his face.

Time passed in a mix of coughs and unfinished sentences and then Andrew seemed to rally. 'I'm free next weekend, I was wondering if you were about? We could have a drink? A meal?'

'Well, I...' Irina felt the loneliness of the workshop around her, pictured his face, expectant and boyish. He hadn't asked to meet for months, he had stopped asking, just rung and talked a while. She wondered if she had been waiting for him to call and ask again. She thought again of yesterday. Them on the beach all those months ago. 'That would be good,' she said as warmly as she could. 'Thank you,' she added.

'Great.' The tone was different now, upbeat, energetic; confidence had been restored. 'I'll let you know a time and place. Great.'

'Great,' she echoed.

'Have a good week then, Irina,' he said.

She could picture him smiling into the phone and smiled herself, feeling her face lift. 'You too.'

He hung up and she stared briefly at the phone before setting it down carefully in front of her. They'd been together a little over two years. His voice was familiar now but also changed somehow, or was that her memory distorting things?

There was a faint whistle, like air through a narrow space and she turned to look behind her. The kettle was off, the room empty. Then a cold gust swept around her, as if someone had just opened a door suddenly, and the smell of pipe smoke struck her and then another sound, slow at first, something sliding on wood, followed by a loud empty clatter that made her spin back.

Her ancient mobile phone was lying on the floor next to the workbench, in two parts. She stared at it for a second and then bent to pick it up, pressed it back into place with a click. She must have left it closer to the edge than she thought. She must have been careless. Her arms prickled and she rolled the sleeves of her jumper down. There was that whistle again, like air trapped in something, coming from nowhere, the cold again.

She backed away, towards the stairs to her flat, reaching behind her for the handle of the door, not wanting to turn around. It opened and she stepped through, quickly taking two stairs at a time to her apartment. The light and heat hit her immediately, the lingering smell of toast from breakfast, the cat limping out to greet her with curious green eyes. She leant back against the apartment door, trying to focus on these things. She hadn't imagined it though; she could have sworn she hadn't left her phone near the edge. She had heard a noise. She hadn't imagined it, she repeated to herself, marching through and turning on the television, throwing herself into her chair and paying particular attention to the comforting voices of the Sunday breakfast-time presenters, cooking up something for the viewers.

ABIGAIL

They said goodbye to Beth and Tom at their gate, promising to drop in on them another time. Then they walked up the path to the cottage. Abigail wiped her hands on her coat, her throat dry. Richard glanced at her, a line forming between his eyebrows. 'Abigail Lovatt, are you nervous?' he teased.

'No, I'm fine. I...' She glared at him through narrow eyes. 'Stop looking at me like that.' But she couldn't hold the expression, her mouth lifting into an unwilling smile as he took her hand gently in his.

'He is going to adore you,' he assured her, another hand on her back guiding her down the path.

Old stones practically hidden by clumps of grass, top-heavy flowers drooping over themselves, signs that the garden had perhaps once been tended but large patches now out of control, strawberry plants peering hopefully from beneath an apple tree, the hard round balls of apples a while away from being ready. Abigail couldn't imagine a lovelier square of garden: modest, colourful, unfussy.

Richard opened the door and she couldn't help glancing at him briefly. A quick swallow and she stepped inside.

'Dad,' Richard called, steering her into a room on the right. 'You'll need to get the best tea things out…'

She found herself stumbling over the compliments the moment she got inside. It was a lovely garden, she wasn't blessed with green fingers, the cottage was enchanting, how nice to hear the rivers running either side, how calming. Perhaps it was the presence of the wheelchair in the corner of the room, the man in the winged armchair, his lips caught in a rounded 'O' that soon morphed into a smile, his legs folded carefully beneath him, smaller than the rest of him.

Abigail stepped forward to shake his hand. His shirt sleeves were rolled up to the elbows, showing tanned, muscular forearms, a scar running along the length of one that she would later learn had happened on a fishing trip.

'I'm Abigail, it's a pleasure to meet you.'

He cut her off with a quick, 'Martin. And the pleasure is all mine. Do sit.' He indicated an armchair opposite and Abigail sat.

Richard had moved through to the kitchen and Abigail could hear the sounds of china and teaspoons as she sat, hands folded into her lap. He returned trundling a trolley into the room and stopping it by his dad.

'That's a very smart set,' Abigail said, taking in the teapot with its intricate pattern painted onto fine bone china.

Martin poured her a tea. 'It was Maisie's,' he said, glancing at the pot. 'Her best. We always get it out for visitors, but we haven't had many of them in a while. She'd hate to see we weren't still using it.'

'I'm very honoured,' Abigail said, holding the saucer reverentially in her hand, a lump forming in her throat, her eyes drawn to the sepia portrait of what must have been Maisie,

Richard's mother, on the mantelpiece. Her hair was in combed-down waves, eyes dancing in the picture, and she wore a straight skirt and suit jacket; one boy was standing behind her, a hand resting on her shoulder, and her arm was looped around a younger Richard, who leant in, head resting on her hip.

Abigail wondered who the boy was standing behind them in shorts and braces, the same-shaped face as Richard, chin tilted up as if he was trying to look taller. Martin saw her looking and indicated to Richard to bring the photograph down. It was placed in his hands and the two men's eyes met for the briefest moment, Richard dropping a hand on his father's shoulder before taking up his tea, the tiniest wink making Abigail feel like he had put his hand on her too.

'She was lovely looking,' Martin said, his mouth twitching as he drank in the photograph. 'And kind. It's a rare thing, to be truly kind, to truly put someone else first. That was Maisie, falling over backwards to help other people.'

Abigail felt suddenly inadequate. Had she ever been truly kind? She pictured Mary back in Bristol, in that bedsit, reddened as she wondered again how she could have left her on her own. Had she always thought of her mum first? Could she have spent more time helping her in the house?

'She had a mouth on her too, Dad, remember. She could put us in our place if she thought we were getting out of line.'

Martin's mouth lifted. 'I'm not saying the woman wasn't a she-witch at times.'

Richard shook his head, smiling. 'Dad.'

'Don't tell me you've forgotten the time you were both locked in your room after eating her WI sponge. Never heard such cursing! The ladies would have been shocked.' His whole face crinkled at the memory, a low rumbling laugh emerging as he replayed that day in his mind. 'Oh I miss her,' he said, looking at the photograph again. He paused, his voice dropping a fraction. 'I'm glad she never knew,' he said and Abigail knew he was talking about the other boy in the photograph.

Richard settled back in his chair, the tiny china cup making him seem like a child playing with a tea set, one finger poking out awkwardly as he sipped from it.

'And you, Abigail, Richard tells me you live with your sister and her husband…?'

'Yes, that's right. Connie and Larry Cowley,' Abigail confirmed, his name sticking in her mouth, his face in her mind then, crowding into the room with her as if he were watching over a teacup too. She put her cup down quickly, the china clinking, the remnants slopping.

'Don't know them, but Richard tells me they live in one of the fancy houses up on the clifftop.' There was no malice in his voice, no chip on his shoulder as he said it. 'You must get great views over the bay.'

Abigail smiled as she knew she should, felt her lips stretch over her teeth. 'Yes, it's a lovely house. My bedroom window looks out on the sea, you can look right across to Wales on a clear day.'

'Richard won't much like the sound of that. Scared of the water.' He shook his head. 'Only fisherman in England who's afraid of the water.'

'Dad!' Richard's neck was reddening as his Dad chuckled again.

'Happened when he was younger, fell in a pond head first. I had to scoop him out by his ankles, covered in weeds and spluttering half the contents out on the grass.'

'Quite an image.'

'He looked at me, all big eyes, so large you could see all the whites round them, one straggly weed still draped over one of them, and he told me solemnly, "I don't want to do that again, Dad."'

Abigail laughed at the thought of the younger Richard covered in weeds, enjoying him shifting in his chair as his father spilled this childhood story.

'Dad, we need to talk about which stories you're allowed to tell,' he protested, but he couldn't keep down the half-smile.

'The girl needs to know what kind of man you are,' Martin said, sipping at his tea and leaning back again.

Abigail settled in the chair, her whole body unfurling in the warmth of the square room with its simple figurines and framed photographs, an oak dresser in one corner, and listened to the two men, back suddenly in Bristol with Mary and her mum as they teased and giggled about tiny fragments of memories, moments they had shared. She didn't want the teapot to end, took her time sipping at cold dregs to prolong it, had a second helping of the malt loaf Martin had made, watched the hands of the carriage clock as they moved steadily, unstoppable, around the face. She would have to leave. Connie would wonder where she was and she couldn't keep lying about the long walks in the forest, on the moors.

Richard stopped her from clearing the crumb-covered plates and empty cups, loading up the trolley with their things. She lingered in the doorway, a goodbye to Martin.

'Come again, anytime,' he said, lifting his hand.

She nodded a thank you, moving towards the front door, the narrow corridor suddenly smaller with Richard standing behind her, one hand on the small of her back as he guided her out. She felt the spot white hot and wanted to turn and lean into him, bury her head in his chest and stay there in that house. She felt her breathing quicken as she reached for the door, not trusting herself to speak.

Outside, the path was slick with raindrops, the day darkening, the clouds heavy above the village. In the window next door she could see Beth jiggling the baby in her arms as she laughed at something Tom said, standing at the sink with his sleeves rolled up. She looked at them, an urge to be part of a similar scene a sharp pain in her stomach.

'I'll see you soon,' Richard said in a low voice, perhaps embarrassed to be heard by his father. 'I'm glad... Well, it's been good to have you round the house and maybe, well...'

He pulled a hand through his hair as he rattled on, his nervous patter giving her confidence to smile, reach up and drop a kiss on his cheek.

For a moment he rested a hand on her hip and then softly pushed her away. 'Back to the big house.' He grinned, redness stealing up his neck.

'Back to the big house,' she repeated, the words heavy on her tongue.

IRINA

She stood before the bureau, appraising it. Patricia was next door and the sounds of her heels on the shop floor, the intermittent noise of the till opening and closing, the occasional snippet of a laugh or a sentence grounded Irina. Everything was as she had left it, the drawers lying on newspaper, the inside exposed. She bent down, ready to run a hand along the bottom edge of the panel again, to find the thing she had discovered before.

It was a small shape, not quite circular. She shuffled forward on her knees now, her head moving deep inside the bureau, the light lost as she scanned the interior. It was a sort of keyhole, a small disc of wood with a single groove in the middle. She wondered if she could insert something into it, force it open. She felt a frisson of excitement whenever she unearthed something like this, always amazed by the ingenious designs. No one would know from the outside that the disc was there; she wondered what it might open if she managed it.

She crawled backwards, making skid marks in the shavings of the workshop floor, her palms coated in dust. Fetching her smallest set of screwdrivers from the side table, she ducked back inside, inserted one into the gap and tried to jimmy it round. It slipped and she tried a slightly bigger one, careful to try and get it to fit into the groove and turn it. It spun round hopelessly and she didn't try again, didn't want to damage it.

As she searched for something smaller in the toolbox, she imagined she could hear chatter, sounds, the blare of a ship's horn. She could almost feel the bureau giving off an energy, vibrating as she approached it with the next screwdriver. This one fitted neatly into the slot and she moved the wood around, the disc turning ever so slowly to the right, pointing now to three o'clock rather than midnight. The disc released and she was left with a circle of wood poking out half an inch. She held onto it and slowly slid out a small compartment, a drawer that was cleverly hidden in the bottom panel of the desk, long and deep but no more than an inch or so wide, like a hollow plank of wood.

Items inside it slid forward, forcing Irina to grab the little drawer with two hands before it tipped onto the floor of the workshop. It wasn't heavy, just unexpected, and she carried it over to the worktop. Switching the desk lamp on above her, she took a breath, realizing she had been averting her eyes from the contents. Forcing herself, she looked down at the drawer.

It seemed unremarkable in many ways and yet she experienced the same unease as she went to sift through the contents, the same feeling that this drawer had meant something to someone and they were somehow watching her do this, were waiting for her to do this. She felt the room hum with the possibilities of what she might find, as if the walls were holding their breath, as if the shadows were jostling to look over her shoulder, and the bureau, now with another empty gap, something removed, like a war wound, the pulsing centre of it.

'Irina…' Patricia burst through the beaded curtain and looked at her.

Irina started; eyes wide as she looked up.

'Reg wants you to fix his carriage-clock case again. I've told him you're working on an important commission, but he needs it quickly and he won't give up.'

'You know I'm standing right here, Pat,' Reg called from the shop.

Patricia turned to call back through. 'If I ask nicely, Reg, it might happen.'

Irina couldn't catch Reg's response beyond some mumbling, directed at Patricia no doubt. They had known each other for years, went to whist evenings together.

'Yes, of course, tell him Friday. Friday, Reg!' She called out the last bit.

'Friday,' Patricia repeated, bustling back through to the shop. 'Hear that, Reg? You're lucky.'

The interruption had given Irina the confidence to focus on the secret drawer in front of her. She needed to discover more about the bureau; she couldn't remember ever having been affected by another item in this way before. It had taken over the workshop, its presence expanding in the small space, suffocating her, overwhelming her focus so that it was all she thought about. This small pile could help her move on; help release her from its strange grip.

She drew out a small stack of postcards and letters, a couple of old photographs. The movement triggered a wave of scent and it was as if she knew the smell from another time. Some were tied with a purple slip of ribbon, others were loose; they were all in the same hand, all seemed to be undated. There was also the stub of a receipt, a handkerchief, a shell in a perfect spiral, a key attached to a keyring made of a threepence piece. Irina tried the key in the lock but it was too big; she felt her shoulders fall with the disappointment. Lastly she drew out a colour photograph with scalloped edges, a posed portrait, three people in a garden. The bottom of the drawer seemed to be coated in a thin layer of powder, granules of something crisp and white scattered and collecting in the corners and edges of the wood. She smeared a finger along it, feeling the tiny bumps on the surface.

Laying out the items, she breathed out slowly. A sudden certainty that she was meant to find these things. One of the postcards was of a sandy bay, still water, a fishing boat in the distance and behind the curve of beach a hill rising out of the picture, buildings perched crookedly up the cliffside. Letters in the top right spelt the name of a place Irina had never heard of. 'LYNTON', the postcard announced. She turned it over in her hand, expecting to see a scrawled message, 'wish you were here' salutations, but instead she saw the words 'Forgive me' written in the centre. Frowning, she stared at the two words, feeling her spine stiffen as she set the card to one side.

She examined the keyring and the shell, both ordinary-looking items. It seemed strange that they'd been secreted away, as if they were enormously valuable. Irina picked up the handkerchief. It was a gorgeous piece of lace, with a delicate square border, something they would sell in the shop. In the corner it had a large letter sewn into it, an elaborate 'A'. She unrolled it fully and then frowned. The middle part of the lace was damp. She looked back at the drawer, which was bone dry.

She wondered again if she'd been meant to find these things, whether something had led her to that drawer and its contents. She looked again at the handkerchief, the small spot of water slowly seeping to the edges and felt her arms prickle.

ABIGAIL

She stepped up to the front door, twisting the key as slowly as she could, hearing the latch turn, cringing as if it had echoed round the valley. She pushed open the door, one palm flat on the wood as she slipped around it, nudged it gently back into place. The house seemed to breathe in and out around her, a distant sound, a footstep? Was it just the wind? She wriggled out of her coat, pausing as she reached up to place it on the hook.

She moved down the hallway, careful to keep her steps light, tucking the key into the pocket of her cardigan, determined to get back to her room before anyone could find out where she'd been. She didn't want to tell her sister, felt that Richard was her secret.

Poking her head around the living-room door, she frowned to herself. The furniture stood like sentries looking out to sea, the French doors bolted, the white lace curtains tied back, framing the scene. Through the glass Abigail couldn't make out anybody on the terrace, just the uninterrupted line, the lawn and the bushes at the back that seemed to melt into the water beyond. The sea was a cloudy grey, the horizon indistinct as fog suspended over the surface of the water inched its way to shore. For a moment Abigail wanted to rush round, check all the windows were shut, block the misty fingers from entering. She loathed the thick fog that distorted shapes and lay on top of things like a dull blanket.

A scuffle, something scraping on the wooden floorboards upstairs and Abigail froze in the stillness of the hallway. Her eyes darted behind her, over to the staircase, its wide chestnut banister polished to perfection, the smell of beeswax stronger the higher you climbed. She put her foot on the bottom step, looking up, as if she could see round the turn in the staircase, see through walls. She decided to dart up the stairs quickly, soft and fast, as she imagined a hare might flee from a predator. The stair runner helped hide the sound and she made it to the carpeted landing slightly breathless, righting herself.

The noises were coming from the bedroom beyond, her sister's room. Connie must be in. Abigail's mind ran through excuses, ready to pour them out. She'd popped out to the post office to send a letter to Mary, she'd wanted some fresh air, she'd picked some flowers for her bedroom. She hadn't brought anything back from her outing, so she scratched the last thought. She thought of Richard's expression as she'd left him and a small smile crept over her face, threatening to expose her secret.

A muffled cry, a murmur and Abigail crossed the landing. She approached the door to her sister's bedroom quickly, her fingers worrying at the outline of the key in her cardigan pocket, the metal hard through the thin fabric of her top. She was holding her breath, unsure whether to knock, whether to just walk in. She would say she had wanted fresh air, her sister wouldn't probe. The door wasn't closed, it stood ajar, a slither of the peach carpet just visible, the bottom of the steps leading to her four-poster bed, which was raised on a platform, like a stage.

Then the sounds changed, became lower, regular, and Abigail realized, with an overwhelming sense that she should not be privy to these things, what she was hearing. She caught herself, one foot suspended in the air, toes of the other on the carpet, heel raised, as the thought struck her. They were on the bed. She could see the top of her sister's head through the crack in the door; he was bent over her. Burning scarlet, she stood stuck to the carpet, appalled, confused, her heart hammering so loudly she knew she would give herself away. Just before she turned, he looked up, straight at her, straight at her through the crack in the doorway, straight into her.

She stepped back, once, twice, a hand shooting out to balance herself, fled up the second flight of stairs and into her room. Trying desperately not to be heard, as if she could silence everything, eradicate the last few moments. Even when she closed her eyes and lay on her bed, covers pulled up to her chin, she could see them still. She felt her body heat up with the shame. She waited, limbs straight and stiff, for noises, for footsteps coming to her room. He had seen her, what would he do? Throw her out? Send her back to Bristol? Did she want that? She thought of Mary, she'd see her again, but where would she live? What would she do? They had plans to travel, but she needed money, more time. Richard's face stole into her consciousness, she wouldn't see him again if she left. She lay there fretting, imagining her door being flung open at any second, Larry dishevelled, throwing her suitcase into the room, instructing her to leave.

Larry left for the town hall in Lynton, a councillors' meeting he'd mentioned a few days before. Abigail watched him walk down the path, adjusting his hat then closing the gate behind him. She ducked behind the curtain, imagining him looking up and catching her staring. She felt jittery, didn't want to go downstairs, wanted to hide in this square of bedroom, remain under the covers as if she were eight again and had had a bad nightmare. She wondered if he would be out that evening too. Abigail had heard him returning in the small hours before, clattering into the hallway, a brief clash with the furniture, keys thrown down, boots on the stairs, whispered words, her sister's weary replies as the door below her opened.

She ached to be able to leave this house, to travel to America. She could find work, she was sure of it, in a big city; there would be opportunities. Another face drifted into her mind and she allowed herself to linger over his features, knowing the more she saw him, the harder it would be to leave. She patted her hair, rolling her eyes at herself in the oval mirror. She would find a way to make things work, she reassured herself, pulling open the bedroom door with a lot more confidence than she felt. Shoulders back, she walked down the stairs, pausing only briefly outside the living room to swallow. She could smell dinner wafting through from the kitchen. Edith had made a casserole.

Her sister was sitting on the chaise longue reading *Vogue* magazine, flicking idly through the pictures, rotating the page every now and again, squinting at the smaller print. 'Do you think I should wear my hair slicked back?' She felt her hair self-consciously. 'They're all wearing it like that now,' she said, holding out the magazine to Abigail.

Abigail, who spent most of the time pinning errant pieces of hair back into some kind of order, did not feel qualified to have much of an opinion. She held out her hand for the magazine. 'Can I see?'

Connie handed it over and Abigail felt her body relax as she searched her sister's face, sure that she would be able to tell if she had seen her earlier, if she was waiting to speak to her about it. Even thinking about it caused heat to pump round her body. Convinced she was blushing, she focused intently on the photograph in front of her as if it were a vital document.

'It's unusual,' she said, not really taking it in, her sister's head on the bed, his eyes looking over at her. She closed the magazine abruptly, Connie cocking her head to one side.

'You don't like it.'

'I don't mind it.'

They lapsed into silence, Abigail getting up to browse the bookshelves.

Abigail skirted round various topics all evening, found herself unable to focus on her sister's face for too long, squirming in her chair as unwelcome images seemed to criss-cross over the present. The beef casserole filled her up, she pushed the rest to the side of her plate, chased peas around with a fork. She made her excuses the moment she could, a sudden headache, she needed to lie down, and left the room quickly, lay staring at the ceiling in all her clothes, looking up at the plaster moulding wondering how long she would live in the house, whether she would always feel like this.

She woke too early, strange dreams forcing her awake at odd hours, imagining eyes in the corners of the room, people where there was clothing, monsters where there was furniture. Her eyes were bleary, she dabbed beneath them with a sponge of cold water, hid the red rims with brown pencil liner. She drew a careful line around her lips, a neutral shade, and smacked them together. Her made-up face making her seem older, more sophisticated, Abigail could fool herself into thinking that she was ready to face Larry.

She found she couldn't even look at him, ate her breakfast in silence, her head burning from his eyes on her. The toast was dry, sticky in her mouth; she felt every grain of it pass down her throat.

She looked sideways at her sister's hands. The manicured nails, neat pink squares, a French polish, busying themselves with the process of buttering her toast. She was talking about the neighbours, she thought they had started planting broad beans in their garden already. She wondered whether they were right to have done so, or whether the weather would turn. She didn't seem to notice that neither of them were responding. Abigail felt the room was as small as the square of table they were sitting at: no escape.

'Well we shouldn't worry about what they're doing, darling,' Larry said, 'and you shouldn't be peeking over the fence at them.' She could hear the smile enter his voice, felt her flesh crawl. 'It's not nice for people to watch other people without their knowledge – is it, Abigail?'

She heard him; she heard her name in his mouth. Her sister turned, the tiniest puckering of the skin in between her eyebrows: a question.

She looked at her plate, at the yolk bleeding slowly out of her egg, dribbling down the edge of the egg cup. 'It's not,' she said in a voice barely louder than a whisper. And then her eyes were dragged upwards.

He raised his egg spoon at her, the white wobbling on top. 'No,' he said with a crooked, closed-lip smile, 'it's not.'

IRINA

None of the letters or postcards were dated, many just had rushed, slanted words tripping over each other. They were full of love, teasing, focusing on happy times. Irina found herself drawn to the author, smiling as she read about a day in 1940, making a fruit cake 'to send to Churchill, to keep his energy up'. There were two small black and white photographs too, both creased and battered as if they'd been carried around. One showed a room in a house somewhere, light filtered through thin curtains, two women on a velvet sofa, cheeks pressed together. Another in a garden, an older woman sitting on a bench, her needlework on her lap, a small smile on her lips.

The colour photograph stood out, different from the rest. It wasn't just the scalloped edges, or that the others were in sepia or black and white. This seemed to be another place, a more formal portrait, a man and two women on a terrace at a delicate wrought-iron picnic table, stone pots filled with lavender around them, a sweep of manicured lawn behind them, a tantalizing hint of the sea beyond. One of the women

Irina recognized, from the sofa in the other photograph, her expression different though, eyes deadened, glancing off to the right of the picture, away from the couple on her left. A pretty woman was sitting in a chair, ankles drawn together, a nipped-in suit and patent heels, her hair twisted into a bun, her rosy lips full, winged eyeliner. The man behind her was standing, one hand resting on her shoulder as he looked directly at the camera, his mouth lifted in a crooked smile. His other hand seemed to be reaching to his right, towards the other woman, standing slightly to the side.

Irina frowned at the picture, something strange about the scene. She felt a coldness seeping into her arms and put it down on the workbench, setting it aside for Patricia to take a look at. Patricia loved mysteries, gossip and secrets and she would have a large number of theories about the discoveries.

She was working late on Reg's carriage-clock case, wanting to get it finished quickly, otherwise he'd be pestering Patricia every day until it was done. He was a regular in the shop, always bringing in bits and bobs. He liked to collect Royal Doulton pieces, so they always set them aside for him to have first option on. He was a big man with a gruff voice but always said thank you, barking it at them both as they wrapped the pieces for him.

She thought he would be about the same age as her father and she wondered then what their relationship would have been like. Her father had a softer voice, used to do all the funny voices when he read to her, used to let Joshua and her sit on his feet and be dragged around the kitchen, even when he was still wearing his smart shoes from work. He had loved to read; she remembered his side of the bed always piled high with books. Would they have found things in common?

She set aside the case, pleased with the job, and shivered as she felt a breeze whistle around her bare ankles. A small window, loose on its hinges, slammed back against the frame. Irina moved across to secure it, glimpsing the patch of garden beyond, the bushes and trees outlined in the light of the large moon. Placing the window back on its catch, she turned to pick up the photograph from the bench where she'd left it.

It wasn't there. Irina stepped across, her eyebrows drawn together, eyes narrowed. She was sure she'd put it on the side. She looked in the drawer again, wondered whether she'd returned it without thinking. She hadn't. She looked down; perhaps it had blown off the bench in the sudden breeze. On the floor she noticed little flecks of white, flakes like snow scattered under the table. She bent down and realized they were tiny fragments of stiff card, a photograph. She picked one up, recognizing it immediately, half of the man's face, one eye looking directly back at her. The photograph had been torn into tiny pieces. Behind her the window let out a groan as if something had been released, then smashed back on its hinges again. Irina wrapped her arms around herself, feeling the cold sweep around her and into her, scared now of what she had discovered.

ABIGAIL

Her sister was sitting on the terrace under a parasol reading a magazine. She looked as perfect as the woman on the front cover, her lips neatly pencilled and filled, her eyebrows plucked and combed, her hair falling in soft ringlets over her shoulders.

Abigail couldn't help blurting, 'You're so beautiful,' feeling clumsy and ungainly as she dragged the other iron chair out to sit on, wiping at an insect that was crawling over the white latticework.

Her sister lowered the magazine onto her lap and shifted in her chair. 'Mum used to let us both put on her lipstick in her bedroom. Do you remember? She used to wear scarlet red and Mrs Harrison from next door called her names behind her hand.'

'I don't remember,' Abigail said, putting two fingers up to her bare lips as if she could taste red lipstick. The mum she'd lived with during the last few years didn't wear red lipstick. But then she remembered a day on the Downs long before the war, before even their dad had left them, so she must have been very young. They'd taken a kite up and their mum had been sitting laughing on a picnic rug, her feet curled beneath her, her shoes abandoned in the grass. 'You're right, I'd forgotten.' The feeling smarted a little, the memories jarring.

'I used to steal out with it in my handbag sometimes,' her sister admitted, sneaking a small look at Abigail as if she might admonish her for it.

Abigail felt a warmth flood through her, her sister drawing her into confidences, the kind of conversations she used to have in Bristol with Mary, one head next to the other's feet, staring at the sky, talking about the future, men, marriage, their parents. She smiled in collusion. 'Mum would have been appalled,' she said, knowing their mother was always too gentle on everyone to ever have been appalled.

'The garden looks lovely.' Abigail gestured, panicking that she was now veering away from their moment, not knowing what she could say to draw her sister further.

The garden did look lovely, it was true. The sloping lawn had been mowed in neat strips of jade and lime, the flowerbeds were bursting with colour, a riot of lilac and fuchsia, clumps of delphiniums and cornflowers spilling over each other, the lavender sticking up proudly in pots. A bee made an unsteady path over them, pausing briefly before moving on.

'I've never seen you wear any,' her sister suddenly announced, picking up her magazine and placing it on the table in front of her.

'I'm sorry?'

'Lipstick,' she said, a tiny frown breaking up the peachy smoothness of her forehead. 'Do you even have any?'

'I suppose I never got into the habit of wearing it, there was none of it around when I took an interest. My friends went through a phase of using beetroot instead, but it tasted dreadful and I always ended up looking like I'd rubbed food dye all over my face.'

Connie's nose wrinkled at the image.

Abigail couldn't imagine Connie's face looking anything other than immaculate. She shrugged. 'I always feel surprised when I wear it, it seems like someone else staring back at me from the mirror and not the girl who lived through the war and put gravy browning on her legs.'

'You didn't!'

'I did, we all did, and drew lines down our calves. I had a terrible hand and mine were always hopelessly off-centre. I used to make Mary do it, but she was just as useless.'

'I did miss lipstick,' Connie mused, 'but Larry used to bring me home other things, powder without the puff sometimes, that sort of thing.'

Abigail swallowed the urge to tell her it would have been from the black market. She plastered a smile on her face as she thought back to a particular day in their Bristol house. 'One of Mum's friends made herself underwear out of RAF silk maps. She rolled up her dress right there in the kitchen to show us and we all fell about laughing.'

Connie giggled softly at this story and Abigail felt that connection sparking again. She edged herself forward in her chair, eager to continue.

Connie gave her a look, her eyes widening as if she had finally noticed her, really noticed her, for the first time since she'd arrived. 'Let's do your make-up,' she said, lightly clapping her hands together, her manicured nails shiny and perfectly trimmed.

'Oh.' Abigail sat back in her chair again, feeling excited at the idea. She didn't normally think too much about her hair or make-up, but her sister's glossy appearance made her wonder what she might look like. 'I'd love to.' She sounded as if she were accepting a formal invitation and felt the familiar heat on her neck as if she were about to blush deeply.

Connie stood up, moving towards the French windows. 'Come on.'

Abigail followed wordlessly, the sudden shock of the inside making her start. She crossed the living room and headed up the stairs, her sister's calves at her eye line until they rounded a corner and she was left looking at the wallpaper, the mahogany trunk on the landing. Connie had already swept into her bedroom and Abigail felt strange as she approached, hovering in the doorway unable to step across the threshold.

Connie turned, her skirt flaring out. 'What are you doing? Come on.' She beckoned her with one hand, crossing the room to pull out a velvet stool at her dressing table.

Abigail was staring at the four-poster bed, images jostling over her sister's words. She shook her head a fraction, as if she could throw them from her mind to the ground, and swallowed, trying to rouse the same enthusiasm she'd felt out in the sunshine on the terrace. She couldn't help but cast a quick glance over her shoulder, as if she were half-expecting him to round the corner or pop out from behind the bedroom door.

Connie was frowning at her now, tapping a silver-backed hairbrush on her thigh. 'You're so slow,' she said, her voice a whine.

Abigail was plunged back through time, to the arguments Connie had had with their mum. She'd stood on the periphery, watching as Connie wheedled and twisted until their mum gave in and Connie got her way with a triumphant squeal.

She walked over to the stool and sat down as Connie moved behind her to start brushing her hair, untangling the knots she encountered. Their eyes met in the triptych-mirror; all six pairs focused on each other. The process felt incredibly intimate and Abigail bit her lip, watching her hair shine under the light in the room.

'I wonder whether I would suit going darker,' Connie mused, patting at her own brown hair, faint hints of blonde running through it.

'I love your hair,' Abigail said. 'I prayed and prayed for lighter hair when I was little, but Jesus never gave in. Mary and I covered bits with lemon juice, which was utterly hopeless. I'm amazed none of it fell out.'

Connie tilted her chin, her mouth turned up. 'We'll pin it to the side in waves – that will really suit you, you have the loveliest-shaped face and a long neck.'

Abigail felt herself glow within at the compliment. She was already feeling more glamorous, sitting on the velvet stool surrounded by glass bottles full of expensive scents, a powdery, rich smell hovering like a sweet cloud over the dressing table.

Connie took an age on her hair, asking her questions, her forehead puckering as she bent down to pat, spray and smooth, the concentration setting them both off into laughter on more than one occasion. Eyeliner was wielded, flicked on in the neatest line of rich brown; eye shadow brushed on so that when Abigail turned it shimmered in the light; mascara built up in layers.

'Right, let's finish by giving you gorgeous scarlet lips,' she said, picking up a silver lipstick case and taking off the lid. Abigail eyed it warily and Connie spotted her expression. 'Trust me,' she giggled, leaning down so that Abigail was forced to look anywhere but at her sister's cleavage.

She stared at the ceiling as she followed Connie's instructions. 'Press your lips together, hold still.' She thought briefly that this was what it might have been like if Connie hadn't gone away and they had grown up together. How desperately she had craved her older sister when she was in her teens, wanting to ask questions, things she was too embarrassed to say to her mum, eager to share secrets and crushes. She felt the emotion build behind her eyes and worried she might make her mascara run. 'Finished!' came the announcement.

Abigail paused briefly, neck still craned back, blinking once before lowering her head and staring into the mirror in front of her. What she saw caused her to take a stifled breath. She didn't recognize the woman in the glass opposite, the woman whose face frowned as this thought moved through Abi's mind. Her lips were full and bold, her teeth the whitest they'd been, her nose and forehead matt and smooth, her hazel eyes popping out of the perfectly applied lines and lashes. She looked capable, desirable, sophisticated. This was a woman who didn't feel insecure or envious, didn't worry about the little things; she exuded confidence, would know French, could run a household, could play the piano. She hadn't been brought down by years of war and worries. The light in her eyes suggested playful thoughts, a carefree life. Abigail could not believe this woman was her.

Connie was walking behind her, her mouth pursed in appreciation, dimples in her cheeks as she stepped back.

'You're a genius.' Abigail laughed, pushing back the velvet stool to sashay across to the four poster bed, standing on the stair beneath it, twirling round the post to dip her head back like the movie stars in films before they get kissed. Her sister making a low whistle and clapping her hands in delight.

Their celebrations were so loud, they missed it. They didn't hear the sound of the front door opening and closing, they didn't hear the sound of keys being thrown down, of footsteps in the hallway, they didn't hear footsteps on the stairs and the landing. In fact the first they heard of Larry was when he was standing in the doorway, the door swinging slowly back to reveal him, his mouth turned down, one eyebrow twitching.

His voice was low, his mouth barely moving and their laughter dropped away. Abigail took a step away from the bed, snatched her hand from the post, biting her lip.

'They might drop an H-bomb at any minute and you're smearing yourself in lipstick,' he said, staring first at Abigail and then at Connie.

They looked down at the floor like scolded children. Connie didn't say anything. Abigail could feel Larry's eyes on the top of her head. Her painted face should have given her the confidence to look him in the eye, to say something. But the carpet swam before her, the peach blurring as rage built inside her. She willed her sister to stand up to him, to tell him what they were doing was harmless. Why shouldn't they? The war was over, they were young and yet still, years later, everyone seemed to be dragging around the guilt of their survival, hands clamped over laughing mouths before the sound could leave them. They should be joyful; what did all those brave men and women die and work for if not so that future generations could laugh until their sides hurt, until tears rolled down their faces?

The room felt crowded as he stepped forward, wearing his brown checked trousers, his shoes scuffed at the toe. The only exit was behind him and she felt dizzy with the thoughts hammering through her mind, the cloying smell of open powder pots tickling her nostrils, her sister's terrible silence, her averted eyes. Abigail was firmly trapped.

She raised her head, her lips pressed together. They felt sticky and unfamiliar as she spoke. 'I'll go to my room.'

'Wipe it off,' he said, unsmiling. 'I won't have you seen outside this house like that.'

'But… I…'

Connie looked at her quickly, tucking a strand of hair behind one ear, her eyes darting left to right. She tore off a piece of cotton wool, pushed it into the cream and pressed it onto Abigail's skin, the make-up leaving orange smears on its surface, her face becoming a sad wash like a watercolour left out in the rain. She felt the tears prick the back of her eyes, the humiliation as Connie dragged the make-up away, brown streaks under her eyes from the mascara, stained lips and uneven skin. Her sister didn't look at her as she undid all her work.

She waited for Connie to say something, the triptych-mirror showing her three selves silent in the middle of the room. Abigail thought back to the hour before, felt their closeness snap shut as Larry moved behind her, blocking her view, meeting her eyes in the mirror.

'And your hair, take it out,' he said.

Abigail removed the pins one by one, her hair remaining in waves down the side of her face, kinked and shiny after Connie had spent so long on it.

She was Abigail again, messier and sadder, but Abigail.

'Better,' he said, one hand reaching out, squeezing her shoulder slowly. 'Isn't that better?' He laughed, his face looser, his eyebrows raised. And Connie, slowly, painfully, started to laugh too.

IRINA

Irina could tell that she wanted to ask. Irina never visited mid-week. Her mother was sitting at the kitchen table, a blanket around her legs that seemed to age her. She'd been embarrassed when Irina had appeared. The flat had seemed too cold: she never put on the heating, even in winter. Irina never questioned why, not venturing into that territory, the place they didn't go. Her mother eyed her over the hot chocolate that Irina had made them both, a film of milk now stubbornly stuck to the pan in the sink. She was waiting. Irina could feel her unanswered questions as she listened to the sound of someone moving around in the apartment above, the noise of a car on the road outside tracking through puddles, its engine straining.

'A piece arrived, a bureau, last week,' she began.

Her mother looked momentarily disappointed, her mouth half-opening and then shutting again in a thin line. She seemed surprised. Irina wondered briefly what she had imagined she was there to say.

'From an American client,' she continued, her finger and thumb rubbing against each other. She noticed her mother looking at them and stopped.

'Oh, right.'

'Well, the thing is... This, well, it sounds sort of silly really, now I'm here, but I think...' She stopped abruptly, perhaps not wanting to admit things aloud, perhaps feeling foolish for saying them in the first place, for thinking them. How much had really happened? It seemed so small.

Her mother leant forward, cupping her mug with both hands. 'Go on.' Her voice was rich with encouragement and Irina gulped and started again.

'Mum, it sounds stupid, but I swear it's not right, it's making things... happen.'

Her mother's forehead crinkled and she leant back a fraction. 'Happen?'

'Well I suppose what I mean is strange things that I can't really explain how they... Things are happening.' She could hear how hopeless she sounded.

Her mother took a sip of the hot chocolate. 'What kind of things?'

Irina took a breath. 'There's a feeling I get, it's odd, I haven't had it before.'

'Go on.' Her mother waved a hand, nails bitten away.

'Like someone is watching, is with me in the workshop. And, well, it's more than that. I... I saw a face... Well, I wasn't sure, but there were footprints and I found photos, a photo and things in a drawer, but someone tore it up and...'

'Hey, hey.' Her mother hushed her in a voice that transported her right back to her childhood. She blinked and looked up. 'Slower. What do you mean, footprints?'

'They were watery,' Irina explained, 'as if someone had walked through water. But no one had.'

She knew she sounded strange. She tried to take hold of herself, check her breathing. The images of the last few days, the feeling she got when she went into the workshop, it was overwhelming and she hadn't even realized the extent of it. It had driven her here, to her mother.

She let a breath out. 'There was a pool of water by it, and someone's face at the window, in the mirror, and my phone was moved, thrown on the floor…'

Her mother didn't cut her off, or laugh, or look disbelieving. It gave Irina the confidence to carry on, like she wasn't being ridiculous, like these things could be happening. As she spoke she realized she didn't feel so alone anymore.

'And there was a photograph that was torn up. I know it sounds crazy, but things are happening and…' She didn't want to admit she was scared, didn't want to say it to her mother, who had been through so much. Her fear would make it real and she wasn't sure she was ready for that. 'Do you believe in that? That stuff?' she asked, not able to meet her mother's eye.

There was a pause that seemed to go on for such a long time. Sounds melted away and Irina strained to just hear her mother's response, not sure what it would be.

Her mother placed the mug down carefully, smoothed the blanket in her lap. 'I… I'm not sure.'

Irina nodded. Her shoulders dropped.

'I suppose things happen that we can't explain.' Her mother pleated the blanket. 'And we don't know everything.'

Irina bit her lip, thought of the torn-up photograph, the footprints, the face. How did you explain them? It seemed so absurd, though, to imagine something had been there in the room with her, that a piece of furniture had done that to her.

Her mother was staring at her lap, her eyes unfocused as if she were caught far away.

Then Irina heard herself asking, couldn't believe she had,

'Do you think they're out there somewhere?' She didn't need to say who 'they' were.

Her mother closed her eyes for a moment, breathing through her nose.

'Sorry,' Irina blurted, regretting the question, or rather the reaction, not wanting to upset her and yet wanting to know.

'No, it's fine, it's...' Her mother put her fingers to her lips absent-mindedly, rubbing them across the surface. 'I have thought about it, of course,' she admitted.

It was Irina's turn to nod. She stared mutely at the table and then back at her mother. She hadn't realized she was holding her breath.

Her mother looked up at her, a grim expression on her face. 'But no, I don't think so, they're not out there.'

Irina nodded once more, trying to convince herself. She thought of the boy in the blue jumper. And the woman at her window.

It seemed to signal the end of the conversation. Irina nodded dumbly, taking both mugs and scrubbing at them in the sink. 'Best get on,' she said, bending to plant a kiss on her mother's cheek, not giving her time to linger over a goodbye.

She couldn't shake the memory of her mother's expression as she left and on the drive home she tilted the rear-view mirror towards herself and caught her own eye in the strip. She was reminded of another journey, the journey bathed in the glow of 'Before'. Irina in the passenger seat next to her mother. They were driving back from picking up her dad's surprise, an enormous cake in a ribboned box, the icing made to look like a putting green. Her mother had asked her about school and Irina had talked about the play they were doing; she had five lines in the first scene and was worried she wouldn't remember them. Her mother had offered to help, touching her leg as she said it, glancing to her left with a quick, reassuring smile.

It had been the last day like that, when Irina didn't carry around all the other thoughts and sounds and smells. When she still had her family. Sometimes her whole body ached to be back in that car with her mother. Some days she wished they had never gone home.

Pushing through the shop, past customers browsing for knick-knacks and Patricia's raised eyebrows, she headed straight to the bureau, her jacket still on, puffing beside it, rolling up her sleeves. Loading up the woodstove with off-cuts, she fetched a strip of sandpaper and started to scrub determinedly at one of the empty drawers, in a rhythm, trying to distract herself with the monotony of the task, something she had done for years, back and forwards, back and forwards, smoothing the surface down, smoothing the marks away.

She worked all day on the bureau, refusing lunch, cups of tea, just wanting to get it finished, not allowing herself a pause or a quiet lull that she could fill with more questions. Her arms were aching, the minuscule flakes of wood suspended in the air, clinging to her clothes and her skin, giving off their familiar smell, warm and comforting. She needed to glue a knife-cut veneer to the front of a couple of drawers but she didn't want to leave the pieces to dry, not today; she wanted the momentum.

Hours passed, with Patricia bustling about next door. The sound of the till rolling open with a rattle of coins as she counted the day's takings nudged Irina into thinking about packing up. She was bent over the last of the drawers, sliding it into the bureau and out so that it didn't snag.

Drip, drip, drip.

The sound was quietly insistent. Irina looked over at the

sink. The tap was dry, hadn't been used all day. She frowned and returned to her task.

Drip, drip, drip.

She looked over at the window. The sky was turning from blue to lilac, the sun having swept past the shop and now setting over the hills beyond. There had been no rain. The gutters would be dry.

Drip, drip, drip.

It was louder this time, close, the noise, so close she could almost see the splashes from the individual drops as they fell. She put a finger up to her ear, wondering for a moment if she was imagining it.

Drip, drip, drip.

She looked down at the bureau, the floor around it, and then dipped her head slowly to peer underneath, not quite making it as Patricia moved the beads aside to call a goodnight.

She straightened up quickly, pivoting on a foot to face the entrance, one hand flying to her chest. 'Oh.'

Patricia was waggling her finger. 'Stop working soon,' she chided as she lifted her bag back onto her shoulder with one hand.

'I will.' Irina smiled, trying to hide her alarm, wondering for a second if she could ask her to stay. Saying nothing more.

Patricia turned and left. The beads fell back with their clicking clatter and she moved through the shop beyond. No noises nearby. The faint bell as she'd gone, the key turning in the lock, the hint of her footsteps as she walked away from the shop. No other sounds.

Drip, drip, drip.

Closing her eyes and then taking the sandpaper again, she carried on, over the edges, making it smoother, in a rhythm, faster. She would finish this piece. There was no noise, it was all in her head. There was no noise. Irina carried on scrubbing at it. She would finish this piece.

ABIGAIL

She picked her way up into the woods behinds the village, the slippery damp of the forest floor forcing her to grab on to gritty branches as she stepped over a carpet of leaves in absurd shoes. She thought of her mum in that moment, clutching her sides with laughter at her city girl let loose in the woods in thin leather heels and a cotton skirt that caught on every bramble and weed. It felt good to be alone, just her and the muted hush of the trees around her, the whole world tinged with greens and browns, the leaves curled and brittle on the branches. She thought of her sister back in the house darning socks on the sofa, Larry by her side, one arm protectively looped over her shoulders, seeming to shield her from other people.

The large house often felt too small for the three of them, the walls hemming her in, her sister glancing over at her, strained smiles, Larry padding into rooms, his footsteps soft, always there. Abigail had been making plans, writing to Mary about the work they could do, where they could stay as they saved up for that first boat crossing. It made her feel better to think ahead, to feel free of the house and village.

'Hello there,' a voice called, Richard's face tilted up at her from the path below.

'Hello,' she replied, feeling her mouth stay open in an 'O' of surprise.

She patted her hair pointlessly, brushing away a spindly strand just as he appeared, red-cheeked and out of breath, his hands pushing down on his thighs as he made his way straight up the slope towards her. He wobbled at the end, which made her shoot out a hand to grab him. She felt his jumper tug away from her and she seized his arm with two hands.

'Woah,' she said, her own shoes slipping on the ground so that for a brief second she thought they both might tumble back down the slope.

'That wasn't quite the entrance I'd planned.' He laughed, putting his hands in his pockets and bouncing on the balls of his feet.

She was aware of the warmth of his jumper now her hand was empty, his flushed cheeks, his breath rising and falling with the sudden effort of running to catch up with her. 'What are you doing here?'

'I'm following you,' he said, his face a solemn mask.

She took a step back, her neck craned back too, and that prompted Richard to look horrified, both hands flying up.

'I'm kidding, Abi,' he said, frowning at her and lifting his eyebrows.

Abi. Her mum had called her Abi. She was distracted by the sound of it.

'I'm actually meant to be getting Dad some castor oil and picking up mince for dinner, but I thought I'd head up here quickly and stop in at...'

His words faded away and it was Abigail's turn to wonder

whether he was acting strangely. 'Yes, oh mysterious one,' she teased, feeling like herself once again, feeling comfortable with Richard, who seemed to be able to laugh and cajole her out of any dark mood.

Richard tapped his lips with a finger before a slow smile crept across his face. 'OK,' he said. 'But it's a secret, you have to promise.'

'I promise.'

'How can I be sure?'

'Because I give you my word.'

'Is your word like rock?'

'What do you mean?'

'Is it unbreakable?'

'You can break rocks. Look...' She puffed in mock-exasperation. 'I won't tell anyone – will that do?'

'Hmm... That will do for now.'

'Good.' She hovered, making her eyes into slits. 'You're not a Russian spy, are you?'

His face erupted into a laugh; quick, sincere. It made her want to hear it all over again.

'Come on then, I need to show you something,' he said, reaching to take her hand and then pulling back at the last moment. 'It's up here.'

She followed behind him, noticed the mud clinging to the heels of his shoes, his corduroy trouser legs wearing thin at the bottom.

'Nearly there,' he said, throwing the comment over his shoulder.

Abigail moved on, chest tightening, legs burning, unused to climbing this quickly. Perhaps sensing she was falling behind, he slowed up, hands on his hips, looking out beyond the branches towards the sea.

She was grateful for it, joining him to catch her breath,

looking at the small squares and shapes of blue in the gaps between the leaves, feeling her chest rise and fall.

They reached another corner in the path and he offered her his hand. 'It's just here but be careful.'

He edged between two sagging fence posts, a useless thin bit of barbed wire holding nothing in or out and perched on a flat rock that jutted out of the side of the hill. She joined him on the rock, looking down at a ledge just beneath them, hidden from the path. He dropped down, turned to help her, held her hips with both hands and lowered her down carefully, one hand reaching up to her face to tuck a piece of hair behind her ear. Then he coughed and let go, avoiding her eyes and moving to sit on a moss-covered trunk lying on the ground.

Flushing, she joined him on the trunk, balancing herself on the edge, tucking her skirt underneath her. The scent of moss, damp and warm, seemed to swirl about her; the gentle chitter of insects hidden from view. She could still feel where he had put his hands on her. Ahead of them was a perfect, uninterrupted scene, the bluish bruise of the sea laid out before them, the tops of the trees beneath them so that when she peered down it made her feel dizzy with the height.

'Is it dangerous?' she asked, worried for a moment that they might both tumble down the cliff face.

'No. I've come up here all my life.'

She licked her lips, feeling a patter of nervousness cross her chest, knowing it had nothing to do with the height and everything to do with his thigh being inches from hers. He twisted round to face her, she felt like someone had turned a gas lamp on her right side, a warmth that started in her left arm and seemed to course through her body steadily and surely. She felt the urge to lean in towards him, rest her head on his shoulder and then laughed at herself for being ridiculous. He was looking out over the water now.

She smiled then, following his gaze. 'It's amazing.'

'It's a good spot,' he agreed, his eyes crinkling as he turned back to her. 'My brother and I used to lean right over the edge and see who would quit first.'

Abigail thought back to the photograph on the mantelpiece, the boy in braces. 'Your brother, is he…?'

He was shaking his head before she could finish. 'El Alamein, '42.'

She nodded once, knowing what that meant. 'I'm sorry.'

'So am I.'

He scuffed a hand along the trunk. 'He was bloody brilliant, my brother. He was one of those people that everyone liked and wanted to crowd around, you know?'

She nodded slowly, thinking of her mum, of people crowding into their house during wartime ready for a cup of tea and a laugh, feeling at ease. She wanted to reach across and take his hand.

'He was good at just about everything: it was my life's mission to beat him at something. He used to make me try and catch golf balls in a fishing net we used for crabbing. Dad shouted at him when one got me in the stomach.' He started laughing at the memory, a brash, confident laugh, as if he was used to remembering the best times.

She imagined the two boys playing in a garden somewhere in the village below and grinned with him. 'I've never had a brother, although I'm not sure I'd be keen on one that fired golf balls near my head.'

'It's still odd being just me, I forget a lot of the time, go in to tell him something, tease him about a girl, talk to him about Dad, but the room is empty and it still pulls me up short. Strange.'

'I'm sorry,' Abigail said, knowing this was so inadequate but not wanting him to clam up. She thought of the days after her mum died, how she'd assumed she was just upstairs or in the next-door room. All the times in the past few weeks she had wanted her there, her counsel, a gentle admonishment. Anything. She thought of her sister back in the drawing room, felt a surge of feeling that she should be there with her. She was lucky she had her left, hadn't lost everything.

'I seem to tell you more and more miserable things every time I see you.'

'You are a joy to be around,' she teased, nudging his side.

'It's what all the girls love about me.'

'I'm sure.' She laughed. 'Irresistible.'

He leant back on his hands, looking out over the sea.

They settled into their own thoughts, watching a seagull hover in the wind, wings motionless, feathers ruffled in the breeze, before dipping out of sight.

'Tell me more about Bristol,' he said, craning his neck up to catch the sun on his face.

'I miss it,' she said after a moment, admitting it quietly. 'Well, I miss certain things, I suppose. The size of the place, you get lost there, on a bicycle, anonymous; you can be anyone. I miss the people...'

'People?'

'Mary mostly.' Abigail felt the guilt sitting in her stomach as she thought of Mary now, all alone. She would write again tonight; they had talked every day for years. 'We were friends, more than friends really. She spent so much time in our house, Mum joked she might as well move in.'

'Does she have family?'

Abigail shook her head, picturing Mary in the single room at the top of the stairs, underwear drying on a line over the fireplace. 'She had me.'

They sat like that for a while, not talking, just looking out through the tops of the trees. She felt her heartbeat slow, a calm spread over her as they stayed there. Larry's face didn't seem as significant when she was with Richard; the hole left by her mum felt less painful. She felt a flicker of guilty confusion, thought of her plans to work, to leave the village. They were fading up here, her resolve melting into the leaves at her feet.

They'd been so quiet, Abigail squeaked when Richard clapped his hands together and announced, 'I know where we should go.'

IRINA

'You look tired,' Andrew said as he pulled out her chair for her and smiled, his eyes crinkling kindly. It was a smile you couldn't help but return, it was so open and honest. He pushed his hair off his forehead, looking like an overgrown schoolboy, the burgundy jumper and brown cords too adult for his youthful face. He didn't seem to have developed any new lines and Irina wondered if he would always look cherubic.

She thanked him and sat down, nodding in acknowledgement. 'Busy week.'

He paused momentarily, wavering, and then sat, hands clasped together, elbows resting on the table.

The restaurant was dim, the dark red walls and oak panelling rich, giving everyone a warm glow. Andrew looked good, she thought; he always had. When she recalled him in her mind he always seemed too heroic, too perfect almost, but the hole in his jumper, shirt peeking through, was a much-needed flaw. She smiled at him as he picked up the wine menu, feeling her body unfurl against the distant clatter of pans and the smell of spices wafting from the kitchen every time the door opened. A waiter appeared and they ordered a Rioja, grinning stupidly at each other as the bottle was produced and the waiter showed it to them on a napkin-covered arm and walked them through its particulars.

'Very good,' Andrew muttered after swilling it around and raising one eyebrow at Irina. His cheeks were reddening, the scrutiny perhaps too much; he had always hated being put in the spotlight.

She felt a flutter in her stomach and the urge to laugh. They both felt relieved as the waiter walked away. Andrew poured the wine into her glass, a thick red wave that soon settled.

'I'm glad you called,' Irina said quietly, fiddling with the stem of her glass. 'I know I've not... well... I don't deserve it.".'

Andrew swatted the comments away with a hand. 'I'm not here to go over old ground: I've missed you, simple as that, and I wanted to see you.'

She was grateful for the easy way in which he'd moved things on. She'd always known where she stood with him as he'd always made things abundantly clear.

'How are this year's students?'

'Hard work,' he said, his mouth twitching. 'We've just had the half-term break and they still know next to nothing. They've got exams, so they keep coming and seeing me for last-minute revision sessions.'

'What does that involve?'

'Mostly panic – me, not them.'

'Oh dear.' Irina laughed, feeling as if she'd been whisked back a year, their easy conversations over a bottle of wine, waving forkfuls of food around as they chatted. 'Well I don't have sympathy for you really, you do have about five months off a year.'

Andrew nodded, raising his wine glass in a toast. 'This is true.'

'Plans?'

'I'll spend a few weeks pretending to work on my PhD of course.'

'Have you still not finished that?' she said, her mouth agape in mock horror. 'You won't be made a doctor without it.'

'Reena, it's eighty thousand words, that is... so many words.'

'That is a lot of words,' she agreed, taking another sip of her wine, trying to block out the heat coursing through her stomach as he used his nickname for her. *Stop it.*

Andrew had an MA in French history and was now exploring the French Wars of Religion of the sixteenth century. At first she had wondered how anyone could be so absorbed in such a small part of one country's history, but he had brought the period to life for her, fired up by the stories of the gruesome St Bartholomew's Day Massacre, the controlling Catherine de Medici.

'How about you? How's the shop? Doing well?'

Irina paused momentarily before answering, the bureau flashing across her consciousness. 'Yes, well, we've had a lot of people through the door and it's busy.'

'What are you working on at the moment?'

'Bits and bobs,' she replied, picking up her wine glass and drinking, her eyes off across the room. Another couple were sitting picking at their food in an enclave. She had a sudden flash of memory, Andrew perched on a stool in her workshop as she glued and sanded, the radio playing, him doodling pictures in wood shavings on the bench as they chatted. She had put away the second stool when they'd broken up, but she pictured it now, dusty and unused in the cupboard under the stairs. She had hated looking at it.

'Interesting bits and bobs?'

She was drawn back to the restaurant a moment before she really heard him. She held her breath as his question opened up a desire in her to share everything with him, wondered what he'd think if she did. She looked at his face, expectant, unhurried. He had never been one to laugh at her over such things.

The waiter was standing by their table again and Andrew had sat back and asked for a couple more minutes. 'We're being hopeless,' he said with a laugh.

'Not at all, sir.'

They ordered and talked about politics then and Petworth, and the food came and they ate and commented on it being delicious, the meat tender, the seasoning exactly right. He didn't ask again and Irina didn't offer anything more. She told him about Pepper and Patricia and her mother. He made her laugh into her napkin with stories about a couple of his more eccentric colleagues. She wanted to relax completely, found herself immersed in this old, familiar set-up, wondering at how easily it came to her. Then she thought about returning to the workshop, her apartment. Andrew stopped in the middle of a sentence, probed again.

'Is anything wrong? You seem distracted.'

She twisted the napkin in her lap, feeling silly, and cross with herself for ruining what had really been a perfect evening.

'I'm being idiotic,' she said, feeling the wine washing around her head. 'I just need some fresh air.'

'Well let me pay up and I'll walk you home,' Andrew said, signalling immediately for the bill, his eyes crinkling again, the irises indigo.

Irina went for her handbag, knowing it would be a futile effort.

'My treat, please,' Andrew said, touching her lightly on the forearm.

She looked down at his hand, the scar on his forefinger, the nails squared off. His touch was gentle and when he removed his hand she placed her own where it had been, brushing lightly at the skin, remembering.

Something had shifted and they walked out of the restaurant in silence. Irina had brought an umbrella and she opened it in the high street when tiny drops pattered around them. She was relieved that she couldn't see his face, hidden as she was, and when he asked her again what was wrong, she couldn't help it, she started to explain. The bureau, the drawer, the feeling that something wasn't right. It spilled out of her in little bursts, like the drops of rain. Andrew was quiet for a while and she watched their feet moving in tandem down the street, her black brogues, his dark brown loafers. When she could bear it no longer, she pushed the umbrella backwards and looked at him.

His face had a puzzled look, as if he'd read something he was still trying to compute or was reflecting on what answer to give her. She felt a strange tug of déjà vu, back to the day they broke up, didn't stay in that moment, worried she would feel the pain again, fresh perhaps, now she had seen him again. She tipped the umbrella back down, listening to their footsteps echoing on the pavement, out of sync with another couple's, further ahead and moving at a different pace.

'Can I see it?' he asked eventually.

Irina felt relief, instant and gratifying.

They arrived at the back door of the workshop and Irina propped the umbrella against the doorframe as she searched her bag for her keys. Andrew stood a little way behind her and there was a second where she wondered whether he was remembering another night when they had stood like this, when he had encircled her waist, dropped his head down onto her shoulder and whispered in her ear. She had leant back towards him, happiness coursing through her as they'd giggled and pushed their way into the room, up the stairs to her apartment. The space now seemed bigger and she gave him a self-conscious look over her shoulder.

'It's in here,' she said pointlessly as they stepped into the workshop. She flicked the switch and the room came flooding into view. Everything seemed so stark and dirty in the light: smeared glass, her coffee-ringed workbench, the shavings on the floor in small heaps, the dust suspended in the air, dead flies collected in the strip light.

She watched him make his way across the workshop, his movements careful, his hair curling over the top of his jumper, hints of reds and browns highlighted by the light above him. He stopped before the bureau, both hands on his hips, observing it like a policeman might take in a suspect, or a teacher berate a pupil, a challenge. The air hummed with his energy, this other person in her space. Patricia nipped in and out on occasion, but Irina wasn't used to this scrutiny. He had tilted his head to one side and was staring at it still.

She stood next to him, silently, her hands brushing her side. She watched him move around the bureau, sucked in her breath, half-expecting something dramatic to happen. She felt her palms dampen at the prospect, her chest tighten. She could hear his steady breathing, which grounded her once more. The atmosphere was changed, with him there it seemed the bureau was simply that, a bureau. She felt ridiculous then. Had she been imagining things? Winding herself up in this space? The wooden top looked smooth, a lighter square patch in the centre where she had removed the leatherette. The pigeonhole drawers were still out on newspaper, only the jammed one sitting stubbornly in its place.

Andrew went to pull on its handle, turning to her as he realized it was stuck.

'I know,' she said, stepping forward. 'There's no key or keyhole, but I can't seem to get it open. There was another drawer, like a secret compartment, along the bottom.'

'A secret compartment...' He lifted an eyebrow at her as he moved his hand across the desk. 'Well, we should find out how this one opens.'

The 'we' made Irina glow from the inside.

'It's funny,' he said, squatting next to it, feeling along the side of it, in the gap from the other drawer, 'it looks like it has a false back, like the drawer is too short for the space.'

How had she missed that?

She crouched down, peering over his shoulder, aware of their closeness for a moment before her curiosity made her forget everything else. 'You're right.' She could feel a spark of excitement as she spotted the gleam of bronze. 'Look.' She pointed at it and he looked at her, a smile forming. There was a small hook attached to a strip of wood at the back.

'Ready?' he said, reaching to lift it up.

Irina knew the drawer would open. She felt her skin prickle again, relieved Andrew was there with her as she reached a hand out. She could feel him suck in a breath, the atmosphere in the room closer. The strip light flickered, as if it were crackling with anticipation. She drew the drawer out, preparing herself for more postcards, or an empty space, a pile of jewels, she wasn't sure what. But she knew that somehow she was meant to open this drawer.

There were items collected in the bottom and she carefully pulled them out. A small feather, light grey, tickling the centre of her palm; a tiny key. She laid them to one side and pulled out a ticket stub, its faded logo indistinct, then went back for more items. She drew the drawer out, her shoulders sagging with disappointment. The contents were strangely sad, yet they'd been locked away in this secret drawer, important to someone.

Andrew had picked up the ticket stub, held it under the strip light as he scanned the letters and numbers. 'It's for a railway,' he said over his shoulder.

It was green, a hole punched through one end, a picture of a carriage in a circle printed on it, 'L & L Clifftop Railway' written in italic scroll around the logo.

'Clifftop?' Irina frowned at the unusual name. On the back someone had written on it in blue ink. 'It's a date. "June 1952,"' she read.

'All very mysterious.' Andrew looked at her, eyebrows waggling, which made her smile. 'I wonder…' He trailed off, looking back at the bureau.

'Wonder…?'

'If there's more.' He bent down to inspect the edges of the desk, feel along the legs. 'It's clever.'

She knew then that he was right, that there might be more discoveries. She had heard of pieces of furniture like this, with cleverly constructed secret compartments and complicated routes to reach them. She remembered her days as an apprentice in Chichester and thought back to a desk there, something sliding about inside it, unreachable; her master had become so fed up that he took a sledgehammer to it until finally they discovered the drawer, behind a false panel at the back, accessed via a button nowhere near it.

'Have you tried contacting the owner? Does he know, do you think?'

'I've just got out-of-office emails.'

'Shame.' Andrew was still staring at it intently, the researcher in him awake. He picked up the ticket stub. 'Would you mind?' He raised it to her. 'Can I keep it?'

She shrugged. 'Of course.'

He looked at it thoughtfully.

'What are you thinking?'

'Nothing. Well, something.' He slid the stub into his wallet, patted his pocket. 'I'll let you know.'

A warmth spread through her stomach, she felt calmer than she had in days, a weight lifted. 'Do.'

'I better go,' he said, his voice lower.

She pressed her lips together, nodding.

He hesitated by the door to the shop, turning to give her a kiss on the cheek. He smelt of their meal, the candlelight, oak and rain. She momentarily shut her eyes and then he stepped back and she smiled at him, gently closed the door. He disappeared down the path to her left.

Resting her head against the glass, feeling the cool seep into her forehead, she breathed slowly in and out, the window fogging. She thought back to his last look before she lost his expression in the shadows. She felt an ache for him that she had spent months resisting.

She was still smiling when she moved back into the workshop, crossing towards the door to her flat. As she reached for the light switch she caught a movement from the corner of her eye; a gasp, she spun round, seeing a blur at the edge of her vision. For a split second she could have sworn she saw a woman running, darting through the workshop. She felt her happiness abruptly drain away, pulled the door to her quickly, raced out of there and up the stairs.

RICHARD

The railway to Lynton was a draw for all tourists to the area and so, to Richard, it seemed the obvious place to take her. He didn't say anything much as they descended the hill, hoping she might think him wildly mysterious. He had a momentary panic that he didn't have enough money for the tickets, imagined himself blustering at the ticket office, feeling hot and red as she sneered at him. He never carried money on him, giving most to his dad and secreting the rest away for his ticket out of the village, when that day came.

Looking over his shoulder at Abigail, he knew he would have emptied all his pockets, run back and fetched all his money to impress her. There was something about her. He'd seen it in her on that first day, leaning against the harbour wall. He'd stood and watched her, haloed in the light, the cottages and trees rising up behind her, wearing that yellow cotton dress that seemed to make her brown hair richer, her skin glow. Men had passed him, hitting him on the shins with buckets, water slopping over his shoes and the stench of salt and tangy mackerel coating him, but he'd just stayed there and watched her. She'd looked straight at him, into him. He'd never met anyone like her before, she'd really lived already, beyond the village, in a city, the likes of which he could only imagine.

He was hungry to know more, kept his eyes on her lips as she told him of the ships in the harbour, the steam train puffing alongside, the river snaking through the city, the hubbub of hundreds of people lining the walkways, looping ropes through the big iron mooring rings; the market stalls, row upon row of produce, and then the city above them, the sandstone buildings, wide tree-lined avenues in Clifton, houses in a huge crescent, manicured lawns, fancy shops.

The girl with the sad eyes but the pulsing energy fired up when she spoke of her friend Mary, the one she'd left behind, her mum. He'd watched her as she stood on that railing over the bridge on the river, her heeled shoes on the first rung, her ankles, her body bent forward, skirt billowing behind her in the breeze, shouting into the wind with such force he thought the river might stop with the shock of it.

The village seemed both more exciting to him and smaller now that she was here. He wanted to see things through her eyes, imagine how they might look, the dockers and fishermen dragging the scent of pike around with them, the sweat of a long day, the gossip, the falling out over prices, the greying buildings hidden amongst the trees that penned them all in.

His friend Bill, rubbing his spectacles dry on his shirt, had nudged him the day before, teasing him for mooning about on the boat in a daze. He was shocked by his reaction to her. Now here he was, tripping down the hill, wanting to show her things, to spark that smile, the wide eyes, see the dimple in her cheek. They rounded the corner, past the Rhenish tower, towards the end of the beach.

He slowed up, walking side by side with Abigail, who

asked where they were headed. Then they were there, standing at the bottom of the cliff, at the ticket booth to the railway.

He pushed two threepence pieces over the counter. 'Two tickets, return.' He didn't need to name the destination, this railway was unique, there was only one stop and one way back. It was a clifftop railway, carved out of the stone more than fifty years before, powered by water and gravity.

The locals didn't use it regularly; the two villages were separate entities, each with its own butcher, baker, garages and shops. People would make their way up the path to the top, the sea on their right, stretching out, grey, patchy with colourful shadows from the clouds above – blue, cobalt, iron, jade, depending on the weather.

They waited in a short queue, watching as the green-painted carriage descended on rails above them.

'My sister told me about this, but I had no idea...' Abigail said, craning her neck to watch the two carriages cross in the middle of the tracks above them, a little boy waving at her from the balcony of one, the other passengers studiously ignoring her, looking through the windows across the Bristol Channel. She waved back, and he gave her a wide grin, one front tooth missing. Richard felt the urge to snatch up her hand, grip it tightly.

'I've never seen anything like it,' she said, spinning round to look at him, breathless with the anticipation.

'It's the only one in the country, unique, opened on Easter Monday 1890...' He found himself parroting an old advertisement he'd once seen.

'Well, it's ingenious,' she remarked, moving aside to let the passengers off, the toothless boy hiding his face behind his mother's skirt, less bold now that he wasn't sailing down the side of a cliff, king of the mountain.

They piled in. An older couple carrying string bags of goods, carrot tops sticking comically from the top, nodded at them; a couple of awkward boys in shorts and knee socks were swept on by a harried-looking mother, chins wobbling as she told them to sit down.

Abigail moved to the balcony outside the carriage so that she could stand in the open air as they moved slowly up the clifftop.

'Nine hundred feet…' Richard said, enjoying watching her widen her eyes and bite her bottom lip as they started to climb. They could see out across Lynmouth to the beach beyond; Countisbury Hill, a motor car moving around the curve of the coast as if about to tumble down it; the cream facade of the Tors Hotel nestled among trees on the other side of the valley. He noticed her attention had been drawn to the rooftop of a house on their left, dormer windows reflecting the light of the day.

'That's the house,' she said, her voice a little changed.

Later, Richard wondered if he should have noticed more, but he was following her eye line, looking at the house between the trees, the twin brick chimney stacks and roof tiles in deep red, distracted then by her arm, slender, bare, stretched out before him as she pointed to it.

'What a spot,' he said, imagining her waking up each morning with the sun on her face as it streamed in dusty ribbons over the bed sheets, making her glow with a soft light. He coughed, carried away with his imaginings. At times he felt like he could write poetry when he was with her.

'Yes,' she said, a momentary pause before she switched on her smile, as if she'd had to think about it.

They'd reached the top and people were filing out past the small ticket office and up a slight incline into Lynton. They'd left the sea far below them and began walking into the small village, its high street snaking around and down, narrow cobbled streets with shops and cafés that seemed precariously clustered on narrow pavements. Richard hadn't been in Lynton for a while, just one or two trips to the cinema on Sinai Hill. As a child he'd come up to the village more, playing war games with friends on Holiday Hill, daring each other to climb down the cliffs to get seagulls' eggs.

Abigail was looking about herself, over her shoulder, searching the high street as if she'd lost someone.

'Are you alright?'

'I was wondering if my sister…' She trailed off, licking her lips and swallowing.

Did she not want him to meet her? The thought forced his shoulders down, made his voice heavy. 'Is she very like you?'

She thought for a moment, a hand quickly fixing a pin in her hair at the back. 'People say we look similar, but it's funny, I think we were apart so many years, we sometimes forget we grew up together. She left just before the start of the war to come here and it became Mum and me, and all my memories from before then seem unreal, as if they were part of this unreal world.'

She seemed more relaxed now that they had turned back around to sit on a bench near the top of the railway. Passers-by bustled past, disinterested; pigeons edged closer, hoping for scraps.

'I miss her. I mean, I miss what we might have been, I think, if that makes any sense.'

Richard thought about that for a moment, pictured his own brother's face, his thick arms, the shaving cuts on his chin, the nose he'd broken when he'd fallen from a tree as a child.

'I'm sorry I said that.' Abigail interrupted, perhaps having seen right through him. 'Your brother, you must think of him a lot.'

Richard nodded, shrugging both shoulders. 'I get so tired of missing him, I'm used to the ache,' he said, moving one hand to his stomach. 'Mostly I miss the everyday things, talking to him, laughing about old memories: how we used to build wigwams in the forest, begging Dad to help us make a tree house, how we used to get a load of school friends to meet in the harbour at the open-air sea pool.'

'Sounds idyllic.'

'It changed at the start of the war. We were all so earnest. It seemed strange when the lads left, would have felt wrong.'

'I know what you mean. We were all so worthy! I learnt to knit things and we sent lots of parcels to the Red Cross.'

'Everyone just seemed sort of broken after the war, even here, and you couldn't avoid it, they were always doing training exercises on Exmoor and you heard the gunfire. Everyone knew someone who had died or been taken prisoner and the stories kept coming.' He stopped for breath, his cheeks reddening slightly as he looked at her.

'It was the same at home,' she said. 'We were so sick of black-out blinds and gas masks and dried milk, but it was the awful feeling that nothing would ever be the same again, that something had gone forever.'

He nodded at her and they rested against the wood; she was picking at some flaking paint.

'So, is it nice being back here with her? You might get your sister back.'

She nodded once, slowly. 'It's been grand remembering the little moments from when we were younger, although I think she just remembers me as this messy, wild thing with sticking-up hair, poking my tongue out at her from behind cereal boxes, and making Mum scold me.'

'You sound a delight.'

'Well I was so young and she was so much older, going off to dances and reading novels, and I thought she was frightfully grown-up.'

'And your brother-in-law?'

She looked sideways at him, an expression he hadn't seen before crossing her face. 'What about him?'

Richard stretched out his legs, his feet sticking up in front of him. 'Did you know him well?'

'Oh.' She turned back to look out at the booking office, where a couple were holding the hands of a child who was swinging between them. 'No, I didn't. I remember him from the wedding, he tied up one of my loose ribbons, but they left for Devon the moment they were married.'

'That's a shame.'

She didn't reply, nodding once. He frowned, wondering whether she was alright. Had he said something to offend her? Was she bored? He ran a hand through his hair. She must be used to grammar-school boys and dinner parties, men puffing on cigars and regaling her with stories from their university days. He had none of that, he had stories about the boat, about Bill and him leaping overboard on sunny days, fishing from the balcony at the back of Bill's house, fires on the beach in the summer.

'I think I better get back.'

He felt his whole body slump as she said it, his shoulders sagging, his mouth turning down. Of course she did. She couldn't meet his eyes then, cleared her throat, swallowed. He briefly considered whether she might be harbouring some great secret, but knew he was reading too much into it, hoped it wasn't simply that she was fed up.

'We should…' He gestured to the railway, wanting to tell her they should do it again soon, that they should meet the next day, the day after. She looked at him, she had thick lashes and he was distracted by them, stumbled over the sentence. 'Yes, we should get back.'

She swallowed again, a small smile, not enough to form the dimple in her cheek. He kicked himself all the way back down the clifftop railway, the carriage descending like his hopes.

IRINA

The whole day had felt unsettled. It was unseasonably cold, had started to spit lightly in the afternoon. Irina had worked throughout, another presence in the room with her. It seemed more obvious now, as if rootling through the drawers had awoken things. As she worked, she intermittently looked around the room, unable to shake the feeling that someone was watching. Without Andrew's easy presence beside her, the bureau had become menacing again, watchful.

A misty bank of cloud hung over the hills around the village and the sky darkened as Irina closed up for the day. Patricia had left, her robust frame almost entirely hidden by an enormous golf umbrella so that only her heeled court shoes could be seen at the end of tan tights. It got worse during the evening, the rain lashing and battering the windows at an angle, drumming on the surface like insistent fingers desperate to get in. Slices of rain tumbled down the glass in a never-ending stream. Irina moved through to the living room, turned on the lamp, the television, the bold flickering colours a pathetic distraction from the sounds outside. A glass of red wine sat on the table beside her.

She focused on the people on the screen, a drama, something she knew she could lose herself in, given the chance. She tucked her legs underneath her and took a sip of the wine. There was a noise, something rolling, metallic, across the street and she ignored it, cross for feeling so jumpy. She felt a breeze tickle the back of her neck, a gust as if someone had opened a door. She found herself checking over her shoulder for something. Nothing, of course. Then the cat appeared in front of her in the doorway of the kitchen, arched back, fur up, watching something in the entrance to the room.

The front door to the apartment was beyond; Irina could see it and it was shut. There was nothing there and even as Pepper started to hiss, she reminded herself of this fact. Pepper wouldn't stop though, her whole body an angry curve, mouth open, teeth on display, entirely focused on something in the empty doorway. Then, slowly, very slowly, her green eyes followed a path across to the sofa where Irina was sitting. Pepper continued to hiss at a spot to her left and Irina held the red wine to her chest as if it could protect her from what was there. The hissing merged with the orchestra of the weather, the rolling metal and she felt her palm dampen on the glass.

Then all the lights went out, the television snapped off with a gasp, the lamp sputtered and died. Irina felt her heart hammering in her chest, against her ribs, felt impossibly hot, clammy, then a cold sensation seemed to run over her body, her left arm, her chest, her face, as if someone had opened a freezer door next to her. The cat's eyes glinted in the half-shadows, she was still staring at the sofa and Irina felt entirely frozen, petrified of looking to her side.

The weather seemed to pause, the momentum gone, the rain almost disappearing, as if it had never been there. It was only her breathing then, just her in the flat, in and out, the cat's stare.

Then the noises started up, instantaneously; everything came back on and in the shock and the surprise of the moment Irina felt a dampness all over herself, seeping through her clothes to her skin, sticking to her. She looked down at her chest, at the enormous red puddle down her top, like blood, all over her, spreading everywhere. The wine glass empty in her hand.

She put the glass down, wiped with two hands at her chest, frantic now. She couldn't be alone tonight, she knew that, she felt she was going slowly mad. The cat padded across to curl up at her feet. The temperature seemed to be normal again, the rain a friendly patter on the roof, the drama on the television still on. She was scrubbing at her top with both hands, her breathing shallow as she finally looked left, at the sofa.

It looked unchanged at first, but then Irina saw it, the small indentation in the seat, like someone had recently been sitting there.

ABIGAIL

She found the bird lying beneath the beech tree in the garden, making a pitiful sound, high-pitched and tiny. It was lying on its side, one wing bent under its body, the other flapping pathetically in the air before dropping back to the ground, its minute chest thrumming with frantic breaths. She couldn't see where it had fallen from and carefully knelt down to gently scoop it into her hands. The unfamiliar feeling of bones and feathers almost caused her to drop it again in surprise. Its pulse continued to beat violently as she slowly walked back towards the house, pushing through the French windows backwards, relieved to see the living room deserted.

She hadn't noticed it at first, had been replaying the previous day in her mind. She had been such dull company, distracted, returning to small talk and then so quiet, answering his questions in monosyllables, the thought of returning to the house too much. Richard was surely used to lively girls, rosy-cheeked women with stories that could make him howl. He was bursting with energy, always on the edge of a joke, wanting to show off the village, point out the details. She loathed herself for having dampened his mood, had left him without a cursory glance back, a muttered thank you.

The bird was hopelessly small, sitting in the palm of her hand, one eye looking out at her with desperation. She cupped her other hand over it as she moved into the hallway towards the stairs. It was silent, her footsteps louder on the wooden floorboards, her eyes adjusting to the sudden darkness.

She had one foot on the bottom step when she heard him.

'And where are you slinking off to?'

She froze at the words, both hands trapped over the bird, holding it out like a religious offering. She wondered whether her own chest beat quicker, whether the bird would sense her rising panic. She glanced to her right, where the words had come from. He was standing silhouetted in the doorway that led to the kitchen. 'Nowhere. I…'

It was no use, he had already spotted her awkward pose, moving towards her now, his eyes focused on her hands. 'What have you got?' he asked.

'It's nothing. It's…' She lifted one hand.

'What?' His lip curled in disgust as he took in the ruffled downy feathers, the tiny yellow beak.

'I found it, in the garden. Please, I think I can help it…' She stopped, embarrassed by the whine in her voice. She should stand taller, look him in the eye. Why was she hunched over herself?

Her answer seemed to amuse him. His face lightened and he stood at her shoulder, close, the smell of burnt toast on his breath as he went to examine the bird. 'Let me see.' He wiggled his fingers impatiently.

She tried not to flinch as he reached out, lifting her hand away, his hand closed over hers, lingered, before he removed it. He placed one finger on the bird as if he were baptizing it.

There was a circle of skin in the middle of his hair, at the top, where it was thinning.

'You can have your plaything,' he said in a low voice, looking up at her. He was so close she could see the individual pores on his nose.

Then with boyish enthusiasm he seemed spurred into action. 'Wait here,' he instructed, moving suddenly away from her, down the hallway. She heard him issue instructions to Edith and when he returned he was holding a glass of milk and a freshly sawn slice of bread.

'Go on.' He nodded at the stairs and she started to climb, aware of him following her, feeling every movement of her body, clenching her muscles as she went, trying not to draw attention to herself.

They reached the landing outside her bedroom and she hesitated at the doorway. He brushed past her with an impatient click of his tongue, opened the door, set the milk and bread on the side, and stood there expectantly. It was strange seeing him standing in the middle of her bedroom, she felt embarrassed to see a girdle thrown hastily over the back of a chair, discarded stockings rolled up on the floor. He turned, rubbing his thumb and forefinger together.

'Come on.' She hadn't seen this look before. He seemed impossibly young suddenly, the years stripped away as if he were a young boy, his foot tapping restlessly. 'Where were you going to put him?'

For a second she forgot where she was, and who he was and she said with a smile, 'Him? I imagined it to be a her.' She blushed at the end of the sentence, hearing her own voice, cajoling, friendly. She straightened, her mind jumbled, feeling wrong-footed. 'The hat box.' With her head she indicated the top of the wardrobe.

He reached to bring it down, the sound of something slipping around inside it. He opened it up on her bed, gingerly removing her best hat and placing it reverentially on the pillow. It looked as if someone was sleeping on it. He rearranged the tissue inside to form a makeshift nest and stood back to watch her lower the little body into it. They stood there side by side, in silence, before he turned to tear off a piece of the bread, dipping it into the milk and returning to place it gently at the beak of the bird.

'Thank you,' Abigail said quietly.

'I'll leave you now,' he said, moving towards the door, into the corridor beyond and down the stairs before she could think any more about the encounter.

Looking down into the box, the grey body in a halo of tissue, one orange eye roving, she said a quick prayer for the fragile thing, hoping she might fly again one day.

They spoke about the bird that evening at dinner, Larry enquiring after its health as if it were an elderly relative. Her sister raised one pencilled eyebrow at the conversation. 'What bird?' she asked, her snub nose wrinkling a fraction.

'Abigail rescued it. Sorry…' He raised a hand, a small smile playing on his lips. 'Rescued her.'

Abigail shifted slightly in her chair, feeling heat creep up her chest and into her face. 'She was in the garden,' she explained to her sister. 'She'd fallen. I don't think she's broken anything.'

'And you brought her into the house? The thing probably has diseases.'

Abigail couldn't fail to notice her sister's hand moving quickly to rest on her stomach as she spoke.

'Nonsense,' scoffed Larry, piercing a piece of pork with his fork before lifting it to his mouth.

Connie didn't respond, looking quickly at her plate instead.

Abigail felt a lurch, as if she had somehow wounded her. Trying to make amends, she said in a light voice, 'This is delicious.'

'Edith made it. It's always too dry.'

There wasn't much talk after that, the sound of the carriage clock far too loud, Abigail feeling that they must be able to hear her swallow, the meat (it was rather dry) rolling slowly down her throat. She was grateful to be free of the table, to be climbing the stairs back up to her room. As she pushed the door closed she could hear their voices moving through to the living room and hoped they were not talking about her.

Perhaps if she had found the bird lying still on its side, all the breath having left her body, she might have wondered whether the bread had been too much, whether the jostling and the unknown territory had tipped her over the edge. Perhaps, if she had seen her chest drumming quickly, she might have thought it had been a natural turn of events. But she didn't find her like that, she found her lying in the perfect circle of tissue, on her side, yes, but with her tiny neck broken, head forced back at an odd angle, her frozen eye looking up at nothing.

Abigail reached into the box, gently lifting out a loose feather. It had the softest feel.

'How is the little thing doing?' he asked her as she emerged from her bedroom, his arms folded, leaning on the banisters on the landing below.

Abigail felt foolish for wiping at her eyes. 'She's dead.'

Larry looked up at her with a steady gaze, not flinching at the news. 'What a shame,' he said, his voice flat. 'Although you don't want to go getting too attached to things, they might not stick around.'

IRINA

'Come in, come in.' Andrew beckoned her inside. His hair was mussed up on one side like he'd been sleeping, which he probably had been when Irina called him, whispering into the phone as if she were being overheard.

She stumbled as she moved through the doorway, a hand out to balance herself, which flattened against his chest. She could feel the heat from him, underneath the brown jumper he had thrown on.

'Are you alright?' He looked concerned.

She didn't feel alright, couldn't remember leaving the apartment, making the drive over there, her head snapping back to look at the passenger seat of her car as if it were occupied, as if something had come with her from the flat. He drew her into a hug and she didn't stop him, her head tilted down so that her forehead rested on his chest, the cashmere soft. He was wearing jeans, his bare feet another sign that she had disturbed him. She froze momentarily, wondering whether he'd been alone when she rang.

'The cat,' she sniffed, in a voice that didn't sound like her own.

He drew back gently, holding the tops of both her arms. 'The cat what?' He smiled then, in a way that reminded her it was only her that was in this mood. It was an easy smile, teasing and light.

'Pepper. I left her there.'

'She'll be alright until the morning, cats are very resilient.' He held her gaze. 'And Pepper can more than take care of herself, she's a minx. Don't worry about it.'

She nodded mutely, glad to be there, glad she'd called him, wanting to thank him.

He walked down the narrow corridor ahead of her, his bare feet not making a sound on the hardwood floor. Her steps clacked in the silence, bringing it all home to her. She had left him and now here she was, arriving on his doorstep, eyes wide, asking for him to comfort her, to let her straight back into his home.

It hadn't changed: the walls were still white, there were still stray dumbbells acting as doorstops, which made her briefly forget her panicky mood. Everything was so uncluttered and modern. She felt herself relax as she moved down the corridor after him, into a kitchen with glossy units and silver pots in ascending order on the counter.

'I've put the kettle on,' he called over his shoulder, his back towards her at the counter as he reached up and brought down two mugs. The patterns were familiar; Irina had a sharp memory of the same two mugs on a tray, a morning about a year ago, both of them under the covers, papers spread out on the duvet, crusts of toast abandoned, mugs topped up.

'Great,' she said after a beat, still back there, a year ago, under those covers. The thought distracting her from the mood she'd arrived in.

He didn't talk about why she was there; she had babbled something at him down the phone but couldn't remember how much she'd told him. He handed her a mug wordlessly and she sat on one of the black leather bar stools, hands wrapped around the mug, feet tucked beneath her, blowing on the tea.

'I'm sorry it's so late,' she said, waving a hand at the window, through which they could see a midnight-blue sky moody with clouds. The lights of the kitchen were reflected in the glass.

'You don't have to explain.'

'No, I want to. I'm sorry, I know it seems silly, but it's like the house has been taken over by something.'

He didn't laugh at her, look scornful. She'd known he wouldn't.

'There's something there. The woman... It's like she's waiting for me to find out more.' It struck her then that this was true, that she felt some invisible connection to the things she'd seen, as if she'd woken something up and now she had to find out why.

'I was going to phone you in the morning actually. I looked up the information...'

Irina seemed to be hearing him from a distance, her brain slow to process the words.

'The ticket stub,' he prompted.

'Oh, of course,' she said, remembering the other evening as if it had happened a month ago.

'It's a railway, quite unique actually, built towards the end of the nineteenth century in Lynmouth, connecting it with the village above it, Lynton.'

'Lynton,' she repeated, thinking of the postcard, the calm curve of the bay, the hills and houses. 'Where is it?'

'It's Devon, Exmoor.'

'Devon.' She rolled the word around slowly. The shell, the smell, the white grains in the bureau, like sea salt. She felt sure this was the place. 'Maybe I should go there. Things seem to be pointing there, and now the ticket...' She hadn't realized she'd said it out loud until Andrew joined in.

'It's something,' he said, taking a sip of his tea, looking at her over the rim of his mug. 'I'll come with you.'

'You don't have to.' Irina jumped in. 'I... Well, don't feel obliged.'

'I'm not obliged, I'm curious. And frankly, I want to know what's going on and I want it to stop.'

His eyes were filled with concern and Irina looked away, her chest squeezing, a familiar pain as she remembered how they'd been together.

'We can talk about something else if you like? Take your mind off things?'

She tasted the sweet tea he had made. The kitchen tiles were charcoal, the kitchen top marble, shapes swirling in the surface. She felt so strange and yet so familiar in this room that she must have drunk a hundred teas in.

They spoke of nothing and when Andrew yawned and Irina couldn't hide the dregs in her mug anymore, he announced, 'I made up the spare-room bed.' He said it quickly, avoiding her eyes.

Was that a flicker of disappointment she felt?

'Of course,' she muttered, putting her mug down a little too hard on the counter. 'Thank you.' She followed him out of the room. Absurd to feel tears prick the back of her eyes.

He showed her to the door of the spare room. It had changed since she'd been there last: a new picture, an old street map of Paris, hung over the bed, the duvet was a different colour, and the pile of gym clothes had vanished from the corner.

'I had a clear-out,' he said, as if he had heard her thoughts.

'It's nice. Thank you,' she said, turning back to him.

He moved to switch on the bedside lamp. 'Right, well, you know where everything is, so… Towels in the cupboard, and the kettle and…'

She wondered again whether anyone else had been there. Nearly asked and found herself clamping her lips together at the last moment. 'Thank you,' she repeated.

He turned to go. 'Night, Reena.'

For a brief second she wanted to follow him, hold the bottom of his jumper as he guided her to his bedroom, get lost in his embrace in the darkness. Tell him why she had come, why she had left the apartment in such a hurry and then why she had chosen to come to him.

Instead, she watched him leave, listened to him cleaning his teeth, washing his face, whistling for a second before he stopped, perhaps remembering she was next door.

She hadn't thought to bring anything really, had scooped up her thick cardigan, pushed her feet into shoes without socks. She took off her clothes so she was just wearing her knickers and pulled the cardigan around her, waiting for him to leave the bathroom, for his door to click closed.

Then she went in, wiped under her eyes with a finger where her mascara had marked shadows, splashed her face with water. She squeezed some toothpaste onto her finger and moved it around her mouth, pausing as she looked at the medicine cabinet, tempted to open it, to snoop, then chiding herself. He could live how he wanted; she had left him, she reminded herself.

The cream linen was ironed and smelt of detergent, the pillows plumped and comforting. She wriggled under the covers, pulling the duvet right up around her shoulders and chin, and turned on her side. The alarm-clock numbers and outline of the lamp were the last things she remembered before falling asleep.

He had left for work by the time she'd woken up, a note on the kitchen table: 'Stay as long as you like, A x'. One of her fingers traced his initial. The note was kind, easy, and she imagined he was there saying it to her.

ABIGAIL

She hovered at Connie's side as she instructed Edith to clear the summerhouse of cobwebs, scrub down the outdoor furniture for them – the wrought-iron chairs were filthy. She studied her sister's face, the peachy cheeks with two spots of blush as if she were one of her old china dolls, the swoop and curl of her eyelashes, her bow mouth puckered now in a line as she watched Edith leave the room with the tea things. Abigail thought she might never go.

She opened her mouth to speak, to tell Connie what she had found, that she felt Larry had known, had been in her room, had done it. The glassy-eyed stillness of the little bird was imprinted on her memory. Her sister looked at her, raising an eyebrow at her open mouth. She shut it again, bit her lower lip, went to sit on the chaise longue, changed her mind and stood again, one fist clenching and unclenching.

Connie had moved across to the window seat, gazing out on a charcoal sea, angry layers of cloud piled on top of each other seeming to weigh down the sky with rain and sadness.

'Maybe I spoke too soon.'

Abigail was a moment late in her response, unaware her sister was talking about the weather. 'Did you?'

'The garden furniture,' Connie said, an irritable flick of her hand at something unseen on her cardigan. 'We won't be sitting outside if it rains.'

Abigail struggled to concentrate, aware she sounded vague. 'Oh, you're right.'

They lapsed into silence, her sister's calmness at odds with the hammering in Abigail's chest. She had to say it, had to tell her, couldn't really understand why she was putting it off.

'Connie...' She took a small step forward, lifted a hand, the palm facing upwards.

Her sister turned a little in the seat to look at her, the tiniest of lines between her eyebrows.

'The bird's dead,' she started. 'It died. Well, it didn't die, it was killed.'

Another line emerged on Connie's forehead as she tried to follow what Abigail was saying. 'How gruesome.' Her nose wrinkled in disgust, giving Abigail the strength to continue.

'No, you don't understand. The bird was killed, her neck was snapped backwards.'

'Don't be so ghoulish, Abigail. I feel quite unwell just thinking about it.' She placed a hand on her stomach, rubbing it rhythmically. 'I hope you got rid of it.'

Connie didn't get it. Abigail realized she hadn't spelt it out and she needed her to listen. She approached the window seat, bending her knees so that she was at her sister's eye-level.

'He did it,' she whispered, looking over her shoulder as if at any moment he might appear in the doorway, then loathing herself for having done so.

'What on earth do you mean?' Her sister's light laugh tinkled around the living room. 'Don't be absurd, of course he didn't.'

'I'm not making it up,' she insisted.

Connie rolled her eyes. If it hadn't been for the briefest of pauses, Abigail might have thought that she really didn't believe her, but it had been there, a fraction of a moment, enough for her to realize that Connie knew exactly what he'd done.

'You're being ridiculous, Abigail. Larry loves animals.' Her voice was false, a little higher in pitch than normal, her eyes now looking out again over the sea as a roll of thunder could be heard in the distance. 'You're imagining things.'

Abigail felt a spurt of anger and straightened up, standing over Connie as her voice quivered. 'He broke its neck. Are you really going to keep pretending? Do you not care?'

Connie didn't turn round but said simply, 'I think I'll go and lie down now if that's all.' She rose and left the room, scurrying past Abigail as if she might be chased by more words.

Abigail's head dropped onto her chest and she felt the breath leave her body. As the rain fell in fat, bold drops outside, she wondered why Connie would want to ignore things, realized then that she was completely alone.

IRINA

In the stark morning light she felt a little foolish, as if the feelings of the night before had been blown away by the new day, with its hint of sunshine, people driving through the streets to work, the chirpy buzz of breakfast television. She picked up her mobile and cardigan, looked around at the apartment. She added a line under Andrew's note. 'Thanks' seemed like an understatement, but she didn't know what else to write. The whole way back to Petworth, his face drifted into her mind until she had to physically shake her head to stop it. He had just been kind; she didn't need to read more into everything.

She didn't stay long in her apartment, topped up the water and spooned food out of a tin into the bowl for the cat, who had licked yesterday's efforts clean. The rolling sound of the boiler as she ran the hot water, the last drops from the tap, the kitchen clock loud and insistent. There were no other noises, nothing for her to feel jittery about. She showered and changed her clothes quickly, throwing on overalls already faded and spattered with old varnish, oily blobs in different sizes. They smelt faintly of turpentine and dust, reminded her of past jobs.

Downstairs, the new leatherette arrived in the post and Patricia signed for it, directing the delivery man to the back with clicks and pointing so that he appeared, disgruntled and awkward, through the beads. She would be able to stick it down with glue, having cleaned the frame around it first, but for now it remained in its packaging, propped against the wall next to the ramshackle pile of off-cuts and planks of wood that Irina used for repairs.

She made a start on the two lopers the desktop rested on, pulling the wooden struts out and down to clean. As she wiped the surfaces with a cloth soaked in white spirit, she felt the narrowest line along the edge of one of them and then the tell-tale bump of what could only be a hinge. Frowning, she realized that the loper might itself contain another secret compartment and, looking on the other side, noticed a tiny keyhole cut into the wood.

Reaching behind her to the wall, where various tools hung on hooks, she selected a small screwdriver that might be able to turn the lock. The key was no doubt long gone. The screwdriver turned pointlessly, unable to catch anything and keep hold of it, and Irina breathed out in frustration. She tried a slightly larger tool, also with no luck. Then, almost smacking her forehead like a cartoon character, she remembered the key she'd found in the other drawer. Bending down to rummage quickly for it, she drew it out as if she were unsheathing a great weapon.

She placed it in the lock, her hand trembling slightly, her fingers feeling fat and clumsy around the tiny key. But it worked, it turned; there was a small click and Irina felt the lock shift. Taking the edge of the wood in one hand, she lifted it up. The whole top of the loper, a mere quarter-inch thick, if that, lifted away and inside was a line of grooves etched into the wood. Thick enough for coins. There were nine grooves in all, running down the length of the loper, and they were all empty. Apart from the last one, near the back. Irina pulled out the loper without a thought. There was something in there, resting in the groove. She brought it out and held it up to the light, turning it slowly around as she examined it. She held her breath, squinting as she took in every minuscule scratch and scuff. It was an oval brooch with a purple background and a cream silhouette of a woman in relief. It looked so delicate sitting in the palm of her hand.

She looked back at the loper, opened and plundered, and placed the brooch back in the groove, closing the top carefully and locking it after her. Lifting the loper back into the side of the bureau, she puzzled at her find. All these objects secreted around this innocuous piece of furniture. She wondered what it all meant and whether anyone knew they were there. Had her American client known about the trove of things she would uncover? She moved across to pull down the other loper, expecting to see the same hole, the same hinges, but there was nothing there at all, just a straightforward block of oak in need of a thorough clean and polish to restore it to its former condition. As she placed it back inside, she wondered what else the bureau was hiding and whether she had been meant to receive it, whether it had found her. She felt like she was being given a dozen clues with no idea where to begin.

'A brooch?' Andrew repeated when she spoke to him later that day.

She'd rung him on the way back to the workshop after lunch; she wanted to say a proper thank you for the night before. He sounded pleased to hear from her.

'Inside the loper,' she confirmed.

'What's a loper when it's at home?'

'The thing the desktop rests on when it's pulled down. They look like chair legs, sort of, but they stick out of it, facing you.'

'What, and it was like another secret drawer?'

'Sort of. It was for coins, I think – originally, that is. It looked like a clever hiding place for them. You could hardly tell there was anything there, the person that designed this thing made sure of that.'

'What does it look like?'

'It's oval, a cameo brooch, no more than an inch long with a silhouette of a woman's profile. There's a hallmark on the back.'

'So, who did it belong to?'

'I'm not sure. I sent another email to my client but got the same out-of-office reply. It doesn't look particularly expensive, it's not quite a diamond ring.'

Irina closed her eyes, embarrassed to have made reference to a diamond ring. Andrew didn't say anything either and she wondered if he'd noticed, or whether he was just thinking about what she'd told him.

'This is all becoming weirder and weirder,' he said, seemingly unaffected by her blundering comment, or hiding it well. 'Send me a photo of the back of it, the mark.'

'OK,' she said, distracted by another thought, something that had been playing on her mind. 'Do you know, it's funny, but I feel like I was meant to find that brooch. There was no need for me to search there, I wasn't really thinking about it, I just knew there might be something there, like someone was directing me to it.'

'Do you think…?'

He didn't say it, but Irina knew he wanted to talk about the woman she'd spoken about. She didn't have an image of her fixed in her mind, she was faceless, but distinct in that she felt real. Irina was more and more sure she was seeing the same person: the face in the steam, at the window of her flat, in the workshop. Today she was sure she was seeing her for a reason; the woman was trying to tell her something. She didn't say anything out loud though.

Andrew's reply came, his voice a little higher than normal. 'I've got an idea.'

ABIGAIL

She waited there all morning, feeling ridiculous and exposed as villagers walked past her, casting glances at the girl on the bench. She stayed on the same page of her book for half an hour, scanning the faces, craning her neck to peer up the high street as people spilled in and out of shops. Tourists were flocking to the village now for the summer months. 'Honeymooners' paradise' they dubbed it and everyone seemed to be eating bags of fudge, licking at ice-cream. The wind was warm today, blowing in from sunnier climes, and she had taken off her cardigan, could feel the sun on the nape of her neck, her hair twisted into a bun, her arms covered in freckles already.

Then she saw him, walking along the opposite bank, chatting with a man his age in round spectacles, waving him off and turning to look out across the sea, then picking his way onto the shingle and almost out of view. She hurried then, her book quickly closed, the page forgotten, tripping as she got up, her shin bruised on the bench, a sharp sound out of her mouth that caused a passing woman to look up.

She crossed the bridge, had lost him; he'd dipped out of

view, his dark brown hair and wide shoulders no longer visible. He couldn't have gone far. She sped up in her heels, a brisk walk, arms pumping. She knew she looked absurd, she could feel sweat pooling underneath her arms, the sun blazing high above her, her palm damp as it clutched her cardigan.

She saw him from the promenade, on the wet sand a hundred yards ahead. She sank into the stones, the rounded, broken shells, lumps of grey, tumbling over each other, impeding her in her heeled shoes as she made awkward progress down to the water's edge. He was skimming stones, watching them bounce once, twice, trip along the water and out of sight. She wondered if he knew she was looking, smiled at the thought. He'd thrown his jacket down on the stones, his shirt coming untucked from the waistband of his trousers, billowing out in the breeze, his shoes and socks off, trousers rolled up, sand sticking to the hairs on his legs.

'Very impressive,' she called out, sitting herself on the stones, feeling the gentle bump of the pebbles as they shifted under her weight, warm to the touch.

He turned towards her, his hair lifting in the wind, the dark strands sweeping over his forehead as he moved towards her, leaving squelching footmarks in the sand that quickly filled with water.

'Come and show me how it's done then,' he said, an eyebrow raised in a challenge. He didn't seem surprised to see her; familiar and confident, he didn't seem to have changed at all. She felt a flicker of hope that she hadn't ruined things completely with her sullen mood that day on the clifftop railway.

'I couldn't possibly,' she protested, 'it would just embarrass you.'

He threw himself down on the stones beside her, his face flushed and tanned. He looked exotic today, his skin hinting at travel and spices. He seemed full of life, itching to throw stones, run through sand, take his shoes off. She couldn't help laughing, giddy with the feeling. She felt an immense relief when she was with him, that she could be herself, not the coiled version that sat nervously on the edge of a single bed, looking out over a grey sea. With him she was Abi: toothy smiles, bold laughter, teasing and jokes. She felt like she was with Mary or her mum back in Bristol, giggling over the everyday things, her chest light with friendship.

He lay back on the stones, his toes wiggling into the sand, disappearing. 'Perhaps best. You look like a girl with a good arm.'

'I shall take that as a compliment,' she said, inspecting her arm with one hand.

'It was meant as one,' he said, shutting his eyes.

'Did you just lure me here to show me how marvellous you are at throwing things?'

'I didn't lure you anywhere, you followed me.'

She felt her whole face flood with heat, ready to make her excuses, to deny it, but he continued, eyes still shut.

'I'm so pleased you did. I was about to come and knock on your door, ask your chaperone for a meeting, force you out of there, like Rapunzel.'

She exhaled quickly, not sure if he was teasing and so glad he hadn't appeared at the house. 'I don't have long enough hair for Rapunzel.'

'Well, someone stuck in a tower.'

'I also don't have a chaperone.'

'You should have.' His mouth twitched. He opened the eye nearest to her, tilting his head to the side. 'I love this bit of beach. Shall we walk along it?'

'Alright then,' she said.

'First you must remove your shoes.'

'It'll be cold,' she protested, a flush of embarrassment flooding through her. Ridiculous to feel embarrassed at baring her feet.

'It's hardly cold and they'll get ruined if you don't. Second option: I carry you, but I'm not sure we'd make it very far.'

'How rude.'

'That's not a slight on your weight, only my inability to act like a strong man.' He made a pathetic gesture with both arms, as if he were trying to lift something enormous with both hands, and she giggled.

'Fine.' She relented, raising both hands in the air. 'I shall remove my shoes.'

'Excellent.' He sat up, then sprang to his feet, perhaps sensing that she was fumbling a little with the straps on her shoes and wouldn't appreciate an audience.

The leather felt slippery in her fingers; clumsily, she pulled them off and then stood in stockinged feet. 'Turn around,' she said, reaching up to unclip her stockings and roll them down. She felt scandalous doing so and peeked over her shoulder for any passing walkers.

She wiggled her toes into the sand, feeling the damp grains seep between her toes. It was heavenly after the sticky heat of the day and she exhaled loudly, sighing in appreciation. Rolling up her stockings, she balled them into her fist.

'The whole village will probably drum me out, but I am ready for walking,' she said, spinning on one foot and walking towards him. The sunlight made his white shirt dazzle and his skin seem a darker brown. 'Come on, strong man.'

They walked along the shoreline, leaving footprints in a trail behind them. The blue sky was streaked with wispy clouds skittering past the sun; a thicker, bruised layer of cloud sat mulishly on the horizon, making the water duller, lurking as if at any moment it could rise up and take the good weather away. Up ahead, trees obscured the road that ran down from the clifftop. Abigail imagined herself looking down at them both from that height. Tiny insects walking on the sand, specks of people. She bent down to pick up a shell shaped in a perfect spiral, the browns and greys washing together, the surface smooth.

'I love this beach. I'll always want to walk along it, no matter how old I am.'

'But…' She stood up abruptly, her eyebrows knitted together. 'You won't always be here, will you?'

He cocked his head to one side. 'How do you mean? This is my home; I've always lived here.'

'Well, yes, but surely you want to travel, to get away?'

He carried on talking. She felt flimsy, weightless, as if someone could send her spinning over the sand, the sea, send her flitting up, caught on the breeze, whirling higher into the clouds and away. She felt the shell, perfect in her hand, squeezed her fist around it. She had assumed he would want to leave the village, had dreamt of persuading him to head to America too.

'… I want to build things, Abi,' he said, pointing to the houses lining the beach. 'I want to build my own house. I've been learning, practising with different cuts of wood and studying how to do the different joints.'

She looked at him then, fully, drinking in his enthusiasm, watching his mouth, full and fast, talking to her about creating things out of wood and other materials.

'What about a boat? You could build a boat. Imagine owning a boat, where you could go, the places you could see…'

She did imagine it then, imagined herself in polka-dot shorts and her hair tied up in a knotted scarf or beneath a wide-brimmed hat, sunbathing under large cream sails, the turquoise blue of some foreign sea behind her, maybe a dolphin or two trailing their boat as they steered a path through the water. Diving off the edge of the boat, plunging into the still sea. Turning in the waves to look at him on the deck, bronzed, bare-chested, his teeth dazzling in the sunshine. She could practically taste the salt on her lips, feel the warmth of the sun's rays, hear the gentle splashing as the boat gently rocked at a standstill. Stopping over in a new port, clambering out to discover another new place.

'Wouldn't that be heavenly?' she whispered, returning then to the greys and purples of the pebbled beach in Lynmouth, wrapping her cardigan around her as a cloud sat stubbornly over the sun and the wind picked up.

'I suppose it would if you didn't hate the sea.' He laughed, scooping up a handful of stones and letting them run through his fingers.

'But…' She felt her body droop then, knowing it was her fantasy, not his.

'I'm saving,' he said, misunderstanding her sudden melancholy, keen perhaps to prove himself, 'and Tom said he can get me the timber cheaply.'

'That sounds wonderful.' The words came out in a monotone. She watched as his face fell, his green eyes dull despite the sunshine overhead.

'I couldn't leave Dad anyway. I'm all he has.' He gave her a lopsided smile and a small shrug of apology.

She didn't reply, wanted to take his hand and give it a squeeze, to recapture his previous enthusiasm, but she didn't do anything, just stood in her bare feet, goosebumps breaking out on her calves. She turned in the direction of their shoes. 'I need to get back.'

'Abi…' She could hear the confusion in his voice.

She bent down to pick up her stockings, pulled them on

quickly, swearing under her breath as one laddered in her hands.

'Abigail, wait,' he said, tying up his shoes, going to pick up his jacket. 'Where are you headed? I can go with you.'

'No. Don't. Stay. It all sounds brilliant. I'm glad,' she trilled, marching back over the pebbles, throwing her remarks over her shoulder, feeling foolish as she sank into the stones, waddling away like an idiot, leaving him looking at her, wondering what had happened and what he had done wrong.

IRINA

'We should definitely go to Devon,' Andrew said firmly, appearing in the shop the day after the discovery of the brooch, an errant bit of hair poking up, his shirt buttoned up incorrectly. 'You're right, it's all pointing us there,' he continued, his voice filled with excitement, catapulting Irina back to other days with him. Andrew always wanted to explore, was an adventurer, had dragged her off laughing to the New Forest, to walks in the Malvern Hills, to B & Bs down rambling country lanes in Cornwall. His cheeks were flushed and his eyes bright. He had clearly been thinking about this.

Irina felt wrong-footed, as she often had, caught on the hop and slow to catch up. 'What else?'

'I looked up more about that brooch you found and, well, guess where they made them? I contacted the assay office and they say the maker was based in Exmoor.' He'd got her attention now. 'We should go there.'

'Oh, I... The shop and...'

Irina hesitated; knew he was right. She seemed to be moving through treacle that morning, had been exhausted by a dream, dragging her unwilling legs through liquid, thigh deep, knowing it would rise and choke her. When she woke, she felt she'd run a marathon, had wearily pulled her legs round her on the bed and onto the floor, pushing her thumbs into the muscle to ease the tension, running a hand up her calf that was aching from the efforts. That was impossible, surely? She'd only been in bed.

Andrew was still waiting for her response, his smile faltering, one hand patting at the errant strand of hair. She didn't want more dreams; she didn't want to feel consumed by something she couldn't place. She wanted to go to Devon with Andrew. She wanted to know more about the items in the bureau.

Her face broke into an easy smile. 'We should.'

The music was on low as they navigated their way past the South Downs, the sunlight inching its fingers over the tops of the hills, dispersing the dark shadows from the clouds that hung suspended in the sky, the greens and lilacs and yellows muted by a mist that cleared as they left Sussex behind and found dual carriageways west. Andrew hummed along to some of the songs, unashamed, starting suddenly at one point, as if he'd forgotten she was sitting in the passenger seat, an embarrassed smile touching his mouth. She giggled with her head back and her eyes closed, feeling the warmth seeping through the glass, a sense that they had left something behind.

'Do you think we'll find anything?' he asked her, his cheeks flushed again.

She opened one eye. 'I'm not sure,' she said, then added, 'I hope so,' in a voice that surprised her with its passion.

'It's funny,' he said, quickly glancing her way. She had opened both eyes now and was looking at him curiously. She noticed the mole on his neck, on the left side, that always peeked out of his collar. 'I felt something in the flat last night. It was strange.' He laughed once, his words tripping over themselves as he continued. 'Like a presence, as I learnt more about that brooch. It was an odd feeling.'

She didn't respond and he gripped both hands tighter on the steering wheel, so she could see the whites of his knuckles, as if he were waiting for her to say something. She should have commiserated with him, soothed him and reassured him it was simply paranoia, the fact that they had been discussing it, the trip to Devon firing his imagination, but the words stuck in her throat. She felt relieved that someone else had felt something, that she wasn't going completely mad.

'It was probably nothing. The mind, you know,' he said without conviction.

'Maybe,' she said after a pause.

She thought she saw him shiver. Then he broke the mood, suggested they stop for ice-creams.

She raised an eyebrow. 'It's barely spring!'

'Reena,' he said, 'we're going to the West Country, ice-cream is an obligation.'

'Right, my bad,' she said, stepping out of the car and feeling lighter than she had in weeks. 'And my treat,' she said, dangling her wallet between two fingers.

They ate the ice-creams in the car as the clouds had started to spit. Feet up on the dashboard, Irina nibbled on the choc chips, the creamy, mint-flavoured ice-cream gorgeous. They looked like little kids, devouring the small cones, wiping the stray drops from the sides of their mouths.

Joshua had loved ice-cream. She remembered them both in the garden hearing the tinkle of the ice-cream van in the street outside, both of them pestering their parents to buy them ice-creams. Joshua tugging on her hand as they ordered cones with flakes, Joshua getting most of his round his mouth as he gabbled on back in their kitchen, their mother spitting on a tissue to clear his face, which had made Irina curl up in a ball and tell her she was gross. Joshua had giggled at the expression, happily allowing her to slobber over him in the clean-up operation. Wanting another ice-cream straight away, making Dad chuckle.

'Ready?' Andrew asked brightly, and she forced herself back to the car and this moment, slow to respond, as if she'd had to drag herself back over the years to him.

A fleeting expression passed across his face, familiar, and she nodded a second later, remembering to smile. 'Yes, of course.'

He went to say something, his mouth open in a rounded 'O', then pursed his lips and turned on the engine. 'Let's get going then.' His voice was louder in the small car, his knuckles white again.

She wondered whether Joshua would have liked him; she wondered why she couldn't tell him more.

They grew quieter the closer they got. Perhaps they'd both been thinking about the last time they were at a beach together. The flash of his back leaving her on the shore in Brighton. She blinked, removing the image, and then took a sideways look at him in the car. His face blank, his stubbly chin unwavering, his nose perfect in profile, his eyes on the road ahead. Did he think back to that time on the beach? Feelings that she hadn't recalled in months rose to the surface again, the hurt she felt when they'd broken up making her eyes sting so that she had to look out of the window, away from him, biting her lip to distract herself.

Her stomach plummeted as they made their way down into Lynmouth, the road into the village at an impossible angle, ominous escape lanes to the side with tyre tracks in the heaped sand left by motorists who had needed to use them. She knew she was holding her breath, her foot pushing at an imaginary brake in front of her, one hand on the glove compartment as they seemed to tumble down the road and out into the openness of the village, the slanted cottages in a higgledy-piggledy line under the cliff of greenery that enclosed the place. They drove around a low stone wall and Irina found her eyes drawn to a bridge further up that was dwarfed by the hills either side of it.

As they climbed up the other side of the village, past idling tourists eating fudge from paper bags, chips from polystyrene containers, she smiled at the holiday image. They had booked two rooms in a small B & B in Lynton and the satnav informed her they were less than half a mile away. She was looking forward to lounging on her bed, the crisp sheets smelling of washing powder, opening her window to let the sea air in, hearing the gulls calling to each other.

Andrew put the car in first gear as the engine strained to get up the other side, the road continuing to turn, hugging the edge of the cliff, guarded only by a flimsy-looking barrier that she noticed was dented backwards on one of the bends. She didn't want to wonder why. As they rounded another corner, the temperature in the car suddenly dropped and she found herself wrapping her arms around her body, shocked by the sudden blast, as if the air conditioning had just been turned up high. She checked the dial, as if she had somehow missed him reaching across to adjust it. The skin on her arms broke into goosebumps as the chill passed right over her, making her clench her jaw and hold her breath. Her heart sped up and Andrew slowed the car, glancing at her without saying anything. The sea was a blank space of grey beneath the clouds that hung stubbornly in an unmoving bank. The roof of a house just below them on the cliff could be glimpsed through a line of trees, its double chimney stacks peeking over them.

Then they were back on a straight road, the temperature rose once more and they arrived in Lynton village. Andrew stopped the car, said without quite meeting her eye, 'That was...' He didn't finish the sentence and she was left wondering if he had felt it too, the cold seeping beneath his skin and into his veins, pumping round his body so that he wondered whether he would ever be warm again. She looked back over her shoulder at where they'd come from; there was nothing there now, the road darkening as it twisted down the hill and round the cliffside. For a second she thought she saw someone standing at the end of the road staring back at her, but when she looked again it was just a lamppost.

'Ready?' Andrew called, heaving her worn leather bag from the boot and throwing it over his shoulder.

ABIGAIL

She stomped back, prickly with the need to talk to someone. Her moods recently had been as changeable as that day's weather, shadows crossing her sun, purple clouds sitting heavy in her eye line. She felt trapped, the house surrounded by thickening trees, obscuring more of the view with each passing day, the sea a drop on the other side, untamed and stubborn. She wanted Mary, Mary's patient understanding, her sympathy, her honest reactions. She wanted to talk everything through. She knew she shouldn't vent her frustrations on Richard. She saw then his bewildered expression when she'd turned on her heel; he was surely cursing her fickle moods, not knowing when she would take offence.

Why shouldn't he plan a life here? It was his home. She should have encouraged him; she should have been gay company. He didn't deserve her petulant reaction. It was just that he seemed to see his future so clearly, and unless she did something, she would be left in the village, stuck in the house with Connie, hiding in her bedroom, avoiding Larry.

When she finally reached the house she was out of breath,

droplets of rain merging with her sweat, hair plastered to her forehead, clammy in her clothes. She forgot to be quiet as she pushed open the front door, wanted to see her sister, to tell her, at least in part, where she'd been. She felt the urge to confide in her. What she was doing wasn't something to be ashamed of and yet the creeping around made her feel that she was being disloyal. She should have mentioned her meetings with Richard a long time ago; instead, she'd hugged them close, not wanting to give them up. She was afraid too that saying something might ruin things, perhaps her sister wouldn't approve, would try to stop her seeing him. She hung up her coat on the hook in the hallway, smoothing her hair back as she pinned another loose strand back into her bun.

'Connie,' she called out, turning into the living room and starting at the figure in the chair, sitting silently, one hand resting on his thigh, half-turned away from the window, his eyes on the horizon. 'Oh, I'm sorry, I...' She turned to go, Larry slowly swivelling his head as if he had only just noticed her there.

'Abigail.' He said her name slowly, stretching out all three syllables as if he wanted to play with them on his tongue.

She felt her body twitch in response as she looked around the room. 'I'm sorry, I was after Connie, I wanted to talk to her.'

Larry was patting the chair next to him with a flat palm, slowly, eyes on her. 'Sit,' he said when she remained frozen in the doorway.

She paused briefly, twisting her hands behind her, both feet stuck in the same place.

'Sit.' He smiled; his lips stretched across his teeth but not revealing them.

She moved forward, tentatively patting her chignon, re-fixing another pin. Her hand trembled imperceptibly, the pin digging into her scalp.

She sat and he folded over the newspaper he'd been reading, leant back and looked down at her shoes, up over her legs and tea dress. She felt flustered under the scrutiny, aware of her ruddy cheeks from the heat of the beach, the brisk walk back, her damp hair, patches under her arms, every lock of hair that wasn't in its right place.

'Is Connie...?' The question got trapped somewhere, her throat tight.

When he leant forward, she imagined the room becoming smaller, everything edging closer to her, shuffling across the rugs. He smelt of smoke, mothballs and spice; the scent seemed to stick in her nostrils so that she felt dizzy with it.

He hovered a hand over her knee then lowered it gently. She looked down at it, moving only her head, not able to move her leg away, not able to do anything but sit there and stare at his hand. Sandy hair, like a baby's, on his fingers, his nails were clipped short, some bitten right down, inflamed red skin on the sides.

'It's been good to have you here, Abigail.' That same smile again. 'Connie likes it, but I wonder,' he said, releasing her at the same moment, so a second later she wondered if she'd just imagined it. 'I wonder, Abigail, whether it suits me.'

He let that last sentence hang there and her eyebrows knitted together in confusion.

'How do I benefit?' he said, reaching to light his pipe, the match steady in his hand, the other cupped around the flame. He shook the match out. 'Connie seems to think the house just goes on functioning without hard work.' His voice sounded brittle. 'That food miraculously appears, that heating costs nothing, the new television set, the turntable...'

'I can get work,' Abigail blurted. 'I would be happy to contribute.'

'A woman in my household working?' The tone dropped, a soft caress of syllables so that Abigail had to strain to hear the last part. 'You would make me a laughing stock.'

She pleated her skirt with two hands, hands not able to stay still, patting, flattening, folding. He was watching them, listening to her breathing, quicker now, her eyes not able to stay on his face but sliding away to the corners of the room, her mouth twitching, biting on her lower lip as if he were admonishing her for something. What could she say? Why did she find herself jumpy and hot?

'My mother had the same hands,' he said. 'Creamy smooth, long fingers like a pianist's, decorated with rings that flashed when she spelt the shapes of words in the air. She couldn't communicate without flapping them around.'

Abigail's hands stopped; she clasped them together, still, as if in prayer, looking down at them, willing him to release her. Why had she left the beach?

'You don't look like Connie.' He sat back, exhaling rings of smoke between closed lips, his eyes narrowed. 'Wispier, drifting through the house.' He rested one hand on his groin, his jaw working. 'Fussing over that pathetic bird.'

She looked up sharply at that, felt a flash of hatred for him. Thought of that bird with its broken neck, bit down the words that were cramming into her mouth ready to fire out and be spat at him.

He leant forward again, resting his pipe on the edge of the ashtray, his eyes not leaving hers. Then came his hand, back on her leg, his grip tightening. Her eyes widened; she could feel the muscles in her legs stiffen. She shifted a fraction, her knees clamped shut like her mouth but her eyes roving, searching his face now.

He released her as quickly as he had seized her and her hand shot out to smooth her skirt, smooth over the memory of where his palm had been. She felt the fuzzy warmth of the room, the close atmosphere as if the sun were leaking into every crack and crevice of the house, filling the room with heat. He licked his lips, dabbing at the back of his neck with a handkerchief, and she started to panic. How would she get out of this room? What did he want from her?

She coughed into her hand, just once, her mind filling with questions, plans to get out. The door to the house clicked and turned, announcing Connie's arrival, and as she bustled into the room, coiffured and rosy, her handbag tucked under her arm, she started, seeing them both there in the silence.

'Darling,' Larry said, standing and readjusting his trousers, pulling the fabric up above his knees with both hands before walking across to kiss her.

Abigail watched him put his arms around her waist, pull her towards him and give her a lingering kiss on her mouth. Connie lost the words that she had, her cheeks scarlet when he let her go, unable to look at Abigail.

'Oh, Abigail doesn't mind.' He laughed, pecking her on the cheek, reverting to his role as dutiful husband.

'Of course not.' Connie swallowed a hiccough of a laugh, still not looking at Abigail, who sat frozen to her chair, staring at them both.

He looked over at Abigail, meeting her gaze, seemingly gratified by the way she held it.

IRINA

She followed Andrew through a small wooden gate, jumping stupidly as the face of an old woman appeared in one of the downstairs windows. The woman held up one hand in a wave and Irina nodded at her. When she looked again, the sun had come out, bouncing off the glass and obscuring the view of the room inside. The door had been left on the latch and they stepped through it into a small reception area.

The narrow space was lined with watercolours of beach scenes and delicate dried flowers, pressed and carefully labelled in simple pine frames. The receptionist was a bored-looking twenty-year-old with a goatee and a toothpaste mark on his jumper. He clicked on the computer in front of him, waiting for the page to load and rolling his eyes at the speed of the connection. 'So slow, sorry,' he said, without sounding it.

She didn't feel tired after their journey; there was something about the village that fired her up inside. The moment she lay on the bed she felt restless, as if there was someone urging her to explore. She unpacked her things, hanging her few clothes on separate hangers, lining up her bottles with gaps between them to take up more space. She stared at the room, the tiny television on brackets in the corner, the dusty pink lampshade, the curtains hooked back to show a hint of sky beyond. She could hear the odd passing car, the tweet of birds and then silence, unnerving compared with the hum of the village beyond the shop in Petworth. She thought of Patricia clucking in the shop just then, whistling round the place with a duster, finally accessing her workshop and trying to create some order in the pungent chaos.

A knock on the door and Andrew was standing there, in a yellow shirt crumpled from his suitcase. He peeked over her shoulder. 'Nice room,' he commented. 'Mine is pinker.'

She turned and grabbed her bag and they left the B & B. The breeze had picked up and her hair was loose in the wind as she tried to draw it into a ponytail.

'Where to?' Andrew asked. He too seemed filled with renewed energy now that they were there.

'We need to find someone old,' Irina said.

'Seems like a solid plan.'

She gave him her best withering look and he threw back his head and laughed, tucking her arm into his as they set off. She peered up through her lashes, feeling her body lean into his, an urge to snuggle into his chest like she always had in the past. Then the jolt as she remembered why they were apart; she pulled back a little, pretending to tie her hair again as she removed her arm.

They passed a shop crammed with sheepskin slippers, woven baskets, postcard racks. A café with a young waitress taking a family's order, a bored barista on his phone next to a large stainless-steel coffee machine. The town hall, steps leading from the pavement up to its double doors. There was an old stationer's opposite, a dated, dusty shop with an old-fashioned bell that rang as it swung open. The entrance was narrow, filled with stacks of yellowing newspapers, brochures and pamphlets piled messily on top of each other so that Andrew was forced to remain propping up the door, standing on the solitary stone step, one foot in, one foot out.

It wasn't a big shop. A large printer littered with more paper sat in the centre of the room churning out copies, a strip of light moving across its surface in a rhythm. On the shelves were an assortment of commemorative mugs and old toy-train carriages in every colour, crests painted carefully on their sides, tracks heaped in piles. A middle-aged man in a cardigan, three large beige buttons down the front, looked up as they arrived. He peered at Irina over tortoiseshell glasses, brow furrowed as Andrew sidestepped in behind her, almost sending one of the towers of paper flying.

'Can I help?'

Irina felt her mouth freeze up as she went to speak. Fumbling in her handbag, she pulled out the postcard, the letters 'Lynton' in bold on the front. 'I found this,' she stammered, 'in a bureau, a drawer. I wondered, well…'

She wasn't exactly sure what she wondered. Did she imagine the man would leap up and instantly recognize the handwriting? Remember the exact client that he'd sold this postcard to? She knew they were on a wild goose chase, with no real idea what they were looking for, but still she found herself holding her breath.

The man had taken a step towards her, skirting round a wire rack that contained an assortment of envelopes in different sizes. 'Come on then,' he said, holding out his hand for it.

She thrust it into them, a sudden flare of hope that everything would fall into place. He looked carefully at the front, tracing the image with one finger, a small smile on his cracked lips.

'It was never posted.' She gestured at it pointlessly, her arm dropping a fraction as she watched him read the back. She could see the words without looking: 'Forgive me'. She wondered again who 'A' was. The handwriting had an energy to it, as if the two words might fly off the end of the card. 'I wondered when it was written. It's hard to tell really, without a postmark.' She knew she was babbling now, knew she should stop to take a breath and let him speak. 'It's a lovely old postcard, don't you think? I adore the image, it's so romantic.'

'Well, the village has changed a bit,' said the man, unclear as to what both of them were doing there in his shop or perhaps disappointed by the lack of business. 'That pub has long gone, it's a gift shop now.'

Andrew tried to peer in the direction he was pointing but was impeded by the stack of papers.

'So, do you have any idea who sent it?' She knew the moment it was out of her mouth that this was an absurd question. How could he possibly have any idea? The overwhelming task ahead of them made her voice wobble with disappointment. 'I know it seems impossible, but we are desperate to know more about it. Anything, really, might be a help.'

The man stared at the card again, as if another look might solve all her problems. Then he shook his head decisively, pushing his glasses up his nose. 'I'm afraid I wouldn't have the first idea.'

She knew it was idiotic to feel so disheartened. What had she really been expecting? She turned to shuffle out of the shop, her face just inches from Andrew's chest, so that it seemed she was about to hug him. He opened the door wider to let her out, setting off the bell once more. She placed one foot on the stone step outside.

'You might,' said the stationer as an afterthought, 'want to see Bill in Lynmouth. He's been around longer than anyone, might be more of a help. He lives above The Rising Sun.'

'Is that a Devon term?' Irina asked, her forehead wrinkling.

'No.' The man's laugh turned into a hacking cough, so that he couldn't get the next sentence out quickly. 'It's a pub. Here, I'll give you directions, it won't take long.' He plucked a stray piece of paper from the top of an unsteady pile and drew a rudimentary map as Irina gushed, turning bright eyes back to Andrew, who looked equally excited.

There were signs pointing down into the village, but Andrew dragged her across the road, curious to see the clifftop railway. For a flash they were back on one of their holidays, he was ready to pull out his mobile and take a photo of her, to snatch up her hand while talking about something he'd seen. For that flash nothing had changed, they'd stayed together, she'd spent the last few months waking up to him on the pillow next to her, his crumpled, open face smiling sleepily at her as she offered to bring him a coffee. For that flash it all seemed possible again, like nothing had happened, like they were just a normal couple.

He bought the tickets – no green stubs but a simple paper receipt – and they waited in a small queue for the carriage to trundle up the cliffside. It was powered by water, one carriage moving up the cliff as the other moved down it at the same rate. Andrew was reading the pamphlet, throwing facts over his shoulder about the engineering. 'So, this is it, the first of its kind… Opened in 1890… It's powered by water from the West Lyn river, hundreds of gallons.'

She smiled at his enthusiasm, his thirst to always find out more, to understand things. She was so pleased he was there with her and for a second she was certain that they were going to find the answers they'd been seeking.

They stepped into the carriage and moved through to the back door to stand on a metal balcony, the rocks falling away beneath them, water running down the middle of wooden tracks. Irina felt momentarily dizzy as she looked out over the rocks and trees on the cliffside to the strip of sea that remained a steely grey, cloud obscuring the horizon. They started to descend, Andrew making the same squeak of pleasure as a seven-year-old girl nearby. Irina rolled her eyes at him before nudging him quickly in the shoulder. He shrugged innocently and looked back out as they sank lower. Then, with no warning, she felt the same cold from earlier steal over her, a sudden breeze, she thought, although she couldn't see the trees reacting to anything. Andrew glanced at her sharply, which only made her skin break out into goosebumps again. And then it was gone, as if it had never happened, and they passed the halfway mark and dropped into the village. Irina glanced quickly up to her left, sensing movement, but all she saw was a canopy of leaves, perhaps the hint of a red roof through them, a chimney stack.

The moment they reached the bottom and entered Lynmouth, Irina felt as if she was surrounded by the sea: the stench of dried-out seaweed, the salt on the wind that coated her, settled in her hair. They walked along the promenade, the wide paving mostly empty of people, the odd walker, a dog straining on a lead, a bench that sat in an alcove facing the water. The waves smashing gaily against the rocks, throwing up surf, the droplets snatched away by the wind. Strands of hair broke free from her ponytail and tickled the side of her face. She put up a hand to tuck them behind her ears, feeling surprised by the ridges on her skin, as if she'd forgotten they were there.

They passed a shop crammed with beach gear, spades and buckets dangling hopefully on hooks, baskets full of wetsuits and swimwear, a rack of postcards showing Lynmouth on sunnier days. A window, slid open, a faded list of ice-creams for sale sellotaped to one side. Past the headland, a tower with a metal brazier on top, and the harbour with one or two rotting wooden boats moving with the waves, faded buoys like bald pink heads poking out of the water. On their right the pavement split into two, one branch veering steeply upwards, above the streetside wall, connecting a row of cottages. The Rising Sun sat squarely in the middle, a painted line above the door claiming it was established in the seventeenth century. Small, square, mullioned windows and a large thatched roof seemed to overwhelm the ancient cottage.

Taking a breath, Irina knocked on the cottage next door, ivy climbing around the small porch, clinging to the house and inching towards the window. The lights were off and Andrew cupped his eyes to peer through the window, shaking his head as he backed away.

'No one there,' he said, stating the obvious. He sounded as deflated as Irina felt, her excitement punctured, her shoulders drooping. All this way for nothing. 'Drink?' He indicated the pub next door.

Irina shrugged, feeling petulant, wanting to stick out her bottom lip and sit on the floor, wait for Bill to come home from wherever he'd gone. Maybe he was just in a nearby shop? Or maybe he was visiting relatives miles away and wouldn't be back for days?

Andrew had obviously clocked her change of mood; he nudged her on the arm. 'We'll find him,' he said with a smile.

The Rising Sun was empty aside from an elderly man sitting by the window nursing a pint of ale at a table covered in water rings. He shifted his glasses up with one finger as they pushed through the door, both dipping their heads automatically as if they would hit them if they stood up straight.

The long, thick beams of the pub seemed to be holding up a sagging whitewashed ceiling and Irina had the strong sense that at any moment the whole place could collapse on top of them. As they approached the bar she noticed the barman, mouth agape, circling a pint glass and staring at her face before remembering himself and walking down the counter towards them. As he took their order he couldn't resist another look, his cheeks reddening as their eyes met. Irina battled the urge to cover her scars with her hand or hair, tried to look dignified and stop the watery sting at the back of her eyes.

'Why were you sniffing around out there?' the elderly man called out, looking up at Andrew.

'We were looking for someone. Bill,' Andrew replied, handing over a note to the barman.

The man's face changed, a subtle widening, a half-smile.

'You're Bill,' Irina guessed with a laugh, joy bubbling in her stomach.

The man looked at her, a brief pause as he took off his glasses, wiped at them with a handkerchief. 'I am as long as you don't want money. If you want money, Bill tragically died last week.'

'We don't want money,' Andrew said, crossing the carpet of the pub and holding out his hand. 'We've been sent down the hill to see you.'

'That old codger in the stationer's sent you, did he?'

Irina started in surprise.

'He sends everyone with questions down to me,' he explained softly.

Irina wondered then who else had come asking.

'Well, come on then, sit down, sit down.' He motioned to the chairs at his table.

Irina picked up their drinks and brought them over. Pulling out a seat, she dived immediately into her handbag, handed him the postcard and watched as he flicked it back and forward, scanning it.

'It's from the fifties…' she began.

Bill turned it over, frowning as he took in the two words, then flipped it back, tracing the cove on the front, the letters of 'Lynton' in bold.

'We didn't really have many dealings with people in Lynton back then.'

'But it's so close.'

'I know it seems strange, but the villages always kept themselves to themselves and we had everything we needed down here, didn't need to go up there. There was a sort of pride in it, I suppose, but now we need them, we don't have the infrastructure anymore.'

Before she could ask why not, Andrew had asked, 'Do you want another?'

He'd indicated the near-empty pint glass and Irina was grateful when Bill nodded. Andrew left them to go and order at the bar and she felt a rush of gratitude. He had always been like that when they were out, settling people, quietly ensuring everyone else had what they needed. She was hopeless, distracted by conversation or drawn into her own thoughts so that by the time she raised her head the moment to notice had long passed. She realised she'd been staring at his back as he departed. Bill raised one rather bushy eyebrow at her and she found herself looking down into her lemonade to avoid his gaze.

'So, do you think you might know? Well, could you guess? I think they were new to the village,' she said, aware she was babbling now but knowing this was true. 'It feels as if they were writing as an outsider somehow.' She sensed his eyes on her and shifted in her seat. 'There was this comment…' She pulled out another postcard. 'About a Richard and a—'

'Martin.'

She looked up at him with enormous eyes. 'Exactly.' Holding her breath, she watched Bill's face, his eyes lowering, the light fading.

'I knew a Martin,' he said slowly, turning to look out of the window. The grey sea beyond, a gull sitting on an iron railing opposite, perfectly still. 'And his son, Richard, I knew him too.' He shook his head, not seeing Andrew as he put the pint of ale down on the table in front of him. 'Still hurts,' he added, reaching for the drink.

Irina gripped the edge of the table, feeling a fizz that they had come one step closer to learning more.

Bill seemed to recover then, staring at the names once more. Andrew looked at Irina, head cocked to one side as she went to open her mouth to speak. Then her mobile started to trill, letting out the familiar ringtone that meant her mother was calling. It filled the small bar, jarring the peace.

She went to answer it, apologizing as she pulled it from her bag. 'I'm sorry,' she said, drawing it to her ear. She would just tell her she'd call her back. Her mother hated it when it went to answerphone, left stilted messages punctuated with short sighs. Irina didn't want her to feel ignored, felt a wave of guilt she hadn't even told her she'd gone away for a couple of days.

'Hi, Mum, I'm sor—'

'Is that Miss Woods?'

The caller had a low Mancunian accent, unfamiliar, and caused Irina to frown into the phone and look up at Andrew, making him pause, hand moving to hover over her forearm, his eyebrows knitted together in a question.

'Yes,' she said slowly, worry churning her stomach so that the lemonade seemed to swirl about in there. 'This is she,' she continued in an absurdly polite voice. *This is she?*

'This is Brighton General Hospital. I'm calling on behalf of your mother...'

ABIGAIL

She didn't like to spend time in the house at all now. She was always looking for signs that Larry was there: the double chimney smoking, his boots propped up by the door, fresh mud on the boot scraper, the smell of pipe smoke, the sound of Beethoven on the gramophone, a silhouette beyond the net curtains. Sometimes, though, there would be no signs and she would convince herself the house was empty: a draught pushing through the empty hallway, the floorboards swept and clean, pictures hanging straight, lamps unlit, no keys on the silver plate. Then he would appear, in a doorway, as if he'd been waiting, his face red with energy behind his eyes, like he was about to burst with the anticipation of it.

She would double-back, one palm up on the side of the door, remove her hat with shaking hands, shrug her coat off, sucking in her breath as he came and helped her, slowly pulled at the sleeves, leaning over her as his hands skimmed her, almost touching, his smell in her nostrils, his breathing seeming to fill the hallway, obscuring any other noise.

She would stay by her sister when she was there, glued to

her side so that Connie would sigh and brush at her, trying to increase the gap between them. Abigail would blunder after her when she left a room, fabricate reasons for wanting to help. She longed to be back in Bristol, longed to feel free.

She could feel Richard's pull, seductive, a rope slowly coiling around her ankle, dragging her deeper into the village, calling her down the hill, away from the house to the harbour walls, the idling boats, the water slopping against the side, the taste of salt on her lips, the wind biting at her face in snatches. They would meet now at the bottom of a road where the two rivers met, colliding into each other, spilling over rocks. She would collect things from their walks and keep them in her pockets: a pressed leaf, the ribbon she'd been wearing, the handkerchief he'd given her. She felt their outlines as she sat at the dinner table, Connie eating in silence opposite, Larry always watching, and she would return to her day with him.

She felt guilty as she pressed down with the pencil on the latest letter to Mary, hasty and pathetic, repeating their earlier plans for Mary to come to her. She had stopped talking about America though, seeing Richard's face as she shut her eyes. She sent countless letters filled with nothings, licking the envelope, listening to them drop into the letterbox crawling with ivy at the end of their road.

She wanted to take the last plea back the moment it was out of her hand, the lightness in her empty palm sending a shot of guilt through her. Mary couldn't come there; Abigail didn't want her in the house. She reviewed her hasty scrawls, the hinting at things that seemed to lurk in the corners of the house, not able to really outline what it was she was so afraid of but knowing Mary would worry if she knew.

She walked slowly back up the hill to the house, its windows looking out over the sea, the trees, bursting with new buds and leaves, dancing in the sunlight, obscuring the lower end of the garden from view. She automatically put her hands on her thighs on the steep part, ready for the ache in her legs, barely there these days. Around the corner, the cliff edge, where, if you leant over, you could make out the jumble of grass and rocks that plunged into the sea. She thought of her mum's grave left untended in Bristol, pictured the wind battering it from every angle, withered flowers long dead, an empty patch as others visited those alongside her. She moved closer to the edge, peered down, reeled back, her breath leaving her body in one enormous gasp.

Larry was in her room when she stepped inside, standing hunched over the dressing table. She jumped, making a noise, sharp and high, enough to make the muscles in his shoulders twitch. He didn't turn round, moved his hands slowly over the handles of the small drawers, over the contours of the wood, one finger inching over the surface.

He turned then, slowly, mouthing the word 'Beautiful,' as he looked at her, one palm flat on the dressing table so she wasn't sure which he was referring to.

'I've been walking.' She gabbled the sentence, the words tripping over each other so that they barely made sense.

'Close the door,' he said. The same expression, the same precise speed: assured.

She didn't want to close the door, hovered by the gap, the brass doorknob marked with thumbprints over time, her hand folding over it, her eyes shutting briefly. She wondered if she could call out, would her sister be here? She knew she wouldn't be. Could she simply leave, walk quickly down the stairs and out? But where would she go?

'Close the door. The draught,' he repeated, adding a laugh, a quick snatch.

Her feet were glued to the ground, her shoes impossibly heavy.

'Let me look at you,' he said.

The light from the window behind him meant she couldn't read his face. She swallowed, pursing her lips, wondering if he could see her throat working, her chest rising and falling.

He made to walk towards her and perhaps it was this that made her step across to him, one, two, her eyes unblinking as if she were lost in some trance.

He held out both arms to her then and for a flash she recalled her father, a memory from years ago in Bristol, she must have been four or five, he had held out both arms to her, twirling her round in their garden at home. He'd left that afternoon, a suitcase in one hand, a woman waiting in an automobile outside. She hadn't seen him again.

She was in front of Larry now, standing, quivering imperceptibly, shoulders tense, her fingers rubbing at their neighbours, the rest of her body still. He had undone a button from the top of his shirt and underneath his paisley necktie she could see individual strands of hair, fine and brown, poking out. His Adam's apple moved up and down as he swallowed, his tongue moving over cracked lips.

'That's better.' His voice dropped a level, softer now as he put a finger under her chin and tilted her face towards him.

Abigail leant backwards, her neck shifting right, not wanting to look him in the eye, her palms dampening, feeling her eyes roll. The smell of sweat and polished wood overwhelmed her. She couldn't avoid his gaze much longer, turned to stare straight at his pupils. He was so close. His breath was warm on her face, stale smoke and something acidic underneath it. She flinched and he cupped her chin now.

'I wanted a good look at you,' he said, his other hand leaving the dressing table to hold her around her waist, pull her towards him so that she was thrust against him, feeling the whole weight of him, his cotton shirt, a roll of stomach, the buckle of his braces digging into her hip. Her body stiffened, straining not to touch him. She was scared now as to what he wanted to do with her; she felt him stir, the shock of him making her curve her back.

He tutted slowly, showing yellowing teeth, laughing softly as he said, 'Naughty girl, don't wriggle, stay still.'

His breath again, seeping into the pores of her face. She could see a scar, tiny, cutting across his left eyebrow. She focused on the mark, tried to take herself away from this scene. If she did what he wanted, he would leave her; if she stayed here like this her sister would come and find her, she would help her.

Without warning he released her, spinning her round so that she faced the wall: a fading watercolour depicting a hunt in a gilt-edged frame, the hounds sniffing along the grass, men on horses, thighs rippling with the effort of holding onto their charges, one leaping over a line of bushes. The image swam before her so that she felt washed into it, as if she might suddenly hear the master's horn, the call to the hounds that there was a scent to pick up, the fox shivering and terrified, racing to escape their pounding after it.

She remained facing away from him, sensed his body still close, the gap between them small. She reached out a hand to the bedpost, took a tiny step away from him. Nothing. He didn't call her back, she could hear him panting a little, his breathing heavy.

'Whore,' he whispered.

The knuckles of her hand tightened on the post, bile rising in her throat as the word crawled over her.

'You think I can't tell what's in your filthy mind. Be sure that I don't tell your sister.'

Her mind ran through every moment they had been together, feeling panicked, palms clammy now, the room closing in, so hot and small, and just him. How had her behaviour made this happen? Mary had told her once before; she'd been smiling, staring directly at a man, challenging, and Mary had told her not to always be as bold. She had brought this on herself. What would Connie say? Would she throw her out? Where would she go?

Footsteps. She clenched and then a rush of air, the door clicking shut, his boots on the carpet, muffled, an even pace down the staircase. She rubbed at her arms, felt her skin crawl, wanted to seize the water jug on the top of the chest of drawers and pour it all over herself as she stood there.

'Abigail.'

Her sister's voice, light, lifting at the end in a question, floated from the bottom of the stairs.

She swallowed, trying to find a reply, her throat like sandpaper.

IRINA

The one time she'd left her mother, the one time she hadn't told her where she was headed and this happened. She felt a deep sense of shame creep over her, the contents of her stomach bubbling in panic as they headed back up the clifftop railway in silence. Everything that had felt so magical and exciting that morning seemed to have dulled and slowed. The railway seemed to dither, the water taking forever to fill up so that Irina was tapping her foot and looking up the cliff as if it might be quicker to climb it herself.

'Hey,' Andrew said, holding her elbow and steering her over to the metal terrace, 'it's going to be OK, we'll get there by tonight.'

She noted the 'it's' not the 'she', and the fact that he couldn't reassure her made her feel even worse. She had the same sense of overwhelming hopelessness as she'd had all those years ago, standing looking at the house, the horrific realization sinking in. She felt her breathing quicken, the start of a panic attack. She couldn't feel the air going in, her head lighter as she gasped at the air; it wasn't going into her lungs, it wasn't helping. Andrew's voice melted into the background and the colours around her seemed to fade as if there was a dial someone had turned down. Her legs wobbled and her head just screamed that she needed more air. She had left her alone, and this had happened.

Andrew steered her over to a seat in the carriage, the other passengers no doubt looking on as she was instructed to put her head between her knees. She felt his hand circling her back, closed her eyes. They left the carriage with her leaning on him, her face red, her eyes blinded by the sudden colours. They walked slowly to the B & B, Andrew looking down at her, speaking to her in a steady, low voice, one hand hovering over her shoulder. She wanted his hand on her, reassuring, she wanted to feel his touch. That thought made her feel worse. *So you're thinking about a man while your mother lies in a hospital two hundred miles away.* She deserved this; she realized then that she'd been waiting for this day. That it felt somehow inevitable that she would be left alone, not have a chance to even say goodbye, to say all the things she needed to say.

She couldn't stop herself thinking back to that day all those years ago, the scenes she'd replayed over and over in her mind for years. She and her mother in the cake shop, loading the enormous cake into the car, singing together as they drove back to their house. They never sang in the car after that.

She would be entering another hospital, recalled the last time she'd done that. She remembered the ambulance, sitting in the back of it as they'd tended to her face, her mother wringing her hands in the doorway, looking inside at Irina, back at the house behind. Her asking after Joshua again and again, her mother crying, being lowered to the floor as her legs collapsed beneath her. Her asking after her dad; it was his birthday, she told them. A fireman bending to talk to her mother; he'd taken his yellow helmet off when he was speaking, he didn't have a lot of hair. Irina remembered feeling that he'd know where Joshua was, expected him to appear in the sliding door of the ambulance, fascinated by it, wanting them to press the siren so the lights flashed and the noises came on. He never appeared in the doorway of the ambulance and they had taken her to hospital, her face covered in dressings, the pain starting to tear at her; they gave her injections and then everything went dark.

The journey back seemed to pass in a fog of old memories, panic, questions, faces. Andrew played Radio 2. Every now and again his hand left the gear stick, wavered inches from her leg before returning; she had seen it as if it were not attached to him, as if they were two other people in a car going somewhere else, somewhere lovely.

He dropped her straight at the hospital, pulling up and putting the handbrake on, cranking it urgently. It had been a five-hour journey, her neck was sore, her backside numb from sitting frozen in the passenger seat.

'Shall I come in? I'd like to,' he said, leaning across as she stepped out of the car.

She looked back at him, wanting to direct her anger somewhere, wanting to get rid of the hurt she was feeling. If they hadn't gone to Devon... He'd been so adamant they should go, she'd been swept along, and look how it had ended. She had left without a thought for anything else.

She blustered a response. 'No, I don't think...'

'I'll drop your bag in and—'

'No, don't. I'll get it now,' she said, moving to the boot to fetch it. She returned with it slung over her shoulder. 'Thanks,' she muttered, trying not to look at him, as if they'd had a row. This was how they'd always left things. Him trying to talk about it all, her batting him away. She slammed the door harder than she meant to. His face, tinged with hurt, was the last thing she saw before she turned to walk up the steps to the hospital, through the sliding doors into reception, relatives and friends waiting in plastic bucket seats, charts and signs indicating where people should go. As the doors closed behind her, she looked back outside, but his car had already gone.

ABIGAIL

She had made her way back to Richard's cottage, a haven. The relief of walking down the hill to Lynmouth, turning the corner, passing the Rhenish tower, watching the water lash at the rocks beyond, seeing the village winding away and up the valley, the river meandering in between the buildings, a babble behind, a man in glasses and a cap fishing from his balcony at the back of his house. She wanted to linger in the small square of garden, chat with his neighbours over the fence, sit on the bench with his father playing draughts and drinking glasses of cold water.

Beth was there as she arrived, sitting on a rug in the front garden, her baby swaddled in layers in her arms, her son roaming around on a search for snails.

'Mama, mama.' He looked up from squatting in the middle of the flowerbeds.

Beth smiled slowly, her face pale but content. 'Don't trample the flowers, George.'

'Not 'ramplin'.'

Abigail moved across to the fence, feeling lighter already, giggling as she saw George watching in fascination as he followed a snail trail with one finger. He looked up at her, blowing his fringe out of his eyes with a puff, then scrabbled backwards to the safety of his mother on the rug.

'I'm sorry.' Abigail laughed, realizing she had scared him away.

'You're not normally shy, George,' Beth chided. 'That's Abigail. Say hello to her.'

He hid behind his mother.

'Are you well?' Beth called over. 'I'd get up, but…' She shrugged from her spot on the ground, a light laugh.

'No, don't, you definitely have your hands full.' Abigail looked at the little boy, his feet turned inwards, dressed in corduroy shorts and a shirt. 'What were you looking for, George?'

He paused, a quick glance at his mother, who nodded encouragement. 'Go on.'

He took a step towards her, not quite meeting her eye. 'Snails.'

'Ahhhh,' Abigail said, peering over the fence and down the wooden boards. 'I bet you'll find one if you keep looking.' She scoured the panels, pretending to search. 'Is that one?' she asked in an innocent voice, gratified that George had trotted over on unsteady legs to crouch down and stare.

'Where? Where?'

'I think he just disappeared behind that pot.' She giggled as he turned his intense gaze on the terracotta pot spilling over with rosemary. 'How are you coping with the two of them?' she called across, watching Beth reach a hand out to tuck the blanket in.

'It's busy. It's his christening next week.' She nodded at the bundle in her arms. 'So we've been making plans, but everyone's been so kind, dropping us in food and all sorts.'

The baby was sleeping, his eyes shut, his pudgy hands clutching at the woollen blanket over him, a solemn expression on his face as if he were in the middle of a very serious dream.

'He's gorgeous,' Abigail said, wanting to walk across the lawn and stroke his skin, impossibly smooth and new, feel his fingers curl around one of her own.

'He was a lot less gorgeous last night! But you're right,' Beth said, unable to stop a smile from spreading across her face as she looked down at him.

Richard emerged from the house and leant against the doorway; his arms folded. Abigail felt her face move into a smile, everything else melting away as she took him in. His shirtsleeves rolled up, his skin browner from the recent good weather, his hair curling over his collar.

'Hello there,' he said softly, walking across to her. He bent over the fence too, grinning down at George, who was still rootling around in the earth near the terracotta pot. 'Digging for treasure?'

George looked up. 'Treasure,' he mumbled, at the same time as Beth called out, 'Richard, do *not* give him ideas!'

'What?' Richard laughed as Abigail nudged him. 'He could find gold.'

George had raised his head, twisting back and forth from his mother to Richard, the whites of his eyes more pronounced than ever. 'Gold?'

'Oh God.' Beth laughed, the baby snuffling as she rocked.

'Right, we need to get out of here before Tom comes back and skins you alive.' Abigail giggled, automatically reaching out a hand to Richard's arm. She felt everything unclench within her, the last few days insignificant in this patch of sunny garden.

He threw an arm across her shoulders as they walked back towards the cottage and she felt herself leaning into his warmth, a thrill running through her body, her breathing faster. They entered the house together, the hallway dark as their eyes adjusted. The cottage was so familiar to her now she'd become a regular visitor, and she felt her whole body unfurl as she stepped across the hallway. The door on the left was open, revealing Martin's bedroom, his slippers resting next to the bed, shafts of sunlight spilling into the room.

'You're right on time,' Martin called out from the living room opposite.

For a second she stared up at Richard, their eyes meeting in the silence.

She moved through, leant down to kiss him on the cheek. 'That's a new tie,' she said, admiring the jaunty yellow spots.

Martin adjusted it with a half-smile. 'See, Richard, a lady of taste. Boy hasn't noticed,' he added.

'Just jealous, Dad,' Richard called from the pantry at the back, the steam from the kettle whistling on the range.

She was fussed over, told to sit, already happier, being back in the small front room, fresh flowers from the garden in a jug on the windowsill, jigsaw boxes piled up on the window seat, the latest laid out on a table in the corner, a painting of a steam engine emerging from the shapes. They sat and chatted and ate coffee cake, Richard missing a spot of icing on his mouth, Abigail grinning at Martin as he pointed it out.

It had started to spit lightly, droplets clinging to the panes of glass, the sky now a milky grey. She knew she had to leave, had to head back to the house. She'd told her sister she liked to walk up on the moors, but lately Connie had started to ask more questions. She wondered if she suspected something, if she wanted to ask. She bent to kiss Martin on the cheek, moved to the doorway, spilling thanks.

'Wait there,' he said, reaching for his walking stick, shooing Richard away with the other hand. 'I'm fine, just let me.'

Richard stepped back, taking Abigail's hand in his. For a second she froze, then allowed her hand to relax in his grip, enjoyed the sensation of their skin touching. Martin was rifling in the top drawer of a dresser, taking things out, placing them on the side, rummaging. Finally, he produced a small box.

Resting back in his chair, his chest rising and falling with the effort, he looked up at her. 'For you,' he said, holding out the box to Abigail.

Glancing at Richard, she released his hand and crossed the room, taking the box from Martin. Looking at him for permission to open it, he nodded almost imperceptibly and she lifted the lid.

Inside, resting on a velvet cushion, was a brooch: the silhouette of a woman in profile, in cream on a lilac background.

'It's beautiful,' she said, not wanting to sound false or over the top. It really was a lovely piece of jewellery, delicate, the cream woman made out of shell.

'She wore it often. She would have loved to have seen someone have it, someone special to us.'

The lump in her throat had returned and she blinked, placing the brooch back on its cushion. 'Thank you. I love it.'

'Well now, don't start crying on me, I haven't made a lady cry in years and I don't plan to start now.' His voice was gruff as he said it, and he clapped a hand on his thigh.

Richard had appeared at her side, one hand on the small of her back, looking at it over her shoulder before she closed the lid. 'She adored that brooch,' he said, his voice low and controlled.

For a brief second Abigail panicked that he was unhappy she'd been given it. It did seem like such a generous gift, and it had belonged to his mother. She felt the box grow heavier with this responsibility.

'She would have loved you having it.' He closed her hand over the box. 'Thanks, Dad,' he said quietly, his eyes watering so that he had to look away.

'Pah!' Martin waved them both away with a hand and a laugh. 'Get out before we all start weeping on one another. You make sure this one looks after you, Abigail, and you come back and see us again soon.'

'Definitely,' Abigail said, leaning down to kiss the old man's cheek again, feeling the bristles under her lips, smelling Old Spice.

He turned as red as the teapot. 'Well don't be expecting presents every time. I'll be wanting you making the tea next time you're about.'

'Naturally.' She laughed as she crossed the room, the box gripped tight in her hand, safe with her: Maisie's brooch.

She clutched the brooch to her all the way back, leaving Richard at the bottom of Mars Hill, his promises to meet again soon still in her ears as she climbed the hill away from him, grinning goofily as she let herself in, straining her ears for noises before taking the stairs two at a time.

Her room seemed different somehow. Had she left the bedspread with those creases on the right? Had she not plumped her pillow even though there still seemed to be a depression where her head would be? She had thought she'd left the window open on the first notch of the fastening, had she closed it without thinking? Had she left her hairbrush resting on its bristles, the smeared silver facing up, throwing reflections onto the walls when the sun bounced off the glass?

She traced a finger along the chest of drawers, straightened the lace doily under the wash bowl, turned the handle of the jug to ninety degrees. The book she had been reading was still resting on the bedside table, a bookmark sticking out. A glass of water, almost empty, alongside it. Her eyes flicked over to the wardrobe, which was ajar an inch. She lifted the brass handle to push it closed, pausing momentarily to wonder why it had been open in the first place. Taking a breath, she pulled the door back, revealing lines of blouses, skirts, pressed and hung in neat order, her cardigans folded up in a pile, the drawer with her underclothes shut.

Feeling silly now, paranoid, she pushed the door shut, hearing the latch click into place. She sat on the trunk at the end of the bed, breathing evenly as she calmed herself. He hadn't been here. And yet the room felt different, smelt different, not hers.

That night she hid the brooch between layers of undergarments, secreted between silk, thinking of Maisie and Martin and their marriage, their sons, imagining the woman in the photograph wearing it.

She wished for the twentieth time that there was a lock on the door and that she was mistress of the only key. She felt fidgety, restless as she went to lie on her bed, reached for her book, tried to focus on the words and stop her mind creating things that hadn't happened. She couldn't help but have one eye always watching the doorknob, a shadow in the crack below, one ear listening for the sound of footsteps coming up the stairs. She chewed her lower lip and lay back. The words, focus on the words. She rested her head on the pillow and, for a moment, imagined the scent of pipe smoke and mothballs filling her nostrils, then she took a breath and forced herself to read.

She pinned it to her chest in the morning, under a cardigan so that it remained her secret, another secret. She knew she would have to tell her sister soon, wanted her to know, yet something stopped her, she felt herself wavering on the edge of a confession. She would wait a little longer.

IRINA

Her mother looked smaller, sunken, surrounded by a sea of white sheets. The doctor had told her she'd collapsed, had been brought in for tests.

As she looked down at her she felt their roles were reversed and she was her mother visiting herself as a child in the hospital. Maybe it was the familiar line of other beds, the distant spluttering, the curtains pulled back to the sides, the smeared windows through which Irina could see waiting ambulances and a couple of off-duty nurses, coats over their uniforms, puffing furiously at cigarettes. The cloying smell of disinfectant and rubber seemed to fill her nostrils and she was transported back to her childhood, to lying in a hospital bed, woozy, lifted gently as someone checked her for other injuries.

Her face had hurt, burning as if she'd had acid thrown at her. She'd learnt about acid in school, the chemistry-lab floor was pockmarked from spillages. That was her face. She put a hand to it, wanting it to stop, but it was covered in a dressing; someone lightly held onto her arm, trying to put a soothing note in their voice to make up for the fact they couldn't soothe her face. Irina realized with a start that it was her mother's voice she'd heard, her mother drawing her arm back to her side as the doctors worked on her. The world had grown blurry and distant after that; she remembered having to count backwards – how silly, she'd thought, wanting to show them she was a big girl and could do that, that it was easy-peasy-lemon-squeezy. It was Joshua who couldn't count, Joshua who always missed out 'seven'.

Irina hadn't realized she was frozen in the centre of the room as the memories washed over her. Her mother had her eyes closed, sheet pulled up to her chin and arms resting on top of it, parallel to her body, face pale. She looked like a corpse. Irina took a step forward, scared that a new chapter in her life was being revealed. What would happen now?

She drew up a small plastic chair to the side of the bed and sat down, feeling comically low down, reaching up awkwardly to hold her mother's hand so that her arm was bent at a strange angle. She thought she saw her eyelids flicker, her chest barely rising and falling with each breath. Irina glanced at the monitor next to her, at the nonsensical numbers and lines that were charting her mother's progress. Were they good numbers? The drip that was sticking into her hand made Irina feel nauseous, liquid flowing into her from a squashed bag by her side. She didn't seem at all like her mother in this environment. She would have hated the stark light in the room, showing up the lines on her face, the creases around her eyes whisper-thin as she rested. Her brow smoother than Irina remembered – was her mother permanently frowning?

'Excuse me, could you tell me what's wrong?'

The nurse looked her in the face, eyes shifting slightly to her right when she noticed, momentarily distracted, even though she must see worse every day. Or perhaps not.

'Doctor Georges will be along shortly, ten minutes or so. Your mother came in a few hours ago, collapsed, but we have her on a drip and we're monitoring her now.'

'Will she be alright?' Irina blurted. A hopeless question, she knew that, the moment it fell out of her mouth, but she needed to know; ten minutes seemed an interminable wait.

The nurse picked up the chart at the foot of the bed. 'Her condition seems stable now and the doctor will talk you through the results of her blood test.'

'Test?'

'She had one when she came into A & E.'

Irina thanked her twice, turning back to see her mother's eyelids fluttering. She scooted round to hold her hand.

'Mum, it's Irina. I'm here, it's OK.'

Her mother's voice was croaky as she tried to focus on Irina's face. 'I'm sorry,' she said, her hand half-lifting from the bed.

And for a moment the words seemed weighted with something more.

MARY

Abigail's letters were still infused with something, a hint behind the sentences. She straightened out the latest one on the table in the pub garden, frowning as she drew her finger along the lines, mouthing the words as she read. She wanted to ball it up in her fist, fed up with letters and words when their friendship was all about shared looks, sounds, chatter. She remembered the days just after they'd found her dad, how she'd moved senselessly along pavements and had found herself wandering into Abigail's house, the whistle of the kettle on the range, a warm embrace from Abigail's mum, Mary's tears falling onto thick woollen knit, being fed soups and scones as they sat with her.

Perhaps Mary had known her dad would be found like that one day. He hadn't been back home a year. He was shorter, stooped, would disappear into that other place as he sat in the chair in the parlour, reliving those bleak, endless hours in the camp. He'd shout foreign words in his sleep, the bedclothes patchy with sweat. She used to stand in the doorway, uncertain, one foot moving towards him, then a step back, knowing she couldn't help him when he was like this. She'd bring him countless cups of tea, digestive biscuits, as he sat unseeing in his chair, not able to work or concentrate on anything as the day darkened and she had to leave for the pub, the braying customers.

They'd found him at the bottom of the gorge. She hadn't wanted to listen to the policeman who'd come to her house, taken his hat off, his hair slick with Brylcreem, matted down over his forehead from the weight of the hat. He had rotated it slowly in his fingers as he told her the details. She had gone to identify the body. They let her look at a bit of his face through a sheet.

'Don't lift the rest, miss.'

She wondered what she would see under the sheet. There were angles poking up in all the wrong places. The head wasn't the right shape and one eye was swollen and the skin all puffed up so his nose and cheeks seemed to merge, blood clotted in his hair. He still had the same glassy expression. People told her afterwards that he was at peace now, but she had seen that look, always the same look. He would spend an eternity in that camp, never be able to escape the memories of what they had done to him.

She'd been given a lift by a policeman back from the mortuary, stood in the doorway of their house, her dad's half-finished mug of tea on the side, yesterday's newspaper crumpled on the sofa, a cushion still indented where he'd rested his head. She briefly wondered whether to try and contact her mum, but she'd walked out years ago and Mary knew she wouldn't care.

Mary hadn't waited around, had walked unthinking to Abigail's, was folded into hugs, Abigail's mother tucking her up into her bed, one hand soothing her forehead as Abigail sat and held her hand, cocooned there. When she'd moved out of the house and into rented rooms it seemed she spent half the week with them both, falling into an easy rhythm, helping prepare meals, scrub the kitchen. She'd been gradually restored; the nightmares eased; she began to see her father's face as it had been before the war. He had always loved nature, insects, had wanted to keep bees, used to show her illustrations in books, explain how they made honey, fascinated by the idea of a colony.

Now it seemed that she had nowhere she could feel at home. She scrawled her news to Abigail, the money she was saving, her plan to join her in Devon, then they could leave, find work together. During the war they'd talked about saving up to go to America, their brief glimpse of the soldiers from there, bolder and bigger somehow; they'd imagined cattle farms and cowboys and had paused at the newspaper stand to stare into the faces of the movie stars on the front of magazines. She reminded her of those things.

She was desperate to see Abigail, knew something was lurking behind the words, her descriptions of the beach and the woods. She talked about Richard, and Mary grinned as she read about fishing from the back of his house, him teaching her which bait to use, her sitting in the sunshine with his father, drinking tea and teaching them their own strange version of gin rummy. Mary could picture Richard now, shirt-sleeves rolled up, hair that curled at the back, broad shoulders. She wanted to know more, a little frightened by the thought that Abigail was experiencing something Mary could only imagine.

She got up, rubbing at the watermarks on the table, moving round to clear the empty pint glasses, the sun warm overhead. There were sweet peas lining the back wall of the pub, in amongst the weeds, cheering up the dull facade. She closed her eyes for a second and imagined someone there whisking her away to the banks of a river, teaching her how to fish, howling as she taught them card games.

'We need you, Mary,' came the call, shouted through the gap in the kitchen window.

'I'm coming,' Mary whispered, eyes opening, wrenched away from a mossy riverbank, somewhere sunny and far, far away.

ABIGAIL

She could feel his eyes on her through the front window, the small panes of glass breaking his body into parts: a mouth, one eye, his shoulder. Watching her as she shifted the basket onto her other arm, as she closed the gate behind her, pressing on the latch, as she dropped down onto the path until she was just shoulders, a head, a hat, and even then she knew he was still watching.

Even when she was ordering sausages from the butcher's, scanning the newsagent's window for advertisements, passing the idle boats in the harbour, looking out over slate-grey water. Even then, with the house high up and hidden from her, she could feel his eyes on her, watching.

Maisie's brooch became a talisman, warding off evil when she wore it. She pinned it to her chest, the discreet bump under her cardigan the only sign it was there, but she could feel it, sometimes raising a hand to finger the outline of it, hard and reassuring. She felt cocooned in a protective layer, it made her feel bolder, meeting Larry's gaze at dinner, answering her sister in a too-loud voice, sitting straighter.

She didn't tell Richard of course, embarrassed when he caught her flinching at his touch on her arm, something uncertain in her voice when he asked what was wrong, her eyes slipping from his face as she replied. She had asked him once what he knew of Larry, kept her voice light, a mundane question in a string of others.

'Have you had dealings with him? What's his reputation?'

Richard shrugged. 'The folks up in Lynton tend to keep themselves to themselves. There's no real cause for them to come down here.' Then he added, maybe to please her, though he didn't notice her face change, her eyes darken, 'Heard he's on the up, a councillor and a businessman. He's not interested in fish, that's for sure. He'll take good care of your sister.'

He wanted to reassure and she nodded emphatically, worried her smile was too thin, that he would delve deeper if she overcompensated, a throwaway smile, a light laugh. 'He will.' She injected the two words with as much warmth as she could muster. They didn't speak of him again. Not until that last night.

She was in the garden when Larry found her, where the lawn sloped away as if it were cascading through the trees to the sea below. The days were long and she had been reading, the sun almost lost to the line of trees in front of her, creating long shadows that reached her bare feet as she rested her head back in the deckchair she had dragged out.

His hand on the top of her head forced her eyes to look up. She lurched forward and was pushed back down in an instant, dropped into the curve of the deckchair, her knees too high, awkward, her skirt slipping to reveal her garter. She snatched her hand back down. She'd been holding the brooch, examining the face as if she could reach through history and talk to the woman in the small oval. She wasn't holding it anymore.

'What's this then?' He plucked the brooch from the ground, holding it out between two fingers, an eyebrow raised.

She leant forward in the deckchair, wanting to cry out, to knock it from his hand, but she felt her chest tighten, her breath freeze as she watched him turn it over and back in slow, minuscule movements. She tried to keep her face set, went to shrug nonchalantly, as if the brooch were nothing to her. He'd guessed it, though, a victorious spreading smile emerging on his face, a languid lick of his lips as he peered at the silhouette on its front.

'Who is she?' he crooned, moving in front of her, one finger outlining the face, a face that Richard loved, the profile so important, and now his finger smeared over it, his tone mocking.

'No one.' The words came out in a half-whisper, clumsy. She couldn't move her eyes from his hand, the brooch held by its pin, flipped back and forwards, as if he knew he were a cat playing with a mouse.

'You won't mind if I take it then.' His hand closed over it and his eyes met hers, daring her to challenge him, daring her to say no.

She reared up pathetically out of the chair, standing awkwardly. 'Please don't…'

'So not no one then.' He examined it for another few seconds. She felt her pulse throbbing at her neck.

'What would you do to get it back, I wonder?' His lip curled as he said it.

She tasted sour milk in her mouth, her stomach churning involuntarily. Her eyelids flickered with the thoughts rushing through her, trying to see her way out, trying to answer this, to end things. She pictured Richard's face back in the cottage when she had accepted the brooch. She remembered the way his eyes had rested on her, satisfied she would be a careful guardian of something so precious. His greeny-gold irises had focused on her.

Larry, impatient now with her silence, repeated his question, taking a step forward so that he was standing over her, forcing her to crane her neck up, his face unreadable surrounded by the darkening sky, a wash of purple haze.

What would she do? What did he want? She swallowed, eyes fixed on the ground to her right, focusing on a patch of clover. Perhaps if she pleaded with him? She looked up, eyes wide and tried to smile, tried to placate. She took on an expression that she had seen her sister use, her voice higher as it came out, girlish, she hoped.

'It's just a trifle. Silly really.' She stopped, then a small laugh. 'But I've grown fond of it.' She was careful not to put too much into her voice, clamping her tongue between her teeth. She felt her palms dampen, looked up at him through her lashes, then coyly to the ground.

He leant forward, his mouth brushing a loose strand of her hair. 'I don't believe you,' he whispered.

Her eyes were on the brooch, still in his hand but now within her reach. Could she seize it? Scrape her fingernails down his arm, force his hand to open and release it? Her head was awash with these thoughts, thoughts that mingled with a spicy scent. She was close enough to see the open pores on his nose, his skin reddening in the heat.

He put his free hand around her waist, pulling her into him roughly. 'What will you do for it?' His fingers gripped her side, she could feel his breaths coming faster, the noise loud in her ear.

She wriggled then, ashamed to feel him harden between his legs, the realization freezing her. 'What would my sister say?' she asked, desperate to remind him who she was. It didn't seem to help.

'She'd wouldn't say a thing.' He said it so matter-of-factly and in that moment she knew that was the truth and she wondered if she would ever feel as lonely as she did then.

'I can't... I won't.' She wriggled again, releasing herself from his grip, tripping over the leg of the deckchair so that she stumbled and had to right herself. She stood on the lawn unable to speak, one hand on her chest stilling her breathing, her eyes trained on his, convinced he would lunge at her again.

But he didn't. Instead, he took one last look at the brooch and then at her, a sneer forming on his lips as he moved his gaze slowly from her feet to her head. 'You think I'm interested in you?' he said. 'You're pathetic,' he spat. Then, after a pause, 'She's ugly.' He tossed the brooch at her feet.

She dropped to her knees as she watched it fall, all pretence gone, snatched it up, closing her hand around it, wanting to rub at it, wipe him away. Tears filmed her eyes but she refused to cry, refused to give him that pleasure.

He was already walking back towards the house, his jacket tight across his shoulders, swatting at an insect in the air, not looking back. She didn't need to see his face to know that he was smiling. She could have sworn she saw movement at the French windows; someone had been looking out at them both, someone had been there. She clutched the brooch to her chest, remaining on her knees as the sun finally disappeared, bleeding into the tree line and letting the shadows creep all over her so that she was now in the dark.

She hadn't realized she was shaking until she was back in her room, both hands pushing the door closed, spinning round to press her back against the wooden panels. She caught herself in the mirror on the dressing table, all three faces wearing the same ghostly expression, the skin wan, the lips cracked, something in the eyes that hadn't been there that morning.

She felt it now, the walls of the house closing in on her, the valley beyond pressing down on her. She was trapped here, in this room, in this house, in this corner of Devon. The tears came then, pitiful sobs that made her body convulse, forcing her to clamp her hands over her face to try and stifle the noise. She thought of her life in Bristol, memories now cloaked in a rosy glow, clattering along cobbled streets with Mary, spooning warm fish pie into her mouth, waving her fork around as she swapped the day's news with her mum, her appraising gaze. She cried for those times, for Mary's face when she left, for her mum's inert body in that sepia room. She cried until she had nothing left, hugging her arms around herself in the absence of anyone else to comfort her.

She needed to get out. She would leave, she would run away. Seized by this sudden thought, she got up from the bed, scrubbed at her eyes, her face a mess of angry blotches. She scribbled a letter to Mary, the start of plans, persuading her to come, persuading her they would go somewhere together. She didn't linger over details, she didn't question whether it was the right thing to do, she just wrote, spilling out her need to escape in ink, the words scrawled and messy, words scratched out and replaced. She needed to get out.

IRINA

She felt as if she had been away for weeks not hours. The moment she pushed open the shop door, the familiar smell of beeswax, wood and polish enveloped her like a parent's hug. The bell seemed loud in the space and she navigated her way through the shop, noting a couple of new pieces packaged up and stacked against the wall ready for her to take a look at. They hadn't let her stay past visiting hours; she would get back to the hospital first thing.

She stepped through the beaded curtain into her workshop. As predicted, Patricia had been in there. Piles of shavings were heaped into corners, the floor covered in dry brush marks, the worktops cleared, tools lined up on the draining board in the corner of the room. The mirror was sparkling, the windows recently cleaned, the evening light giving everything a lilac sheen. It should have felt warm, familiar, but in the corner the bureau lurked, its bulky presence an unwelcome extra person in the shop. She found herself staring at it, unable to turn her back as she shuffled to her apartment door, reaching behind her to put the key into the lock before stepping inside.

It seemed the bureau's influence was leaking beneath the gap in the door, slowly spreading up the staircase, across the hall landing and into her apartment. She scooped up Pepper the moment she pushed open the door, pleased to bury her face into her soft fur and feel the healthy throb of her heartbeat, her ribcage pulsing with life.

She clattered through the apartment, opening cupboards and slamming them again, turning on lights, the television, the radio, wanting to be surrounded. She stared at the telephone on the side table, imagined picking it up and calling him. She had been so rude to Andrew. She would have to phone him and apologize. Why did she always have to be so unpleasant to him? It was incredible that he still returned her calls. She felt a momentary warmth as she thought back to the clifftop railway, the closeness of him on that narrow metal balcony, the urge to lean towards him and nestle into his chest as if nothing bad had happened between them, as if they were still together. She couldn't call him, not tonight.

Should she phone Bill? He had thrust his number into Andrew's hand, asking him to let him know how she was. She had registered it all in a far-off way, as if it were happening to someone else. What had he been about to say? He seemed to have known the two men mentioned in the postcard; she was sure he would be able to shed more light on things. She worried then that she had frightened him a little. Her reaction to her mother's collapse had been extreme and Bill had pushed out his chair and stood up as she gabbled at him, as Andrew helped her out of the pub.

She felt better as the evening wore on, got sucked into some reality show with Z-list celebrities doing humiliating things. She had a glass of wine in her hand; she would see her mother again tomorrow.

Her eyelids were drooping as she scanned the channels for something else, a last mouthful of wine in her glass. A gust of cold air made her turn her head towards the door and the voices on the television were drowned out by an enormous crash from her bedroom, as if her wardrobe had fallen down, her clothes and belongings scattered. The noise had been so loud, it was as if something had pushed its way through the walls of the house. She lifted her legs off the floor, the last of the wine slopping onto the sofa, a noise escaping from her mouth. She stayed in the pose for a few seconds, slowly lowering her legs onto the floor as the temperature rose.

Her heart was beating hard and she wished Pepper was there with her. She didn't want to get up and go and look, but she knew she had to. She stood up, putting the wine glass down on the table and then wishing she had something to hold onto.

Creeping forward, she checked the hallway before walking into it. Nothing had fallen over: the side table was full of the usual clutter, a line of shoes, a row of hooks with coats, all exactly as she'd left them. The door to her bedroom was down the corridor to the left. It was closed. She hadn't been in there since returning home. She wondered what state she would find it in.

She swallowed, glancing back at her mobile on the sofa and wondering if she could phone Andrew. Pepper appeared in the doorway, making her start. She lifted her into her arms and walked forward slowly. She couldn't phone, not after the way she'd left things. She was here alone and she would have to deal with it. Something had fallen, that was all. She was just scaring herself. A brief thought: that she was edging closer to discovering the truth behind the bureau and that this had stirred things up somehow; that this would only end if she could find out more.

Reaching out for the doorknob, her palm felt slippery on the metal. She lifted her chin, tried to inject confidence into her stance. She pushed, the door swung away from her and she stepped inside. The cat twisted in her arms, digging her claws in, legs stretched, body tense, hissing as she leapt down onto the floor and raced back into the living room. Irina moaned, feeling lost and alone.

The room was dark and Irina quickly switched the lights on, convinced she would see her things strewn on the floor, maybe some broken furniture, a collapsed shelf.

There was nothing out of place. The room looked exactly as she had left it. The bed was still crumpled in the same place, the cat's sunken imprint in the throw at the end, her books lined up neatly on the shelf over the desk. The wardrobe stood in the corner, perfectly upright, and the chest of drawers with one top drawer slightly open seemed to be the same.

She walked round the bed, still certain that she would find something. She went to the window, wondering if she'd been mistaken and the noise had come from outside. Perhaps someone had had a terrible car accident near the flat? There was nothing there: a couple walking, a streetlamp leaving its pool of light. It must have been outside, she reasoned, despite the little voice in her head insisting it had come from in there. She silenced the voice, trying to ignore her clammy hands, hairs standing to attention on her arm.

She went to leave the room, taking a last look round before reaching for the doorknob. As she turned to close it, from the corner of her eye she saw it. Her bedroom wall, smashed, a gaping hole through to the street, the garden laid bare, her belongings spewing from the room, the window frame splintered and bent at an odd angle, the bricks exposed, half-fallen away. She spun back around to the wall. The neatly painted wall, a framed picture of a field of poppies, the cushions plumped on the window seat, the glass blank. There was nothing wrong with the wall at all, yet the image followed her all the way to the living room, made her sleep curled up on the sofa under a throw, with the cat clutched to her. It appeared in her dreams that night, she could feel the wind ripping through the hole and around her, her skirt billowing, her legs and arms cold, and her face, unscarred, not her, wide eyed in the broken fragments of mirror opposite.

RICHARD

He hadn't told her where they were headed, simply that she was to find some sturdy boots, heeled shoes wouldn't cut it. They met at the top of the village, the river tumbling through the trees somewhere behind them, the houses like a line of wonky teeth poking up towards the sea beyond. The temperature had dropped in the last couple of days and she arrived in a thick winter coat. She pulled it around her, the wool damp, tiny droplets sticking to every strand. She licked the water from her lips, rain misting everything, coating everything with a sheen of water, clinging to their skin like an outer layer. The bottom of his hair beneath his hat was curling over the collar of his wax jacket. He had brought along his mother's waterproof cape that she had often taken on walks.

'Come on, Abigail Lovatt.' He smiled, handing it over with a bow.

She threw it on, getting the ribbon at the throat stuck in her hair so she couldn't fit her head through it. 'Get me out of this thing,' came the muffled response as he reached to tug it gently over her, her face appearing, hair askew, cheeks red, a head out of nowhere; a face he wanted to cup with both hands, so precious.

Instead, he straightened up, laughing as she did a slow rotation in front of him, like she was at a coming-out ceremony.

'Where are we going?' she asked for the tenth time, knowing her questioning would get her nowhere.

He enjoyed her exasperation as he again refused to tell her. 'Patience is a virtue.'

'I wouldn't know.'

'Clearly.'

He felt better the higher they climbed. She had seemed nervy again when they'd met, peering over her shoulder in the direction of Lynton and flinching when he went to hand her the cape. Sometimes she reminded him of one of Exmoor's red deer, liable to race off into the undergrowth at any moment and never be seen again. He felt it was his job to keep her there, try to anchor her to the moment, to him.

They walked up the path that led into the trees. She was getting slower to respond, her answers briefer the higher they climbed, and he enjoyed shouting questions over his shoulder, laughing as she clutched her sides, not able to speak from the slight stitch that was making her gasp between choked laughter. 'Stop... asking... me... questions...'

He waited for her on a tree stump, producing a pasty from a brown paper bag, still warm, the meat a gorgeous, spicy explosion in her mouth, the pastry crumbling to perfection.

'Where are we going?' she asked after the last gulp.

He rolled his eyes, screwing up the paper bag. She licked the smallest flake from her lips and as he looked at her he felt excitement bubbling in his stomach. He couldn't wait to show her. He couldn't wait for her reaction. He hadn't shown anyone, no one knew, not even his father. She seemed different though, her movements jumpy, lines of worry crossing her face when she was lost in her thoughts. He worried about the serious look she took on, as if she were steeling herself for something terrible.

He guided her over to the tree stump, settling her there. Her eyes were darker, her face jade green from the shadows of the trees around them. He stood before her, eyebrows knitted together, one hand on her arm. 'Abigail, what is it? Sit. I was teasing, we shouldn't go so quickly, there's no hurry.'

'I'm fine,' she insisted.

He stayed crouched down beside her, his hand still on her arm. 'It's not far now.'

She returned then, her face tipped to the side, eyes flashing in shades of green. 'I'll stop lounging about on tree stumps then,' she said, going to stand and letting him help her. 'Right, where are we going?' she asked yet again, the question and his bark of laughter driving out the sombre mood.

He stayed by her side the rest of the way up, skirting round puddles filled with stagnant liquid, holding out a steadying arm at points where it got steeper.

They reached the top, where the trees thinned out and the moors stretched in front of them. Away from the cover of the trees the wind was colder, surrounding them, and Abigail hugged her woollen coat to herself.

'We're almost there.'

Ahead of him the land seemed to spread for miles: russets, reds, clumps of gorse, bracken slanted by the force of the wind, mud and green blending together, thin lines of fences beyond where the road ran. On their right, horses chewed at the ground; one, a chestnut, munched slowly, one yellow eye on them, tail flicking in the air sporadically, then it turned towards the rest of the group, its plump backside keeping them away. He loved being up there with that view, the sky seeming to stretch for miles, the fields and grass an uninterrupted blanket beneath.

'This way,' he called over the wind, holding his hat down as he turned to her.

She was standing in her own patch, arms now out by her sides, her eyes closed. Her cheeks were pink, her eyelashes clumped together from the wetness of the air, not quite rain but able to soak you right through if you let it. He found himself staring; she looked like a sprite, soon to spring off into the heather, lost in the deep green of the trees like a wild thing. She nodded at him, strands of hair loose from her chignon snatched this way and that by the wind, and he felt his stomach turn again. What would she think?

He panicked then, wondering whether she would sneer at what he was about to show her, whether he wanted to risk it.

He knew the route well, made his way down one side of a hill, the ground spongy, the air smelling of rotting leaves and damp. He felt clumsy, aware of her following him, her footsteps in the same spaces that his had occupied moments before. He slipped at one point, almost losing his balance as he tried to avoid the thorny tendrils that would snap back into her path, tear at her stockings, scratch her legs.

He could make out the roof up ahead, practically obscured by an oak tree that now towered above it; the gate was missing, the posts standing blankly with empty hinges, the pathway covered in moss and thistles, the grey paving stones long covered. He turned to see her standing under the tree, one hand on the bark, looking up at the house. Something in her face, a weariness, and he wondered again whether this had been a good idea. He drew back, towards her, holding out a hand.

'I want to tell you about this place,' he said and then, as if the expression had never crossed her face, she looked at him with wide, clear eyes and smiled slowly, taking his hand. He wanted to hold onto it long after they stopped at the peeling front door, already ajar.

'Ready?' he asked and she nodded once, quickly.

He let go of her hand to push open the door, the memory of her skin still on his as he stepped inside.

It was almost completely dark, weak light coming from boarded-up windows, thin lines highlighting a dusty stone floor, abandoned benches, a rusty bucket, roof tiles shattered in a pile. Fumbling with a match, swearing under his breath as it was blown out and then trying again, he watched her take in the room, running a finger over the back of a chair, the woven seat punched out as if someone had fallen through it, noting the low thick beams above them, the stained corners, the damp rising up the walls.

He stood in silence, hands in his pockets, as if waiting for a schoolmaster to pass judgement on his work.

She turned, her expression quizzical, one eyebrow raised. 'What is this place?'

'It's nothing yet, but it could be,' he said slowly, wondering if she knew where he might be headed. 'Look!' He drew her across the room, ducking through a doorway, a stone step walking them down a level.

Inside, the butler's sink stood abandoned under large, flaking windows; it was the view that made her suck in her breath. Even with the cloud, and the raindrops sticking to the glass, she would be able to see how far it extended, to the sea and the land beyond, south Wales a hazy strip, fields directly to their right, a line of trees to the left, and a secluded garden grown wild with weeds and long grass.

'It could be so much more, with some work.' He paused momentarily, waiting for her to remark or snort or something, but she simply looked at him with those calm eyes, listening, drinking it in. 'I want to buy it. There's a workshop too, well, a shack with holes in the roof. Here, let me show you.'

She followed him wordlessly as he pushed open the back door, dried-out leaves and mud making it stick. They stepped across an old terrace: a wooden bench, the slats long gone, a skeletal frame remaining; plant pots, empty and chipped. He wanted to show her it all, wanted her to feel the same excitement he did at the chance to make this house beautiful again. He wanted her to be swept up in his vision, to see things as he did, the house repainted, patches fixed, the bench lovingly restored and polished, the plant pots bursting with greenery.

The workshop was in truth a decaying outhouse, its thatched roof almost entirely caved in, the door propped up, unattached. He pulled it to one side to show her the empty damp space, the stench of compost and rotting wood filling their nostrils.

'I know it doesn't seem like it…' he said, noticing her face shift as she took in the dirty floor, suspicious-looking droppings in the corner. She pulled her arms around herself then, perhaps imagining rats in the corners, their yellow eyes trained on her. She stepped back and he felt his own face fall a fraction, his mouth turn down.

'I know it looks bad…' he started again.

She stepped forward; her whole body silhouetted in the doorway. 'I trust you,' she said simply. 'I can see it.'

And then she turned and looked back across the garden and up to the house and it seemed to him as if she really could see it, could picture him sitting on the roof, hammering nails into tiles, crawling over its surface to assess the damage, repairing and reworking things, bringing them back to life, could see herself in the bedroom looking out over Exmoor as she idly rearranged flowers in a vase.

He didn't know how it happened, but he moved towards her, his vision entirely made up of her face, his heart hammering as he bent down, slowly at first and then, a hand on each side of her face, smelling misty rain and the garden, he kissed her gently, brushing her lower lip. As she responded, he kissed her more urgently, pressing his body against her, pulling her into him. Then, just as suddenly, he pulled away, one hand still on her cheek.

'I'm sorry,' he breathed.

He waited for her to slap his hand away, but they seemed to stand like that for the longest time, their bodies pulsing with the moment they had just shared. And then she reached up to place her hand on top of his, drew him back to her with the other, pressed her lips against his again. They stayed like that for a minute until, laughing, they broke apart.

Something had changed on the way back down from the moor; he felt like a different man to the one who had led her up there. Older somehow, his body feeling more solid, his own. He could see his future taking shape, images flooding into his mind, a sense that they could be together. She glanced over at him, and he wondered if she too had felt things shift, wanted to know if the moment in the garden had had any effect on her. He scanned her face, relieved to see it open and bright, a different smile, a new smile for that day, this time her eyes crinkling with it, and he knew something had changed for her too.

IRINA

She had woken tired, her neck cricked from lying on the sofa, bunched up and uncomfortable. She left for the hospital immediately, not staying in the flat a second longer than she had to, whisking through her workshop and out via the beaded curtain and the shop before she could explain much more to Patricia, who hadn't expected to see her at all, full of sympathy for her mother, promises to look after the shop, for her not to worry.

She walked quickly to the car, shivering in the dress she'd been wearing the day before. Her jumpers were all in her bedroom and she hadn't wanted to go back in there. Lynton seemed like a lifetime ago, had they really been walking along the seafront less than twenty-four hours earlier? Being back in the apartment seemed to have returned her to the mood she'd been in when she'd left. She had to know what had happened. She knew that now. She hated feeling like this, as if she were being followed, watched. If she could find out more, it might stop.

She sent another email to her client, a snippier message

than before, bashed out on her mobile as she squinted at the screen. She knew he was probably out of the country on business, but she insisted he get in touch. It was urgent and she never used that word. The same out-of-office response was sent back and she puffed in frustration, her teeth gritting together to stop herself from crying out. She drove, with questions flying around the car, unthinking, into the hospital car park.

She was there when her mother stirred. It was mid-morning and Irina had been about to get coffee, her eyes red-rimmed from the lack of sleep. Seeing her mother again had made Irina feel guilty for worrying over absurd sounds and things that weren't there when her own mother was lying ill in bed. She felt more objective away from the apartment.

The machines were still there, blinking and bleeping, lines moving, numbers changing, up and down. Her mother was propped up on another pillow and the blanket had come loose along one edge, so Irina reached out to tuck it in. She was stretching across, her hair falling over her face, when she heard her mother say his name. She started, shocked.

'Joshua.'

Irina bent over the bed again, eyes darting from her mother's closed eyes to her mouth. Her lips were cracked. Had she heard her correctly?

'Joshua.'

Irina sucked in her breath, frozen over her mother's face as she watched her lips form the letters.

'I'm sorry, Joshua. I'm...'

Irina leant in closer, her hair tickling her mum's face, knowing what she had heard and desperate to hear the name spoken again. She couldn't remember the last time she'd heard her mother say it, it was a forbidden topic.

Her mother was shaking her head a fraction and Irina rested her hand on her forehead. 'It's OK, Mum. It's OK.'

Her head moved more violently; her eyes screwed up tight as if she were in pain. 'No, I need… I'm sorry, I can't…'

Irina looked on in horror as a small tear sloped down her mother's cheek and around her ear, hanging there like the saddest earring. Her eyelids fluttered and another tear fell, dripping onto the pillow.

'Mum,' Irina said in a low voice, circling her mother's hand with a thumb, 'I'm here. It's OK, you're OK.'

Her mother seemed to settle down at that, exhaling in one long breath as if she were at a yoga class and they were doing relaxation exercises. Her head stopped, her eyes remained still and then, in the tiniest voice, she whispered Irina's name.

Irina leant over again. 'Yes, Mum?'

'I'm sorry.'

Irina didn't want to leave her, but an hour passed and her mother was sleeping and Irina had to resist the urge to shake her shoulders, to wake her up, to force her to say his name again. She wanted something, needed to feel that her mother would talk about it. Was this the moment? She had to confess, to hold her mother's hand as she told her the truth that had festered inside her all these years.

She needed to get out. Looking back at the bed, she shrugged her handbag up on one shoulder. She bought a coffee from the café inside the hospital, moved down peppermint corridors hung with jaunty pictures, past signs heading every which way, to the double doors and the outside world beyond, surprised to see cars driving by, people going about their day. She finished her coffee, lingering as she stood by the entrance, making the automatic doors open and close, a nurse looking up at her from the reception desk inside.

She pulled her mobile out of her pocket before she could

change her mind, wanting to hear his voice. 'Hi, it's me,' she said, knowing her name would have flashed up on his mobile.

'Hey.' He sounded weary. Those three letters dragged out of his mouth.

She cupped one hand over the mobile as the wind whistled round her. She swallowed, knowing he wouldn't make this easy for her. She didn't blame him. 'I'm sorry. I was rude.'

'Your mum was ill, you were worried.' He sounded robotic. It wasn't in his nature to be cruel, but she could hear that he was reciting something, as if he knew she would ring and had his script prepared.

She closed her eyes. 'Yes, but I didn't need to be such a bitch.' She hoped that last sentence might make him laugh; he was always the first to break into a low chuckle, a grin spreading across his face when he was amused.

'You weren't. Look…'

He sighed and the sound made her stomach plunge. She had lost him again, he wasn't going to play her game, back and forwards, lend her a hand. She was desperate to break this tense exchange, to bring him back. 'Something happened in the flat last night. It was bizarre, a huge crash…'

'Are you OK?' he said.

She felt a sudden flare of hope. He cared. 'I'm fine, there was nothing there, but the sound was… enormous. Like the house was being torn apart.'

He had wanted to find things out, believed her when she'd told him things before. Would this pique his interest? She tucked her hair behind her ear and waited for him to reply. Perhaps he would agree to come over there? Perhaps he would invite her to stay with him again? 'It was scary,' she said, 'hearing it.' She knew she'd put on a too-high voice, a little girl needing to be cared for; his frosty silence was prompting her.

'Look, Irina—' he said. That sigh again.

She didn't let him finish. 'Will you come back with me? To Devon? I know Bill was going to tell us about the postcard and, well, I hoped—'

'There's no point,' he said quietly, cutting off whatever she was about to say next. 'I can't.'

'You can!' She laughed, it sounded forced. 'Please, I—'

'Will you talk to me about your past, what happened?' He asked the question in a firm voice. She'd heard him use that tone once before, on that beach in Brighton.

She thought of her mother in the bed upstairs, the name on her tongue. For years they had danced around each other, Irina not able to say the things she should have said all those years ago, not wanting to cause her mother more hurt. 'I… It's not as simple as… I can't…'

'I thought so,' he said in that low, steady voice.

She didn't continue; they had been there before, the same circular conversation. She knew she wouldn't tell him anything and he would get frustrated and keep probing. It wasn't that she didn't want to, a large part of her did want to, craved having someone to listen, but the moment she thought about it, actually thought about telling him, she knew she couldn't. She would have to tell him the whole truth and she couldn't let anyone know that. He would never think of her the same way again, he would hate her and she couldn't face him hating her.

'I'm sorry you feel like that,' she said, aware she was sounding sniffy, as if he'd rejected her choice of wallpaper. She sounded absurd and stiff. 'Take care,' she said, wanting now to end the phone call on her terms, lick her wounds.

He sighed slowly. 'You too, Reena.'

She felt tears thicken her throat and she swallowed, hanging up so she didn't have to reply. She blinked at the phone. Familiar feelings threatened to choke her; they had been here before.

Staring out at the car park of the hospital, cars reversing slowly, people moving between vehicles, a man at the pay station, she felt hopelessness wash over her. Exhausted from carrying around all these memories, the guilt. She thought of her mother lying a few floors above her muttering the name they never said out loud. She thought of the times Andrew had asked her, pleaded with her to talk to him. She thought of the number of times she'd lain in bed running through the events of that day. She reached up automatically, putting a hand to her cheek, the skin rigid beneath her fingertips. Would she ever be free of it?

ABIGAIL

He was waiting for her when she got back. Standing next to the hat stand, his expression lost to the shadows. She started, her body jerking involuntarily, then half-turned as if she could escape him. He had stepped forward, one flat palm closing the door, trapping her there. Her eyes rolled backwards as she took in his scent, mingled now with beery fumes, the first few words slurred before he righted himself.

'Doctor's been.'

She looked at him then, noticing a bloodied hand towel. 'What's happened? Is Connie alright? Is she hurt?'

'*She*'ll live,' he said, stressing the first part, his eyes dead.

'I should go to her.' Abigail moved to push past him.

He stepped in front of her. 'She's not here, she's in the hospital. And we don't want you scurrying away again, do we? What entices you out of the house, I wonder?' He went to put a finger to his lips, the finger slipping to one side, tapping his cheek.

She didn't answer him, her body rigid, arms thrust downwards, head strained backwards, the brim of her hat bent as she pushed against the wood. Did he know? Had he followed her? It was such a small place, eyes everywhere, had she really expected him not to find out?

'All these secrets.' He tutted, shaking his head slowly. He drew the bolt across the door, after the second attempt at ushering her in front of him, so that she was forced to move.

Did he know about Richard? About her visits to see him and his father?

She cleared her throat, eyes darting to the silver tray in the hallway, hoping that he was lying, that she might see her sister's key, her distinctive keyring, a threepence on a chain. There was nothing there, the glimmering surface containing a few pennies, nothing more.

'I should visit her, take her some things, she'll be scared.'

He shrugged, eyes crossing. 'We'll have a drink first.'

If she agreed, maybe she would get away from him quickly. She nodded once, unable to look at him now, feeling the weight of him, unsteady by her side, his eyes roaming loosely over her.

'A drink's allowed, isn't it?' His voice mocked her. 'God knows, I need one. You can tell me where you scuttle off to.' He lurched backwards before standing up straight, rolling his shoulders back and heading towards the living-room door in as straight a line as he could manage.

She followed him, not knowing what else she could do, tentative.

He was pouring whisky from a crystal carafe, the stopper already resting on its side, one glass already half-full. She had never drunk whisky before but took it when he held it out, a little off-centre. She sniffed at it cautiously, which seemed to amuse him. She looked at him as she drank, quickly, the liquid firing down her throat, the urge to cough and splutter it back up all over the carpet overwhelming, but she swallowed, kept drinking. Tears filled her eyes, her face screwed up as if she was drinking a glass of lemon juice. Her head ached with the shock of it.

He sloshed more into his glass, picking up the tumbler and directing it at her. 'You're quite different to your sister, you know.'

Were they? She wondered. She thought of her sister, impeccably turned out in her cotton dresses, the waist cinched in, neat polished shoes, her hair clipped back in a chignon, the rest of it framing her face in pinned waves. The softly spoken women who hosted coffee mornings in her beautiful living room, who had taken her in. She thought of Connie now, in the hospital, knew then what had happened, the hand moving protectively over her stomach in recent weeks, her grey face in the mornings, her trips to the bathroom after breakfast.

She wanted him to be reminded of her sister, so she asked, 'How did you two meet?' realizing as she did so that she didn't know, vague memories of him appearing, clutching drooping carnations for her mum in Bristol all those years ago.

Something flashed across his face, the expression gentler, wistful, a whisper and then gone. His mouth moved into a thin line as if he were suddenly afraid the words would tumble out if he didn't lock his lips tighter.

'I remember your wedding day. I couldn't believe there was anything more perfect than how she looked that day.' The dress she'd had hanging in her bedroom for weeks, the veiled hairpiece worn on glossy, dark hair. Her rosy pink lips full, her eyes trained on Larry, never leaving him, blushing as he took her gloved hand, as they posed for photographs on the steps of the registry office in Bristol.

'She was the prettiest girl in Bristol.' He said it as if it surprised him, clamming up again, then taking another sip of his drink. 'You were... what? Eight, nine? A little girl, a little flat-chested girl with a posy of flowers and a high laugh.'

Abigail smiled, one side of her mouth lifting, unnatural. She thought of that girl in her high-waisted dress, a satin sash draping along the floor. How had that little girl ended up here?

'Just a little girl,' he said. 'Not so little now, are you.'

He moved quickly then; she had no time to react as he removed her tumbler before it could slip from her grasp and smash into a thousand pieces. She felt light-headed, the alcohol swirling in her veins, clouding her thoughts, stopping her voice. He had taken both her hands; they felt too small, too smooth. Richard's hands were bigger, rougher, more welcome. He circled a finger on her palm in deliberate, slow movements, the pressure and feel of him making her momentarily nauseous. Her nostrils were filled with his breath, her mouth with whisky and fear.

He guided her over to the chaise longue, its cheerful peppermint shade at odds with the moment. He pushed her down onto it so that her face was level with the buttons on his trousers, the bulge of the material forcing her eyes to slide right to left before he took her chin in one hand and held it steady. With the other hand he reached down and undid the buttons one by one, his waistband loosening, the creases in his shirt imprinted on her memory. She seemed unable to move away from him, her breathing coming thicker, her chest rising and falling, her body getting hotter, palms damp, the roar of blood in her ears. It seemed that everything had slowed down then.

'You've wanted to do this since you arrived.'

Where was her sister? Where was Edith? She couldn't hear anything except the sounds in her own head, the room blurred, just him in front of her, this moment. She had to get out.

He paused, removed his hand from her face, looked down, briefly distracted, and she took her chance, pushed him away, making him stumble as she lurched past him, across the room to the French windows, which had been left open. She imagined him turning to stop her, a hand gripping her arm, his fingers round her flesh, trapping her in that room. She made it into the garden, onto the terrace, weeds starting to peek through the cracks in the paving stones, the scent of lavender overwhelming as she moved to the grass, down to the gate. He followed her, stumbling through the French windows and, as she clicked the latch down on the gate, she dared to look over her shoulder. He had fallen, one knee on the paving stones, half up. Then she was through the gate and away down the path, her head woozy from the alcohol and fear.

She wasn't aware of the path, the people walking past her, just her heartbeat and the certainty that she had to get out of there, she had to leave. She knew she was also running away from her sister, but she couldn't stop herself. With every step she felt the thread that tied her to the house stretched, stretched until, as she looked across at the turquoise strip of sea and the tops of the houses of Lynmouth, she felt it finally snap and she was free again. She couldn't go back there. How could she go back there?

IRINA

'You went with Andrew?' her mother breathed, her voice smaller in the bustle of the ward. Irina had to lean forward to catch what she had to say.

'Hmm.' Irina was brisk, getting up to pat at the bedclothes, going to fetch the nurse to fill up her mother's jug, it was nearly empty.

The corridors of the hospital seemed to stretch on forever, unfamiliar signs pointing this way and that, a vending machine, plastic bucket seats in a row. It was the smell that made her remember being there, aged eight, getting wheeled on a gurney, staring up at the strip lights above her, her face burning, her mother's heels somewhere on the linoleum behind her. Disinfectant. The scent clinging to the hairs in her nostrils, tickling her throat. Layer upon layer of bleach, over blood, over fluids, over the smell of a hundred different strangers. She was back there, men leaning over her with masks, hands tucking her into scratchy blankets, talking all around her, instructions issued, the sound of metal on metal. It made her pause for breath, one hand on the wall of the corridor as the signs swam, blurred, Irina's breathing faster, her chest constricting.

She returned, fiddled with the lamp by her mother's bed, moving it this way and that, not wanting to remain still.

'Leave that,' her mother said, lifting a hand to wave her away, the effort seemingly so momentous, she dropped it again.

Irina sat, smoothing her skirt, searching her lap for something to say. They didn't have a game to distract them, a view to look at. She heard someone cough in another room; a beeping, rhythmic but quiet, seemed to grow louder from a machine in the corner of the room. A family were huddled into a curtained cubicle, a bark of laughter and lots of shushing followed.

'I want to meet him,' her mother said, looking at Irina with her milky-blue eyes.

'I know,' she said. 'Maybe, although…' She trailed off, not wanting to admit to how she'd behaved, to see the disappointed look on her mother's face as she tried to make excuses for her rudeness. 'One day,' she said finally.

'I thought he was out of the picture,' her mother said innocently, then shooting her a quick look.

'He was.' She squirmed in her seat. Absurd to feel so uncomfortable talking about it, but they didn't delve too deeply into things like that; her mother had given up asking after him months ago. 'We're not…' She let the sentence hang, the suggestion clear.

'Oh, I see.'

A nurse walked in with a trolley and a small plastic cups of pills and handed one to her mother. She felt relieved at the interruption.

Her mother was smiling at the nurse, thanking her and for a moment she seemed like a different woman. She hadn't seen her mother around other people for years, hadn't watched her interact. She was so open, grateful for the pills, asked after the woman's son. He was fine. Irina blinked as the nurse passed her, smiling and bending down to say, 'Lovely lady, your mum.'

'How old's her son?' Irina asked, watching her mother's face change, cloud over, the familiar lines between her eyebrows, around her mouth, as she took the pills, sipped at water, let the silence stretch.

'He's six.'

They both looked away. It hurt, hearing it.

'I miss them,' Irina said suddenly, when the nurse had left, overwhelmed perhaps by the memories of the last time she was in a hospital, when she'd asked every nurse and doctor about her brother. Was he somewhere, in another room? Was he with their dad? She was older, you see, and it was her job to look after him, the worry gnawing at her.

Her mother tutted, just once. 'Let's not,' she said, in her brisk voice, looking over at the family behind the curtain.

'I want to,' Irina said, picturing Andrew's face in the car when he'd dropped her off the other day. He wanted to help her and she needed to talk about it, and one of the people she had to talk to was lying there in front of her. 'I need to tell you something… about that day.'

Her mother physically reeled, her eyes rolling into her skull so for a second Irina rose out of her chair ready to call for a nurse. Then her mother swallowed. 'I really don't think… I'm not sure…'

'Excuse me…' A head appeared between the curtains and a tall ginger-haired man was staring at her. 'I'm so sorry, but could you possibly get a nurse? I don't want to leave my wife.'

Irina got up from her chair. 'Of course,' she said, her voice strained. She went to the door of the room, looked out into the corridor at the nurses' station. Why did her mother insist on avoiding things? Couldn't she see she needed to purge herself of this thing?

'Excuse me, could you come?'

The nurse who had spoken to her earlier smiled and came over. 'Everything OK?'

'I'm not sure. It's the woman in the bed next door.'

She walked back into the room, the nurse already over with the family, the curtains still closed.

Perhaps it was being there in the hospital that made Irina bolder than normal, perhaps it was the weight of the last few weeks, the feeling of unfinished business, the presence in her shop, but she wasn't keen to drop things, to stay quiet. They needed to talk about the past, she needed to speak about it before the faces and the shapes and the secrets drowned her.

'Mum, I need to talk about it. I need to tell you—'

'Why are you doing this now, Irina?' her mother said, hands shooting up to her temples, massaging them in small circles.

'Because we never do,' she said, her voice rising in frustration. 'We just bloody skirt round things, never bloody talk about any bloody—'

'Don't! Don't!' Her mother was rubbing at her eyes. 'Don't swear.'

Irina's hands clenched into fists, her skin was sweaty, her breathing heavy. 'I'm sorry but this is ridiculous. It's what we do and I can't do it anymore, Mum.'

'I know, I know.' Her mother's voice was low, her head nodding from side to side as if she was trying to shake things free.

'Please, Mum.' Irina felt the fight drop away, her mother in a hospital bed, her anger ebbing as she glanced at the IV drip in her hand.

There was a long silence, her mother's hands raised, shielding her eyes. She looked impossibly young as she looked up at Irina.

'We will talk, next time.'

Her mother's voice seemed stronger then and for a second Irina really believed her. She was ready to get up and walk away, to give her mother one more day. Then she thought of all the other times they'd ducked out of saying the words, and her eyes filmed over as she nodded, pushing the plastic chair back against the wall.

'Next time,' she repeated in a hollow tone, knowing that they wouldn't talk about it next time, that this thing would keep chewing at her insides, burrowing into her limbs, weighing her down. 'Next time.'

ABIGAIL

She hadn't been sure where she was headed until she found herself climbing the path again, winding round corners, pushing herself on so that her chest felt tight, her breathing heavy, constricted, the rain a light sheen on her face, falling between the canopy of leaves beneath her, bouncing off the puddles on the ground, droplets dancing in the air, clinging to her face, her hands, resting on her lips, in her hair.

She had moved through Lynmouth without stopping, not able to face the cottage in the middle of the two rivers, needing time to think without their faces confusing her. She would have to leave and she couldn't have anything stopping her. Richard's face, his gentle kiss, swam into view, replaced now by another face, a hand gripping her shoulder, breath full of beer and ugly words. She swiped at her eyes, realized she was crying.

When she approached the abandoned cottage, she startled a rook. It dropped the twig it had been carrying and swept off to her left, landing a safe distance away in the branches of a tree, eyeing her warily. Ducking into the house, she stepped down onto the cobbled floor, dust collecting around the skirting boards and in the corners, lining the cracks in the walls, which bulged inwards so it seemed the house was sinking in on itself. The air was thick with the scent of neglect; she heard something rustling in the corner, turned to see a yellowing newspaper laid out on the floor for a job that had probably never even been started. Through the windows, smeared and dotted with watermarks, the outside seemed distorted, the sea and gardens, trees and bushes merging into a single wash of green and blue, the colours duller in this space. What had he seen here?

She rested her hands on the edges of the butler's sink, the ceramic cool under her hands, and closed her eyes. She pictured the windows in front of her scrubbed and cleaned, a herb pot stuffed with basil, rosemary, thyme, the smell wafting round the room, a loaf cooking in the range. The light from the kitchen throwing long rectangles of yellow onto the manicured lawn beyond, the border clipped and cut back to reveal the view to the sea, a silvery strip of calm.

Perhaps it was possible. She imagined herself then with a purpose. She would be rolling out pastry on a scrubbed pine table, Richard would be bringing in logs from outside. They would have children, rushing around by the range; she would lean down to brush flour from the little one's face and kiss him or her on the top of his head, before she, yes she, raced off again.

They would eat in the garden in the summer, looking out across the tops of the trees to the thin line of sea beyond. There would be insects chirruping intermittently and her head would be light with the cider they had made in kegs, syrupy and delicious, that clung to their lips as they kissed.

Larry wasn't there in her imaginings and her sister wasn't in a hospital. Connie would visit, she'd be relaxed, and they would sit on a blanket at the bottom of the garden and watch as their daughters played together. They would do their hair in long plaits and talk about their mum, and about the dreams they'd had before the war had ruined everything. They would walk back up to the house arm in arm, Abigail's head resting briefly on her shoulder; she would smell of honeysuckle and wine and they would giggle and sing along as Richard played music on a turntable, a lively tune that would make them kick up their legs and twist around the pine table, bringing beads of sweat to their brows, sounding out across the moors behind them, and the whole house would throb with their laughter.

Standing there now, eyes open again, she returned to the present, to the walls streaked with damp and the pockmarked wooden beams above her head. Preparing to go, she walked across the stone floor and pushed at the door, felt it give, swing out, the path now slick with heavier rain, large lumps of cloud, fat and full, hovering over the house. And yet, if she turned and half-closed her eyes, there they were in the kitchen, dancing round the table, their mouths open, the light giving them a warm glow, teeth flashing, alive and laughing.

IRINA

She didn't want to stay in the apartment and she didn't want to visit her mother again in the hospital. She prickled with the feeling that she might explode; the atmosphere between them had shifted back to exchanging shallow comments in light voices, pretending they were normal. They had years of experience. Nothing more had been said about the past and everything seemed to have fallen back into the same pattern.

Her mother would be allowed home soon with a supply of needles, insulin and a strict list of instructions on how to handle diabetes. She was shown what to do in the hospital, Irina looking away as the needle went in, squeamish at the thought. She promised herself she wouldn't let things drop this time, she would tackle her mum when she was at home, not in the hospital. She wondered who she was fooling. How many more years would go by in this strange silence, their faces growing more shadowy?

The apartment made her restless too, and the workshop was filled with questions; she knew that the feeling wouldn't disappear until she got some answers. She traced a line over the postcard, the face in the brooch, placed the feather in the palm of her hand, closing it in her fist. She needed to go back and, after writing a rushed note to Patricia, she found herself in the car again, the empty seat next to her a reminder that she was alone once more.

The hill down into Lynmouth seemed even steeper, the escape tracks making her grip the steering wheel even tighter; she edged her body forward as she inched down the hill, imagining winter months when ice would make it even more precarious. She was relieved to reach the bottom and cross the low stone bridge, the river babbling underneath. She looked across the road, out along the harbour wall and to the sea beyond, the still water, the outline of Wales in the distance. One of the postcards lying on the passenger seat beside her showed the same view. She felt her hand hovering over the objects she'd brought along to show Bill. She'd phoned him the night before. She felt certain that he could help her, that the sightings and sounds would end once she'd found out more, that everything was connected to the bureau.

Turning into a side road, she wound her way round houses, shops and a hotel, wrought-iron balconies lining its first floor, large floor-to-ceiling windows on the ground floor opening onto a terrace. On the outside wall she could make out a small circular plaque but was too far away to see what it said.

The car dipped down, following a slope in the road, the sun obscured by a row of cottages on her right. She went to press the brake. Something was wrong. She cried out at the shock of it. Her foot felt wet, drenched suddenly, her other foot submerged too, dragging through icy water in the footwell. She lost sight of her surroundings, her speed, didn't have time to think before the water seemed to be up to her knees, making her gasp with the cold as she felt her jeans sticking to her, the water reaching over her thighs, pooling in her lap, her left hand snatched from the gear stick, her hand dripping. She glanced down, not understanding: everything looked dry. She was pressing the brake now, pumping it hopelessly, feeling her bottom lift from the seat as the water rose over her stomach, over the steering wheel, her hands, over her breasts, up to her shoulders.

She was taking great gulps of air as it inched over her shoulders; she cried out as the freezing cold hit her bare neck, ran down the collar of her jumper, watery fingers of ice. She knew she had to get out of the car, she was going to sink beneath the water, was moving her face up towards the roof of the car, felt the water creep over her chin, her right arm, as she scrabbled for the door; needing the release, she took a breath and the water leaked into her mouth and over her nostrils. Her hand gripped something, she pulled on it, her brain a fog of panic; the door released, the water receding as she toppled sideways, choking on it, pressing with her left hand for her seatbelt, needing to get out. She found the catch, dragged her body through the door, felt the rough pavement underneath her rising up, her hands on grit, the shock of the ground. She was gasping for air, blinking, aware of the water still clinging to her, her clothes sticking and heavy.

Somewhere nearby someone was speaking to her, the voice distant, incoherent, her ears still full of the water, the cold. She was shivering.

'Are you alright? Miss? Are you alright?'

She looked down at her hands; they seemed pale against the tarmac of the road, blurred. Gradually she focused: the knuckles, the small scar on her right index finger, her fingernails, bitten. She could hear the voice, louder now, closer.

'Can I get someone? Do you need me to call for help?'

She looked up in the direction of the voice, saw the hem of a skirt, pleated in the middle, a long brown coat, mohair, buttoned, a woman, grey curls, a worried look on her lined face. Her mouth opening and closing as the words tumbled from her, leaning on her stick.

'I could call someone.'

Irina found her voice, the ground hard beneath her, aware then of the cool of the day, looked about her at her car, the door open, a car edging past, the driver peering round at her. She wasn't wet. There was no water. She looked at her hands again, her breathing coming a little more easily now. There wasn't a puddle.

'I...'

She couldn't explain it, her chest tight, rising and falling quickly.

'I... It was...'

'There, there...' the woman said, a hand on her shoulder. 'You've obviously had a shock. Come on now, you catch your breath.'

The feeling was returning to her body, her knees were hurting, scraped on the rough surface of the road, the pain sudden and acute, making her wince. She shifted on the ground, placing a hand out in front of her to push herself up.

'Take it easy now,' the woman said, stepping back.

'Thank you. I... I'm not sure...'

She felt light-headed as she stood, swaying slightly, one hand on her car door to steady herself. The day came into focus, clouds scudding above her, someone emerging from one of the cottages, nodding at them both as he passed. Her car was sitting in the road, the handbrake on, though she didn't remember applying it, the upholstery dry as a bone, the items from the bureau lying on the passenger seat. She wavered, gripped by a sudden fear. She couldn't get back in the car. The older woman was hovering near her now, clearly not wanting to leave her there.

'I'm sorry,' Irina said, sluggish, the words slow, deliberate. 'I don't know what happened, but I'm fine now.'

The woman pursed her lips, lifted a gloved hand as if she were about to say something, then dropped it back to her side. She adjusted her collar. 'Well, if you're sure...' The woman's eyes lingered on her face, an almost imperceptible flick to the scar, questions swallowed.

'Thank you, you are kind,' Irina said, feeling a blush building, realizing traffic had slowed behind her, a car tooting as it passed. The woman shook her bag at it, muttering something.

'Well then...' the woman said and turned to leave. 'You take care now.'

Irina took a breath, stared at the open door to her car, saw that it looked the same as it always did, the same faded patch on the driver's seat, the same map thrown carelessly in the passenger footwell. Everything as expected, and yet she imagined herself back in there, her body suspended in the cold water, her hands finding glass, feeling their way along, her vision blurring as the water seeped over her face, the fear that she'd be trapped there.

She shook her head, determined not to return there. It had been a strange daydream, that was all. She glanced at the brooch, feather and postcards on the passenger seat. A daydream, that was all. Ducking down, she started the car quickly, fumbling with the seatbelt, releasing the handbrake, a glance in her mirror, a moment where she thought she saw something else, an enormous mound of debris, then a blink and it was simply the street, the row of houses winding away from her into the hills behind. She reached the bottom of the slope and turned left up the hill and away to Lynton, her body seeming to let out a sigh as she emerged back into the sunshine.

ABIGAIL

She hadn't wanted to go back, descending from the hill, her head pounding with a dull headache but calmer than when she'd left. The rivers were higher with the recent rain, the water flowing effortlessly around stones, carrying loose leaves and branches, sweeping things up and moving them on and out to sea. The three cottages stood between them both, a haven away from the water. She found herself hammering on the door, the windows looking blank, the curtains pulled across, hanging still. A seagull perched warily on the gatepost, eyeing her like a watchman. She turned her back on it and knocked another time, wanting to see Richard, needing to see him. As the silence continued, she felt foolish for having come, standing there miserably, goosebumps on her skin as the wind washed round her, through her coat, played with her hair. There was no other door for her to hammer on, no one else she could turn to. Even if there had been, she would still have chosen this door.

As if someone had heard this last thought, a voice called out, 'It's on the latch,' and she realized with a quick lurch of guilt that Martin would be struggling to get to the door. 'It's open,' the voice persisted and with that last sentence she felt courageous enough to nudge at the door, pushing it open to reveal the clutter of the hallway, Richard's cap tossed on a side table, muddied trousers hanging up to dry, salt marked in streaks up the legs, still wet around the hem. The place smelt of dirty ocean and men, seaweed and mothballs.

'It's me,' she said, relieved to be inside.

Martin's expression when she turned into the room was a complex mixture of annoyance and surprise. It was replaced almost instantly by the warm smile he then conjured, but for a moment she panicked. Of course he didn't want her descending on him in this way, disrupting his peace and quiet, forcing her company onto him.

'These damn legs,' he said, smacking the flat of his palm onto a thin thigh. 'I forget sometimes, go to get up and then realize they're bloody useless to me. I'm sorry for the language, but...' His words petered out, the palm going down again, fingers plucking uselessly at the fabric of his trousers as if he might coax his leg back to life. He brooded for a few more moments as Abigail lingered in the doorway, one hand up on the doorframe, not sure whether she should make her excuses, not wanting to, wavering.

'Well, now you're here, let's have a glass of something,' he said, reaching round to pull on the handle of a narrow oak drinks cabinet and drawing out two crystal tumblers and a bottle of reddish liquid with something bobbing around inside it.

'Sloe gin,' he explained, chuckling at her expression. 'Stop standing over me as if you're about to check my spelling.' He indicated the armchair opposite, the worn headrest.

When she sat, she breathed in deeply, imagining herself inhaling Richard's scent, his curious mixture of the outside, the salt water, and his skin, warm and deep, like oak. She reddened as she realized she'd closed her eyes and Martin grinned at her, one front tooth overlapping another as he handed her a glass.

'Lovely,' she said, worrying about the berries floating on the surface. She peered at the glass with narrowed eyes and a low chuckle came from opposite her.

'Richard gives me the same look, but you'll see,' Martin said, toasting her before raising the glass to his lips.

She sipped at it, warmed instantly by the liquid that soothed her throat and left a fruity residue coating her tongue. She sipped again, sinking back into the armchair, feeling her muscles loosen, from her throat down, so that she was soon wiggling her toes in appreciation. She had tried two different drinks in one day, but here the alcohol made her feel relaxed, slipping into her stomach effortlessly, leaving sweetness on her lips. The whisky had felt like it was burning her insides, tearing through her body.

'A convert,' he said, a satisfied expression on his face.

They sat for a while in perfect silence. She could have been back in Bristol before the war, with her own mum. Both bundled up in the sitting room on the velvet sofa, the odd cough or comment bringing them back to each other but mostly her mum silently sewing, Abigail curled up reading. Just the gentle rhythm of the grandfather clock in the hall, the odd sound from someone calling outside, and their steady breathing.

'So, you going to tell me why you tried to batter my door down then?'

'I didn't.... Well, I...' She flushed as she spoke, hiding behind the rim of her glass, not sure what she could share. 'I'm sorry. I was passing and I wanted to see Richard.'

'I sensed that from the knocking, thought your fist would

break through the wood.' He chuckled as he continued. 'He left an hour or so ago and he won't be back till later, they're checking the salmon traps.'

She nodded, wanting to hide there forever. She took another sip, half-finished sentences clogging the back of her throat.

He let her drink her drink, one hand absent-mindedly rubbing at his knee. 'All alright up there on that hill then?' he asked, turning to look at her.

She wondered if he could see inside her head; for a moment she was sure he understood. 'All alright,' she repeated in a quiet voice.

'Your sister looking out for you?'

She took a gulp of her drink, one hand pleating her skirt. The answer emerged in a whisper. 'Yes.'

She felt a dull ache in her stomach for her sister, alone in the cottage hospital in Lynton. She knew she had to get back, needed to see her, to be there for her. She wondered if it had happened before, and how many times. She thought of the longing hand placed on a stomach, the lingering look at a baby in a pram and felt her own insides wrench.

Martin tapped a fingernail on the glass, his mouth opening, a brief pause, before lifting the drink to his mouth. 'You know you always have a place to stop by if you need it,' he said, his face kind, his words wrapping round her like a scarf.

She swallowed. 'Thank you, and for the drink,' she added as he waved her words away with one hand.

'Pah, think nothing of it.'

She walked over to him then, bending to kiss him on the cheek. He had missed a bit shaving, had a patch of bristles on his neck and chin, which was now quickly reddening.

'You get along,' he said. 'I'll tell Richard you stopped by. And Abigail…'

She paused in the doorway, one hand up on the frame, her back to him.

'If you need us, you know where we are.'

She nodded, feeling hot tears at the back of her eyes as she headed out of the front door. All around her the two rivers wound round the village, Richard out there somewhere checking salmon traps. She imagined him then, standing knee deep in the water as the river rushed past him, the wind whisking his hair into spikes. She breathed in slowly, taking in the whole village, houses rising up around her, the trees cocooning the place, keeping it safe. This felt more like home. She started down the path, the rain gone for now, the sky made up of ribbons of lilac and pink. It was going to be a beautiful evening.

IRINA

She shouldn't have booked the same B & B. It felt all wrong. She couldn't help but compare her mood now with her mood then, with Andrew, fresh-faced with a hint of possibility. Had he forgiven her? Would he want to see her again? She was still shaky after the episode in the car. If he'd been there, it would have been so much better. She remembered the receptionist, bored and unwilling, being brought round by Andrew talking about the match he'd been streaming on the internet; it was a Manchester derby and the receptionist had money on City to win. Andrew had the ability to do that with people, to put them at ease, whereas she had the opposite effect – they would look anywhere but at her face, eyes darting across the floor because they didn't want to be seen staring, then a last peek before they left, as if they wanted to remember how awful it really was, and the eyes flicking away again, cheeks flushed with embarrassment. Or pity, she was never sure.

She threw her bag on the bed, not caring if she unpacked or not, keen to get down to Lynmouth and meet Bill. She walked down the cliff path this time, wanting to avoid the jaunty railway, the tourists gabbling about its unique status, how much water was used, how it was the only one of its kind. The path was steep, some parts had steps carved into it, iron railings to help the descent. A stone wall blocked her view of gardens beyond, the backs of houses tantalizing: dormer windows, slate roofs, chimneys hinted at as she passed.

She looped around and down, winding her way gradually, her legs wanting to run, the weight pushing her forward, propelling her down the path. She paused at a lookout point, the sea framed by a canopy of trees, a ledge just beneath the path, the trunk of a tree creating a perfect resting place for admiring the view. Today she could see the outline of south Wales ahead, the land enticingly close, almost near enough to touch. She stopped there, convinced for a second that she heard the voice of a woman, just once, a sentence and then a giggle, infused with warmth. She looked down at the ledge, nothing there, then behind her, wondering if it was someone further up the path. Only the birds chirruped back. Speeding up, she told herself she was being hyper-sensitive to the sounds. A gull swooped across her field of vision, its wings straight out, buffeted by the breeze.

She arrived outside The Rising Sun and looked at the cottage next door, sensing movement behind the thin lace curtains on the ground floor. The flaking cottage door opened and Bill, putting on a flat cap, moved onto the stone step outside.

'Let's get a pasty,' he said, as if he'd known her for years.

She looked up at him and smiled. 'Good idea.'

They walked together down Mars Hill and onto the high street again, Bill shaking his head as she made for a nearby shop that sold pasties.

'It's an easy mistake to make, but you don't want to be

doing that. Come on,' he said, linking arms with her as if it were the most natural thing in the world.

She drew back a fraction, worried about his proximity and smiling as he stopped to ensure he was on the side of the traffic; her father had always done that. The thought brought with it the sting of pain she had come to expect, perhaps faded slightly over the years but still enough to take her next breath away.

'I used to work down on the boats.' He indicated the harbour to the left of them. 'Not so much work anymore.'

They bustled into a café on the corner of Watersmeet Road and Bill refused her money and headed to the counter, depositing her and his hat at a table by the window; it had a small sprig of daisies in a flowery vase and a plastic menu in italic script. She could smell toast and freshly baked bread. Large cakes were scattered over the counter in see-through cake domes, all thick icing and soft-looking sponge. She hoped they might have time for something sweet. Her mother's favourite was coffee and walnut, Irina used to make them for her regularly. She thought of her mother with her insulin injections and her new diet; she needed to learn some new recipes.

She watched Bill as he ordered, leaning heavily on the counter, wiping his glasses as he talked to the waitress. Irina wanted to burst straight into her questions, devour everything he knew, or could guess, about the writer of the postcards, try to work out whose brooch it was, whether any of the items had any meaning to him. He had known a Richard and a Martin but she had left before finding out what he knew about them.

She got up to pull out his chair for him as he returned from the counter.

'That's my job,' he said, but didn't sound displeased.

She went to speak, but the waitress interrupted with two plates, a pasty chopped in half so that the meat and onion were spilling out, steam rising, instantly filling her mouth with the flavour, and a side salad that seemed more for show. Bill was already scraping his away as if it were infecting the pasty with its healthiness. He picked up one half in his hands, holding the crust. 'That's how they used to eat them in the mines, like a handle,' he said, before biting into it.

Irina cut into hers with a knife and fork and earned a roll of his eyes. 'I'm not a miner,' she protested, which made him smile; a warmth spread through her.

'So, what happened here?' he said, indicating her cheek.

For a moment she didn't know what he was referring to and then it sunk in as she followed the path of the half-eaten pasty in his hand, which was pointing at her face. People didn't usually ask her so directly, not like that, and she found her mouth opening and closing as if she were a guppy fish.

'Accident,' she said, 'when I was young.' She swallowed the pasty, the meat sticking in her throat as her head screamed at her, 'Liar. Liar. Liar.' She licked her lips, forcing a smile onto her face as she said to him, 'I wanted to know more about Richard and Martin.'

There must have been something in her expression because he didn't pursue it. As he started to speak, she realized she had missed the start, her mind still turning over his question and her reply. Her lie. It had been no accident. It had been her fault.

'... Richard's dad, Martin, we worked together on the boats, he were a great fellow, bit older than my own dad but younger in spirit, if you know what I'm saying?'

She nodded, back with him, imagining them in the harbour together working on the boats.

'Then his accident, he couldn't be on the boats anymore, his legs.'

'What happened?'

'He fell, between two boats, crushed them, they never set properly.'

'And Richard?'

'His son,' he said quietly, putting his pasty down on his plate, taking off his glasses to rub at the lens. 'We were friends.'

He said this in a different voice and she was already bracing herself for what would come next. Then Bill smiled, popped his glasses back on. 'Neither of us much liked the work. I got terrible seasickness and he was always happier on dry land. You know,' he said, looking up suddenly, 'it's the oddest thing.'

'What is?'

'I thought I saw him, a few weeks ago now, up on Lynmouth Hill. I got such a shock, he was so old. I suppose he'd think the same about me, but it couldn't have been him, not really, it's been more than a lifetime. Maybe you conjured him!'

She felt a little buzz of shock that somehow she had stirred things up and was making Bill see people from his past he hadn't thought of in years.

'So, who is "A"? She seems close to the pair of them?'

He took the postcard from her once more, turning it this way and that as he read the words again, slowly this time. His mouth formed the letter 'A' as if he were running through the alphabet and trying to find the right connection. Perhaps it had been another friend of theirs? An Alistair or an Andrew? She shook that name from her immediately, she didn't want to think about him. She felt strongly that the writer was a woman.

'Did he have a girlfriend?'

'Was he stepping out with someone? That's what we called it then.' Bill chuckled, seeing her expression. He thought about it, raised one finger to his lip, his eyes scanning the air above her as he recalled those days.

'There was a girl,' he said. 'She was new to the place, I remember that.'

Irina found herself edging forward in her chair. A couple of letters had hinted that she was new to the village, as if the writer was remembering finding their way around the place.

'Abigail,' he said suddenly, seeming far younger than his eighty or so years. 'There was a girl called Abigail. It was years ago, mind. I might be mistaken.'

He wasn't: she knew it. The moment he said the name, Irina felt a tingle in her limbs, a tiny shock, as if someone somewhere had switched her on. That's right, it seemed to say, that's the name.

'Abigail.' She tried it out, slowly rolling the name over in her mouth. She felt a spark of recognition and was certain. That was the girl, the girl who had written the postcards and letters with such warmth. Abigail, who seemed so full of life, so open and generous.

'I didn't realize she knew Richard and Martin. I'm amazed Richard kept that to himself, he was always one for talking...' Bill chuckled as he said it, Irina feeling her toes curl in excitement. Then Bill stopped, a line appearing between his eyebrows. 'I haven't thought about that name in an age, they used to say... Well, we shouldn't go into all that – what did you want to know?' Bill asked, seeming to wrench himself back to the little café.

'When do you think she was writing?' Irina asked. 'When were they courting?' Her voice stuck on the old-fashioned word and she suddenly wished Andrew were there to nudge her with a smile. There was no address, no dates to go by, just the words 'Lynton', and the fact they were all written in the same hand.

'Well it must have been the start of the decade, before it all, because Richard left after that.'

'Before it all?'

'Things changed after 1952.' He tapped his lips with a short-stubbed pencil.

'Why was that?' she asked, frowning as she thought back over her history. It was the year before the Queen's coronation, but beyond that she was blank.

Bill looked up, his eyes widening in surprise, as if the answer were perfectly obvious. 'That was the year of the flood,' he said simply, glancing again at the front of the postcard.

'Flood?' she repeated.

Bill stared at her, nodding. 'You been living under a rock here? A terrible thing. Lynmouth were never the same again.'

'How do you mean?'

He took the last bite of his pasty and wiped his mouth with a napkin. 'I think you better come and see something.'

MARY

Joe was already in the pub before her shift started, sitting on a bench at the bar staring into his tankard. She moved around him, wiping down the surfaces, restocking glasses, checking the barrels. She imagined briefly that his eyes were following her around the room, exaggerated the sway of her hips, snatched glances at him through lowered lashes. She had wanted to fool herself into thinking he might be interested, but she couldn't forget the way his eyes lit up when she pulled out the latest letter from Abigail, the wistful way he spoke about her, reminding her of the time she'd played carols on the upright before Christmas, when she'd dragged them all out of the pub to look at the full moon, hugging herself as she stared up into the navy sky.

Abigail had always been the one to turn heads; she had something about her, in an arched eyebrow, a snatch of laughter, a touch on a stranger's arm. She shimmered. That was the word; everything was a bit brighter with her. Thinking about her now gave her an ache again. She had saved the money, had written to Abigail telling her she'd arrive on the tenth of

August, felt her shoulders lighten with the thought that soon they'd be together again, that life could begin again, as if she'd just been treading water, waiting for things to start.

She topped Joe up, moving back behind the bar, pulled on the barrel tap to fill another glass, her mind busy with steamers and beaches and sunshine and foreign languages. She couldn't help grinning as she tapped at the till and wiped the surface.

'You're happy, Mary,' Joe commented, raising a glass her way.

She looked at him, feeling her chest expand. 'I am.' A small laugh burst from her. 'I absolutely am.'

ABIGAIL

Abigail hadn't the strength to reply and say no and as the tenth crept up she wondered just what she was going to do. Mary in the house? She wouldn't allow it. She fretted, played with the fraying sleeves of her cardigan. Where could she take her? How would she explain?

She hadn't left her sister's side since Connie had returned home, white-faced and even thinner, her eyes filling with tears when she thought Abigail wasn't looking. She had tried to hug her, but her sister froze in her arms, her body stiff as Larry watched them both. Connie was quieter than normal, silvery strands at her temples, her face unusually bare. They seemed to spend days in the living room, rain streaking the French windows, Edith bringing them endless pots of tea. Larry appeared, making Abigail slosh the liquid, move across the room to sit at her sister's side. Connie, observing her, a small frown creasing her forehead as she looked at her husband, then back at Abigail.

She wouldn't bring Mary to the house. The day arrived and she met the coach, bundling Mary down into the shade of a line of trees, along the path that ran next to the river. Recent rain meant it was patchy with puddles, their shoes sticking and sucking at the earth, specks of mud flecking their calves as she kept up the pace, Mary shifting a carpet bag on her shoulder.

'Wait,' Mary called from behind her. 'Abi, stop!' she huffed.

Abigail didn't slow up, pulled at a gate and beckoned her to follow. They were walking behind the cottages, the small gardens empty, sheets hanging, billowing in the breeze that wafted down the valley, the sound of a baby crying from the upstairs window of Richard's neighbours. She pictured Beth rocking him back and forth, whispers in his ear, soothing nonsense so that his eyelids drooped and he slept, a fist curled tightly on top of her chest, his breathing calm. Abigail almost wanted Richard to look out of his bedroom, to see her and Mary so that she could share her secret. Instead, she continued on, with Mary straggling behind her, taking her out of the village to the path that led into the trees and up onto the flat stretch of the moors where Richard's cottage stood, smiling crookedly at them from its perch overlooking the valley.

Mary was holding her sides, red in the face, one hand up to fan herself between snatches of words. 'Some of us aren't used to hills like these.'

'It's Park Street, just with a lot more trees and fewer shops.' Abigail laughed, feeling lighter now that they were out of the village and away from prying eyes. She ran over to her friend, grinning like a lunatic as she seized her in a hug. 'It's good to see you, Mary.'

Mary shook her head, her breathing laboured. 'What's going on, Abi?'

It was too soon to tell her everything and she didn't want

to cloud the moment. 'Come on,' she said, hauling her bag up and carrying it the rest of the way. 'We can talk there.'

'At your sister's?'

She stopped abruptly on the path, Mary stumbling into her. 'We're not going there; we're going somewhere else.'

She could sense Mary's questions all the way up the path, felt her eyes on her as she deliberately remained two paces ahead, moving the bag from shoulder to shoulder, her hair sticking to her dampening forehead.

They arrived at the cottage, the door snagging as she put a shoulder to it.

'Who lives here?' Mary asked, holding her bag to her chest and stepping into the dark interior.

Abigail turned and took a breath. 'Right now... you do.'

Mary stood staring at her, slack-jawed, looking around the space as Abigail fretted over lighting the edge of the paper, the wood taking a while to catch as she blew on it. She had spent an hour scrubbing the table, the floor, but the room still seemed dingy and rough and she felt her toes curl inwards as Mary moved around it, running a finger along surfaces, half-opening her mouth and then closing it again.

Abigail made them both tea with lemon, heating the pan over the fire she'd built, revealing two Eccles cakes she'd bought in the village. They took their mismatched plates and cups out into the garden, which was littered with weeds, dandelions and flowers of every variety. It was an incredible sight and she enjoyed watching Mary's face as she took it all in: the wild borders shot through with bright colours, the sea dancing with light as the sun smashed through the clouds before dipping behind them again, the colours faded and mute, always changing.

It was a strange day, the sun hot when it emerged, and they sat feeling the full heat of it on their cheeks, faces tilted towards the sky as they breathed out, sipping at their tea and wiping crumbs from the Eccles cakes off their skirts. The grass itched under their legs, sweat now collecting under Abigail's knees and armpits. She didn't want to leave their spot, she felt carefree once more, as if she and Mary were back on the Downs in Bristol, without a care in the world. She plucked a daisy from the ground, tucking it behind her ear, telling herself all this would work.

'So, tell me,' Mary said cocking her head to the left, her feet stretched out on the grass.

Abigail removed the daisy from behind her ear, tugging at each petal until she was left with just the green stalk. 'I didn't want you staying at the house.' Her throat moved up and down as she swallowed.

'I can see that.' Mary laughed, clearly trying to lighten up her friend. 'I wanted to see the peppermint chaise longue.'

Abigail didn't return the smile and Mary's mouth turned down too, her voice lower as she took her friend's hand. 'Just say it. What's happened? What is it?'

Abigail took a breath, her chest rising with it, filling her with the confidence she needed perhaps. Then in a rush, as if she were expelling it, she said, 'It's my brother-in-law, it's Larry. Well…' She looked away, a frown on her face. 'I don't want you living there.' Her neck felt hot and she flapped her hands like fans in front of her face.

Mary had started a fraction, her eyebrows shooting up. She licked her lips, a nervous tic that Abigail had forgotten about until that moment. 'He's violent?' she asked in a slow voice, watching Abigail's reaction as she said it, glancing at her bare arms, as if expecting to see faded bruises, finger marks.

'No, he's not violent.' Abigail was speaking carefully, every syllable a struggle. 'He's… He's something else.' She felt the blush creep into her cheeks and looked away, out at the horizon, the solid line of Wales in the distance, not wanting to look back at Mary.

'What's he done?'

Abigail paused for a second. 'He is… It's small things sometimes, but, well, the other day he tried to… He was going to…' She glanced up at Mary, not wanting to speak the words, but one look at her friend and she was transported back to Bristol, to all those times they had shared every thought. The desire to finally say something allowed it all to burst out in a great rush of fits and starts. She told her everything, the looks, the feelings, ending with Larry pinning her to the couch, how she'd run.

'I'm frightened,' she admitted, staring at the grass, tears pooling in her eyes before she swiped them away. 'Stupid, I know. I know it sounds… Well, I know nothing…'

Mary knelt up and shuffled across to her, leaning down to wrap her arms around her, resting a cheek on her hair. 'It's not nothing.'

Abigail's body juddered as she felt Mary's arms around her. 'How silly.'

She felt Mary's body stiffen. 'It's not silly.'

Abigail pushed her away, tried to smile, to laugh, dabbing at her eyes and wiping her nose. 'I'm a mess.' She took Mary's hand, squeezed it tightly. 'I'm so glad you're here.'

They looked back at the house then, the roof caved in in one corner, the tiles missing, broken on the floor around it, the cracked glass smeared with years of grime.

'I know it's not perfect,' Abigail said, the worry creeping back into her voice, 'but the weather is warm and I can try to bring some more things. It won't be long and we can make a plan.'

Mary looked around her, one eyebrow raised. 'Can you stay with me?'

'Soon,' Abigail reassured her, her voice firm, 'we can leave. Exeter perhaps. I can find work as a secretary or a typist. I'm a little rusty but I can learn.'

Mary nodded. Abigail could see she was trying not to worry about the moment she'd be left alone, trying to be strong for her.

'I'm so sorry, I should have stopped you coming,' Abigail said, feeling the guilt twisting her stomach, wishing things could be simpler.

Mary put a hand over hers. 'I want to be here.'

Abigail gave her a watery smile. 'Me too.'

'Well,' Mary said, getting up and turning towards the house, arms folded as she assessed it, 'tell me what I need to know.'

Abigail pulled herself up, feeling the sun on her back. 'There's a well at the bottom, but you'll have to boil the water. Richard has a small gas heater and I've found a couple of saucepans and things. I've left tins in the cupboards, not much, but I can bring you up fresh bread from the village and keep you supplied. Long enough for us to make a plan.'

'Ah yes, Richard…' Mary tipped her head, amusement in her eyes.

'He's been… Well, he's…' Abigail trailed off, not sure how to describe Richard, feeling a warm glow in her stomach as she said his name.

Mary nudged her and laughed.

Then Abigail really was back in Bristol, before her mum died, and anything seemed possible. For the first time in an age she felt her shoulders lighten, as if she had set down a great weight.

'Come on then, city girl, I better explain things a little better.'

IRINA

She followed Bill back up the high street, towards The Rising Sun. Below them to their right, some hopeful soul had lined up striped deckchairs along the grassy bank next to the river. Irina was too caught up in Bill's mood to take in anything more. He was walking with purpose, headed straight to a building opposite the harbour. She was right behind him, shrugging her handbag strap back over her shoulder, her mind full of questions.

He indicated a staircase to the left of the building and stood to let her move past him and up them. Irina pushed open the door at the top, struck by the smell of wood and furniture polish as she stepped inside. She could have been back in the shop.

They walked into a small rectangular room lined with old newspaper prints and posters. A large model of the village in a glass case dominated the centre of the room. It was incredible, so many intricate details on display, roads, houses, locations marked out on it, the green hills and trees surrounding it. People moved around the display, reading the words below the model, pausing to watch an old newsreel playing on a television set in one corner. Irina looked around at Bill; he'd removed his hat and was staring at two plaques on one wall. She moved over to join him, slowly scanning the names, many with the same surnames, ages written next to them, a realization building.

'Oh.' She felt the breath leave her body as she understood what she was looking at.

Bill shifted around to look at her. 'It's a memorial hall to remember that night. I haven't been in here for a while.'

Irina touched his upper arm as she moved away from him. She circled the room, other visitors nodding at her as she passed them. She sat and watched a loop of newsreels, the images all in black and white but no less shocking. She read the newspaper articles collected in a folder, studied the model, recognized some familiar places, confused by the layout at times, realizing how much must have changed. Bill hadn't left his spot, was waiting for her to move back over to him, pushed his glasses back up his nose as she approached.

She gestured at the door and they left in silence, crossing the road and making for a bridge over the river, both instinctively needing space, somewhere to sit and reflect. They settled themselves on a bench just before the bay curved away from them, Wales clear in the distance, a navy silhouette ahead of them over the sea.

'So now you know,' he said, eyes on the horizon, a sad smile as he turned to glance at her, seeming older suddenly, the bags under his eyes more obvious, his shoulders drooping.

'It must have been terrible.'

Bill nodded slowly. 'Terrible. It took years for the village to recover. So many people left.'

'Not you.'

Bill gazed at the curve of bay, at a family sitting on towels eating sandwiches. 'Not me, no. It's always been home.'

'So, you think "A", Abigail, was caught up in it all?' She realized as she said it that she hadn't seen Abigail anywhere on the plaques.

'Did you see the name at the bottom?' Bill asked. '"An Unknown Woman"?'

Irina nodded. She had spotted the words, wondered briefly how it was that someone hadn't been identified. The spot where her age should have been written had been left blank, just two dashes where the numbers should have been. 'I thought it might have been a tourist.'

Bill nodded. 'It might have been, and some think it was, but…' Irina turned to look at Bill as he went on, twisting his cap in his hands. 'Well, the body washed up some miles away and was hard to recognize, but this woman, a very smart sort, married to a councillor, she was convinced. I remember her, that day, looking at the body. She said it was her.'

'Abigail?' Irina whispered.

Bill nodded. 'Abigail.'

'I don't understand, why did no one believe her? Surely someone else could have identified her too.'

'Well this woman's husband was there, thought she was wrong, and others were missing too, it was tourist season… It wasn't like now, Irina, with DNA tests and more. No one else came forward, no one was sure, so she was buried with the others up in Lynton. But I never forgot that woman's face. She was certain.'

MARY

Mary found the silence disturbing at first: no neighbours, no chatter, no buses, no bicycle bells. The moor stretched out behind the house, mist stealing over the fields, animals silhouetted in the early-morning light. Then the cacophony of the birds nesting in the trees at the bottom of the garden, swooping for twigs, a caw and a flap if she tapped on the glass, watching them fly up and away.

Bristol had never been quiet, Bristol had been full of children playing hopscotch in the street, bounding down the cobbled roads, sellers moving door to-door, men bustling along the harbour, crowded into the pubs, spilling into the streets holding tankards and making noise. She hadn't noticed the hubbub of traffic, the distant sound of a ship's horn or the hundreds of footsteps marching places until they were gone.

Now she felt as if the whole world could have sunk into the sea and she was the last woman alive, walking over the moors, face flushed, her hands brushing the top of the grass. She built fires in the evening and tried to hum and talk aloud to fill the silence, had never been one for reading, unlike Abi, who had spent days with her nose in a book. She found an old croquet mallet in the shed, and a ball, and batted it across the lawn back and forth, rain coating her arms as she played on, desperate to be moving. She wanted to be angry at Abigail – the start of their grand adventure and she was stuck in a wet corner of north Devon waiting for what? Then she thought of Larry, knew she needed to stay, to help Abigail.

She had only been there a few days and yet it felt like she was the witch in the cottage in the forest, ageing and gnarled. She jumped on Abigail when she arrived with bread and supplies, desperate to hear her news and fill the house with their voices. She couldn't visit every day, so when she was there it felt like heaven, them curled up on the sofa together, their voices chattering. Yet every time Mary outlined a new plan, a new chance for them to leave, she felt Abigail withdrawing, not wanting to meet her eye, something tying her to the village.

The rain was insistent today, driving her inside, stuck on a sagging settee making shapes out of a discarded load of newspapers, folding and tearing and propping them up on the floor around her so it looked like she was making paper companions.

Getting up to boil more water, she heard a noise and ducked down by the sink, one eye on the garden. Abigail always came in from the side path, she knew Mary wouldn't want to be startled and so she'd whistle or call her name.

This was different. A cough, foreign and loud, forced her to dart her eyes around the kitchen for something she could protect herself with. A muddied trowel sat on the table and she snatched at it, emerging from the kitchen holding it aloft, the figure in the garden leaning over a patch of earth to her left. 'Who are you?' she called in the most authoritative voice she could muster, as if she wasn't the one encroaching. She wondered for a second if this man owned the house and she would be turfed out.

The figure yelped and tumbled straight into the nettle patch, scrambling back out, eyes all white, one hand to his chest. 'What the…? Who…? Jesus… Sorry…'

Mary lowered the trowel. The man was around her age, good-looking, with ruddy cheeks and green eyes, flecks of yellow in the irises.

'Richard?' she asked, Abigail's description in the flesh.

The man's eyes widened and he scrambled to his feet, trying to seem relaxed, perhaps, as he walked towards her. 'I am. And you are…?'

'Mary.'

'Mary!' His face broke into the most enormous grin. 'Mary, you seem a very long way away from Bristol.'

'I suppose so,' she said, her heart not quite settled in her chest. She reached up and tugged her fingers through her hair in a makeshift comb.

'And do you always creep up on unsuspecting visitors ready to brain them with a trowel?'

She realized she was still holding it aloft, smiled shyly as she brought it to her side. 'You would have been perfectly safe. I would have been hopeless; I really loathe the sight of blood.'

'Well that's a relief,' he said, holding out a hand to her.

She took it, unable to stop smiling at him as he let out a low rumble of laughter. It seemed to fill the garden.

'How long have you been here?'

'I'm not sure, the days seem to merge now. I arrived on the tenth.'

'And you've been staying here?' he asked.

She nodded, worried then that he would be angry.

His eyes widened a fraction before his expression returned to normal. 'Well you must be wanting to see the village a bit. Is

Abigail here?' He peered round her as if Abigail might emerge from the house.

'No. She tries to come as much as she can, but it's hard...' Mary hesitated, wary of being indiscreet, feeling a loyalty well in her chest.

'Let me fix a few things here and we can get down to the village. I imagine you could do with a break from the place.'

'I...' She had been cooped up in the cottage for days and the thought of a trip to the village below with its quaint shops and rolling sea was too much to resist.

She smiled at him. 'I'd love that, let me get my coat.'

They talked all the way down into the village, Mary feeling guiltier with every step. Abigail had made her promise she would stay in the cottage until they'd decided what to do, was desperately worried Larry would find out, wanted to be with her sister, wouldn't explain why. Richard was pointing out shops and pubs, asking her questions about Abigail when they were younger, laughing at her stories, aglow when he told her more.

He took her to the line of cottages they'd walked past on that first day. The three of them tucked neatly next to each other, the sound of the river surrounding them. Clematis hung over the latticed porch on her left, a woman stopping to nod at Richard, a brief pause, forehead wrinkling slightly before smiling at her, a baby in her arms.

'Hi, Beth,' called Richard, tipping his hat at her.

She gave a sleepy, slow wave, bending over to peer at her baby swaddled in a blanket.

He turned around to face her, the front door behind him. 'This is us. You'll stay here for now,' he said, nodding once, his mouth set in a thin line.

Mary looked up at him sharply. 'No, I couldn't. I...' She felt thrown, flapping one hand to her chest.

'You can't stay up there, it's not safe, you'll get ill. The weather's been terrible and there are holes in the roof.'

'I can't.'

'Of course you can, just while you visit.'

'I won't be up there much longer, we're leaving soon, it won't be long.'

He stopped then, mouth loose, jaw dropping. When he spoke, his voice was quieter, the energy ebbed away. 'She hasn't said anything.'

'She didn't want anyone to know,' Mary explained, panicking now. She shouldn't have come, he'd tell people, Larry would hear and she'd have to leave. 'Please, I….'

'Where are you going to go?'

'Exeter. We can share rooms there and—'

'But why?' It exploded out of him at first, then he hushed the second word, aware of his neighbour peering round at the voices. Richard couldn't hide the hurt on his face, his mouth turned down, his eyes dulled. A line emerged in the middle of his forehead as he looked at her.

'She'll have to explain it to you herself,' Mary said, refusing to be drawn on that secret. She wouldn't betray Abigail.

He seemed to accept that, sighing as he turned back around to push open the front door. 'Watch the step there,' he commented as she followed him. 'It's me, Dad. We've got a visitor.'

Martin was sitting at a table in the window, the light cutting across the wooden surface, highlighting the dots of dust suspended in the air.

'This is Mary,' Richard said, pulling out a chair for her to sit in.

It was wonderful to feel the warmth of the room, to sit and smell chestnuts and furniture polish. She became conscious of her own appearance, tangled hair and hand-washed clothes.

'Mary.' Martin inclined his head, the smallest of lines creasing his brow as he looked back at Richard, his mouth half-open.

'She's a friend of Abigail's,' Richard explained. 'And she needs somewhere to stay.'

RICHARD

He hadn't felt like this before, this strange bubbling anger that seemed to simmer in the pit of his stomach, leaping and burning as he saw her pick her way down the path towards him, edging round the puddles that were ebbing from the day before.

She stopped in front of him, wary, as if she were a fox he had caught in their garden, staring him down before she scampered off. She tried to smile at him, one side of her mouth lifting, but he cut her off.

'Mary is staying with us.'

She hadn't expected that, her eyes widening so that he could see all the whites around her iris. 'Mary? But—'

'I went to the cottage the day before last. She couldn't stay there.'

Abigail had changed colour, a blush creeping from the neck of her cardigan up to her face. 'I didn't know where else she could go.'

'To your sister's,' he said, throwing his hands up. 'There must be, what, six, seven bedrooms in that house and you keep your best friend in a leaky cottage with no heating, no way of cooking for herself.' He could feel his face distorting as he spoke, his lip curled. Had he been so oblivious to this selfish streak in her? That she would hide away her best friend, not share all the comforts of their home. He thought of Mary then, her unwashed hair, the water boiling on the stove, the dust swept into corners, some semblance of order being created.

'I couldn't... I didn't...' Abigail's chest was heaving, words jumbled and incoherent, her eyes not able to hold his for long.

'It's absurd. She looked utterly bedraggled and you were just going to keep her there, not take her up to the big house, afraid to have her embarrass you in front of your smart sister, I suppose?'

He could feel the bubbles leaping into his throat, his voice louder, teeth clenched as he looked at her, waiting for answers, to understand. She remained stubbornly silent. This girl who he thought had such a generous heart, who wanted to make the world a more joyful place, she was a lie. She stood there now, dumbly, arms by her side, no explanation, no excuses. Then the truth, the fact that stung the most, spilled out of him before he could stop it. 'You were going to leave without saying anything?'

It made her flinch. 'Richard, I wasn't... I didn't... We had to...'

It stung, the pain of hearing her squirming, unable to deny it because it was true.

'Were you going to let me know? Leave a note perhaps? I thought...' It was his turn to stumble now, choke on the words he couldn't form. 'I thought we were planning a future.'

Tears sprang into her eyes and he stood there, fists clenched at his sides, waiting for her to respond, to deny it, to throw herself at him and tell him she was never going to leave.

It was a hideous mistake; Mary had been wrong. She stayed there; her eyes lined with unshed tears. She took a breath, looked up at him.

'I would have told you. I have to leave, we have to.'

'But why?' Richard didn't want to beg, didn't want to plead. A part of him wanted to apologize, to persuade her to stay, to propose to her, to do something that would mean she wouldn't leave, that he hadn't glimpsed his future only to discover it was make-believe and with a woman who didn't exist. The larger part of him was telling him to turn around, to return home, to leave her there and not look back.

It had begun to rain, to spit; a cloud like a blackened bruise lingered over the tops of the trees and soon there would be a downpour.

'Do you really have nothing to say?'

Tiny droplets were clinging to her hair, to her eyelashes as she stepped forward, one hand up on his chest. The rain became heavier and she shook her head as if to clear her thoughts. For another second he prayed she would deny it all, it was a terrible misunderstanding.

'I don't know what else to do,' she whispered and he was unsure if she was crying or if it was the rain. Then, without warning, she turned and walked straight back up Mars Hill, head down, into the wind, the rain making her dress stick to her legs as she went. And he was left there, looking after her, seeing the girl he loved leave him.

IRINA

She pushed through the lychgate, ivy growing up the sides, two worn stone benches facing each other, onto a winding path that led to the door of the church. She moved off the gravel onto the grass, narrow lines flattened where other people had come and gone. There were newer graves, marble, stone, different names engraved, inscriptions, pots of well-tended flowers beneath them. She looked down at one tombstone and inhaled sharply as she saw the age of the boy who was buried there, feeling as if she was at the graveside of another boy.

Irina moved on, knowing where she was headed as she made her way around the side of the church, past a beech tree, tombstones crooked among its roots, the names long faded away. Emerging from the shade, she made her way to a corner of the graveyard, to a line of tombstones, the smell of freshly mown grass in the air, a seagull's cry in the distance.

This was the spot: a line of tombstones, some askew, some blank, some with flowers, wilting now, past their best. She was struck by the fact that all the dates matched: August 1952;

understood the enormity of what Bill had told her as she padded silently down the row. At the end of the line, a little way off from the rest, she found what she was looking for.

Her head was full of all the things she'd learnt as she stopped at the grave and read the inscription on the tombstone, partly obscured by lichen. The unknown girl who had lost her life. She lowered herself to her knees in front of it. She was sure now that something in the bureau had led her here to Lynton, that she was meant to be sitting in front of this grave. Sounds dissolved around her as she reread the words, thought of the young woman who had died that night.

She pulled things from her bag and examined the letters. There was so much passion and energy in them. She wanted to lay them in front of the grave, but something was stopping her. She still had questions. Why were the postcards not dated? Why had they not been sent? If they'd been written by Abigail, who had she been writing to?

She looked through the photographs one more time, the faces as familiar to her now as if they were her own relatives. She wondered at the shell, its delicate colouring, the keyring with the threepence, the brooch. She had emptied the bureau of its secrets but she still felt there was more to discover.

She knew she needed to get back to her mother, to face her own past, to finally tell her mother the truth.

She stayed for a while longer, hoping the visit would help, placing the items back in her bag and reaching out a hand to rest on the grave. Going to stand, hands on her thighs, she looked down the line of tombstones once more, the date leaping out at her, over and over, repeated on each stone.

She felt a whisper in the wind as she stood up and turned slowly back towards the village, sensing eyes on her as she left the row of graves, as she walked back out through the gate.

ABIGAIL

The walk down to the Pavilion was slippery and Abigail gripped the iron railings, taking care in her heeled shoes, forcing her footsteps to be smaller, lighter. The rain was bouncing off the ground in sharp bursts, sinking into the material of her shoes, her toes unpleasantly damp beneath her stockings.

'This is disgusting,' her sister said, sounding more like herself these last few days, clutching her umbrella and wrinkling her nose as she looked down at her feet. 'They'll be ruined,' she commented, the suede already two shades darker than usual.

'Not far to go,' said Larry, seemingly oblivious to the violence of the rain. It abated in sections where the trees provided almost impenetrable cover, allowing only a few stray drops to make it through. The light had faded and it was more like a winter's evening than a night in August, the sea somewhere below them a murky grey, a bank of cloud bruised and heavy above them.

They arrived with soaked shoes, hair frizzing in the

sudden warmth of the Pavilion, its foyer busy with chatter as the rest of the audience turned up, shaking out umbrellas on the steps, stamping their feet on the large bristled mat, swiping at their hair, men removing their hats.

Abigail hadn't wanted to go, had spent an hour hiding her red eyes under brown eyeliner and silvery eye shadow, trying to disguise the fact that she'd been crying. She had left Richard in the rain, her thighs burning as she climbed back to the house, rubbing at her eyes, as if she could erase the look he'd given her. She had never seen him like that before, expression dull, her own terrible reflection in the curl of his lip, his words biting into her. She wasn't aware of Connie's comments on the way down, responding too slowly to questions, replaying the day, Richard's look, again and again.

Connie squeezed her gloved hand and Abigail emerged from her daze, instantly transported to another world: the glowing chandelier, the carpeted steps that led to a wide landing, doors to the theatre on either side. They were there to see *Seaside Notions*, a cabaret, a mixture of dancing, songs and skits, and she thought back to the times when she and her mum had gone to shows in the Bristol Hippodrome. They used to sit in the stalls, her excitement mounting as the orchestra warmed up in the pit, then the hush as the thick red velvet curtains opened to reveal an intricately painted set and the story unfolded, swelling around her so that she was immersed in the scene, lost among the warm bodies of others staring enthralled alongside her. She was looking forward to losing herself in the show tonight, forgetting things for a while, ignoring the thoughts that jostled at her.

Larry went to pick up the tickets from the square window, squeezing past Abigail so that his hand lingered briefly on her waist. Her eyes darted to Connie, she was sure she'd seen, but when she glanced across, Connie was looking pointedly at a nearby usher, who moved towards her and handed her a programme.

Six women huddled under the awning outside, commenting on the rain, laughing behind their hands as they shook their heads. The sound of the rain and the sea, insistent and unforgiving, seemed to merge and their laughter was lost to the outside, snatched away within seconds. The foyer felt calmer, everyone bathed in a sepia glow, earrings and necklaces flashing in the light, lipstick brighter, teeth whiter.

They moved through to the auditorium, a general quiet descending as they shuffled along the row to their seats. Abigail tried to ensure she was sitting at the end, next to her sister, but somehow Larry had lingered, made a quick greeting to another Lynton councillor, and he guided them along, placing himself in the middle of the sisters, a hand on the small of her back so she was forced to arch away. Her sister looked at her sharply then and colour flooded Abigail's cheeks as she sat, burying her nose in her programme, wondering where Richard and Mary were at that moment, together no doubt, in the snug sitting room. For a brief second she felt a sliver of jealousy that they were together, then loathed herself for it. She realized with a terrible sinking feeling that perhaps Richard didn't care anymore.

In the breaks they could hear the insistent patter of the rain, still falling outside like a far-off soundtrack, a record player whirring with no record. When the next scene started up, the singing drowned out everything and Abigail could forget the person next to her, leaning towards her, his breath hot on her neck and cheek, a mix of mint and pipe smoke, as he commented on the performers, offered her a humbug from a paper bag. She refused; her body pressed desperately against the other arm rest.

The show hadn't been going for long when there was a

gasp as the lights went out, the whole theatre plunged into darkness, a shot of laughter in a row behind her and then, when it was clear the place had lost power, voices rising everywhere. She was about to ask her own question but was silenced by a hand, firm on her thigh. She froze, feeling his fingers grip the inside of her leg, so high, stroking slowly with a thumb as, in a clear, calm voice he asked, 'What's that?'

Her sister somewhere to her right. 'The power's gone. The power.'

Clucking voices behind her merged. 'There's a storm… We should have stayed… I wanted… I know you wanted… Sorry, can I get out… This is horrid… That's my coat… I'm sorry…' The voices faded in and out as she tensed her thigh, aware only of his hand. A roll of thunder brought her back, the rumble seeming to surround the building, hushing everyone for a moment, but then the voices started up again, louder now, panic injected into some of the questions. 'We can't just sit here in the dark… How awful, do you think it will have to be cut short…? This weather, it's been hopeless all month, this rain…'

The performers were exchanging muttered whispers on the stage and then a man with a huge voice started to sing before words from someone behind the scenes caused him to come to a stop.

There was a voice from the back, loud over the hubbub, and the hand lifted from her thigh as soft candlelight shifted the room from black to a dark grey, faces now half in shadow, outlined in the light.

'Ladies and gentlemen, I'm terribly sorry to be cancelling tonight's show, but I'm afraid due to the inclement weather we are unable to resume the production. If you could kindly help those around you to leave, we could start from the back row. I am terribly sorry for the inconvenience.'

There were apologies as people stepped on strangers' coats, fussed over handbags, readjusted hats, shook out umbrellas. There was mumbling at the management, the sudden cancellation, they'd been enjoying it, would they get a refund? It all seemed rather silly as they tutted and side-stepped along the rows into the aisle, the light not good enough to stop people from tripping, arms on elbows, guiding. The damp heat made Abigail's head feel clammy, the smell entering her nostrils and turning her stomach.

She was grateful to emerge into the foyer, jumping at a sudden flash of lightning which fired up the scene outside for a second before everything was plunged back into darkness. A couple of ushers were standing holding candles as they moved through the foyer, but there was an eerie silence as people picked their way carefully down steps, held out hands for someone elderly, stood hovering at the top, looking into the street outside.

She was shocked by the amount of water on the road, the drains no longer able to cope, the road a stream of water. The darkness made it even more disconcerting. It seemed the whole village had lost power, the effect of the storm, no doubt, another enormously sonorous roll of thunder drowning out the other noises for a moment.

She had drifted to the doorway, the dark sea ahead of her. She could hear the churning sound of the waves over the persistent drumming of rain, the moans and talk from people escaping into the night, heads down, bowing under umbrellas, hopelessly soaked within a second.

'We need to get up Mars Hill.'

'It's dreadful out there,' Connie said, her mouth puckered as if she'd just tasted another of Edith's burnt offerings.

'Well we can't stay here, it isn't going to stop,' Larry said, shaking out the umbrella and holding it up. 'Get under, Abigail.

You too.' He steered her with one hand on her back and they left the Pavilion, Abigail stepping out from under the umbrella, happier to feel the rain wetting her scalp and running down her neck than to smell Larry's damp tweed, feel his hand tightening on her. Her hair was plastered to her head in seconds.

It was worse than she had thought, the darkness so disorientating. Connie had stopped still, crying out at her shoes, her coat, her voice faint in the howl of the weather. Abigail had started to shiver; she moved past them, calling behind that she would wait for them both in The Rising Sun, gasping as she continued down the pavement, water running over her shoes.

She arrived there in a steaming mess, to be met with more red-cheeked, sweaty faces, people huddled in corners, waiting in groups by foggy windows to face the outside. Boats were smashing into each other in the harbour and a couple of the older men were frowning as flashes of lightning illuminated the mess and splintered wood. For the first time Abigail felt a cold fear shiver through her, one hand reaching up to the pane of glass, leaving finger marks on the surface. She thought of Mary and Richard in the cottage, the river running past them.

Larry arrived with Connie, drenched and shivering, her pale face and livid red lips smeared from the rain, her mascara leaving marks on her cheeks. She was holding onto Larry's arm like a life raft, wide eyed and starting to tremble. Abigail pushed her way towards them.

'We need to get back home,' Connie said. Abigail could see the whites of her eyes and held out her hand for her. She dropped her key on the floor, the threepence piece glinting as Abigail picked it up.

'I...' The noise was unbelievable, a distant crash making her prick up her ears like a deer about to leap away. 'I...' She couldn't admit to where she wanted to go, but she needed to see if Mary was alright. She wanted to be with her, check she wasn't frightened. She sent up thanks that Richard had brought her down from the cottage; she couldn't imagine what the place would look like tonight, the pans and buckets for the leaks hopeless against this onslaught.

They loitered in the doorway, jostled by others not knowing what to do and which direction to go in, linking arms.

Larry looked at the road outside. 'Let's go,' he said, indicating Mars Hill.

There was silence for a moment as a huge crash further up the valley seemed to block everything else out. There was a whimper from a woman sitting perched on a bar stool clutching a handkerchief to her mouth, a glass of brandy untouched in front of her. Abigail tried to smile at her, but her face was stretched with worry. She had to check on Mary and Richard.

Larry and Connie went out into the darkness, down the steps. Abigail followed them, then as they turned to climb back up the hill, she veered the other way, back down towards the high street, gasping at the cold, feeling water run around her shoes, her ankles, shocked that the road had turned into a stream, wondering for a moment whether she had made the right choice. She could hear her sister calling for her, shouting her name into the night. She couldn't see her from that distance, already lost in the rain and the wind.

'I'll catch you up,' Abigail called, the words snatched into the wind. She had made her choice.

It was impossibly dark and the sounds were enormous in the pitch black, tearing, screeching. Abigail's hair was plastered to her forehead, her eyelids struggling to stay open as the rain pounded down on her. She was drenched, moving slowly now, pausing to cling to a lamp post, clutching a rail as she continued down the high street.

The six women Abigail had seen clustered around the Pavilion steps had split into two groups. She could just about make them out up ahead, moving through the churning water that used to be the high street, a faint row of figures momentarily picked out by a flash of lightning, all linking arms as if they were a chorus line. It was a comforting sight and she focused on them as they made progress up the high street, to one of the hotels no doubt. The water was deeper now, washing around her feet, spattering up her calves. Then there was movement, more sounds, close, loud, wrenching and thundering, voices calling, shouting over the rush of the water, and they were no longer all walking. One of them had fallen.

Abigail watched in horror as she saw her tumble into the flood alongside them, twisting, one arm loose, her hand up to cling onto something, anything she could seize, being swept down the street towards Abigail. She lost her, disorientated, the pale arm no longer visible, the familiar houses and shops jumbled for a second in the thick darkness, then a glimpse again, hand, hair and she was turning towards her, trying to find a way to reach her, to get something for her to grab, watching as if in slow motion as she passed her.

Up ahead, two lights moved steadily down the high street, impossibly green. They drew nearer, throwing a ghoulish glow across the scene, shapes taking form as she realized they were the lights from a motor car that was now rolling down the high street in the water, lights submerged as if it were an underwater monster. Abigail couldn't look away as it made its way down, bumping slowly along as if it were being driven by somebody, disappearing into the rocks and the river, the lights suddenly extinguished. For a moment she thought she might be lost as she looked to her right, expecting to see a shop up ahead, the landscape entirely altered. Another flash of lightning made her skin break out in goosebumps; the carcass of a sheep swept by, a jumble of trees, rocks ahead, the river wider and higher, the roar all around her.

She looked up, sucking in all her breath as something reared out of the darkness and came towards her.

IRINA

They were sitting opposite each other in the apartment, the peach curtains pushed back, exposing the narrow stone balcony, the car park just below them. Her mother had brought down the Yahtzee set and Irina felt as if it could have been any time on any day in the last ten years. Her mother's medication was lined up on the kitchen counter behind her, the notes from the hospital clear, cartoon diagrams and leaflets walking them through this new world.

'It's nice to be home,' her mother said, throwing a dice. 'Oh, a two. You start.'

Her mother looked up at her, but Irina didn't take the dice. She swallowed slowly, the strength she had felt on the drive back from Devon to Brighton ebbing away. She had wanted to face her own past, finally lay open her own secrets.

Her mother took a tentative sip of her tea. 'Irina,' she said, reaching forward, placing a hand over her daughter's.

Irina dragged her eyes up, looked her mother in the face. Her hair needed cutting, the ends of her normally neat bob were curling under.

'What you said to me before, in hospital, about that day...' Her mother's voice was scratchy, each word a struggle.

Irina felt her breath suspended in her body. Was this the moment?

'You needed to tell me something. Well, I...' Her mother hesitated. 'I need to tell you something too.'

Irina's insides dropped. She knew. Her mother knew. How long had she known? Had she dragged around the knowledge for years? Had she looked over at Irina every time she visited and loathed her for it? Now that the moment was here, Irina wanted to cry 'Stop!', to insist on pushing the genie back into the bottle, locking the box, hiding the key. It had seemed urgent before, when she was fired up by Andrew's questions, the discoveries in Devon, the need to cleanse herself. She hadn't thought then that her mother already knew. She dropped her head, stared at the floor, waiting for her mother to tell her how much she resented her.

'This isn't easy,' her mother said, a small laugh escaping, a bubble of nervousness. 'I've been remembering the last time we were at a hospital together, and I suppose it got me thinking.'

Irina hadn't realized she was holding her breath until she felt herself go light-headed, a nauseous sensation, bile in the back of her throat.

Her mother coughed. 'You won't remember, I imagine? You were in the hospital after...' She indicated Irina's face with one hand. 'They had to dress your face twice a day.' Her voice broke as she continued. 'You were being so brave. Biting down on your lip to stop yourself from calling out, and you just kept asking after your brother...'

'Joshua,' Irina whispered.

Her mother swallowed and nodded. 'Joshua.'

It was her saying his name. That was the moment when

she began to cry, and once she had begun she found she couldn't stem it. Her body shook as the tears fell. Years of tears for Joshua, for her baby brother, the brother she should have protected. Her dad, her lovely dad, who used to growl at her from behind cereal boxes, tickle her as she raced squealing up the stairs. Her mother was crying too, slow, steady tears that leaked out of the corner of her eyes, pooled along the rims, then streamed down the sides of her face, tearing pale scars through her make-up, leaving track marks as they fell.

'He was precious,' Irina said, smiling now, a half-smile, bittersweet. 'I never thought...'

The pain was filling her up, burning her face all over again, moving down her arms as if she was on fire, pain coursing through her veins into every limb, making her ache with it, doubling over. 'It was my fault,' she sobbed through her hands. 'My fault.'

Her mother reached out for her hand again, stroking the skin in small rhythmic circles, and Irina hated her for it, for showing her pity. 'No, no, I have... I have to tell you...'

Her mother drew back, something like fear in her eyes and Irina wiped at her face, straightened up, took a breath. 'The fire,' Irina said in a wobbly voice. 'The fire...' She swallowed, twisted the bottom of her jersey in one hand, her voice dropping to a whisper. 'Was all because of me.'

MARY

Richard left quickly, following his friend, his hair already flattened by the rain as he hurried down the path to the street. They'd turned the lights on at 4 p.m., the sky a strange colour, a large grey cloud tinged with red hanging stubbornly over the village, the rain insistent. She'd stood in the garden, her hands sinking deep into the pockets of her cardigan, feeling the rain on her face, clinging to her eyelashes. It had got worse since then, fat droplets that slid down the roof, filled the drainpipes, rattled the windows and streaked the glass so that the outside was a moving-picture show, nothing solid, everything slipping away and re-forming before her eyes.

Martin had strained his eyes at the blackness outside. 'Absurd. It's August.'

This was her third night in the cottage. It seemed strange that only a couple of evenings ago they'd been sitting in the small garden watching the sun sink lower, turning the sky to a dusky pink, a pale grey, and the clock had told them it was nearly nine o'clock. Now it felt like a winter's night, both sitting in the armchairs by the fire. Mary was playing solitaire, fascinated by the simple game, enjoying removing the marbles, hearing them roll around the edges of the board as Martin read, looking up to comment occasionally.

Mary wondered what it might have been like if her father had never left for the war, if he'd never had to come back a different person. He had once been like Martin, able to look her in the eye when she spoke, amused by her stories, offering words of appraisal in a low, steady patter. She knew she would have to make plans to move on, couldn't stay in this house for too long. She'd tried to pull her weight since Richard had brought her down there, a pie, the pastry neatly pierced, ready to go in the oven for dinner.

Richard was Abigail's, she knew that immediately; his eyes grew softer when he spoke about her. She'd been to the pictures and watched the love stories and she imagined them on a blustery hilltop, Richard holding her face in his hands, leaning down to bring his mouth to hers. She didn't tell him about Larry; Abigail had made her promise not to share the hints and whispered words of her postcards. Mary hated knowing the truth.

Richard to her was the older brother, someone to look up to, to please. She'd helped him bring in logs earlier, stacking them up for a fire they couldn't believe they would need in August, gutting the fish he'd brought back in a basket, laughing at the relief on his face when she'd offered, renewing the water in the teapot.

They hadn't worried at first. The rain was loud, the thunder ominous, and the first flash of lightning had made her start, the two of them glancing at each other with nervous smiles. She went to the front door, looked out into the darkening evening, the lights of the Lyndale Hotel a little way along a comfort.

'It must be the wettest summer on record,' Martin said,

wanting her help to move him around so that he could see out of the window.

'It isn't half loud,' she said, hating the relentless drumming of the rain, the flare of lightning that seemed to light up their small room, and the noise of the river rushing past the house, normally a gentle sound but tonight overwhelming.

Martin looked at her, his worn face creased with worry as they both heard a louder noise in the distance. Then the lights failed, everything sputtering and then out. The room suddenly a black space, vague outlines fooling them. Mary made a surprised yelp and then Martin's voice drifted out of the dark.

'There's matches,' he said, 'on the mantelpiece, on the left there.'

She moved across, feeling her way, arms outstretched, wondering for a moment which direction she was facing. A bolt of lightning, firing up the room and their startled faces for a second so that she giggled, she couldn't help it.

'Careful,' he said as her calf hit something. A coal scuttle, metal; her skin would be marked. 'Go slow.'

'Oh, darn this. Sorry,' she said, patting at the mantelpiece, feeling round ornaments, framed photographs, worried that she might bring something precious crashing to the floor. She wouldn't want to break anything; it would be so embarrassing.

She found the box, careful to slide out the drawer and take a match out, feeling the end and drawing it quickly along the side. She held it up for a second, caught Martin trying to get out of his chair. The surprise made her drop the match and start forward, burning her fingers, the smell instant, then she stood on the red outline so that she wouldn't start a fire.

'I wanted to get the candles.'

'Let me help.'

'No, don't you worry, I can manage.'

He had reached for his stick; she could make out his outline as her eyes adjusted. He sat back down abruptly as another rumble took them by surprise.

'There are candles in the hall, in the table.'

'I'll get them.' She turned to grope her way back across the room, matches clutched in one hand, body stooped, feeling for the velvet of the armchair, straightening up as she took a step towards the door.

'Give me the matches.'

She held them out, squinting to try and make out his hand, side-stepping towards him inch by inch. They desperately needed light. She felt his fingers close over them, the rough skin, the hand bigger than hers.

'Take care,' he said as she turned in the direction of the door, bending down slightly to feel her way around the furniture, blushing as she realized she had hold of his knee.

'Alright!' He laughed.

'Sorry,' she said, giggling again.

She made it to the door, pulled it open. The table should be straight on and to her left. She walked straight into a pool of water, stepped backwards and smacked her elbow on the doorframe, crying out with the pain and the surprise of the water, which had already soaked her feet.

'You alright?' came Martin's voice.

'There's water—'

Another roar froze her to the ground, a deafening crash from outside and she couldn't help the sounds that came out of her mouth. She imagined the house being circled by a giant. She thought back to the fairy tales. He was stomping through the valley now, one foot planted, lifting another, tearing things up in his path. She felt her heart racing faster. She had to stop the water; she could find things to put in the gap under the door. She moved towards the table, alarmed by the size of the puddle, more water seeping under the door, faster. She tried the drawers, feeling past pencils, paper, until her hands came up against the waxy smoothness of a candle. She seized it and turned back around, both hands on the table behind her so that she could get her bearings.

'The holder's in here.' Martin sounded different now, more urgent, and she tried to stay composed. She made her way back to him, her feet sopping, and handed him the candle. He lit it as he sat in his chair and the sudden warmth of the circle of light calmed both of them down; in that moment she thought she had never seen anything more welcoming. Their eyes met in the orange glow; respite for a second.

'Get the holder.' He had to raise his voice to be heard, pointed to a table. She popped the candle inside, cupping the flame as if it were the most precious thing in the world. 'You're going to have to help me up.'

'Let me try blocking the door,' she said.

'I can help.'

She could hear the frustration in his voice and saw him smack a hand on the arm of his chair as she moved quickly to try and shore up the front door. The candlelight revealed an ever-widening puddle that was moving into the living room and to the bedroom opposite, where Martin slept.

'We need to go upstairs,' Mary said in a voice that she didn't recognize as her own.

She had seen Richard do this ten times and yet now she felt the awful awkwardness of their situation.

'I can't...'

'You have to. I can manage,' she said, trying to swallow down her embarrassment and help him to the door.

He leant all his weight on her, trying to keep hold of the candle. It felt strangely familiar, to have a man's body leaning heavily on her, as if she were turfing out one of their customers from the pub. He smelt of spice and tobacco. She coughed and chattered until she had to fall silent, concentrating on every step, the light wobbling, throwing up strange shadows around the room. The water had leaked into the living room now and when they got into the hall it had got deeper, the water up to their ankles, swilling around their calves, the rug beneath it ruined, a shoe bumping gently into her. Her breathing was heavy, her body struggling to take Martin's weight; they stopped on the stairs, him twisting down, his back against the wall, a pained expression on his face. She took the candle higher up, leaving him at the bottom in darkness, surrounded by a black, glittering pool, as if he were sitting on the stair about to fish.

He managed to move up the stairs without help, hauling himself up on his hands on his bottom, moving backwards slowly. The water had reached the first stair and he protested when Mary moved quickly back down to the living room with the candle, wading now, up to her calves in water.

'What can I move? What will be ruined?' she shouted up.

He protested for another moment and then started calling out to her from the top stair, directing her until she had collected a small pile of items: the photographs from the mantelpiece, the letters from the right-hand drawer of the dresser, the photograph album from the left-hand drawer, the carriage clock on the table behind his chair, his sheepskin slippers.

'It will ease off,' she said, one hand on his arm as he sifted sadly through the album, not able to see the details in the soft light. 'Come on,' she urged, 'let's get settled.'

She helped him onto the bed, bent to remove his shoes, dripping onto the rug, his socks sticking to his skin, a hole at the top where one of his toes poked through. She helped him shift so his back was resting against the bed frame, tucked his feet under the woollen rug.

'I haven't been up here for two years,' he said softly, his expression calmer for a moment. 'This used to be our bedroom.'

'Richard told me.' She nodded, glad they were talking normally, worried about the sounds from outside.

She put the candle in the window of the bedroom, embarrassed by the sight of her underthings draped on a chair in the corner. She discreetly moved to put them in her bag, wishing she had tidied up better that morning. They perched on the edge of the bed, surrounded by the water. The lights from the hotel had gone out too and they could hear shouts and voices in the darkness.

'Richard will come back and help us,' she said, her voice high and bright.

Martin was quiet for a few seconds. 'You must go, Mary, get to the hotel. Get help.'

'I won't leave you, and anyway, Richard will be back soon, we'll be safe here till then.'

'Go to the hotel, they'll have a ladder, they'll have men who can help.'

She agreed, a terrible part of her knowing she wanted to get out of the bedroom; she wanted the security of more people, wanted to be herded and instructed. She lit the gas lamp by her bed, the room now suffused with light.

She took the candle, walking slowly, her face lit up from below as she looked back over at him. 'I won't be long. I'll be back with help,' she said, stepping into the corridor, turning slowly and heading down the first short flight of stairs.

She returned moments later in silence, her face pale even in the candlelight. She didn't tell him that the water had reached the landing just below them, that the whole of the ground floor was submerged. She simply returned the candle to the window and sat back down on the bed, trying to reassure him with a smile. She could feel it on her face, wonky. She couldn't jump from the window and they didn't have a ladder, and anyway, Martin wouldn't be able to get out. The water wouldn't come any higher, they needed to wait for help, someone would come.

'The river's changed course, that isn't right,' Martin said, looking out into the darkness as another flash of lightning illuminated the outside. He turned back to her, his face different now, steel in his eyes. 'We have to get help.'

'People will see the light; they'll know we're here.'

'No, you have—'

'And Richard will come,' she assured him, feeling better as she said the words aloud.

More voices then, in between the roar and screeching from outside, someone calling, persistent, closer. Mary stood up, straining to hear, moving towards the small square of window. There was a figure in the cottage next door, silhouetted by a weak light behind him. It was Tom, shouting something across the gap between their cottages. Mary fumbled to open the catch on the window. She could make out Beth behind him, pacing the room, the baby in her arms. The noises seemed to enter the room then, swirl around them, screaming, thudding, tearing. Mary took a step back, frightened of the tumult outside. She couldn't make out what Tom was saying, he was waving an arm at her. She wanted to lean out, reassure, but she felt frozen to the floor now, the curtains lifting with the wind, his shouts merging with the other sounds in the darkness.

'We… help… the house… going…'

'Who is it?' Martin asked from the bed.

His question seemed to rally her. She shook her head as if

she had water in her ears, her mind clogged with the din. Then, as she turned, an enormous crash came from somewhere behind the house and she whipped back round, unable to see Tom's outline in the darkness anymore, unable to see the cottage at all.

'Oh my God.' She squinted into the night, unable to believe the gap that had opened up in front of her.

Martin had twisted round on the bed as water started seeping into the room, a terrible slow puddle oozing over the wooden floorboards.

'Mary, go! Get away, try to climb down. You could go to the school, it's higher up…'

'I won't.'

'Go!' His voice rose, fist hitting the mattress. 'You must. You need to get out.'

'I wo—'

They both looked to the side as the most enormous noise seemed to hurtle towards them from the valley. A wrenching, screeching, terrible sound and then they couldn't see each other and they couldn't hear each other and the candle went out.

IRINA

Her mother had been looking at her for the longest time. Irina was waiting now, waiting for the moment when she would turn, swear at her, scream, tell her to get out: do something. Her mother stood up, her mouth opening and shutting, no words coming out, her arms slack at her side as Irina gabbled again. 'I caused the fire: it was my fault.'

She couldn't look at her mother, babbling now to herself. 'If I hadn't tried to make pancakes, if I hadn't left the hob on, they'd... still...' She couldn't say it, even now, she couldn't finish that sentence. She felt her body tearing into a thousand parts as she replayed that day, over and over.

She had woken early to make pancakes for her dad. It was his birthday. He was going to be forty, totally ancient. They were his favourite breakfast and he always had them with syrup. Joshua was meant to help, but when she pushed open the door to his room he was fast asleep with his mouth wide open, diagonal on the bed. He had kicked off his dinosaur duvet cover and was almost dangling off the edge. She didn't wake him, crept down to the kitchen on her own.

She had been so proud, remembering where the recipe was written, dragging a chair over to the dresser, turning the hob on so she was ready. She stood on the chair to search the cupboard. She needed plain flour, not self-raising. Then her mum had called her from the hallway. She was going to take her to pick up Dad's surprise and when Irina heard those words, everything else went out of her head. She loved surprises. So she left the kitchen, forgetting everything.

If she had just turned it off, if she had just remembered.

'The smoke alarm didn't go off, I don't know why it didn't go off, they would have woken,' Irina said, clutching her sides, trying to squeeze herself into a smaller space, disappear.

Her mother sat back down, slowly, one arm reaching behind her for the bench, stumbling briefly. She bent forward, taking a breath. 'I'd taken the batteries out.'

Irina wiped her face with the back of her hand, wondering if she had correctly heard the words her mother had whispered.

There seemed to be a pause then, only the roll of waves, the screech of a seagull.

'The week before. I'd forgotten, your father always hated the sound, and I'd burnt bacon, pulled out the batteries. I meant to put them back, but I hadn't...'

Irina's mind was a roar of noise, memories, but her mother's words were filtering through it all. The alarm, the batteries.

'Dad was sleeping, you know how he could sleep. They found them...' Her mother swallowed. 'They found them both, they hadn't woken. They told me they died from smoke inhalation.'

'I thought... I never knew.' Irina stumbled, her tongue suddenly too big for her mouth, her mother not meeting her eyes.

'I should have told you. We should have talked years ago. I never wanted to, I didn't want you to know.'

'Know what?'

'That it was my fault. I didn't want you to hate me.'

Irina started at her comment, confused as to what would come next. Her head was spinning with the revelations, the bitter joy of being able to talk about her brother and her dad, to feel them standing some way off as she and her mother finally spoke about their deaths.

'I don't understand.'

'I've blamed myself for years. For how I behaved, for not stopping you, not protecting you. I couldn't help them. But you, I could have saved you.'

Irina held her breath, too shocked to cry.

'For years I've had to think about you racing towards the flames, screaming for Joshua and Dad, rushing straight into the fire; you were so determined, fearless. Even when the heat got too much, you were adamant you could rescue them. And all that time, when you were running at the house, I was standing there, watching, afraid, stuck to the ground while everyone else did something.'

As her mother finally spoke about that day, Irina stood listening. The fire that had torn through their house, the sirens that swept past them, the fire trucks at strange angles on the pavements in their street, the people rushing back and forth, the heat.

She remembered them arriving back from the bakery, her dad's cake in the boot; she'd been so excited to see his face. Then her mother braking hard, Irina lurching forward in the car. Their house hadn't looked right. There was smoke belching out of the windows at the top, both windows, puffing out in huge clouds because the house couldn't contain it.

Her mother had got out of the car. She didn't say anything,

just got out, walked into the middle of the road and stared. She was wearing a skirt and a pink cardigan and she looked so small. Irina had undone her seatbelt, clambered out after her.

She only paused for a second before racing towards the side gate. It was hot, sizzling hot, but she had to find Joshua and it was Dad's birthday and they hadn't been gone long. And it was all her fault. She ran down the path by the side so she could get in through the kitchen then up the stairs. She dodged round a man, he shouted at her, people called out, but she was quick, they'd said so at school, and she could reach him; he was small, he'd be scared.

She thought of Joshua's face, all pale, his floppy hair in his eyes, surrounded by the black smoke, and she reached up to the door handle of the kitchen. Beyond the door were noises, things falling, something bursting, the sound like a wine glass on the floor but ten times louder. She tugged on the side door, pulled it open. She felt the whole house suck in a breath, and then, in a roar, it spat her straight back out onto the side path. The last thought she had before she felt someone drag her backwards was that the house had eaten Joshua.

'They pulled you out, you were so… Your face…' Her mother had started to cry now, bigger sobs that left her shaking. 'And I hadn't even taken a step forward to try. I'd let you go, too afraid to try myself. I should have been with you; I should have stopped you going.'

Irina took a step forward.

'Every time I see it, I'm reminded,' her mother said, turning to look at Irina, reaching out to draw a line down her face. 'My brave, brave Irina.'

RICHARD

He hadn't been able to stay in the cottage that afternoon. The drumming of the rain against the windows, a saucepan on the kitchen floor catching a new leak he needed to fix. His father sitting reading, Mary insisting on making supper in the kitchen, rolling out pastry, her forearms covered in flour. She was wearing the apron his mother used to wear, it was smaller on her, the yellow flowers so familiar he wanted to reach out and touch it. He hadn't told her he'd seen Abigail, that he knew she was leaving.

The thought shrouded him; a bleak, heavy realization that she would be gone and he would be left there. He felt the urge to get out, to head back into the village, up the river, to walk somewhere. He left quickly, pulling on the galoshes that stank of fish, oil-stained, his coat smelling of salt and guts. He rested a hand on his father's shoulder, felt it covered momentarily.

The darkness came as a surprise, the sky swelling with heavy clouds, the rain blurring the scenery, the river higher, sweeping past the house with energy, the road pockmarked with huge puddles. He walked up the path, into the trees, heading up, the ground slick with mud that clung to his boots and splattered up the side of his trousers. He felt his muscles burn with the effort, breathing in the smell of rain, the forest, the soaked soil, losing the village behind him, toy houses somewhere below. He wished his brother was still alive, that they could be off on the moors, on the beach with a football. He kicked at the ground, seeing his future uncertain and empty.

The rain was falling hard now and on the moors the peaty soil was saturated, the spongy heather heavy with water. The clouds were dark and threatening, a purple tinge along the underside, layer on layer of cloud and rain so that he could barely make out what was ahead of him. He knew he should get back, alarmed at the wind that battered him, the storm clashing overhead, lighting up the moor in a ghostly scene. For a second he imagined he saw cattle bloated and lowing for help, a moaning wind; he blinked.

When he arrived back, the fire had been lit, the cottage full of the smell of wood smoke, and he removed his sopping layers in a puddle inside the front door, hanging them on a row of hooks to dry. He moved through to the kitchen in his socks, leaving damp patches on the flagstones, putting the saucepan on to boil. Mary's pie was sitting finished on the side, the counter spotless, wiped down, pans washed and put away. The sight lifted him; he brightened as he returned to the front room, the scene in front of the fire, her shy smile as he asked if she wanted a pot of tea.

'I should do that,' she protested, half-rising out of the armchair.

'Stay put, I'm up. Dad?'

'Have you ever known me to say no?'

Richard switched on the side lamp and stoked the fire before returning with the tea things, wheeling over the trolley.

There was a momentary flash from outside and it seemed the rain became thicker still, impossible already to see out into the front garden, some blurred lights of the houses and hotels opposite. Richard imagined the holidaymakers, here for the sand and the ice-cream, looking out miserably at the weather.

He'd barely sat down, the lamps turned on as if it were a winter's evening, when someone was hammering on the cottage door. He lifted himself out of his armchair, moving in his socks to open it.

Bill stood there, the rain flecking his glasses, lost in a long cagoule, a hood obscuring his hair. 'They're saying the bridge is awash up near Ilkerton Hill. Some of the lads are up there, thought we could be helpful.'

Richard was pulling on his galoshes as Bill spoke, the sky black and grey behind him, the rain pelting the pathway, bouncing off the surface. He poked his head back around the sitting-room door, Mary already on her feet, wringing her hands. 'Can I do anything?'

'No, I won't be long. Will you both be OK?' He looked with concern at his father, who waved him off. Richard was glad Mary was there.

'We can wait to eat,' she said, hovering in the doorway to the sitting room as Richard finished tugging on his boots.

'Thanks.'

'Rich, I might drown waiting for you,' Bill said, stamping his feet. 'Let's go.'

'I'm coming.'

He swept out of the door, into the weather, surprised by the height of the river, which had risen rapidly in the last couple of hours.

'If we head out towards Barbrook we might be able to get up on the road there and see what's happening…'

Richard called back a reply, head down as the rain battered

them from all sides. It was as if they were on their boat in a storm.

They hadn't gone more than a few hundred yards when they heard an almighty crash further up in the valley. A sudden darkness descended as all the lights went out in the village.

'What the...?' Bill swore as he fumbled in his pockets, pulling out a box of matches that became sodden and useless in seconds.

'Brilliant!' Richard laughed, stuck on a piece of road, disorientated and soaking. 'We better head back,' he called.

They crept back down slowly, surprised at the rising water, linking arms as they crossed the road, back along the side of the village, the water already ankle-deep in places, washing around their calves. They made their way round the back of the high street, Richard keen to get back and check the cottage. They'd been gone for an age and had barely got anywhere. Candles flickered in the windows of The Rising Sun, the noise so loud now, they had to cup a hand next to each other's ears and shout to be heard. Bill motioned to the pub, Richard only able to nod in reply.

The room was steaming as they piled in, filled with people, the light low, candles flickering on every table, in windows, along the mantelpiece, bodies clustered in groups, talking in murmurs, the rain ever present as it lashed outside. He started as he made out Abigail's sister, huddled in a corner, her ringlets sticking to her neck, thinner than when he'd seen her last in the village all those weeks ago, an untouched drink in front of her. He couldn't see Abigail, scanned the room quickly for glossy brown hair, the flash of her teeth.

He shouldered his way over to the table. 'Where's Abigail?' he asked, aware of his dripping clothes, the goosebumps on his skin.

The woman looked up, pale, a man's coat draped over her shoulders, still shaking in spite of it, hair plastered to her skin. 'So, it's you.' He didn't know what to say to that. The woman shot a look over at the bar before leaning forward, saying the words quickly, in a half-whisper. 'She left,' she said, returning to stare at her drink. 'I wondered.'

A man with wide shoulders and a receding hairline turned away from the bar and a semi-circle of men. 'And who are you?' He stepped forward; one eyebrow raised. Richard felt foolish in his muddy, wet clothes, shivering a little underneath the layers. The man looked at Abigail's sister; Richard flinched.

'I'm… no one. I just… wondered…'

The man had already turned away from him, was continuing his conversation. 'Bloody girl ran off. We had to come back, wait for her here. Ridicu—'

Richard was moving away before the man had finished his sentence, knowing where Abigail would have been headed, scared now he knew she might be out there.

He paused momentarily in the doorway of the pub. Bill called to him from the bar, his eyebrows drawn together, a question on his lips, rubbing at his glasses. Richard looked back at him, then out at the rain, plunged back into the dark chaos of the high street. He had to find her.

His eyes couldn't adjust, his limbs numb now; the water seemed to be inside every layer, weighing down each step, his hair matted, water dripping into his eyes, from his nose, and each footfall accompanied by new sounds, terrifying sounds. Flashes of lightning showed the river, impossibly wide, carving its way through the village; trees, rocks, masonry, cars, jumbled and stacked high in those flashes. Then the darkness, so he could almost convince himself nothing had changed.

Boats smashed against each other in the harbour somewhere below as he stepped back onto the road, returning to the centre of the village, voices in the darkness behind, shouts; the tear and rumble seemed to encircle him. He was disorientated, the water pushing round him, relentless, forcing him to grab onto railings, windowsills, anything, always rising. He prayed she was somewhere safe, needed to get back to the cottage.

He passed the fruit shop, pausing as he heard cries, the sound of breaking glass. Peering into the dark, wiping at his eyes, he called out. 'Hello, who's there?' The cries continued and he moved across to the building, clutching the walls as the water grew in strength. Climbing up, he could make out a skylight, an arm poking out and a voice shouting something. There was barking as he clambered over the flat roof to peer down into the square of glass.

An older man looked up. 'My dog,' he said, lifting the terrier up towards the gap.

Richard lay on the roof to reach down, the tiny body wriggling in protest as he clamped both hands around it. He could feel its heartbeat through the fur; he pulled it out and sat it on the top. 'Stay!' he ordered, the dog leaning his head to one side, his fur matted immediately by the rain.

'Come on,' Richard called, reaching down to pull the man up, grunting with the effort. He heaved him up and out and they lay momentarily, chests heaving, on the roof.

The man struggled to his feet. 'We need to get to higher,' he gestured.

Richard shook his head. 'I need to go on,' he called back, pointing further up the valley.

The man clasped his shoulder with one hand before he left. 'Good luck,' he called, heading down and across the back of the building to a bank higher up, clutching his dog in both hands.

Richard lost sight of him almost immediately, scared now by the darkness all around him, making the crashing noises even more terrifying.

He dropped back onto the road, the water everywhere, swirling around his calves as he moved forward. He wasn't sure how much time had passed, his whole body shaking with the cold, the wet as he grabbed at buildings, railings, windowsills, his progress impossibly slow. The bridge over to the cottages was out and he felt marooned, unable to get back, to check on his dad and Mary, too far on now to turn away, his breathing quickening as the water rose over his knees, the air filled with unfamiliar sounds. He needed to find somewhere safe, somewhere on high ground.

Then, up ahead, where two roads normally met, he could make out a shape, near the bank; a flash of lightning and he realized it was her. He pulled himself through the water, shouting her name, telling her to hold on.

'I'm coming. I'm coming.' The words were whisked away before they could be heard, his voice hoarse, lips numb.

She was sobbing when he found her, her tears mingling with the rain. She was clinging to a railing as the water whirled and sucked and rushed past her. 'Hold on!' he shouted, looking for something he could use that she might hang on to.

'The woman...' She was crying, pointing down towards the harbour. 'She was... I could have...'

He couldn't hear what she was saying, just shouted again, 'Hold on, Abigail.'

She had lost her footing, both hands now gripping the railing. He turned this way and that, seeing nothing in the inky black. He had lost his bearings; things he would have recognized in daylight had morphed into something else. Roads he walked every day had become unknown streams, the East Lyn river weighted with tree roots, debris and boulders, a roaring, terrifying beast moving down the valley, no longer the gentle river he had splashed in as a boy, fished in, idling on the banks in a deckchair as fish nibbled on his rod, no longer the river whose banks he'd walked along with her, the insistent burble of it an accompaniment to their chatter. Not this, not this thing that was screaming over the top of everything else, screaming inside his head, threatening to destroy the village he loved.

'I can't...' She was mouthing things he couldn't hear, not able to look up at him. She was an indistinct form in the shadows; he could make out the cream of her dress, then she was lit up like a black and white picture, comical almost, sideways. He shook his head, wondering what he'd seen. There was a rumble further along, something giving way and he knew he had to get to her.

He clambered down, one hand over the other, moving along the railing, his fingers slipping on the cold metal. When he reached her, he had to lean forward, shift his weight. His feet were sliding as if he were standing on ice, the water nudging at him, moving around his feet and calves, cold, so cold. An enormous sound above them forced him to lurch forward; grabbing at her arm, he shouted at her to let go of the railing. Hauling her back to him, they fell back up the bank, on top of each other, and his mouth was in the water and his hair and everything was in his eyes, but her body was with him. She was there, lying on top of him, shouting words which were lost as something crashed past them, another tearing sound, wrenching metal and when they looked back the railing had gone, swept down the river.

She was crying now, repeating to him the same words. 'The woman, she was lost.'

He was panicked now, scared like he had never been before as he pictured his father, hopelessly inert in the cottage. Were they safe? Had Mary managed to get him to an upstairs room? He pictured them bobbing around the living room, their belongings floating round them, then he shook his head, throwing the image off, urging her on. 'We have to go home.'

They couldn't get across to the other side of the village, stood staring at the spot where the bridge had been, the river swollen, forcing them to scramble up behind the high street, weaving between the backs of buildings, holding onto each other for support, feeling comforted that at least they were together. They could make out the Lyndale Hotel up ahead, a mass of debris banked against it, windows faintly glowing on the top floor.

They made it there, clutching each other, clambering over silt, a tyre, trees, to a window further up, everything catching, scratching at their arms, their legs. Men in the window of the hotel, candles lit behind them, reached out both arms, one man dangling, straining his fingers to claw at the air in front of them and snatch them when he could. Abigail had reached him, she was hauled through the open window, he could just make out her head and shoulders, hear people calling to him.

He wavered, looking over his shoulder in the direction of the cottages, imagining Mary and his father huddled together, frightened. The Lyndale was a big hotel and he was clambering higher and higher; he imagined his father buried beneath the rubble below, everything was wrong, too high, the river too loud. Then he felt hands on his upper arms, voices around him, his body and feet sliding through the window.

They crept together across the room. Abigail was silent, stripped of her cardigan, teeth chattering, mud on her face and in her hair. Someone thrust towels and blankets at them and they were steered to a corner of the room, people piled everywhere about them, holidaymakers soothing their children, the building vibrating as the bawling outside went on, everyone crammed now onto the top floor, nowhere else to climb to, the pale faces, wide eyes and intermittent sobs making the room feel alive with a crawling fear. Richard clutched Abigail tightly to him, whispering things into her hair, not sure what he was saying now, prayers, sentences, assurances, trying to block out the thud and screech, the constant shout of the water as it battered the building. A silence as they heard a terrible jarring sound, the walls reverberating, the hotel seeming to shift. He wondered which part of it had been swept away into the torrent. He realized then that they might die that night. He held Abigail even tighter, praying for the light of dawn, praying for the interminable night to end.

IRINA

The day had drained her, she and her mother talking over each other, clutching hands, sentences spilling out, the sounds of the apartment block fading into nothing. As she left the building she'd felt a weight lift, the stone she'd been dragging round with her for twenty years; staring up at her mother's flat, feeling her hair ruffle in the breeze, the weather whisked it all away, breaking it apart.

On the drive home she felt calmer, her body relaxing, a sense that things would be different now. She opened the shop door and lugged her bag through the beaded curtain. The workshop seemed different, late-afternoon sunlight spilling through the windows, dancing in the air, the wood warm, the room smelling of polish and shavings. The bureau stood in its place in the corner and she walked over to it and pulled back the dust cloth to place a hand on the leather. She needed to finish it now.

She left her bag in the doorway, not bothering to unpack, feeling the old spark of excitement at getting on with a project, fetching her polish and cloth for a last layer of varnish. She worked deftly, humming a snatch of a song as she rubbed at the wood, tested the drawers, which ran smoothly and freely, pressed down lightly on the leather in the centre of the desktop.

She didn't know what made her look up, but something dragged her eyes away from the bureau. They were there in the mirror behind, as if they were in a room in another house. Two women sitting on a bench next to a river, one younger, with thick brown hair and round eyes, the other much older, her face lined, her hazel eyes crinkled, a warm smile as she rested a hand on the shoulder of the younger woman. Both familiar. Irina stared at them for the longest time, her body still, her mind calm, until their forms became indistinct, merging into the light reflected in the mirror, until there was just the empty glass, the wall opposite, and Irina wondered if she'd imagined them.

Before, she would have felt on edge, but there had been something about the scene; she felt that something had shifted and, with a slow realization, remembered where she had seen one of the women before. She threw a dust cloth over the bureau, admiring the finished piece as she did so. Taking her bag, she crossed the workshop to the stairs to her apartment. Settling herself on the sofa, laptop open, she logged into her email, a flutter as she looked at the latest address. Finally, she had received a reply from the owner of the bureau. Opening it, she started at the name and knew there was only one thing left to do.

ABIGAIL

Light crept through the windows gradually. A dirty, grey light that highlighted the sleeping, exhausted children, their mothers bent over them, small fists clinging to fabric, blankets, tear-stained faces. Men stirred, protective arms around their loved ones, all crammed together in a damp, shocked mess. Abigail opened one eye, Richard shifting his arm, rubbing at it, a dead weight from where she'd finally fallen asleep. For a few seconds she couldn't place them, was grateful for being held by him, and then she sat up abruptly as she remembered, hair released from its pins, dried mud still on her cheeks and streaking her stockinged legs, ladders running up, shoes ruined.

'Mary,' she said in a half-whisper.

It seemed Richard had the same reaction. He pulled her to her feet, looked down at her, one hand reaching out to cup her cheek. He was damp and muddied, his face and neck smeared like a coal sweeper's. They moved over to the window, and she hoped for a moment that they might have dreamt it all, that they would look down on a high street waking for the day, the familiar clink of milk being delivered, people pulling back shutters, women on the doorstep beating rugs.

There was a crowd of men clustered around the window, a circle of smoke above them, serious faces. What she saw over their shoulders, in the gaps, seemed incredible. The silt, rocks, trees they'd clambered up were impossibly high, reaching the ledge, straining against the building. Beyond that, the village, the river swollen, shattered remnants of houses, overturned vehicles, uprooted trees, mud. Wordlessly she reached for Richard, clutching his hand in horror, fingers cold and inert. The look he gave her forced her to ball her other hand into a fist, hold it over her mouth. She didn't want to scare the children. One girl, no more than eight, was looking at her through sleepy eyes. Abigail swallowed, trying hard not to panic, feeling her heart smashing against her rib cage.

'The cottage,' Richard whispered dumbly, looking across the river to the right, and a man in the circle turned to him, pity inching into his eyes.

Abigail looked in that direction, her brain not making sense of what she was seeing.

Carefully they clambered down the debris, hands reaching out to help them. Men were standing at intervals below, on the piles of rocks and mud pushed up against the building. Weary faces as they helped others down, arms around them guiding them mutely. At the bottom a cow's carcass, bloated and disgusting, legs frozen towards the sky, one oddly bent; a tyre, twisted metal somewhere underneath and then, as they looked out to sea, the extraordinary sight of trees standing upright in the water a mile out, as if the forest had been relocated, the seawater brown. The house opposite spewing forth its insides. A washbasin perfectly intact, the rest of the room belched into the street, floorboards hanging down like a great dirty tongue, belongings strewn, limp, dangling. As if it were ten years ago and it had been bombed.

They stumbled, the river still churning past them, travelling its new path, where the road had been. Around the corner, careful to avoid the crack, where gullies had opened up. Then the smell, the stench that met them, of open drains, disgusting and human, clinging to their nostrils as they moved unspeaking through the changed landscape. Abigail couldn't help tripping as she stared at the devastation around them. Everything mud-soaked, dripping. A ragdoll in the branches of a tree. She stopped short, her legs unwilling. A shop, front wall ripped away, the till standing at the counter still showing 3s 7d, a shelf, the tins intact behind it. A child's bicycle mangled beneath masonry, stones. She knew she would never forget these things.

She was confused, couldn't recall what had been there before, knew Richard knew every brick, house, path in the village, squeezed his hand tighter, tears pooling in his eyes, his face grey. He came to a sudden stop, looking out across a swirling, muddied section of the river, impossibly wide where before it had meandered around and behind houses, trickled underneath wrought-iron balconies, children treading over rocks, palms flat on the stones as they played.

A gate, on its hinges that led nowhere. A sign for a B & B in a tree opposite, pointing to nothing.

'The cottages… Oh God, the…'

She looked down, along, backwards. She realized then what they were looking at, seeing the school on the cliff on the other side, the gap where the four cottages should have stood. Richard staring, mouth opening and closing, no words coming out. His house, completely washed away. The riverbed scoured. Nothing there now. Nothing.

Slowly, a terrible lurch in her stomach as her thoughts tried to catch up. They got out, surely they got away?

'They might have got out… We don't know…' She whispered it, unable to stop herself turning away from the river, staring out towards the sea, across the stretch of water, splintered wood, boulders, branches, trunks, twisted metal, silt, feeling her stomach churn as she wondered if their bodies lay there, in amongst the wreckage of the village. She jerked away from Richard then, bent down, expelled the contents of her stomach, her mouth acidic, her gut aching, wiped at her mouth.

Richard had taken blankets from the Lyndale Hotel and she carried one under her arm. They turned away from where the cottages should have been, picked their way wordlessly up the path, both needing to get out of the village. He held her hand in his, silently, at one point squeezing so hard she had to put a hand on his arm and remind him she was there. He was holding an umbrella over them, a flimsy thing that seemed almost comical in the moment.

Their feet and legs were soaked when they reached the cottage, the windows now tinged with the faint orange of dawn, the glass outlined in gold. The sun had started to creep across the moors towards them, the saturated ground spongy as they stepped between the heather, their footprints making noises that sucked at the earth as if they might be sucked right into the long grass.

They lit a fire, Richard prodding at the flames, causing them to crackle and spark. Without blushing, Abigail stripped down to her undergarments, took off her stockings and shoes, leaving them to dry over the fireplace like ghostly clothing, wrinkled and thin. Richard had created a space for them on the floor in front of the hearth and they lay down together in the living room, her head on his chest. She felt empty, unresponsive, and then suddenly her mind was full of her friend's face. It had been her idea that she come to the village, if she'd been with her in Lynton she would never have been caught up in all this.

'We'll go back, we'll look for them, they might not be...' Richard stopped, pulled her towards him, her cheek resting on his bare chest, his pulse loud in her head.

She felt the first tear fall, marking a trail down her face. She went to wipe it away and then realized that Richard was shaking silently, his own tears falling in her hair.

IRINA

She swallowed as she stepped out of the car, reaching back in to grab the neck of the wine bottle. She felt her stomach turn over as she stared up at Andrew's house.

She was wearing a yellow dress, her hair tied back. She'd got ready in the mirror in the apartment, pressing her lips together, smoothing the bags underneath her eyes as if she'd woken from the longest sleep. The scar on her face had seemed less livid as she traced it with one finger.

He opened the door, distracted by something behind him, before taking her in. He had a two-day stubble and was wearing a jumper with a stain on the sleeve. His dishevelment gave her a little more confidence. She didn't want to mess this up again. He seemed wrong-footed as she asked in a small voice, 'Can I come in?'

'Of course,' Andrew said, standing back. 'I'll just get on some—'

'Don't do anything,' she said, one hand on his arm. 'I just want to talk.'

RICHARD

He stood up, confused, eyes red from the tears, mouth dry, head pounding; it was a moment before he realized where they were, that they had slept again, a few short hours. His voice was slurred with the shock and tiredness of the night before as he nudged Abigail awake. She was clutching the blanket, biting on her lip, her face pale. It was mid-morning now, a new day, but he felt frozen in the night before, the last night.

She raised herself up into a sitting position, her chin on her knees, her arms wrapped around her legs. They stayed like that for a moment, him looking down at her, strands of hair loose from her chignon. The sun was making ribbons in the air, dust dancing in strips. He felt grateful at least that she was there, that he had found her. He knelt down to sit on the blankets, folded her into a hug, exhaling slowly as they held each other.

'We should get you back to your sister's…'

'I can't go back.'

She whispered the words into his chest, so, for a moment, Richard wondered if she'd actually spoken.

'I don't understand.' He pulled back from her so he could look at her. She had a streak of mud on one cheek and he reached out to wipe at it with a thumb.

She didn't look up at him but stared ahead, unseeing, at the fire, long dead in the grate. 'I can't.'

Richard felt his lips move into a rounded question; her voice was barely there, a new expression settling on her face.

'What if they never knew?' she continued, biting her lip again, her eyes darting left to right and then up at him.

The ferocity of her gaze forced him to move round and kneel in front of her, tipping her chin towards him. 'If they never knew what? What are you talking about, Abigail?'

Her whole face transformed, a blush creeping up her neck and into her cheeks. She swallowed once, then took a nervous breath. 'If they never knew I survived.'

He reeled back on his heels, his voice sharper than intended. 'What do you mean? Why?'

She reached out to him, her expression desperate, as if she was starving and he was holding the last morsel of food. 'Richard, please. I can't go back.'

He felt a surge of anger at this girl he thought he knew. Had he been mistaken? Why would she say such a thing?

'I don't understand,' he repeated, wanting to understand, feeling overwhelmed with everything that was happening, still not able to keep up.

'My brother-in-law…' She spoke in the smallest voice so that he was forced to lean forward. 'He…'

Richard must have made a noise because she looked up at him sharply. 'He, well, I…' She started wringing her hands, trying to get the words out.

He was thinking the worst things, watching as her eyes flicked left to right, her mouth stumbling over the sentences.

'He tried to force himself on me. He is... If I could leave, I could... I don't want to go back there. They'll think I've gone... I'll be free.'

He didn't know what to say, his head too full of everything, aching, the light pressing on him. His world seemed to be tilting, making him clutch the blankets to keep himself grounded. He thought of his father in the cottage, leading Mary down to him, leaving them there. His fist tightened, he closed his eyes, picturing them in the house, trapped, the water rising.

Abigail was holding her breath and he looked over at her as if he was trying to recall who she was, what she'd been saying.

'Please, I don't want you to think... I didn't want to tell you, but...' She pleaded, brushing the back of his hand.

He snatched his hand away, too many noises in his head. 'Don't, Abi. I can't think now, I can't.'

She nodded, looking down, the exuberant girl who'd screamed at the river now broken by it. 'I'm sorry, I shouldn't have asked.'

He hated to see her like that, her shoulders drooping, her eyes dulled. He reached a hand up to her face and she leant her cheek into his palm as he kissed her, for a brief second trying to believe that it was a normal kiss, that nothing dreadful had happened. He closed his eyes, made a promise. 'It will be alright, Abi.'

'Will it?' she whispered, tears filling her eyes before she looked away.

He stood, walked out into the garden, returned with a bucket of water. Moving to the butler's sink, he splashed his face, rubbed at his neck and cheeks, feeling drops dampen his collar.

'I need to go back down; I need to see if I can find them.'

Abigail nodded, wiping her face with the back of her hand as she sat in the nest of blankets on the floor.

He walked over to the door, pausing as she called his name in a voice filled with a pain he recognized as his own. 'Please try and find Mary.'

He gulped as he looked back at her, trying to give her a reassuring smile but not managing it, then gently closed the door behind him.

The village seemed worse in the harsh daylight, brighter and more exposing than the hours before, or perhaps the shock was wearing off. Even the glimpses as he picked his way down the path – the ground saturated, moss clinging to stone walls, reeking of the recent rain, droplets on leaves, puddles at every turn – didn't make sense to him. He wasn't sure what he was looking at, his brain moving through the images he knew, the places that were so familiar to him now distorted, twisted, smashed. Some not even there.

All across the village men with rolled-up shirtsleeves carried buckets, removing rocks, calling to each other, exclaiming over the crumpled wreckage of another automobile, a house, its contents gaping. In the sea beyond, the line of ghostly trees remained, propped up by their roots, splintered wood on the shore, the tide revealing more objects, masonry, bricks, upturned chairs, smashed bowls.

There was a line of bodies under blankets, a small hand peeking from the side of one. Richard found himself staring at the little finger; a man slopped mud on his shoes as he lingered, muttering an apology, not able to look away. He stood there until someone steered him gently away, gave him a bucket, a hand on his shoulder, words in his ear. Bill rubbing at his glasses as he looked at him, his own face grey, bags under his eyes.

They worked in silence, filling their buckets, clambering over boulders, staring up as shouts in the distance indicated something else had been found.

He spent an age clearing the area around the cottages, the foundations gone, Richard having to look back up at the valley to get his bearings, touching the ground where the houses had once been. His father was found later that day in amongst the slabs of brick, the rocks pulled up gently by Bill and a couple of other lads, carefully muttering to each other in low voices, one holding a handkerchief over his mouth and nose, his eyes on Richard, who felt his world temporarily stop turning. Bill next to him then, a hand on his shoulder again as he fought to hold back the tears building behind his eyes and in his throat. He had needed to see him, to know. He didn't look like his dad anymore. Richard felt something lurch in his stomach, held up a hand to his mouth, grateful for the sheet they put over him.

The next morning he found himself heading down to the village again, in a trance, leaving Abigail sitting in the cottage, pacing up and down as she waited for him to return with news. More bodies found, no sign of Mary. An eleven-year-old who lived over a mile away had been found under the butcher's slab on Watersmeet Road. They hadn't located the body of his little brother. The tide swept in and out, crammed with broken wood, wheels of motor cars, misshapen metal. At times he felt completely disorientated, as if this was an entirely different place and his father was somewhere else, a village up the coastline, untouched.

There were huge stone boulders that Richard craned his neck to look at. They entered his dreams: he was pushing at one hopelessly, imagining his father underneath it, pinned, sinking into the silt, the rock weighing him down. He woke to that image, moving around and around, until Abi held him, told him where he was, brought him back to her.

Enough water to supply both villages for a century had hurtled down the two river valley in a few short hours, destroying their idyllic home, the honeymooner's paradise. The rivers had turned roads into streams and streams into rivers that flowed with furious energy down to the sea, taking everything in their path. There were dozens of mangled motor cars settled upside down and crooked. On the third day Richard stopped short, his breathing thick as he recognized the navy hood of a pram, its metal frame distorted and barely recognizable nearby, wheel-less. He sank to his knees, patting at the debris below it, not wanting to imagine what was hidden there.

Uniformed men from various agencies roamed amongst fishermen and villagers. People stood in the midst of the chaos, carting debris, lifting buckets, picking through the wreckage, returning to salvage belongings from broken homes. A lot of movement and then stillness as they suddenly stopped and stared at the devastation, observing it as if for the first time, as if for a second they had forgotten, that it couldn't have happened, then starting up again, filling another bucket load.

He returned to the cottage every evening, Abigail waiting for him with questions, the cottage swept and tidied. He knew he should make her leave, should make her return to her sister, but as he folded her into his arms, he couldn't bring himself to do it. So she stayed and they didn't discuss it.

On the third day there were rumours that the body of a young woman had been found further down the coast; a little girl had discovered it in the water that morning. There was talk of who it could be. She was being brought back for identification, worried relatives hoping the interminable wait for news might be over. There was a small crowd around the body when it was carried into the village on a stretcher. One man, keen to lay claim to a maid in his service, stepped forward to survey the body. Richard lingered at the edge of the group. A bloated arm, brown hair. Her flesh was exposed, shoes long gone, but Richard recognized the scrap of material found with her, the sleeve of a light pink blouse she'd been wearing that night.

The man shook his head, stepped backwards, and Richard recognized Abigail's sister, standing behind her husband, a startled bird. The husband moved forward, looking strangely out of place in a clean shirt and a bowler hat; he raised a thick eyebrow at her as he turned to steer her towards the blanket, one hand on the small of her back. She remained frozen, had to reach out for his arm at one point or she would have stumbled. Her pale lips were bitten down, her eyes the same shape as Abigail's; she had the same slender neck but was somehow still, as if she were behind a pane of glass, whereas Abigail would have been vivid, breaking through it with her stare.

The man asked for the blanket to be removed from the face. He tipped his head to one side, assessing it, as if he were about to buy a barrel of fish. Richard felt his fists curl into themselves as he stood there, wanting to launch himself over the rocks at him. That was the man.

As if he had shouted his thoughts, he sensed Abigail's sister glance over at him, start at the sight of him. She held his gaze, a steady look. Richard felt himself heat up, his skin itch. He should say something.

'It's not her.' Her husband stepped backwards, interrupting Richard's thoughts, his voice loud, bouncing off the debris, giving others hope that they might recognize the woman.

'Wait.' Abigail's sister spoke quietly, her voice indistinct at first and then growing stronger. 'I want to see.'

Richard watched her closely, his feet planted, unable to move at all, knowing he should go to her but finding himself immobilized, his eyes unable to leave her.

She walked forward, slowly, carefully, stumbling a little on the uneven ground, a handkerchief pressed into her mouth as she stared down at the body beneath the blankets. There was a beat and then she announced it in a quiet voice. 'It's her,' she said, not looking at her husband but rather at the man with the clipboard.

Richard saw her husband take her elbow in one hand, forcibly steer her away. 'Woman's mistaken,' he said.

'I'm not. It's her,' she said, and as she repeated it she looked over her shoulder, straight at Richard. 'It's Abigail. She's dead. She's gone.' She held his gaze, urgency in her voice.

Richard couldn't look away, stared back at her, hearing the words as if from a great distance.

Then there was movement; her husband marched across, seized her arm. 'It's not her. My wife's overwrought, she doesn't know what she's saying.'

The man holding the clipboard frowned, looked from one to the other. 'If you're sure...'

Abigail's sister was muttering now, people's eyes swivelling to the pair of them, voices in the crowd. Bill glanced up at Richard, a question on his lips as he searched his face. Her husband drew her away, his hand firm on her arm, his face set in a line.

She looked back once, meeting Richard's eye again. 'She's gone.'

IRINA

He had sounded surprised when she'd phoned him and asked if she could deliver the bureau to him personally. She told Andrew everything on the journey down and his jaw dropped when she explained where they were headed and who the client had turned out to be.

They found the cottage reasonably easily, although they had to abandon the van in a nearby lane, a locked five-bar gate blocking their way.

'Let's check we're right before we unload it,' Andrew said, looking down the dirt track.

The cottage sat a hundred yards or so along on the right, an oak tree at the entrance to it, the house itself on a cliff looking out over the village below. A patch of the moor was laid out to their left, the heather and grasses shifting in the sunlight, an endless palette of purples, greens and browns.

He answered the door dressed in burgundy cords, a moth-eaten navy jumper and a faded yellow shirt, a walking stick in one hand. His green eyes crinkled as he ushered them both in, shaking Andrew's hand and kissing Irina on the cheek.

'It's wonderful to meet you in the flesh,' he said, his voice a curious mix of accents, part American and part something else she couldn't place.

'It's good to meet you too,' Irina said.

'And you've come all this way to deliver it personally,' he said, lifting an eyebrow.

Andrew and Irina swapped a look, 'Well… it has been a bit unusual.'

'Unusual has it?'

Irina didn't think he looked surprised, more curious as he turned and called behind him, 'I think you better come in.'

They filed into a large room on the right: an enormous fireplace on one side, a neat stack of logs piled high, a square of rug in front of it, a battered leather sofa, an abandoned book on a side table. Across the room a kitchen counter, various utensils hanging from hooks, a sink beneath a window, herbs in a pot on the windowsill.

'Please…' He gestured to the sofa. 'And would you like a drink?'

They both refused, Irina perching on the edge of the seat in her eagerness to talk, Andrew relaxing into the sofa, a hand reaching to touch the small of her back.

Richard lowered himself into an armchair opposite and looked at Irina with interest. 'I should apologize for having been so hard to pin down. I did get your emails but all in a rush. I've been moving everything over from the States, travelling here and there, staying with children, and I'm pretty hopeless anyway when it comes to emails and things. So what is the great mystery?'

Irina thought she might fall onto the carpet as she leant forward to look at him. 'The bureau, I was wondering how it had come into your possession?'

'It was my wife's,' Richard explained. 'She bought it in New

York; she loved to write. She wanted it restored, told me a month or so before she died that she wanted me to have it, to bring it here.'

Irina sat back a little. 'I'm sorry. I hadn't realized.'

Richard held up a hand. 'That's OK. I'm looking forward to seeing it again, it reminds me of her.'

'We found things.' Irina blurted it out before she could think.

Richard frowned. 'Things?'

'It had secret compartments; we found things inside it.'

Richard's eyebrows lifted and it was his turn to edge forward. 'What things?'

Irina twisted round, opened her handbag and drew out the items, laying them carefully on the coffee table in front of her.

Richard picked them up one by one, rotating the shell in his hand with a frown, stroking the feather, unfolding the handkerchief, tracing the letter 'A' with a finger, before turning to the brooch, staring at it for the longest time. His hand closed over it, 'She… All this time.'

Andrew had got up and she joined him, feeling the need to give Richard some privacy, something about his expression making her realize he should be alone. They stood looking out of the window over the butler's sink, down to an overgrown garden, the sea glittering in the distance beyond. Irina was restless as she turned back around. 'What an amazing view.'

'Isn't it? I've missed the place desperately: the village and the moors. I always wanted to come back, and Abi loved the sea.' Richard said it without looking up, still gazing at the brooch.

'I thought…' Irina fell silent then, thrown by his use of the name, the woman she had convinced herself had died the night in the flood.

Richard stared up at her. 'You thought what?'

'Well, Bill told me that Abigail... That she didn't survive... in... in the flood.'

'Yes.' Richard settled back into his chair as Irina waited for more. 'I need to go and see Bill, I've missed him.' He tapped a finger to his teeth.

'So, Abi, um... who was Abi?' Irina asked, feeling Andrew tense next to her, just as keen to know.

Richard pointed to a photograph on the mantelpiece showing a woman with dark hair and a wide smile surrounded by children and grandchildren; in another she was standing next to a young girl with long brown hair dressed in a cap and gown. 'My wife, Abigail. She's there with our eldest, with Mary.'

'Mary,' Irina whispered, pulling the pile of letters out of her handbag. She leant forward to hand them to Richard. 'But I don't understand, did she write these to her?'

Richard seemed taken aback now, his brow creasing as he took the pile from her and looked through each letter, turning them over, reading the words as if he were thirsty for knowledge.

'I had no idea,' he said after a long time, his eyes watery as he traced the words, lingered over the flamboyant signature. 'She wrote to her, for all those years.'

'But Mary looks so young...?'

'Mary was named after Abi's best friend. She... she wanted desperately to keep her memory alive.' He wiped at his eyes. 'All those years.' He was staring at the 'Lynton' postcard.

'Abi must have loved her, this friend.'

Richard didn't respond at first, had flipped over the postcard to see the two words on the back: 'Forgive me'. When he finally answered there were fresh tears in his eyes. 'Oh she did,' he said. 'She did. It was a terrible thing, but it was her way out of here.'

'Way out?' Irina asked, her turn to sound confused.

Richard was nodding slowly, eyes still fixed on the postcard. 'She had to leave; she couldn't stay.'

'So, who was Mary?' Irina asked. 'Is she the Unknown Woman?'

Richard looked over at her, a slow, crooked smile lighting up his face. 'I suppose I better tell you the rest.'

Historical Note

I was on holiday with my husband in the West Country and we decided to stop for a couple of days in Lynmouth. Walking through the streets, we noticed a museum and went in to investigate. I hadn't heard of the Lynmouth flood before that moment, but immediately we were inside it was obvious it had had a catastrophic and lasting effect on the small seaside village. A scale model showed the buildings before the flood and newsreels from the 1950s were being played continuously.

There was a plaque showing the names of all the victims of the flood. The same surnames sprang out at us. The details of one family – the Richards – seemed particularly upsetting: a couple and their two children, who were aged three years and three months. At the bottom of the plaque was the simple line, 'Unknown Woman', a blank next to her age. I paused in front of it, feeling an overwhelming sadness for this victim that no one had claimed or identified.

Who was she? Why had she been in Lynmouth on the night of the flood? Why did no one know who she was? Had no one missed her?

These questions were on a loop for the rest of the holiday and I knew I wanted to write her story.

Why did it happen?

Most reports state that the flood was caused by heavy rainfall due to low pressure over the Atlantic. This seems likely; there had been an exceptional amount of rain across the West Country that day, and Lynmouth had been flooded in previous centuries. Some had warned against building too many houses in certain areas of the popular village, anticipating that they could be affected by severe flooding.

There is also a conspiracy theory about the disaster, which was explored in a BBC documentary in 2001. The theory holds that the flash-flooding was in fact due to Ministry of Defence experiments in rain-making. Project Cumulus was looking at ways of starting heavy storms to hinder enemy movement. This involved cloud-seeding – dropping dry ice into clouds to trigger storms. Supposedly the RAF had been running such experiments in southern England just days before the Lynmouth flood happened. According to the documentary, classified documents on the trials have gone missing. Survivors of the flood called for an inquiry, but this never happened. The Ministry of Defence denied that these experiments had taken place.

The night of the flood

On 15th August 1952 ninety million tons of rain fell on Exmoor. The topsoil, already saturated from terrible weather two weeks previously, could not take it and the water was channelled down both the West and East Lyn rivers, sweeping trees, bridges, boulders and other debris into their path. The two rivers merged and the water and debris tore through the picturesque village of Lynmouth, destroying buildings, cars and infrastructure. The official death toll was thirty-four.

There are no photographs of the flood itself, largely because it happened in the hours of darkness. Locals state that it was already pitch black that day as early as 5.30 p.m., even though it was the middle of August. Others talk about the sky that afternoon – a disturbing bank of dark cloud tinged with red. There is no doubt that one of the most terrifying aspects of that night was the darkness; the village lost power around 7.30 p.m., when the hydro-electric plant faltered, and the only light came from candles and the constant flashes of lightning. One woman making her way through the village in search of safety ordered her children not to touch anything metal as they moved through the water.

The noise was so loud that shouting was pointless, so

throughout the night desperate people used torch lights to signal for help. Residents spoke about the ghostly sight of motor cars rolling in the water, their short-circuited headlights like green eyes. It took days for the body of one woman to be found; she was still inside her car, which had been obscured by debris and rubble.

'We watched a row of cottages fold up like a pack of cards,' local fishermen Ken Oxenholme said. As the water rose, trees, telegraph poles, ten-ton boulders and even whole buildings were washed away. The next morning, trees could be seen in the sea, standing upright, their roots in the muddy water. Not even the foundations of some buildings survived the night.

The Rhenish tower, originally built at the end of the harbour to guide fishermen home, was completely destroyed in the flood. It was reconstructed in 1954, using picture postcards to get the design right. The wrought-iron beacon on top of it was found amongst wreckage on the foreshore and can be seen today.

The Pavilion

There was a seven o'clock performance of *Seaside Notions* with Scottish comedian Al Raie in the Pavilion that night. When the lights went out performers and spectators started a sing-song, but during 'Unforgettable' an increasingly anxious audience left. The esplanade was awash, so some went back up the steps to Mars Hill and others headed for the hotels. Around the corner in the high street, they were hit with a knee-high torrent of water. A group of six women linked arms to get through the water. One woman, fifty-six-year-old Elsie Cherry, on the edge of the group (the lady Abigail sees) was washed away.

The Lyndale Hotel

The Lyndale Hotel (where Richard and Abigail spend the night) was in the direct path of the flood. When the West Lyn broke its banks it pushed rocks and debris against the side of the hotel. The guests had to move up from the first to the second and then the third floor. During the night, huddled on the top floor, they heard the floor below give way and one side of the hotel fall into the river. One guest described the building as 'shuddering all night.'

The next morning they walked out onto the debris and boulders that had been pushed up against the side of the hotel. The watermark here measured fifty-five feet above the normal river level. The only casualty was a budgerigar that had been swept out of the lounge in its cage.

The Unknown Woman

So, who was the Unknown Woman?

The coroner's report produced the following description: 'An unidentified female aged between 18 and 25, length 5′ 2″, weight approximately 9 stone, well-developed, dark hair, natural teeth (some knocked out), well-kept hands and feet, was recovered from the sea on 21st August.'

The short answer is that no one really knows. However, there are many theories. Most argue that she must have been a visitor to the village as all locals were accounted for. Some say she was an Australian, travelling in England and caught up in the flood that day. This seems plausible; certainly no one would have been able to identify her if she was only passing through. However, two other flood victims were Australian tourists, which made me wonder whether this was the case. Other people claimed she was one of the many Irish maids that lived and worked in the village, but it seems unlikely that no one would have identified her.

The most compelling rumour I was told was that the unknown woman was from the Midlands and had been staying in a hotel with her married lover. It was suggested that the man, not wanting to confess, decided not to declare her.

And when her sister back at home found out, she didn't want to put a name to the body either, for the shame it would bring on the family.

After some more research I discovered that in 2005 a local historian, Tim Prosser, was approached by a woman who believed her aunt was the 'Unknown Woman' on the plaque. She claimed her aunt had been disowned by the family for taking up with a married man. Supposedly he had also become estranged from his relatives and his wife was an in-patient in a mental institution. The woman claimed that her mother had received a postcard a week before the flood postmarked Minehead stating that they were planning to head to Lynmouth as her partner remembered it being a pretty village. The family never heard from her again. Their circumstances would perhaps explain why their deaths weren't reported.

The truth is that no one seems to know who she was and to this day it remains a mystery.

Printed in Great Britain
by Amazon

55941243R00226